I0663429

HEART OF STONES

LANNA RICHARDS

Heart of Stones

Publisher: Blue Opal Press

This book was printed in the USA.

Author may be contacted @ Lanna1202@gmail.com

ISBN 978-1-7352708-0-7

With Special Love to My Family

Jennifer, Randy, and Hannah
Kathy, Mike, Morgan, and Trevor
Jay and Dana
Jacob, Sarah, and Oliver
Cailie and Tyler
Patricia and John

ACKNOWLEDGEMENT

Three women molded me, and to them I owe my deep gratitude and love…my grandmother, Lela McCreless Turner; my mother, Kathryn Richards; and my Senior English teacher, Miss Gladys Miller.

Thank you to my beautiful daughter, Jennifer Bullard, who believed in me even when I didn't think I could write, who inspired me to step out in faith, and who loves me without reservation. You are my guiding light always, and I treasure you now and forever.

Also to my sister and brother-in-law, John and Patricia Nelson who made me believe I can tell a story.

And special thanks to James Olson, an amazing author, who has always encouraged and supported me, to my special friend, author, and confidant, Marsha Faulkner, and for all those men and women, friends, family, and classmates who either traveled this journey with me or met me along the way, helping me and extending emotional support, I can never repay my indebtedness, but please know I am eternally grateful to you.

CHAPTER ONE

Scottsville in the summer baked under an unrelenting Mississippi sun. Abraham Sullivan stood on the front verandah staring into space. Not a single cloud interrupted the expanse of sky, and currents of heat rose in an undulating rhythm distorting the landscape. Breathing in the sultry air, he felt as though his lungs would explode. Too bad he couldn't convert the humidity into moisture for the crops. In the fields, sorghum and cotton begged for water, and the vegetable garden lay limp and wilted.

Sarah sauntered out to join her husband and handed him a glass of iced tea. "I thought you'd enjoy a drink. Miss Daisy just made it."

Abe nodded his thanks. "I don't know what we're going to do if it doesn't rain soon."

"We should have stayed in Ireland, or gone to England. I'd rather have starved in the Great Hunger than to have gone through these last few years."

"You don't mean that."

"No, I suppose I don't."

Abe gazed into his wife's misty, blue-violet eyes. "We chose to come here, and the majority of people accept us now, whether they like us or not. Or rather, they accept our money."

"But the ridicule our children have endured hurts me. At least you removed the O from the front of our last name, making us sound more American."

Abe drew his petite wife into a tender embrace. "They just don't understand our Irish heritage, but I didn't want our children to be branded as foreigners, and O'Sullivan would certainly have done that. Most of the gossip is over, and we're living a good life now. I know many men who would give half their land if our daughters would marry their sons." He kissed Sarah's forehead releasing her as they moved toward the oak swing suspended from the ceiling of the verandah. Suddenly a rumbling noise erupted from somewhere in the distance announcing a full-blown stampede. A wide line of darkies covered the horizon running toward the house, waving their arms and screaming.

Abe willed his brain to make sense of the commotion, to no avail. He'd heard of slaves turning on their masters, but his servants had no need for an uprising. What had upset them? Was his family in danger? Before he could react, the foreman rushed up, too winded to speak. The old darkie bent over and wiped his face with his bandana until he caught his breath.

"What is it, Jeremiah?" Abe yelled, looking from one face to another trying to ascertain the problem. They seemed to be in a state of panic and looked scared, but not angry.

Pointing to the east, Jeremiah screamed, "It's da fi-er, Massa, da fi-er!"

Abe's gaze followed the Negro's finger. Curls of dark smoke blotted the clear afternoon sky, and reality hit him like a cannonball to his gut. Trying to remain calm, he asked, "Which field is on fire?"

"Da lower sisty, Massa."

Waving his arms toward his body, Abe motioned the excited darkies to the front steps while he addressed the foreman and his son. "Jeremiah, take everyone to the river and form a line. Jim, grab anything that'll hold water and meet them there. Hurry!"

The activity drew young Grace and Margaret Sullivan outside, followed by the servants who stood behind them, eyes wide as if trying to comprehend the turmoil.

Abe turned to the house servants. "Hurry! Fire's in the fields! Gather quilts or anything heavy you can find and take them to the back porch. I'll get a wagon."

Sarah, Grace, and Margaret rushed into the house pulling down draperies while Essie Mae and Lavitica June, young house servants and Daisy's daughters, darted to all the bedrooms, grabbing old bedding and rugs.

Obadiah, the butler, carried the heavier items and led the troop to the back of the kitchen. Poor Daisy moved along as fast as her three-hundred-pound, arthritic frame would allow, but she was too slow to be of much help other than to mumble a prayer as she lifted her hands to the Lord.

Grace and Maggie ran to their father, and no amount of persuasion would prevent them from going with him, so Abe helped them into the wagon while he waited for the quilts and rugs from the house. He glanced toward the river. Jeremiah had formed a brigade, and Jim's wagon brimmed with containers of water. As soon as Abe's wagon was loaded, he headed down to the water line.

"Go, Jim! Everybody else, get into my wagon! Hurry!" Abe turned the horses, whipping them into a trot right behind Jim. By the time they reached the field, the fire roared out of control. Jeremiah organized a group of women into an assembly line to pass the water while Grace and Maggie helped their father smother the smaller flames with the drapes and quilts.

Jim organized a crew of men and boys to dig a ditch around the field as Essie Mae and Lavitica June stamped out some of the perimeter flare-ups. Adrenaline surged, and the people worked in a state of frenzy, attempting to overcome the hell brimming in front of their faces. After an hour of fighting the blaze, Abe realized it was too big to contain. Jim had the right idea. Dig a ditch and let the fire burn itself out.

Abe yelled for Jeremiah.

"Yas, suh?"

His voice felt parched, but Abe bellowed above the noise of the fire, "Gather the women. Go back to the river. Fill the containers with water again, so we can pour it into the ditch. Go!" Abe saw Jim halfway down an outside row and sent Grace to get him.

"Yas, suh?" The young man ran toward Abe.

"I've sent your papa to draw more water for the ditch. Think we can dig around the field before the fire spreads?"

"Yas, suh, I thinks we kin iffen we works real hard. Iffen the wind don' pick up, it won' go nowhere."

Abe nodded, fingering his jaw. "I'm sending the girls to the house for drinking water. Go back to work, but let me know if you need anything."

Jim bowed and turned to go, but Abe stopped him. "One more thing."

"Yas, suh?"

"Thank you."

The young darkie grinned and bowed. "You's welcome, Massa."

*　*　*

Eyes glued to the window, Sarah paced watching the flames lick the sky, rising higher with each passing minute. Not only was she concerned they would lose the entire plantation, but she worried about the safety of the people. When she couldn't stand the suspense any longer, she headed down the hall, across a small walkway to the kitchen yelling for Daisy. The old cook resting on arthritic knees had her ample frame bent over a chair praying but looked up as Sarah entered the room.

"Yas 'em?"

"Do we have any food we can take to the field? Everyone must be hot and tired."

Lumbering to her feet, Daisy rummaged through the food in the pantry. "Let's see, we gots some roast beef I was a fixin' for supper, some hog's head cheese, and prob'ly some jerky out in the smokehouse. They's fresh bread, and we gots some fried pies."

The kitchen buzzed with activity. Sarah poured water into large pitchers while Daisy made sandwiches of meat and buttered bread. They packed the food into a rectangular basket, jumping when the back door flew open, startling them.

Grace and Maggie burst into the room. Soot and dirt covered their once beautiful dresses, and the odor of smoke hung heavy in the air. Heat had reddened their arms and faces, but neither girl seemed to notice.

Grace addressed her mother. "Papa sent us for water. It's too hot to even breathe down there."

Daisy brought in a large washtub to pack with the pitchers of water. She handed it to the girls to load on the wagon while she shuffled out with the basket of food. As the girls started toward the door, Sarah rushed in front of them.

"I'm going with you."

"No, Mama. You'll get all dirty, and it's too hot." Grace tried to move her aside.

"I'm going." Sarah grabbed a bonnet and followed her daughters to the wagon.

The entire population of the plantation, with the exception of Miss Daisy and some of the elderly servants and younger children, fought the inferno throughout the night, digging the ditch or hauling water as well as beating down flying embers to keep them from spreading to other areas. Blistered skin, singed hair, and scorched clothes didn't stop anyone. Masters and servants worked side by side pushing back the exhaustion threatening to incapacitate them. As the fire subsided to smoldering ashes, thin streaks of light emblazoned the sky with a magnificent, golden-pink sunrise.

Abe sat on the ground beside Jeremiah. "It could have been worse."

"Yas, suh, we wuz fixin' to go to the other field when we sawed it. We come arunnin' right away."

"What could have caused the fire? Was anyone smoking around here?"

"Naw, suh, ever' body knows better'n to do that."

"Then ask everyone if they saw anything before the fire broke out and come tell me."

"Nobody saw nuthin' from what they done tole me. But I'll ast again."

"Okay, round up everyone, and let's take the day off. After this kind of night, we all need some rest. We'll serve breakfast at the Big House and please tell the workers how much I appreciate their help." Abe stood and reached for Sarah's hand as Maggie and Grace followed them to the small wagon.

By the time they washed up and changed clothes, Miss Daisy had a hearty breakfast on the table. Abe patted her arm. "Fix enough food for everyone. Have Jeremiah and the men set up some boards on saw horses for tables on the porches and get Essie Mae and Lavitica June to help you with the cooking and serving."

The old cook nodded and sent Obadiah to find the girls while she started cooking again.

Too restless to eat, Abe left the table. Sarah followed him to the parlor.

"What do you think caused the fire?" she asked.

"I don't know. If the darkies had thrown a cigarette on it, they should have had time to put it out. But the fire flared up so fast. There's no logical explanation."

"Could someone have deliberately set it?"

"Maybe, but who would have done such a thing? Can you think of anyone who hates us enough to destroy our plantation?"

"No, but I'm worried for our safety."

"I'm concerned, too, but give me a few days to sort through what's happened. While I go to town for supplies, why don't you rest?"

*   *   *

Abe rode into Scottsville and pulled up in front of the general store. Entering, he waved to Richard Miller sitting with a group of men gossiping and discussing upcoming events. Abe exchanged a few pleasantries with them before mentioning the fire.

"Darkies, most likely," Oliver Simpson said. The others nodded in agreement.

Abe acknowledged them, but didn't reply, and moved away from the circle. As he began gathering supplies, he noticed Richard motioning him to a corner of the store out of earshot of the other men.

"I'd like to talk to you. In light of the fire, I think this would be a good time. Some planters have let me work with them, and each of us has made some money. How would you feel about doing business together?"

"I'd have to give it some thought."

"We could sign a contract. You've got some undeveloped land as well as the field that burned. I'd stand good for clearing, buying seed, and even hiring slaves from neighboring planters, if we need them, in return for a portion of the profits."

"That's an interesting proposition. Why don't you and your family come to dinner next week? We could discuss it then. Sarah and Ellen can work out the details at church Sunday."

"That sounds fine."

Abe took his time going home. He mulled over Richard Miller's offer but concentrated the majority of his thoughts on the fire. Why the eastern acreage? The most remote of all the fields. If someone wanted to hurt them, wouldn't the house have been the target? The servants seemed happy, and it was inconceivable that they would willfully torch the field. Would they be too afraid to tell Abe if it had been an accident? That made the most sense, but what nagged him was the intensity. He'd never seen a fire burn so hot in such a short time. Abe shivered as cold terror swept up from his feet, settling in his throat. Was his family in danger?

Fear of the unknown rattled Abraham Sullivan, and he couldn't shake the foreboding feeling. Who was doing this to him? Would it happen again?

CHAPTER TWO

A week had passed without incident since the fire, giving an almost surreal quality to the atmosphere. Though the trees surrounding the house formed a leafy stanchion of protection from the merciless heat, the tension in the air and the Sullivans' moods hung as heavy as black velvet draperies.

Sarah sat at her small Queen Anne's desk planning the final touches for dinner with the Millers, but her heart wasn't in it, and her body ached from lack of rest. Not knowing the origin of the fire frightened her, and she felt Abe toss and turn every night. Walking out to the kitchen, she spoke to Daisy. "I've decided an egg custard with fruit would be a good dessert. Cake seems too heavy for this weather."

Daisy nodded. "Yas'em."

Looking out the window, Sarah noticed Abe coming toward the house and went out to meet him. He put his arm around her as they walked toward the front verandah.

"You look tired, Sarah. Is my restlessness keeping you awake? Would you like to sleep in one of the other bedrooms?"

"No, I think we're both worried because we don't know anything definite about the fire."

"I'm doing everything I can to find out how much danger we're in and whether our house is going to be next.

I'm not having much success, but you don't need to lose sleep over it."

"I love our home and the fact that you built it for me, but it can be replaced. Our family and workers can't." She looked at the huge dwelling they'd lived in for the past few years.

The majestic, two-storied, antebellum mansion stood as an architectural masterpiece, fashioned from hand-chiseled limestone with large, Grecian columns encircling the entire home. Massive double doors designed with etched oak trees in the center of beveled glass inserts marked the front entrance. A wide balcony crowned a large wraparound verandah.

Waist-high, boxwood hedges edged the perimeter of the carriageway, and a formal English garden to the left of the main house added to the opulence of the residence. To the right, the terrain sloped down to a large pecan orchard, but the plantation took its name, Oak Hollow, from the plentiful oaks scattered throughout the property. Waxy-leafed Magnolias laden with abundant flowers flanked a wide trail, providing a shady canopy to welcome guests.

Sighing, Sarah took Abe's arm as they mounted the front steps. "I suppose we need to get dressed for dinner. The Millers will be here before long."

* * *

Grace and Margaret Sullivan sat on the verandah, dressed in formal gowns, awaiting the arrival of their guests. True to her name, Grace, elegant, refined, and mature beyond her years sat erect with her hands folded in her lap. Her long, blonde hair hung straight and unruffled down her back.

Margaret, the tomboy of the family, was vivacious and outspoken. Blonde ringlets highlighted with red tones framed her face with tightly coiled spirals of hair going in all directions giving her a somewhat comical appearance. She tugged on her dress, flipping up her petticoats in an attempt to fan some air underneath the tent of lace and net. Her lips turned down at the corners as she looked at her older sister, whining, "I'm so hot I think I'm going to die."

Grace, no more enthusiastic about the upcoming event than her sister exclaimed, "Stop pouting. We have to be on our best behavior for these people because Mister Miller and Papa are going to discuss an important business deal. You know we have to entertain Jane and act like young ladies."

"But I don't want to be proper. It's too hot. Let's at least take off our stockings. Please?"

"Have you taken leave of your senses? Do you know the trouble we'd be in for showing bare ankles?"

"Jane's a snob, and I don't want to see her." Maggie stood with her hands on her hips. "Well? Stop being so proper, Miss Grace, Your Highness. You need to learn to have some fun."

"No, this isn't the time to be silly, no matter how uncomfortable you are."

"You're stuffy, just like Jane. Seems to me, you could stop being so serious for a little while."

Before Maggie could persuade Grace to remove her stockings, the distant drumbeat of horses' hooves indicated company approaching. Not wanting to be seen, the girls ducked to the side of the house and peeked around the corner. They gasped as the coach-and-four came into view, an impressive, black carriage, ornate with gold trim and bright, shiny lanterns glistening like old gold in the ochre and amethyst sunset. Stopping in front of the mansion, the short, stocky driver jumped down, straightened his waistcoat, and opened the door, bending low. A gentleman exited before extending a hand to his lady. A young girl alighted last, dressed in a garish gown much too old for her age. Her air of pseudo sophistication made Maggie feign throwing up, grasping her throat and casting her eyes heavenward.

Grace grabbed her sister's hand pulling her to the back of the house and down the hall to the parlor.

"There you are, my darlings." Abraham rose as his daughters entered the room.

"Margaret. For goodness sake, your hair's a mess." Sarah began smoothing the unruly, corkscrew tresses with her hands, trying to make her younger daughter look more like a lady.

"Mister and Missus Miller," droned Obadiah, opening the large door to the parlor, bowing extra low.

Abraham crossed the room to greet the Millers. "Welcome. We're so pleased you could join us." He bent and kissed Ellen Miller's hand.

Richard Miller extended the same courtesy to Sarah. "We're so sorry to hear about the fire. Have you found out what caused it?"

Without embellishment Abe replied, "No, not yet."

Putting his hand on his daughter's back, Richard pushed her toward Grace and Maggie. "I'm sure you girls remember Jane? She's eleven now. About your age, Margaret?"

"Yes, sir. We know each other, but I'm fourteen, and Grace is fifteen."

Abe's look and firm voice quieted Maggie. "I'm sure you'll have a nice visit."

Taking their cue, the girls moved with their guest to the verandah while the adults seated themselves.

Richard turned to Abe. "Did you tell me your boys go to school somewhere?"

"Yes. Both Matthew and Joseph are in Clinton attending Mississippi College, but it won't be long until Matthew graduates and returns to help me run Oak Hollow."

A few minutes into polite conversation, Miss Daisy appeared in her crisp, black uniform overlaid with a stiffly starched, white apron. She carried a sterling silver tray of tall, crystal glasses filled with iced tea. After serving the adults, she shuffled from the room to the verandah and set the tray on a serving cart for the girls.

Jane took a glass, placing it on an end table beside a white wicker chair. With inflated decorum, she sat down arranging her gaudy, brocade gown over numerous, bouffant petticoats making it difficult for her to sit in a ladylike fashion. In her best grown-up voice, she addressed her hostesses. "I'm ever so pleased to be here. I had to leave my embroidery and voice lessons, but visiting you was so much more important. We had such a pleasant ride from town, and I have so looked forward to seeing both of you. I was just ever so thrilled when we arrived." Her eyes fluttered faster than a moth around a lantern.

Grace dared not look at Maggie knowing she swallowed laughter behind her dancing eyes.

"We've been playing down by the river with the darkies all day, but we had to hurry and get dressed for your visit."

Maggie placed her hand on her chest with an exaggerated flourish.

"Maggie! Stop teasing Jane."

Jane spoke as if Maggie weren't present. "I guess she'll grow up soon enough." Emitting a loud sigh, she drew a lace-edged handkerchief from her flat bosom and ostentatiously patted her forehead trying to appear older than her years. "My, my, it's ever so hot, isn't it?" She sighed again.

Grace tried to make conversation but wished she could knock the young girl off her lofty pedestal. Visualizing those petticoats fanning out and the lace-edged handkerchief flying out of her bosom as Miss Proper Jane toppled from her lofty perch, her feet in the air, her pantaloons showing, and her painted-like-a-woman face upside down caused Grace to smile. She stole a glance at her sister just as Obadiah announced dinner.

The girls entered the house, following the adults to the large dining room with its lavish furnishings. Soft light from tall tapers cast a warm, inviting glow and lent a mellow ambience to the room.

A pale pink, linen cloth with a cutwork pattern covered the table, one of the few things Sarah had left of her mother's handiwork. It provided a perfect backdrop for the Sullivan's best Wedgwood china. Crystal goblets etched with intricate geometrical designs caught the flickering candlelight sparkling like tiny stars just born. Gleaming with a soft patina from years of careful polishing, heavy, sterling flatware added to the splendid table appointments. The elegance and sophistication of the Sullivan household permeated the entire room, a tribute to a family who had overcome the prejudice of a small town and risen to the top of the social stratum.

The girls sat in silence throughout the meal exhibiting impeccable etiquette while conversation among the adults was muted, but cordial. The five-course meal, a gourmet masterpiece, reflected Sarah's expert planning, and the servants presented it in the precise and flawless manner typical of Southern hospitality.

Following dessert, Abe and Richard retired to the study for a business discussion and to enjoy a cigar while Sarah invited the girls and Ellen Miller to the parlor. When the men had finished their meeting, they joined their families for coffee and obligatory small talk.

After an appropriate length of time, Richard Miller spoke. "This evening has been most enjoyable, and we're sorry to see it end, but we should be getting home."

"We'd be honored for you to stay overnight and travel in the morning light."

"Thank you, but it's only a few miles to town, and with the full moon lighting the way, it should be a pleasant ride. I also have some pressing business to take care of early in the morning."

The Sullivans walked the Millers outside and waved goodbye.

Back in the parlor, Sarah turned to her husband. "The Millers are nice, but I'm glad the evening is over. Did you and Richard sign a contract?"

"Yes, but I'm a bit leery of him. They may not be as affluent as they would have us believe, my dear. I just hope he can come up with the money when we need it to clear the trees and overgrowth from the western section of land as well as restore the sixty acres that burned. This could be good for both of us, but time will tell if he can keep his end of the bargain."

"Ellen is rather cool. I have the feeling she looks down on us, but if Richard can help us, then I'll be cordial to her."

Before her parents could ask, Maggie blurted out, "I don't like Jane! She puts on airs and stinks. If I hear 'ever so' one more time, I'll scream." Putting a make-believe handkerchief to her brow and imitating their young guest, Maggie mimicked Jane in a high-pitched voice. "I'm ever so pleased, I'm ever so thrilled, it's ever so hot." She struggled to suppress her laughter. "What a spoiled girl."

"That's enough, Margaret."

Turning to her older daughter Sarah asked, "Did you enjoy her company?"

"No, I'm afraid Maggie's right. She is spoiled and she must've drowned herself in her mama's rose water. She smelled awful, but we tried to be polite."

"I'm proud of you for being courteous and ladylike to our guests, regardless of your feelings."

After goodnight kisses, the girls climbed the stairs to their room.

Even though there were eight large rooms upstairs, Grace and Maggie had always shared a bedroom. They undressed, happy to be out of their burdensome gowns, petticoats, and leggings. The heat had created a steam bath underneath the layers of heavy fabric, and the girls let out sighs of relief as they released their legs from the fiery grip of the stockings.

They slipped into thin chemises and washed their faces, soaking up every trace of coolness from the soft washcloths. While brushing their hair, they discussed the dinner, read their Bibles, and wrote in their journals.

A slight breeze played with the sheer, white curtains, and the luminous moonlight shining through the tops of the trees illuminated their room with interesting and grotesque patterns. They took turns making up stories as dancing shadows flitted across the ceiling, transforming the shapes into nature nymphs and the Wee Ones so prevalent in tales from their beloved Ireland.

Grace awoke before Maggie. Since the fire, she hadn't slept well. Though she was thankful they had escaped the potato famine, Grace didn't like America. How she longed to return to Cork, but that would never happen. Time to rouse Maggie. "Wake up, sleepyhead."

Maggie opened her eyes and smiled. "I was having the most wonderful dream. We were back in Ireland, and the grass was so green. Remember how it used to smell?"

"Oh, yes."

"I try not to think about when we lived there, but I saw our home as clear as any picture." Maggie propped her elbows on her knees, resting her face between her hands.

Grace sat on the edge of the bed. "I miss Cork. Do you?"

"Sometimes. But I like America too. Everyone's nice to us now. And there's no famine here."

Grace shivered as vivid scenes enveloped her. She wouldn't talk about the sights she saw before leaving the Emerald Isle and prayed Maggie's memory would wane until she no longer remembered it at all. Rubbing her nose, trying to rid it of the stench the visions brought to her senses, Grace spoke in a weak voice, "Hurry and get dressed, or we'll be late for choir practice."

Essie Mae only helped the girls dress on formal occasions. Most days they just asked her to lay out their clothes and collect the garments that needed to be cleaned or pressed. The young servant was a quiet, frail-looking girl of fifteen. Her sixteen-year-old sister, Lavitica June, took care of cleaning the rooms downstairs and assisting Sarah in dressing. Both girls acted polite and reserved, evidence of Miss Daisy's rearing.

"Do you remember going to Blarney Castle and kissing the stone? Do you know where the Wee Ones live and why they make little shoes?" Maggie dawdled over her petticoats.

"Of course, but you'd better hurry. You're going to make us late."

"What if I forget how life was there?"

"You won't. Mama and I won't let you."

"But already, I've forgotten a lot of the Celtic songs we used to sing. And the blessings. I can't remember how they go."

"Maybe we can get Mama to tell us some stories this afternoon."

* * *

During the practice, Grace noticed a twinkle in Maggie's eyes but waited until they started home to ask, "Did talking about Ireland this morning put you in this good mood?"

"Guess it did. I can't wait to talk to Mama."

Almost before the buggy came to a stop in front of the mansion, Maggie jumped down and rushed into the house.

"Mama!"

Sarah dropped her knitting and hurried to the front door where her youngest daughter ran soundly into her, almost knocking her down.

"Are you hurt? What is it, Margaret?"

"Oh, nothing." Maggie flashed a demure smile as she caught her breath.

"Margaret Anne Sullivan, you do not come rushing into this house, shouting, run into me, almost knock me down, and then say, 'oh, nothing,' as if you were nonchalantly passing the time of day."

"I'm sorry. I just had a wonderful dream last night. Won't you tell us stories about how Cork used to be? Before the blight? Please?" Maggie looked to Grace to help her.

"Yes, please, if you have time." Grace took Sarah's arm to calm her.

"Why in the world are you in such a hurry to hear about the Old Country?"

Maggie took a deep breath. "I don't want to forget our real home."

"Oh, my dear, that makes me very happy. Where would you like me to begin?"

"Anywhere." Maggie took Sarah's other arm, and the girls led her to the parlor.

They settled themselves at their mother's feet. Sarah's bright, blue-violet eyes sparkled like sunlit water as memories surfaced, covering her like a warm, fisherman's knit afghan.

"Well, let's see. You remember Papa's father was a farmer. Raised potatoes. My father owned a shop, kind of like the general store. We lived above it, but since Mama helped Papa, I spent most of my time downstairs with them. They did a lot of business with Papa's father, so when he'd bring Abe with him, we'd play while the grown-ups talked. As we got older, it just seemed natural for us to start courting."

"Did you ever meet or court any other boys?" Maggie asked.

"I met a whole line of them. Some would come into the shop with their parents. Others, I met at church but never courted them."

"What made you like our papa?"

"He made me feel warm and safe, and we laughed a lot."

The girls shifted positions before Sarah continued.

"The next thing I knew, he'd asked my father for my hand." She paused and gazed out the window.

Grace broke the silence. "Did Grandfather give you his blessing?"

"Oh, yes. My parents loved your papa. We had a lovely wedding. Do you remember our church in Ireland? St. Fin Barrie's Cathedral?"

Grace pictured it in her mind. "Yes. It's beautiful."

Maggie closed her eyes. "I remember bells and music."

"Yes, there's a beautiful organ, and those bells pealed on our wedding day."

Maggie looked at her mother. "I wish our church here had bells and was as grand as the one in Cork instead of plain, old wood."

Sarah patted her youngest daughter on the head. "That would be nice, my dear. I do miss our Anglican traditions from home, but even though our community church here is small, it's warm and pleasant."

Maggie fidgeted. "Did you have a large wedding?"

"It wasn't like an American wedding, but a lot of people came to the church and walked home with us for the feast my mama cooked. I wore a beautiful, sky-blue dress with

Celtic embroidery and a white wedding cloak. The most important thing to me, though, was starting life with your papa. He worked hard, and we saved everything we could to buy land. As our crops flourished, we bought more land with the profits. Later, Papa's father and mother gave us their land because they were too tired to work it anymore, and they didn't want to hire tenants. Do you remember when they moved into the little house next to ours?"

"Yes. We used to go over to get little cakes." Maggie's excitement made Grace smile.

Sarah called up the memory. "Your grandmother loved to bake."

"Wish we could have stayed." Grace's eyes clouded.

"We never intended to leave. The land was fertile and produced good crops until the famine hit, but we had to make a choice. That's when we decided to come to America so you wouldn't die from starvation."

Maggie looked up at Sarah. "Do you like America?"

"Yes, we have a good life here. The only thing upsetting me is the way some planters treat their slaves. I miss Cork, but Scottsville is our home now." A small tear moistened her cheek.

"Don't cry." Grace blotted her mother's face with a handkerchief.

"You're right. There's no time for being sad. We should be grateful we had the means to come here."

"I remember how New York felt as cold as Cork." Grace shivered.

"Yes, but the nicest part of the whole journey was the beautiful boat we boarded to sail down the Mississippi."

Grace touched her mother's hand. "Do you think we could take a trip on that boat again sometime?"

"Perhaps. But now, I need to see Daisy about dinner."

Sarah went to check on preparations for the meal, and Maggie headed for the swing on the verandah, leaving her sister some rare time alone.

The fire had unnerved Grace, and she couldn't dispel the feeling of doom haunting her day and night. What destiny, she wondered, lay ahead for the family?

CHAPTER THREE

Besides piano lessons and occasional activities at the church, Maggie occupied her time with needlework while Grace read or wrote in her journal. Sometimes, they went for walks or visited with Miss Daisy or her daughters.

On a particularly nice day, Grace and Maggie strolled along a path beside the river. It ran just behind the kitchen of the Big House before curving to flow in front of the cottages where the Negroes lived. The river looked magnificent, replete with dark, cypress trees that stood as silent sentinels, providing a cool, refreshing shade.

Grace had hoped they would settle in Vicksburg on the Mississippi River, but Papa insisted they come fifteen miles inland. He said if the great river flooded, it would ruin their crops. How ironic their fields now needed water. The stream running through Oak Hollow had never flooded, but provided hours of pleasure for the family.

Maggie looked at Grace, a puzzled expression on her face. "What do you think it feels like to have black skin?" She dropped down to sit in the soft grass by the riverbank, motioning her sister to join her.

"I guess it feels the same. Although Essie Mae has the most glorious, silky arms. Maybe black skin feels better than white."

"Yes, Miss Daisy's skin feels smooth too. Wonder why we weren't born Negro?"

"Because Mama and Papa aren't Negro, silly girl." Though slave history had interested Grace for a long time, she was surprised that Maggie showed some curiosity about the Negroes and their culture.

"Do you think it's fate the way people are born?" Maggie's brow furrowed. "Do you ever wish you could be a Negro?"

"Sometimes. Our Negroes aren't like other people's slaves, though. Some masters are so unfair and cruel, it makes me want to kill them."

"Grace! You've never talked like that before."

"But it's true. People should all be treated the same." Grace crossed her arms, adding emphasis to her statement. "Papa treats our Negroes like family. If I thought about being a Negro, I'd want to be like one of ours."

"Yes, it would be nice to be able to wear plain dresses without petticoats or stockings and go barefoot, but it must be hard not being able to go to school. I'll bet they wish they could read and write." Maggie changed the subject. "Are you sweet on Paul?"

Grace blushed. "No. Just because we sit together sometimes in church, and I let him carry my books to our buggy after school doesn't mean I'm . . . uh . . . fond of him, or anything."

"You've got a beau!" Maggie's eyes twinkled as she shouted at the top of her lungs.

"Why don't you tell the whole world, Miss Smarty Pants?"

"Do you like him a lot?"

The question had plagued Grace for a few months. She couldn't answer it to her own satisfaction, so what was she to tell her nosy little sister? "I know Papa and Mister Scott want us to marry when we're old enough, but I haven't made up my mind."

The girls started back to the house with Maggie's question reverberating in Grace's mind. Why couldn't everyone leave her alone? Maybe she wouldn't ever marry.

* * *

Slavery appalled Abe Sullivan. He'd read and heard about cruel treatment of slaves in America but assumed the mistreatment seldom occurred. What reason could owners have to abuse workers who tended the crops and kept the plantations running and solvent? Going to the slave marketplace had opened his eyes to the reality of the situation. Since he and Sarah agreed families needed to be together, he'd bought spouses and children of the slaves he'd acquired when he purchased Oak Hollow, but the ordeal of seeing people on an auction block saddened and angered him.

Since the fire, Abe had noticed a change in the servants who worked the fields. Even the house servants appeared more reserved. Riding out to the eastern field where the laborers turned the soil to bury the charred crop, Abe called to his foreman. "Something seems to be bothering you. Can you tell me what it is?"

"Naw, suh."

"Tell me the truth. You won't get into trouble, but I have to know about this fire. Was it an accident?"

Jeremiah's eyes mirrored a depth of sorrow he couldn't hide.

Abe softened his voice. "Tell me, please?"

Shaking his head, the foreman turned to Abe, keeping his eyes lowered, his voice barely audible. "Naw, suh. I ast ever'one. No one done it, but we knowed we'd be blamed. Is you gonna take away our ce'tificates and sell us, Massa?"

The apprehension of the Negroes fearing for their stability disheartened Abe. "I'd never do that! Don't you remember when Miss Sarah and I united all the families here and freed you? Everyone chose to stay with us."

"Yas, suh. But you kin take back the ce'tificates."

"No. All of you are free to go anytime. I'll even help you if I can."

"Naw, suh. Mos' folks get caut and kilt when they tries to leave. We thankful you got our fam'lies together and gave us the bes' gif' in the world...freedom. We wants to stay here."

"Your gratitude is why I know no one set the fire on purpose. And we've always agreed to keep your freedom secret, so none of you would get lynched. Most Negroes are treated worse than animals. We didn't have slaves in Ireland, and this is hard for me to understand."

"Yas, suh."

Returning to the issue of the fire, Abe said, "If you give me your word no one here started the fire, that's plenty good enough for me."

Relief washed over the old man's face. "Yas, suh, Massa."

"The reason I asked is because all the homes may be next. It's always puzzled me how hot the fire got and how fast it spread. We need to get to the bottom of this and find out who caused it."

"Yas, suh. I didn't say nuthin' 'bout it, but I post a man ever' night to watch the Big House. Iffen you want, we could get several men to ride along the edge of the property of a night, too."

The loyalty of his employees touched Abe. "That's a good idea. Have them watch your cabins as well as all the fields. And tell them to pay attention to any little detail that might give us a clue."

"Yas, suh."

School would start soon, and Scottsville prided itself on having a large school open to any student who chose to enroll. Most towns had only enough resources to offer education to boys.

After they were settled in Oak Hollow, Grace and Maggie were allowed to choose between a live-in tutor and public education. Thinking they could make new friends, they opted to go to school in town. Within the first week, their classmates began calling them names and shunning them.

Abraham's livid response prompted him to hire a tutor, determined to shield his daughters from such hatred. However, before the teacher arrived, the girls persuaded their father to let them continue at Scottsville's school, knowing that facing their enemies was the only way to overcome the bigotry. The taunting only lasted a few weeks before the winning personalities of the two girls had elevated them to the standard of the most popular young ladies.

* * *

Summer was drawing to a close, and they were busy preparing clothes for the coming year. Grace had noticed some subtle changes taking place in her body. She was thin like her mother, and her sapphire-blue eyes were as easy to read as a first grade primer. The physical changes didn't bother her as much as the emotions that were confusing and hard to control. Her sister had begun to irritate her. Grace wanted her own room.

Maggie seemed cross, and rather than listen to her complain, Grace decided to read in the parlor. Much to her dismay, Maggie tagged along behind her.

"I'll embroider while you read."

Though Grace opened the book, she felt restless and couldn't concentrate, going over the same words, trying to get into the flow. She closed the book, placing it on the table beside her chair. Watching Maggie work on a table scarf, pangs of remorse swept over her for wanting to distance herself from her younger sister. The impetuous, spontaneous nature of Maggie was like a sudden breath of fresh air. She was a little more endowed than Grace and had inherited their mother's curly hair and cupid's-bow lips. With her cornflower blue eyes, her little sister would win the heart of any man she chose.

Sighing, Maggie stretched her arms above her head. "I can't get my stitches smooth."

"Want to take a walk?"

"No, I'm just giving my hands a little break before finishing this section."

"Then I'll go by myself. Be back soon."

Grabbing her shawl, Grace almost ran from the house. The evening breeze intoxicated her senses, and she stopped to take a long, deep breath. Letting the smells of the Indian summer drift into her dainty nostrils, she enjoyed the gentle gusts of wind blowing strands of hair against her face. Feeling alive and alone, Grace reveled in the privacy she'd longed for in recent weeks. She twirled pretending to dance with the Wee Ones for a while and then dropped to her knees, stretched out, and stared up at the beautiful, pastel sunset blending together in eddies of watercolor. Closing her eyes, her thoughts ran free.

Paul Scott bothered her. He was too persistent in trying to court her, besides being boring. Just because he would follow his father and grandfather in running the bank one day, didn't impress Grace any more than the reverence the town bestowed on the Scott family, especially the grandfather, who had founded the town and named it after himself.

Then there was Missus Scott. Grace's blood tuned to ice thinking about the woman. She'd met Paul's mother a few times at church, but Louise Scott didn't go regularly or socialize with other women. Gossip had it she was frail and sickly, afraid of getting an infection if she attended functions with large crowds. But there was something else, something portentous Grace couldn't pinpoint.

Still, it would make her papa proud for her to be the leading socialite in town. As the most affluent planter in the area, Abe and John Scott, president of the bank, talked many times about their children. Grace and Paul were almost predestined to marry.

The breeze picked up and swept over Grace like a cool, cotton sheet clearing her head of Paul and his family. Turning her thoughts to Cork, she vowed to find a way to return to her magic island now that the famine was over. The bog where her father planted potatoes and the noise of the little leprechauns making shoes called to her in stolen moments.

The sounds around her quieted, alerting Grace to the approaching dusk. She opened her eyes and bolted upright. Daisy and Jeremiah's son, seventeen-year-old Jim, stood about five feet from her.

"My goodness, you scared me half to death," Grace said, catching her breath.

"I be sorry. Jes' wanted to be sure you wuz breathin' and all 'cuz you so still." Jim removed his cap and stared at the ground.

Grace laughed as her adrenaline returned to normal. "Sit down."

"Oh no'm, I couldn't do that. I bes' leave you be. Jes' came to check on you."

"Don't be silly. Of course, you can. Besides, no one can see us here."

"Yes, ma'am, but iffen your papa wuz to see me, he'd be powerful mad at me, and my family might haf to leave. We like it here better'n anywhere else we ever stayed." He looked troubled. "My mama shore wouldn't want me messin' anythin' up."

"Who's going to know? Besides, my father might say something to us, but he wouldn't be angry enough to make you go away."

Grace's smile must have calmed his fears because he sat down quite some distance from her, keeping his eyes lowered, except when she spoke to him. Grace took stock of him. He was tall and lanky with beautiful brown-black eyes that seemed to see right into her heart. His hair reminded her of chocolate curls, and his creamed-coffee skin was highlighted in the deepening veil of early evening. The low, mellow tone of his voice had a hypnotic quality, matched only by the slow, easy way he moved.

During the time the Sullivan family had owned Oak Hollow, Grace and Jim had engaged in some friendly conversations, but they'd never been alone. How strange. She wanted to sit closer, but it was taboo for white girls to socialize with, much less touch, the hired help, especially the male laborers.

All the silly rules of Americans infuriated Grace, and she decided to rebel against them, even if no one else knew.

Her Irish temperament would always be part of her, no matter how long she stayed in Scottsville. A long time ago, she'd promised herself to follow her heart…not a strange country's rules. But she'd keep up appearances for the family's sake, so she kept her hands in her lap. Besides she knew any gesture would have caused Jim to bolt. She couldn't have reached across to him anyway because she seemed glued to the spot where she sat. A sudden, defiant thought occurred to her, so dangerous it took her breath away for a moment.

Collecting herself, she asked, "Can any of the Negroes read or write?"

"No'm, we ain't 'lowed to go to school. Why is it you was askin' 'bout that?"

"Then when you have your Sunday services, how do you know what the Bible says? And if you can't read, why do you have Bibles?"

Jim smiled, his white teeth sparkling almost as much as his eyes. "It's the Good Lord's book, Miss Grace. Just holdin' it is a honor. We can't read, but our old folks has heard the Word. They pass on down what they know, and we learn real good."

"It's not right to keep you from learning to read and write. Someday, all of you may decide to leave Oak Hollow, and you'll need to know how to read papers you may be asked to sign."

"Well, ma'am, I don' think we's gonna leave and I's jes' a dumb darkie. Besides, my mama tole me iffen the lawmen found any books, 'cept the Bible in our house, they'd make it real bad on us. Maybe even kill us. Slave peoples 'posed to work, not read."

Grace knew he spoke the truth. Educating a Negro was against the law, and Jim could be dismembered or lynched. Her father could also get in a lot of trouble. She was ambivalent because she didn't want to put Jim in jeopardy, yet keeping the Negroes illiterate was another method of controlling them.

Weighing the consequences, Grace realized it had to be Jim's decision. "There's nothing I would like more than to teach you, but I don't want you to do this for me. You need to decide if it's something you want. I promise I'll never tell anyone. And don't call yourself a slave. Remember, my father freed you."

"Yas, ma'am. I be doin' some powerful thinkin' on it. I's real scart and don't know iffen I could learn anyway."

"Of course, you can!" Looking up, Grace noticed the darkening sky. "Time for me to go. You think real hard about it, and I'll meet you here tomorrow afternoon, okay?"

"Okay, ma'am." Jim bowed but looked at Grace's face before turning to walk home.

She saw a change in his eyes and at that moment, knew she'd be his teacher.

* * *

The next afternoon, Grace found Maggie in the kitchen. "Come sit with me on the back porch. I'd like to talk to you."

Maggie followed her sister to a small table on the back porch. "What's on your mind?"

"There's no easy way to say this. We've been having more disagreements lately, and I feel terrible, but I'm growing up and have decisions to make, so I'm going to start spending more time by myself."

"Well! I might not want to spend any time with you, either." Maggie's lip turned downward as her face contorted into a pout.

"You're taking this all wrong, but I expected you would before I said anything."

"Leave me alone. You won't have to worry about me chasing after you, ever again."

Guilt reared up like a nightmare monster, and Grace almost yielded to her sister's controlling behavior, but she pushed it aside. As the youngest, Maggie always got her way. Now it was Grace's turn.

CHAPTER FOUR

Abraham walked to the barn, preparing to go to town for supplies and the mail when he saw Jeremiah pulling into the barnyard in the work wagon. Abe turned to greet him.

"You ast me if we found anythin' to come tell you." He produced a tin can. "We foun' this in a clump o' bushes on the other side of the burned field. That part you wuz thinkin' 'bout clearin' for new crops."

Abe looked at the can and doubted its significance, but before he could speak, Jeremiah shoved it in his face.

"Smell it, Massa."

A faint odor of lantern oil wafted past Abe's nose.

"This can still smells, so's it can't have been there long."

Abe nodded. So the fire had been an intentional attempt to wipe them out. The time had come to tell Sheriff Morris Robertson. He thanked Jeremiah and kept the can, but didn't mention anything to Sarah.

* * *

Abe walked into the sheriff's office, handed him the can, and reported the fire, but the news had already spread through town, compliments of the men at the general store. "Somebody wanted to ruin me," Abe said.

"I've heard you're pretty easy on your slaves, but you've got to know, they're probably the ones who did this. This is how they get back at you." The sheriff pushed the can to one side.

Keeping his promise not to mention the freed status of his servants, Abe replied, "That may be true, but why would they bring me the can?"

"To throw you off. I'll keep my ears open, but I think the slaves did it."

Abe left town, more worried than ever. He knew his servants didn't set the fire.

* * *

That afternoon, Grace met Jim in the grove where they sat on a carpet of grass inside a sheltered circle formed by old, stately pecan trees.

Jim fumbled for words. "Okay, Miss Grace. I prob'ly gonna be kilt or my hand cut off, but I'll try real hard to learn. We can't never tell nobody, though."

Breaking rules appeared to make Jim nervous, so Grace attempted to allay his fears with a smile. She patted the ground beside her. "You have to sit next to me, so you can see the book I brought."

With hesitant steps, he inched toward her where they sat side by side for over an hour. Grace showed him the alphabet, sounding out each letter for the first lesson. Jim repeated the sounds over and over until he sounded almost like Grace. She smiled at the thought of Jim with an Irish brogue to replace his African dialect.

When it was time to end the session, Grace suggested they hide the book in order for Jim to have access to it when she couldn't be with him. Rather than arranging specific meeting times, they agreed to a random schedule, so no one would get suspicious, especially Maggie.

Grace discussed the first day of school with her sister. "Did you notice most of the girls had finishing school and coming out parties on their minds?"

"Yes. Wonder why they get so excited?"

"Tradition. Seems social graces hold more importance than book learning for young ladies in America."

"Paul Scott and Daniel Winston both like you."

"I don't know anything about Daniel, except his father owns the plantation next to ours. We've passed on the road a few times."

"Paul acts jealous."

Grace frowned. "He's getting more possessive of my time and always walks me to the buggy. Sometimes, though he's never said so, I think he'd fight to the death for what he wants, and that bothers me."

Maggie's attitude had remained friendly but somewhat cool toward Grace following their discussion on the porch. On occasion they had some long conversations, but Maggie didn't infringe on Grace's time.

Using her new found freedom to full advantage, Grace met more often with Jim and showed him how to put sounds together to form words. He practiced the simple exercises she gave him when he could find a spare moment and absorbed the lessons like a towel soaked up water. After only three weeks, he could sound out and pronounce most one syllable words by himself.

Jim's accelerated progress both delighted and amazed Grace, confirming what she'd already observed. Jim was bright, very bright.

Just as Abe began to calm down, Jeremiah reported a light-colored horse, like one Samuel Winston owned, had been spotted in the wooded area across from the eastern field. A night guard had surprised the rider, but he'd whipped his horse into a dead run before the Negro saw his face.

Scouring the land, the Negroes found a broken whiskey bottle with only a small part of a private label still adhering to it. Smoothing out the crumpled paper over the bottle, Abe made out half of a coat of arms and the letters W-I-N-S.

* * *

Heading into town, Abe gave Sheriff Robertson the details and showed him the bottle. "Tell me what you know about Samuel Winston, other than he's my neighbor."

"I was just coming to see you. George Johnston told me that Sam came into the saloon last night and got pretty drunk. He bought George a drink and let it slip off his tongue that he didn't want his son courting Miss Grace. Said he'd intended to put you in financial ruin, so you'd leave town, but you put out the fire before the rest of the crops burned."

Abe mulled over the information. "That doesn't make sense, Sheriff. Why would he want to destroy an entire plantation over my daughter? He could keep his son from seeing her, or I could have. We could've talked about it. And why didn't he burn the house? There's more to this."

"You may be right. I guess you didn't know Samuel Winston planned to buy Oak Hollow before you purchased it but hadn't been able to raise the money. And he'd give his soul to live in your home, especially if you were forced to leave. Maybe that's what this is all about. The man's jealous."

"Then my business is finished here. I'm on my way to pay Mister Winston a call. We're going to get a few things straight."

"I understand you're upset, but I think it would be a good idea for me to go with you."

"I want you to put him in jail and not let him see daylight for as long as you can keep him there. He could have killed my family."

"All we have is a drinking man's testimony and a slave's description of a horse that resembles one of Sam's. You don't have much of a chance in court, but I think I can get it through his head he's not to bother you any longer."

"I don't mind if you go, Sheriff, but no one hurts my family again. We've had enough suffering to last us the rest of our lives and then some. I'm more than weary of it."

* * *

As Abe expected, Samuel Winston denied any involvement, but the guilt that washed across him left no doubt in Abe's mind. His neighbor had set the fire! Sheriff Robertson threatened the planter, telling him he had it on good authority that Sam was the perpetrator and gave him two choices—be arrested with his plantation going to Abe as payment for damages or pay up now.

Abe spoke in a low, deliberate manner. "I don't want any more trouble, but my family is the most important thing in my life. We've endured more pain and ridicule than you can imagine, so I'm warning you. I have guards posted. You or your family step one foot on my property, and I'll kill you. Do you understand?"

Sheriff Robertson's stare could've bored a hole in Sam's brain. "Well? What's your choice? If you pay Abe for his damages, you'll be getting out pretty light since only one field burned, but it's up to you."

Sam walked to the window and stared out, deep in thought. After quite some time, he said, "I'm not saying I did it, but I'll pay damages rather than go to jail. Tell me how much it'll take." Abe gave him a figure, and Sam disappeared into his study. When he came out, he handed Abe a check for the agreed amount.

Abe looked at him. "Don't forget what I said."

Leaving Sam's house, the sheriff seemed confident that the matter had been resolved, but Abraham didn't share his view and made a mental note to keep the guards on duty day and night.

The two men dropped the subject of the fire and discussed the latest news in town.

* * *

Returning home, Abe told Sarah and the girls the whole story, assuring them there'd be no more trouble. While Grace felt relieved to know who caused the fire, she couldn't relax. Putting her hands on her hips, she turned to her father. "I know one thing, Papa. If Daniel Winston even thinks about looking at me, much less courting me, he'll be sorry."

The family laughed at Grace's determined look as they sat down to a light lunch.

* * *

Grace stole away a couple of weeks later. Jim sat waiting for her with an open book in front of him, moving his finger over each word as he read aloud. "I been practicin' and tryin' to pick out words in the Bible."

"That's wonderful. You're doing quite well. I'm so proud of you." Grace produced some additional books, and they studied for a while but spent a lot of time just talking.

As their session came to a close, Grace said, "When you feel ready, I'll bring a slate, and you can learn to write."

"Oh, I'm not ready for that."

Grace laughed and waved goodbye. For the first time, she admitted to herself what started as her disobedience against American rules could be turning into a bond of friendship.

* * *

Days flew by. A mild October guaranteed the success of the Scottsville Fall Festival, but November arrived cold and blustery. The boys couldn't get home for Thanksgiving, so the day passed with little difference than any other day, except for the feast Miss Daisy prepared.

Grace looked forward to meetings with Jim, and even with the harsh weather, they met every two or three weeks. The shortened days left little light for studying, but Grace found enough time to instruct him in the basics of writing. Just as he had done with reading, he excelled in mastering the lessons in record time.

Their friendship moved beyond teacher and student. Grace couldn't really define it, other than to acknowledge a special kind of understanding, like some kind of telepathy that seemed to exist between them. An inner knowledge of when the other one would be in the circle, and she wondered if Jim had noticed it.

"Do you watch the Big House?" she asked.

"Sometimes, I does, when I's not in the fields, jes' to make sure ever'thin' is okay." Jim fingered the edge of a book.

"Is that how you know I'll be here?"

"Sometimes. But other times, I kinda feels you. I come here, and you jes' shows up. Why you askin' me that? Is somethin' wrong?"

"No, I just wondered." Grace shivered as a brisk wind whipped through the trees, urging her toward the house and its warmth.

* * *

The cold winds continued from Thanksgiving to the middle of December but then quieted down as if preparing for Christmas. Matthew and Joseph arrived home from college, and the house became a swirl of activity and noise. The boys cut the tree, making a big production of letting their sisters help decorate it.

On Christmas Day, Daisy and her girls prepared the traditional meal and served it in the beautiful dining room. After dinner, the young people gathered in the parlor to play dominoes on the last night before the boys returned to school.

The rest of the winter passed without consequence. Grace saw Jim for brief meetings as often as she could sneak away, devising ways to hide books for him when they couldn't spend time together. Many late afternoons when they did manage to meet, they studied very little, preferring to talk and share feelings.

Grace told Jim about Ireland. He recounted his perspective on slavery and what it had done to his family. Their bond grew tighter though neither voiced that they noticed.

*   *   *

As a promise of spring approached, Scottsville came to life. The school held a box supper on Valentine's Day to raise money for more textbooks, and ladies of all ages scurried around getting ready for the social event.

"What are we supposed to do?" Maggie asked.

Grace explained, "We decorate a box with colored paper and whatever else we want on it and put food inside. The auctioneer puts a number on it and gives us a piece of paper with the same number."

"And?" Maggie tapped her fingers on the table.

"Boys bid on the box. The highest bidder has the honor of eating with the girl who made it."

"So that's why Charles Burton wanted to know what mine would look like."

"You're not supposed to tell!"

"Are you going to tell Paul?"

Grace's eyes twinkled. "Let's just say, he'll probably get my box!"

*   *   *

A local band played, and the gala raised more than enough money for books. Paul spent a tidy sum but had the highest bid for Grace's box.

Knowing Charles had very little money, Maggie made a plain box with little embellishment, and as Grace had expected, her sister's box went to him. Watching them eat together gave Grace a warm feeling. They seemed to be unaware of anyone else in the room. She had never had that feeling for Paul and wondered if she ever would.

* * *

Mild days continued as February came to a close, but a howling wind heralded the Ides of March, an unpleasant evening punctuated by a somber-looking Abe. The girls had been called to a meeting, and as they entered the room, they went straight to the sofa, sitting without a word, waiting for their father to speak.

"Your mother and I have made an important decision."

Sarah sat with her hands clasped in her lap, no expression on her face.

Grace determined that something had happened with Mister Miller and expected imminent doom to descend on them at any time. She felt Maggie stiffen and watched her fingers fly into her mouth, as they did when something upset her. Her eyes filled with tears.

Sarah looked at her husband. "Oh my, you've scared these girls out of a day's growth." Turning to Maggie, she patted her hand. "Don't cry. It isn't bad news at all."

Abraham's countenance softened. "Don't be upset. This is about finishing school. We want you to go since you'll be a prominent part of Scottsville's society upon marriage, and your debut will establish us as the all American family."

Maggie wiped her hands across her cheeks. "Papa. . . ."

Abe raised his hand. "Let me finish, Margaret. We haven't said anything because Mister Miller has had some financial problems, and we knew we'd have to dip into your finishing school money to accomplish planting we need to do. We were sure we'd have to postpone your going, Grace."

Sarah couldn't hold back her excitement any longer. "But your papa talked to Mister Miller yesterday. All his affairs are in order now! He'll be giving Papa money to clear and plant big crops on the lower land. So Grace, you're set to go and should be well prepared for marriage after Miss Bouvier finishes with you!"

Abraham looked from one daughter to the other, taking his time. "Margaret, we also need to make plans for you. If you don't want to finish formal schooling, you and Grace could go to Miss Bouvier's together."

"I . . . I'm not going!" Tears streamed down Maggie's pale cheeks. "Not to finishing school or any other kind of school. Don't like it, and I'm not going."

Grace sat in silence. She didn't want to go either. But she had the reputation of being sensible and dependable while everyone considered Maggie to be headstrong and impulsive. How little her parents knew about their older daughter.

Abe's tone changed. "Your mother and I expect you'll do the proper thing." Those words ended the discussion.

Sarah stood. "We'll talk more in the morning."

In the bedroom getting ready for bed, Grace weighed the difference between herself and her sister. Maggie knew what she wanted and would go after it, regardless of what anyone thought. She'd planned out her whole life...even down to the number of children she'd have. Grace envied her. Why couldn't her life be that simple? Why did she keep her desires secret? Too concerned about appearances, she guessed.

"My goodness, what are you thinking?" Maggie asked.

"About the future. What do you suppose Papa and Mama will do when they find out you're planning to become a seamstress?"

Maggie giggled. "Mama will probably faint, and Papa will turn red and pound his fists, but I don't care."

"Of course, you do."

"No, I don't. If I tell you a big secret, will you promise not to tell?"

Grace crossed her arms over her chest. "Cross my heart. What is it?"

"Remember Charles Burton?

"The barber's son?"

"Yes. He shared my box with me. He doesn't know how I feel, but every time he talks to me, my head goes all dizzy."

"You silly thing. That doesn't mean he's the one for you!"

"Yes, it does. Wait and see!"

CHAPTER FIVE

Grace couldn't sleep. She wanted to experience how it felt to walk under the stars. Slipping out of bed, she drew her lace-edged batiste wrapper around her and on cat-like feet, felt her way to the door. Taking her time, she made her way down the stairs and out the back door.

The full moon seemed to flirt with her, winking as heavy clouds passed in front of it. Tonight would be the first time Grace had ever gone barefoot outside. Trying to quiet her nerves, she took a deep breath and cautiously extended her small, naked foot to the carpet of natural elements, anticipating how it would feel. Fearful, she drew back, held her breath, and tried again. Determined, she raised her wrapper and placed her tender foot flat on the ground. She shivered, not from cold, but from the unfamiliar. Small, thin, dew-kissed tendrils of grass crept between her toes as crisp, dried leaves crunched under the pressure of her heel. Her weight pushed her feet against tiny, hidden sticks and planed surfaces of pebbles, which gave her a thrilling, tickling excitement that was most exhilarating.

The sensation almost overwhelmed her, and she had to put both hands to her mouth to choke back a squeal. She imagined herself a darkie as the wind whipped her cotton

chemise against her skin under the light robe. Grace felt free—
no confining stockings, petticoats, or heavy dresses. Wisps of
hair blew in all directions from the saucy breeze as it ruffled
through each strand performing a pantomime dance with
her golden tresses. Smiling, she picked her way by the erratic
light of the moon to her favorite spot, the outdoor classroom
where she always met Jim. Sitting on the grass and peering into
the darkness, she realized she'd never known that stars really
twinkled, or that the sky was so vast. The firmament reminded
her of a bowl, an upside down bowl of sparkling, faceted
diamonds swimming in a deep, ebony sea. Moisture began to
creep through the thin clothes to her legs and buttocks, a new
and pleasant experience. She relished this moment. Looking
across the river, pinpricks of light coming from the darkies'
huts reflected on the water like tiny chandeliers.

Grace's ears picked up the faint strains of a Negro
spiritual floating on the air. The strong breeze muffled the
sound of the already hushed voices, and though she couldn't
understand the words, the music soothed her soul, calming
the jitters she couldn't define. Trying to get nearer to the
music without being seen, Grace edged her way from tree to
tree along the riverbank toward the huts. As she got closer, a
large boulder blocked her way, but hiding behind it gave her
a perfect panorama of events unfolding across the river. The
music grew a little louder. She noticed a crowd had gathered
in the tabernacle the Negro men had built for their church
services. Wednesday, that's it. The mid-week service was
winding down.

Please don't stop the music she begged in a soundless
voice, hoping her thoughts would influence the meeting.

Lanterns hung from the rafters of the octagon-shaped, open sided structure. Large willow trees, scattered in a haphazard pattern around the area, seemed to be keeping time with the music as their branches ebbed and flowed with the breeze.

The wind quieted, and Grace heard the first clear note. She didn't know Jim could sing, but his deep, melodic voice surged through her body, touching the inner core of her heart. Grace didn't move until all the lanterns had been extinguished. Sitting alone in the silence with a circle of light from heaven's ceiling, her thoughts kept her company.

She had left the house to formulate a plan for her life, but the music consumed her, leaving an unshakable longing in her heart. The deep spiritual bond she'd felt with the Negroes stirred a long forgotten chord in her soul, echoing what she'd never acknowledged. She missed the closeness of life the way it had been before the famine in Cork. Given her choice, she'd make her way back to Ireland, so she wouldn't have to become Paul Scott's wife in America.

Grace's thoughts cleared, replaced by a peace she hadn't known since leaving the Green Isle. Lingering, she enjoyed the contented feeling until the dark elegance of night faded to a dull gray, signaling sunrise.

She had to hurry to get back to the house before anyone woke and missed her. With agile feet, Grace flew over the damp landscape. She made it back into the bedroom unnoticed. Her date with the velvet night played out in her mind. What if she'd been found out? Her antics would have displeased Papa, and Mama would have been disgraced at her daughter wearing so few clothes outside.

* * *

After school, Paul caught up with Grace and grabbed her books. "When are you going to let me call on you?"

"I'll ask Papa. Maybe it won't be too long,"

"I'd like to call on your birthday next week."

"Let me see what I can arrange." Taking her books from him, she scurried through the big oak door of the school and spotted Maggie animatedly talking with some of her friends.

"Grace!" Maggie shouted. "Come here. Susan told me a traveling circus is coming to town next week. Isn't that great?"

"Yes. I'll wait for you in the carriage." Grace's voice lacked enthusiasm as she nodded to Robert who had opened the carriage door for her. Though he was too old to work very hard, he was still a good driver, and Abe had given him the job of transporting the girls to and from school.

Maggie cut her conversation short in order to join her sister.

"I want to talk to you." Grace turned toward Maggie who fussed with her petticoats.

"What? You want to know about the circus?"

"No, not that. So many things are whirling through my brain. Finishing school, making a debut, and what to do if I don't marry Paul. He's getting more persistent by the day. I'm confused and afraid of keeping you from resting when I can't sleep. What would you think of having a door opened between our room and the one next to it so I could have my own bedroom?"

"Why?"

"I'm going to be sixteen next week. It's time we each had some privacy."

"I want you with me."

Maggie's face turned red, but Grace refused to give in to her sister's anger or her own pangs of guilt. "You're so creative, and with my bed out of the way, you'll have more room to spread out your fabric."

Maggie's face contorted. Though she tried to control her temper she screeched, "No! What could you do in your own room that you can't do now?"

"Have some time to myself." Grace stole a brief glance at her sister, but softened. "If you ever find the need to talk, I'll be right next door."

Maggie didn't speak the rest of the way home.

As soon as the carriage stopped, Grace greeted her mother and headed alone for the circle. Hurrying as fast as she dared, she still couldn't keep up with the racing of her heart, knowing Jim would be waiting.

"Hey, ma'am," he whispered from behind a tree.

"You can come out in the open." A little laugh escaped her lips. As he neared her, a faint fragrance floated past her nose.

She closed her eyes, trying to ascertain the scent. Hay. The sweet smell was just like fresh-mowed hay. Clean, wholesome. Jim had bathed before meeting her. He didn't seem to want to study. Instead, he narrated the horrible memories of having his father taken from their family. Grace wanted to scream as he described the beatings both his parents had endured and the humiliation they'd all suffered.

"The other massas treated us worse than dogs. Jes' 'cuz we's not white, they thinks we can't feel nuthin' through black skin. That's why we gots it so good here, Miss Grace. When Massa Sullivan bought my daddy, my mama said he was a pure angel come straight down from heaven."

"Why are people so cruel? Treating another human being, or even an animal, that way breaks my heart, but one of these days, I'll find a way to pay them back."

"It's okay now. Don' you fret. We's real happy here."

"What about your friends?"

"They's not so good, but Mama says one of these days, the Good Lord'll take care of them awful massas. What the Lord'll do be worse than anythin' they could do to us. He's powerful big, ma'am."

"Still, I wish I could do something." Grace reflected on the cruelty and insincerity that defined America for her. "Promise me something."

"Yas, ma'am. Anythin' you wants."

"Promise you'll continue reading and writing and you'll teach as many of your people as you can."

"Yas, ma'am, I do that. Some of my peoples runnin' away to the North. Lots of 'em don' make it, but them that does gets hired jes' like they's white folks."

"Then it's even more important that they're educated."

"Yas, ma'am."

The setting sun reminded Grace and Jim the time had come to end their visit. Bidding her friend a hasty goodbye, Grace lingered for one last look before starting home. She saw the gratitude in Jim's eyes before he turned and ran toward the river.

* * *

"Grace, you look radiant tonight. You and Paul must've had a nice conversation at school." Sarah blushed, giving away her curiosity.

"Maybe it's because I've been talking to the teacher about a suitable career."

Abraham stopped eating, "My dear, don't give it a thought. You'll marry well and carry on the tradition of the family, you and Margaret both." The discussion was ended.

To keep from smiling, Grace looked down at her English peas. No sleep last night, wandering around half-naked, teaching a darkie to read for the last several months, and her mother thought she looked radiant. Grace took great delight that no one knew her secrets. In her heart, she knew she'd never again set foot in Ireland, and Jim's education would be the only thing to come from their meetings, but being in control of part of her life that no one knew about gave her a sense of herself. She'd keep this part of her life private even though her public life had been arranged. She'd live up to her family's expectation and marry a leader in Scottsville. That meant Paul, whether she liked him, or not.

Maggie described the upcoming circus. "Papa, may we go, please?" she pleaded.

"No! You absolutely may not go. Why, I've heard some of the women show their ankles and more, and if you think one of my daughters will be seen there, you'd better think again, young lady."

Abe's mood changed as a heavy weight of despair assaulted him. Failure lay all around him. The crops were going to die if it didn't rain soon. Though he didn't need any resources at the moment, he had a disquieting sense if money became an issue, Miller might never come through with his offer. The knowledge Abe might not be able to send the girls to finishing school after all engulfed him, further darkening his state of mind. How he longed to go home to Cork, but he'd never let anyone know. America lacked a lot in being the promise land as he'd been told. Problem was he'd severed all ties making returning impossible.

"Abraham?"

Sarah's sweet voice interrupted his thoughts, but Abe couldn't dispel the sadness pervading his soul. He rose, lowered his gaze, and half-whispered, "Please excuse me." He rushed toward his study.

Sitting at his desk, Abe fingered a letter that had arrived a few weeks ago, one that if he were not careful, could change their lives forever. He pushed most of his thoughts aside. The major obstacle that confounded him right now was how to tell Sarah the contents. Yet he had no right to keep secrets from her. There never seemed to be a right time. After returning the envelope to the middle drawer, he locked it and pocketed the key. The secret remained safe in his heart as he left the study to join his wife in the parlor.

"What's troubling you?" Sarah rose and hugged him.

"I'm a little worried that Oak Hollow is too big an undertaking." They sat down, and Abe put his arm around his wife's shoulders.

"I wish we could've stayed in Cork, but we did the right thing. At least, we brought our parents with us. They had a comfortable life here in America and died with full stomachs instead of starving."

Abe rubbed his jaw. "Yes, but I wonder what really caused the famine. Did the British send the potato blight as a way of controlling us as people say? Or did the Americans cause it in order to get us to sell our grain at a low price to afford passage out of there?"

Sarah leaned closer to her husband. "I don't think we'll ever know, but I never understood why the farmers let their families die, so they could send grain to America. Guess it doesn't really matter who was responsible. In the end, people starved, regardless. Working in the shelters, watching people die a slow, agonizing death is a memory I can't erase."

"When you stopped eating and collapsed, my decision was made to leave. I couldn't bear to lose you, Sarah. My only regret is not investigating a little more about plantation life before I uprooted us. We have some good people with this place if I can just make it pay."

"You will. Freeing the Negroes was a beautiful gesture, dear. People shouldn't be chattel."

"Let's go to bed, Sarah."

Abe couldn't sleep. He'd ignored the intermittent chest pains flaring up over the past few weeks. Though the discomfort had let up some, it still interfered with his rest, an alarm that it was time to put his affairs in order and tell Sarah the truth so he could relax. Try as he might, though, he couldn't quiet his mind.

The children invaded his thoughts. Matthew and Grace didn't worry him. They'd be faithful stewards of the family name and do the proper thing. But Joseph and Margaret didn't seem to have a care in the world. Abe wouldn't have been surprised to find them working as a team in that transient circus. Just had to get them settled and make them understand the meaning of responsibility. After all, they had his name to uphold, didn't they?

He crept out of bed, heading for his study. Maybe a shot of Irish whiskey would settle his nerves.

Sarah heard Abe get up. She worried about him, knowing he, alone, carried the burden of responsibility for this plantation. She wanted to help, but he always turned her away. What else stood between them? Why hadn't Abe shared what troubled him? For the life of her, she couldn't imagine what it could be. When he left the bed, her first inclination had been to run after him to soothe his soul, and hold him, but she knew he'd resist and brush her away with a flick of his wrist. Tiptoeing to the door of Abe's study, Sarah listened to her husband pacing. Intruding would only intensify his inner turmoil. Instead, she turned away, wondering if Abe would ever tell her the secret that tore at his tormented soul.

CHAPTER SIX

Bright sun and warm days coaxed shoots of wildflowers out of the ground, forcing them to bloom early, their sweet perfume delighting the senses. Their vibrant colors adorned the table for Grace's sixteenth birthday dinner, and as a surprise, the Sullivans had invited Paul and his parents to join them.

Waiting for the meal to be served, Paul gazed at Grace. "I'm so glad you have seven people here for your birthday because seven is such a sacred number."

Louise Scott smiled as she addressed her son. "Grace probably hasn't studied the significance of numbers as we have, but there's plenty of time to teach her." She turned to Grace. "Paul has always been curious about life around him. We've done some reading on the way numbers interact with each other. Seven is the perfect number."

Grace didn't understand but decided to dismiss it rather than get into a lengthy conversation.

After dinner, Paul presented her with a box of pastel stationary while Maggie gave her some pearl encrusted combs for her hair. Abe and Sarah handed her a gold broach inlaid with sapphires.

The adults moved to the parlor, and Maggie, sensing Paul wanted to be alone with Grace, made an excuse to go for a walk. Paul winked at Maggie before leading Grace outside. "I'm very pleased your father is going to let me see you even though you haven't made your debut, and surprising you on your birthday was wonderful. Are you enjoying yourself?"

"Yes, I'm having a grand time." Grace hoped Paul didn't detect her lie.

He spent the evening talking about taking over the bank and making money. His arrogant attitude bothered Grace, and the forced conversation lulled, making the minutes drag. When he held her hand, instead of feeling close and warm, Grace felt as if she were a prisoner, his hands being the bars preventing her from running.

After what seemed an interminable length of time, Abe and Sarah led the Scotts to the front verandah, and after a brief conversation, Paul and his parents took their leave.

* * *

Grace hadn't realized Maggie felt neglected until several days after the birthday dinner when she begged in her most convincing voice, "Please, will you play something with me?"

"What?"

"Checkers or something. Anything. You never have time for me, and when you do, you fuss at me and make me feel terrible."

"Pouting has always worked for you, hasn't it, little sister?"

Grace pulled the game from the storage chest in the hall. As she set the board on the large, intricately carved oak table in the dining room, Grace watched her sister. Maggie had always loved the table and asked many times to eat on it without a tablecloth. Grace noticed as she sorted the checkers, Maggie ran her fingers around each swirl of the complicated Celtic design forming the border around the outer edge of the table. The pattern absorbed light in one place, reflecting it in another, bringing the design to life. At times the patterns gave the impression the swirls were moving. Abraham had the table made by a master woodworker and presented it to Sarah just after they moved into the house.

"Your move," Grace said.

"I don't really want to play. Can we just talk? I need your help."

"Of course. What's wrong?"

"I'm sad and happy all at the same time, and Papa's going to be mad at me."

"What makes you think that?"

"Charles asked me to be his girl next year, and I promised."

"Honey, if that's all that's wrong, don't worry about it. A year is a long time, and you know Papa won't let a fellow court you until he thinks you're ready. That may not be until you're out of finishing school."

"You don't understand. I am not going to finishing school, and no one can make me. I'm going to open a shop, sew, marry Charles, and have six children."

"I wouldn't suggest you tell Papa about this anytime soon."

"But he's letting Paul court you."

"Yes, but Paul is the banker's son, and if I decide to marry him, Papa would benefit a lot."

"It doesn't sound to me as if you love Paul. Don't marry him if you're not sure."

"I'll think about that. But right now, I'm sleepy. Think I'll turn in."

"Me, too."

The morning light awakened the girls early. As they descended the stairs, Sarah met them. "Don't forget Matt and Joe will be home today, but they won't be able to stay very long. They have to get back for some summer courses they want to take." Sarah fluttered around like a hummingbird in a garden of red trumpet flowers.

*　*　*

After school, as they neared home, Grace looked out of the carriage window. Her brothers stood on the front steps of the verandah waving as Robert pulled the buggy into the carriageway in front of the mansion. Matthew looked more like Papa every time Grace saw him.

Tall, slim, already a wrinkle between his eyebrows. His steel-blue eyes under straight, jet-black hair gave him a striking appearance, and he always stood out in a crowd. In spite of his smile, Matt looked serious and withdrawn as if his heart carried a burden too heavy for his twenty-year-old body.

The girls alighted, and after excited embraces, moved with their brothers to the outside furniture on the verandah. As they sat down, Joseph and Maggie tried to outdo each other with wild, and sometimes not-so-truthful, stories. They waved their arms, laughing at their tales and even managed to draw Matthew and Grace into the revelry.

The gaiety filtered throughout the house. Daisy's dancing eyes and wide smile gave testament to her happiness at the boys' homecoming as she plodded outside with a tray of lemonade.

Grace couldn't define the difference in Joseph, but his midnight-blue eyes no longer seemed to be laughing at the world. His happy-go-lucky attitude had vanished, replaced by a sadness that spoke louder than his joking with Maggie. Joe, at nineteen, was the epitome of an Irish lad, short and stocky with curly red hair to match his ruddy complexion, making his seriousness seem out of place. A persistent gnawing usurped Grace's thinking, and she swore to uncover her brothers' secrets.

"Joe," whispered Maggie, "did you know there's a circus coming to town? Papa says we can't go, but you could take us. Will you, please?"

Maggie's begging must have touched Joe's heart and sense of adventure. He threw his head back, giving a big belly laugh that almost shook the verandah.

"Be quiet, Joe. You'll have Mama out here for sure."

"Okay, Magpie," he said, using the pet name only he was allowed to call her. "I'll think about it."

Matthew interrupted the jovial gathering. "I'm going in to read a while before dinner if you'll excuse me."

Grace wanted to see Jim if only for a short visit. Matt's leaving gave her the perfect opportunity to go to the circle. "You two keep telling your little tales. I need to write something down." She rushed up the stairs two at a time, grabbed her journal, and bolted out the back door. Running down the path with her petticoats flying like an inflated circus tent behind her, she headed straight for their meeting place.

Jim sat in the grass, turning over a pecan leaf in his hands. He appeared to be studying it.

"Hey," gasped Grace, trying to catch her breath and regain some semblance of her dignity.

"Hey, ma'am." He stood and bowed in one perpetual motion.

My, he looks elegant and genteel, even barefoot and in tattered clothes, she thought. His voice seemed to start way down deep in his soul before flowing from his throat. Jim's presence worked its magic on Grace, and she relaxed, though her knees felt weak, and her heart pounded. Running must have caused her to feel this way.

Together, as if directed by some unseen force, they lowered themselves to the ground and sat facing each other.

"I'm so glad you're here, so I didn't have to go looking for you."

"I seen your brothers come in. I knowed you'd be busy with family, but I jes' come here to think."

"There are a couple of things bothering me. The first is why you call me ma'am all the time. We're friends now, and you can just call me Grace. The other thing I need to know is if you're afraid someone will find out I've been teaching you?"

"No'm, it ain't that. I jes' hadn't had nobody who wanted to teach me nuthin' 'sides how to pick cotton or hoe or somethin' like that. I ain't had no white folks want to be my frien' in my whole life."

Jim fumbled with his fingers, splitting the leaf in two. He tossed the pieces to the wind, trying not to call attention to his shaking hands. Nervous and uncomfortable, sweat began to blot his shirt, and his brain went fuzzy. Though wanting to explain to this beautiful angel how he felt, he didn't know what to say. "Sometimes, ma . . . uh, Miss Grace, feelin's come up from way down deep in my soul that's so powerful, they make me feel funny, almos' make me fall over. Makes me feel my heart jes' gonna blow up, but I ain't never talked 'bout it 'cuz mens 'posed to be strong." He tried to cover his embarrassment at letting his emotions show.

"I know the feelings you're talking about."

"Sometimes they's sad, sometimes happy. Sometimes so, so . . . I don' know the word, Miss Grace, but so..."

"Spiritual?" she asked.

"Yeah, spiritual. Like church. Like close to God where you dump down yore burdens, so's He kin pick 'em up and carry 'em for you. Do you understand what I'm tryin' to say?"

"Yes." Grace turned her head. With a quick swipe of her hand she brushed away the tears on her cheek. "That's the most beautiful thing I've ever heard. I so wish I didn't have to go back to the house. Promise you'll meet me here the minute you see my brothers leave."

"Yes, ma'am . . . uh . . . Miss Grace, I be here when you come back."

He stood, waiting for her to position her petticoats and dress, so she could rise in a graceful manner. If only he could help her up, but that was forbidden. He ached to touch her skin, so white, so perfect, so pure. The setting sun's soft rays framed her beautiful, flaxen hair that sparkled like burnished gold. Jim knew he shouldn't be having these thoughts, but he couldn't help it. No one, except his mama, had ever been this concerned about him. Most white folks never even bothered to look his way, and here she was calling him a friend. He was just too baffled to sort it all out. There'd be time enough for thinking while waiting for her to return.

Grace got to her feet. How nice it would have been if Jim had given her his hand to help her up, but she knew he wouldn't initiate such a familiar action. Her father had never been prejudiced, but Grace knew he wouldn't understand if she and Jim entertained the notion of touching each other, even just as friends.

Suddenly, nothing seemed real. Grace couldn't figure out what was happening, but she didn't care, either. She reached for Jim's hands, and they stood, stone still, shocked, their gazes locked on each other, sealing a profound and indescribable bond. The moment was suspended in time, carrying the weight of hundreds of years, thousands of tears, and millions of smiles, of their ancestors, of the present, of future generations. Nothing mattered, yet everything took on utmost importance. A magical sketch had been drawn on the canvas of time, and Grace felt she would faint at any moment. The only audible sound came from Jim. A slow, deep sigh, caressing her with a breath so sweet and light, she knew she would surely die.

This had to mean nothing and could never happen again. They shouldn't even be friends, much less share intimate moments together. She was white. He was black. Jim squeezed her hands with a gentleness that stopped her heart for a second, dropped his eyes, and turned to go, but looking over his shoulder, he raised his hand in salute to her. Grace couldn't walk. Not one part of her body, with the exception of her heart, seemed alive. After a few deep breaths, she thrust herself forward in an awkward motion.

By the time she reached the house, she had regained most of her composure, ready to join in the festivities of celebration of her brothers' visit.

Sitting at the dinner table, Abraham turned to his eldest son. "Matthew, after dinner, I'd like to discuss the project Mister Miller and I are working on for the cotton crop."

"Sure, Papa." Matt's easy manner exuded his confidence. "I'd like to talk about some ideas I have, too."

Staring at his family, Abe was struck by the picture they presented. Each one different, yet with a thread of similarity holding them together. His beautiful daughters who would carry their heritage well. His sons, the bearers of his name, his pride and joy. How blessed he felt to have such wonderful children and a wife beyond compare. Abe smiled as his spirits lightened. An unexpected happiness washed over him, sweeping away his worries.

Sarah watched Abe relax, noticing a softness creep into the crevices of newly formed wrinkles on his face, puffing up his skin, so that he looked younger and more peaceful than she'd seen him in several weeks. She offered a prayer of thanks that her sons had returned to the fold, knowing their presence uplifted her beloved husband as only a father's sons could do.

Abe's voice softened as he turned toward Joseph. "My fine, young son, how have you been doing in school?"

"Well, sir, my grades are good, and I've been trying to find a career that would make you proud of me." Joseph allowed a nervous laugh to escape him.

Sarah's hand went to her face. "Don't even say that. Your father will be proud of you no matter what you choose to do.

You don't need to find a career that pleases him." She looked distraught at the idea her younger son might forego his own dreams in an attempt to please his father. "Tell him, Abe, tell him it doesn't matter what he does, you'll still be proud of him."

"Of course, I will, Joe. You know that. If you want to come home and help Matt and me run this business, there'll always be a place for you. My sons working side by side. But if you find striking out into uncharted waters is your calling, do that. Your mother and I will always be here if you need us. No matter what you do, you'll always be my son. I love all of you equally." Abraham swept his hand to include all the children. Though emotional issues made him uncomfortable, the look on Sarah's face told him he'd said the right things.

Following dinner, Abe invited the boys to his study. Joseph declined. "Think I'll go for a walk to stretch my legs." The house had become stifling, not from the heat, but from Joe's melancholy, urging him outside to ruminate over the past few months. He knew his father loved him, especially after his little speech, but Matt taking over the plantation seemed to be all Abe wanted to discuss. Joe felt like the spare in case something happened to Matt. He followed his mother and sisters into the parlor and gave them each a hug before going for a much-needed stroll.

CHAPTER SEVEN

Coming back to Oak Hollow, Joseph felt tense, as if he'd stepped into someone else's home, but as soon as he left the house, he relaxed. He loved walking under the sloping branches of the pecan trees, feeling the little hills and valleys of the earth beneath his feet. Evenings had always been his favorite time, and the dark stillness of this particular night gave Joe the solitude he'd dreamed about for the past few months.

School had turned out to be harder than he'd imagined with all the subjects involved, but living with so many other students proved to be more difficult. He realized, after the first week, that a lot of young men had come to college just to have a grand adventure before returning to their old-moneyed families where they'd be set up for life.

When he first arrived at school, he'd shared a room with Matt, but since they moved in different social circles, they'd decided to find separate living quarters. Of the two brothers, Matthew was more gregarious, socializing with the wealthy, spoiled playboys, while Joseph opted for the more creative and intellectual students. Since Abe wanted the boys to live together, Matt and Joe had made a pact to give the impression they shared an apartment.

Joseph had some serious concerns about Matt, but he attributed them to immaturity. His brother had a good heart and a strong sense of fairness. He would carry the Sullivan name well, once he gave up his wild behavior. At least, Joseph hoped so.

A subtle noise startled him. He squinted into the darkness, trying to discern who shared the night with him. The moon shed its light through half-closed lids with drifting wisps of clouds superimposed on its mantle, making it difficult to see into the shadows. When the clouds dissipated, he noticed a squirrel passing in front of him, trying to climb a nearby tree. The creature kept falling backward, emitting a soft, whimpering sound. Mental alarms sent adrenaline surging through Joe's body. Perhaps the little animal was sick or injured. He'd heard about fevers and infections that could spread to humans, but he refused to leave a creature in distress.

Pulling a handkerchief from his pocket, he bent down and gently picked up the squirrel that seemed too weak to resist. After wrapping it snugly with the handkerchief, Joe held the diminutive tree dweller to his chest trying to calm the tiny creature's racing heartbeat. Moisture seeped from the handkerchief, and Joe realized the squirrel was injured and bleeding instead of sick.

Holding his little charge close, Joe searched in the dim moonlight until he found what he thought was a stand of comfrey, the healing weed Negroes used. Making his way back to the tree where he'd found the squirrel, he sat down at the base of the big oak, placing the weed in his mouth. Nothing could quite compare to the taste of comfrey, and he chewed it until his saliva formed it into a sort of mush. Feeling for the wound, he spat the herb into his hand and applied the poultice along the length of the animal's back where he felt the blood. He rewrapped his handkerchief around the squirrel, leaving the little nut eater's legs exposed, so it could walk if it started healing and had enough strength to move around. Joseph laid it on a soft stand of grass at the base of the tree and said a silent prayer as he continued his walk.

He followed the river, walking close to the edge letting his thoughts wander. Just like Grace, he'd always been drawn to the gurgling stream and found solace there. Sometimes, he even imagined he could decipher words as the water splashed over the rocks. On rare occasions, he thought he saw the Wee Ones and heard them tapping their tiny hammers, making little shoes. Knowing most Americans would think him a bit daft, he kept quiet about the subject.

Joseph had wanted to think about his future, but the squirrel unnerved him, not from fear of being bitten or becoming infected, but because of not knowing for sure if what he did would help. He made a mental note to check on the little creature the next morning. Somehow, he felt a strange kinship with the small, furry animal and decided if the squirrel had died, he'd give it a proper burial.

Without realizing it, Joseph had stepped too close to the bank of the river and felt his foot slip on the wet mud. Gee, he really did have feet of clay. Amused with his own thought, he bent over, dipping his hands into the river to wash the squirrel's blood from them. Then he used a stick to scrape his shoes, removing most of the muck.

Joe started for the house when an eerie, high-pitched sound that seemed to last forever jolted the silence, sending raging chills through his body. Glued to the earth beneath his feet, his senses tried to sort out what he'd just heard. Quiet now. Surreal, measurable, minute-by-silent-minute quiet. Then another one. High C soprano wailing. Loud, deafening screaming. What could be happening? Was someone being hurt? The Negroes must be drinking and fighting, or maybe an unhappy husband was beating his wife. Or had someone died?

Did the darkies practice keening with wailers like folk do at an Irish wake? Another scream. This time it sounded deeper, more solid, and had the distinct characteristic of a loud groan. The sound had come from across the river where he could see lights in the huts. There seemed to be a lot of activity with people milling around. Men congregated outside one particular hut while women kept going in and out. Through a large open window, he saw several women scurrying around inside, cooking something in a big pot, but he didn't smell food. After a few minutes, he saw a woman poke a stick into the steaming container and lift out dripping rags. When they cooled, she wrung them, and gave them to another woman. They couldn't be washing clothes at this time of night.

What was happening?

The screaming stopped, and Joe picked up enough of the conversation among the men to learn that a woman was about to give birth. At that moment, Joseph heard another high-pitched wail. The baby's first cry! Bringing a new life into an Old World. He dropped to his knees and whispered a prayer for the mother and her newborn child. How terrible it was women had to suffer so much pain when producing such beautiful miracles. But then again, he reflected on how God chose Mary to give birth to His only Son, the greatest gift ever given. Not that he compared women to Mary and God, but it helped him to understand the pain without all the sadness.

Something triggered his memory as vivid scenes played out in his mind. His father had headed a committee to organize a community church in Scottsville soon after they arrived. Ministers would come, but seldom stay. During the interim when they had no pastor or during inclement weather, church services in town were canceled. Sometimes, he and Matt would go down to the river, hide behind a big bolder, and listen to the gospel services of the Negroes. Nothing made him feel quite as good as their music. The darkies had church all day long every Sunday, no matter what the weather. They'd sing and clap, shouting Amen, Praise God, Hallelujah, Glory Be, and Yas, Lawd. Then the preacher would get wound up with the sermon, and they'd do it all over again.

Every once in a while, they took a break. Mothers nursed their babies while the older women and girls served food to everyone. Small groups of people sat under the big, shady, oak trees or the droopy weeping willows that grew near the river. After lunch, the men catnapped while the women and older children tidied up. The younger children played with homemade toys or made up games. When everyone had rested, the singing started again. Before long they raised their hands, women chanted, men preached, everyone swayed about, some talked and some sang, all at the same time. The Spirit of the Lord sent shivers of joy through Joe's body, and Matt told his brother he felt it, too.

They'd talk about their experiences as they walked home. Both of them had expected a chariot to swing down any minute and carry them up to the streets of heaven. On Sundays, he and Matt wanted to be darkies. Joe remembered praying to be allowed to go up with the Negroes if God did send that chariot.

Reminiscences faded when Joe reached the house where he cleaned the soles of his shoes on the handmade iron scraper outside the door, abraded his immortal soul on the reality of the moment, and entered a house where he didn't belong. Painted smile, jovial attitude, and all was well in the world as far as the Sullivans were concerned. Now the jester was home for the evening.

Abe and Matt emerged from the study just as Joe walked in. Sarah, who'd fallen asleep in her favorite chair, awakened with a start at the closing of the back door. Screaming, she jumped to her feet when Joseph entered the parlor. She ran to him, grabbing his shoulders. Abe and Matt rushed to her side.

"What on earth happened to you?" Her voice shook as she spoke.

Joseph looked down at his shirt and saw the bloodstains near his heart area. He began to laugh. "Sit down, Mama. I'm not hurt. I just tried to make an injured squirrel that I found comfortable." Joe hoped his voice sounded unconcerned, but the incident with the squirrel and the birth of an unknown baby had confirmed his career choice in a single, magical night.

"Let's have our famous Sullivan nightcap," suggested Abe.

Sarah went to the kitchen to prepare the beverage since Miss Daisy had long gone home, and the girls were already asleep upstairs. She stoked the fire in the wood cook stove and put a kettle on. While the water bubbled, she took down four of the very special cups she'd brought over from the Old Country, filled well used tea balls to place into each cup, and poured boiling water over all of them. Saucers went on top while she sang a nonsensical tune under her breath. The little ditty her grandmother taught her when she was a child was written to last just the right amount of time for the tea to steep. Waiting, Sarah wondered if her daughters still remembered when she taught the tune to them. She placed the steaming cups on a tray and carried them to the table.

The cadenced ticking of the grandfather clock in the hall and the spiced tea served to relax the group around the table, prompting each person to head to bed.

*   *   *

The girls had a few more days of school, but amid the chaos of the boys' visit, Maggie forgot about the circus. On Wednesday, Joseph sat on the porch sipping lemonade, waiting for them.

"Hey," he called, waving.

"Where's Matt?" asked Maggie.

"Inside helping Mama untangle some yarn."

Maggie hugged Joe. "I'm hungry. Think I'll go to the kitchen."

Joseph turned to Grace. "Are you hungry?"

"Not at all. Are you?"

"No. Just had some pie."

Grace put her books on the swing. "Want to go for a walk?"

Joe took Grace's hand to help her down the stairs.

How she wished she were holding Jim's smooth, worn down hand, softened by bacon fat rubbed in at night. But Joe's hand felt just fine.

As they walked, Joe broke the silence. "What are you going to do with your life?"

"Standard answer. Go to finishing school, marry Paul, have three children, join auxiliaries, and be the bank president's wife. Why do you ask?"

"That's not what you want, is it?"

"No." Grace couldn't keep the dejection out of her voice, but what bothered her at the moment was the sadness in Joe's eyes. Kind of like a lake that looks crystal clear on the surface, but on closer inspection, the opacity below becomes visible. "What about you? You're always joking, but I can see deep down inside where you keep your secrets, you're sad. Why?"

"To be honest, I've always felt weak since I haven't known what to do with my life, but the other night, I realized what I want more than anything."

"What?"

"Medicine, but please don't say anything to Papa."

"Why?"

"Not sure how he'll feel about it."

"It's a wonderful profession! Why on earth would he be upset about you being a doctor?"

"He might think I'd be leaving my roots and the Sullivan name for Matt to defend alone. And my lifestyle would be far different from the one we're living now. A physician is a servant—a servant of mankind, just like the slaves. But my servitude would be voluntary. The money would be next to nothing, but the real reward would be to heal people. That would make me happy."

"How did you come to this decision?"

He told her about the walk he'd taken. "Your turn. What would you rather do than marry Paul?"

"Promise not to tell?"

Joe crossed his arms over his chest. "Promise. Besides, I trusted you with my secret."

"Yes, but please tell Papa about your decision. He'll be so proud of you."

"I will when the time is right."

"As for me, if I could have anything in the world, I would be a Negro. Not a slave, but a Negro like those who work for us. I like the bonds they have with each other, the warmth and trust. And the real freedom they have. No pretenses, just being God's child." Grace paused and took a deep breath.

"I never thought of their life as being like that, but you're right."

"I even walked barefoot in my gown the other night. No shoes, no petticoats, and I felt true, honest freedom from the bondage of society. You know, don't you, we're the slaves, not them. We think it's the other way around, but it isn't. We're Americans now, bound to tradition, to doing what society dictates. Have you ever considered how fake we are, agreeing with someone to prevent embarrassment to our families? We're cold, calculating, and predictable. Boring is what we are. But since my color or social standing can't be changed, what I'd like to do is leave America and return home to Ireland. Papa still owns the land over there, doesn't he?"

"I'm sure he does. Maybe that's where I'll go to medical school. Then you and I can go home together. I'm glad we talked and have safe secrets."

"Me, too." She released a deep sigh as they started toward the house.

Grace valued the secrets she and Joe had shared. If only she could get Matt to open up and tell her what was on his mind, but Papa had kept him busy meeting with people and staying up late talking about business. And Matt had seemed agitated since they'd been home, so Grace resigned herself to waiting until he settled down before attempting to talk to him.

* * *

Days blended together in a frenzied sort of way. One afternoon, Grace sat on the sofa in the parlor reflecting on Joe's decision and how relaxed he'd appeared since sharing his thoughts with her. Maggie, on the other hand, had become more distant since the boys came home.

Peering out the window, Grace noticed that Joseph and Maggie were sitting in the swing on the verandah. He said something to her, causing Maggie to laugh. "Maybe he can bring her out of her mood," Grace muttered under her breath. She watched as they started down the steps, walking toward the orchard.

"Now, let's see," Joe said, assuming a serious look, "you must be about . . . uh . . . eight or nine now?"

"Joseph Sullivan!" Maggie exploded, "You know better than that. I just had a birthday. I'm fifteen!"

"Goodness," he exclaimed, teasing her, slapping his face with his hand as he'd seen their mother do a hundred times, "and bless my soul. You're a bona fide almost adult."

"Yes, I am," Maggie retorted haughtily.

They came to a dock the boys had made one summer. Sitting down, pulling off their shoes and socks, they dangled their feet in the cold, jade-green water of the river, watching minnows dart around to avoid their toes. Bits of slimy, olive-green moss, broken loose from a rock or a small root, passed by, tickling their feet on the way downstream.

Maggie cocked her head and studied Joe. "I know everyone thinks we're the ne'er-do-wells of the family, but do you think if one of us made a choice to do something against The Sullivan Solemn Declarations, we'd still be accepted as part of the family?"

"What on earth are you talking about Child . . . uh I mean Magpie?"

"Papa's probably going to disown me because I'm not going to finishing school."

"Why?"

"Because I'm going to become a seamstress, marry Charles, and have six children."

"Well, sounds as if you have your entire life planned out. Have you, by any chance, informed this Charles about these decisions?"

"No, that's another reason you can't mention it. Promise?"

"Have you told Gracie?"

"Yes, I told her the other day."

"I have a secret, too."

"What? Tell me."

"Grace and I discussed it the other day when we went walking. Papa may be disappointed if I don't help Matthew run Oak Hollow, but I've decided to go to medical school. I don't want you or Grace to say anything until I've had time to tell Papa."

"I'll keep the secret, but it's a great thing to be a doctor."

The sun had begun its slow descent, sliding from the sky, leaving a trail of pink and purple ribbons interlaced with gold and orange highlights as it made its way to bed. The river took on a somber mood and darkened with the deepening shade of twilight. Time had come to tuck in their secrets for the night and go back to the house.

* * *

The whole Sullivan clan rose bright and early Saturday morning to see the boys off. The girls smothered their brothers in hugs and laughter as Abe prepared to take them to the train depot.

"See you next time," Joseph yelled.

CHAPTER EIGHT

Sarah settled herself in the parlor. As much as she missed Cork, she liked the soft, easy, sauntering through the grass, sipping a mint julep, graceful kind of way people moved, and the way they drawled their words. She patterned herself after the women who were as soft as a summer breeze and as strong as a mighty oak tree. The Southern gentlemen amazed her. The way they could be so cold and calloused when dealing with business matters, how their eyes took on the appearance of some lethal weapon if their lady's honor came into question, but how in a tiny fraction of a second, they could change back into the most gentle and charming men.

Her world, an ocean away, beckoned almost every day. Visions of the noisy family pubs and the jolly, red-faced, loudmouthed men raising their steins to anything and everything that would give them an excuse for another drink caused Sarah to smile. She recalled the women, their tongues wagging like a new puppy's tail over a bowl of warm milk, going to fetch their men home. The husbands would weave their way along held up by their wives, only to get up the next morning, work until quitting time, and head back to the tavern to start the cycle all over.

Not all families were like that, of course. Sarah hadn't wanted to marry a man who spent his evenings in a pub, but she dreamed of the day when she could control her husband while making him believe he ruled the whole world.

The sobriety of the Sabbath starkly contrasted to the frivolity of Saturday evenings. Though men dressed up in their best clothes, sometimes their eyes looked like blood-colored highways on a map.

Nothing could compare to a choreographed Irish wake. How she missed the camaraderie of the women gathered in one part of the house, the men in another, and the young people playing games. And the wailers who carried on as long as food and drink held out amazed her. Yes, her culture had different traditions, and Sarah missed them.

Here, people marked death as a sad, solemn event. Everyone wore black and talked in hushed tones. Never had she seen a wake in America with glasses raised in tribute to the dead. In the American tradition, men sat up with the body day and night until the funeral, and it sometimes got rather eerie if an animal happened to get in through an unprotected window.

A few superstitious men had upturned their chairs, making a run for the outhouse upon hearing the mournful wail of an animal who'd jumped into an open coffin in the dead silence of the night, within the tomb of the darkness of death and finality.

Thinking of death brought the famine to the forefront of Sarah's memory. The stench of the corpses in the streets, the flesh separating away from light tan bones, covered in maggots, falling in jagged strips to the ground where the bones would be bleached as white as icy snow the next week assaulted her senses. The undetectable faces that looked like parts of a jigsaw puzzle with pieces missing made her sick. The greed, the inhumanity of it all. To think it might have been a political move, according to the powers that ran her beloved country.

Sarah didn't know who to blame, but she hated the unnamed enemy. Hate was a strong word, but so was murder. Hunger taking its victims was not pretty. Dying was slow, insidious, and cruel, painting a dark picture on the back of her eyes that couldn't be forced away, no matter how hard she tried.

Then Abe brought her to America. Now she was a Southern woman. He'd also brought their parents and built houses for them in town. Mister and Missus Sullivan died the first year when lightning struck their home during the night, burning it so quickly there was no time for them to get out. Her mother died six months later and her papa this past January. She and Abe donated her parents' home as a library. Sarah was glad their parents got to live in and see America.

At least Abe had kept the land in Cork. She knew if things got too harsh here, they could always return home, since the country had started rebuilding. Sarah vowed to learn more about business affairs, but there'd be plenty of time for that later.

Enough of this, she admonished herself as she took up her knitting to wait for Abe's return from the depot.

* * *

Matthew and Joseph sat in silence as the train rumbled along, each staring out opposite windows. The train belched, forcing them together. They grabbed each other to keep from being thrown onto the floor.

"What in tarnation is happening here?" Matthew roared.

"Sorry sir," replied the conductor, clinging to the back of a seat to keep his balance.

"Sorry sir," Matthew mocked. "We could be killed before ever getting back to school."

"Speaking of school, why even finish?" Joseph asked.

"What's that supposed to mean? Papa wants me to have an education. Besides, he's not ready to give up the reins of the business yet, and I'm certainly not ready to run it his way."

"Have you told him how you feel?"

"Not exactly, but as soon as I get my hands on it, there'll be some changes made. I'm going to take care of us a lot better than Papa's done. I'll make us the richest people in town."

"We're already the richest."

"Not as rich as the Scotts. Banking is lucrative. We'll be that rich."

Joseph knew the Scotts weren't as rich as they let on, but he didn't press the point. "You'll share with us, big brother?" The sarcasm, evident in Joseph's voice, apparently didn't faze Matthew.

"Of course, I will. The girls have to be protected and cared for, no matter what. It's just that Papa's too lenient with the Negroes, and he's let a lot of land lie fallow. Producing larger crops will give us bigger profits and using fewer slaves, forcing them to work longer hours, will make harvesting more productive. Papa freeing our slaves was a mistake, so he needs to step down and let me take over. We have a name to uphold, and I can do that by becoming a leader in the community."

Matt's words rang false and Joe's heart seemed to lodge in his throat. The way his brother had changed since going to college shocked and angered him. Never would he have thought Matt would be power-hungry and selfish with a cruel streak toward the darkies. If Matt ran the estate the same way he'd managed his life, he'd lose Oak Hollow within a year. Then, where would they be? Matt's voice interrupted his thoughts.

"Don't worry, and don't say anything to anyone. Everything's going to be okay once my plan is finalized. You can't make money if you don't give it all you've got by trying new things. What's wrong with that? Times change. Papa hasn't learned to move forward."

"I understand that. Oak Hollow is a business, but it's a farming business, and you don't seem to have the desire to work the land…to be a farmer. I think you just want to own it, and could care less about the land or employees as long as it makes money."

"That's pretty close to right. I want to own it and run it, but if you think that means I'll stay out in the hot sun and the freezing cold tilling the soil and getting my hands dirty, then think again. I'll do it for a while, but only until I have enough money to buy you three out. You'll be rich when I buy your portion."

As Matt rambled, Joe became more morose. Never once had his brother acknowledged their parents' presence on the plantation in a positive way. Matt acted as if their parents were dead, so Joe changed the subject, talking about lighter topics.

* * *

Once the boys decided to obtain separate living quarters, peace spread through every cell of Joe's body. He couldn't wait to get away from a brother he realized he didn't know. When the train finally pulled into Clinton, they secured their luggage, and Matthew, giving Joe a speedy handshake, almost ran the opposite way, indicating the need to separate was mutual.

Joseph took his time walking to the small cottage he'd occupied for the past few months. Entering the dark interior, he didn't even bother to light a lantern, but sank into a chair to mull over the conversation on the train. What had led to the change in his older brother?

The time had come to acknowledge Joe's concerns. He knew Matthew had been socializing with unscrupulous characters, letting his studies slide in favor of partying and courting girls of questionable reputation. More than once, his brother had been called to the dean's office, but since Matt could charm himself out of almost any trouble, he'd managed to stay in school. When Joe had first come to Mississippi College, Matt had offered to show him around and took him to a few parties, breaking the rules of the Baptist college. That started the rift between them.

Joe had to devise a plan for his own future and that of the girls. While he didn't expect anything to happen to his parents, he knew Matt wouldn't take care of any of the family. How Joe longed to talk to his father. But what could he say? Would his father believe him or take Matt's side? The answer lay written in the rich soil of the farmland and the one who'd till it.

Knowing Matthew had been gambling, drinking, and visiting brothels when he couldn't find a young lady to satisfy him would break Papa's heart, but it seemed Matthew didn't care about anyone except himself.

Joe had witnessed the girls Matthew had used and discarded along the way, never looking back. Girls left with broken hearts and fractured bodies that might never heal. Thinking about his brother disgusted Joe.

The darkened room felt hot, and he'd forgotten to eat. A soft knock sounded on the door. When he opened it, Rebecca Taylor stood smiling, illuminated by the moon.

"Rebecca, I'm sorry. I should've come by to see you the minute we got back, but I got sidetracked. Would you like to come in?" Joe lit a lantern on a table by the door.

Lifting her head to meet his eyes she said, "No, I just came to see if you were home. My family is having a late supper if you'd like to join us."

"I'd like that a lot." He closed the door, taking her elbow to help her down the steps while she lifted her gown just enough to keep from tripping. Her carriage and driver sat just outside his door. After helping her, he climbed inside and sat across from her.

Before the horses even started moving, Joe became cognizant of how much more comfortable he felt in a carriage with her than on a train with his brother and was amazed that this beautiful, young woman now sat across from him. Rebecca. Her name sounded like a symphony to his ears. Her petite beauty refreshed his tired mind, but more than that, her sweet spirit caressed his soul and healed his heart. She was intelligent, pleasant, and the most refined, young lady Joseph Sullivan had ever known. They had met last winter in an indirect way through Matthew. Though their first meeting hadn't been ideal, it had paved the way for a real, trusting friendship. Matthew had courted her but became disgusted when Rebecca wouldn't drink with him or allow him to bed her. They had a confrontation, ending with Rebecca fleeing the party Matt had taken her to. She had run headlong into Joseph who had been on his way to the school library. They'd both fallen and tumbled down the sloping, rain-soaked lawn of the mayor's estate. Joseph had thought the incident funny and laughed until he saw her tear-stained face.

"I'm sorry. Are you hurt?"

She shook her head but didn't refuse his hand as he'd helped her to her feet. She'd straightened her petticoats and dress, taking the handkerchief he'd offered her.

"I'm Joseph Sullivan, he'd said. And you are?"

She'd looked at him with a frightened gaze, reminding him of a cornered animal, about to bolt. Instead, she'd taken a deep breath and asked, "You're Matthew's brother?"

"Yes, why do you ask?"

"I must go."

"Wait, please. A young lady should not be walking at night by herself. Please let me see you home."

Rebecca hesitated for a few minutes before attempting to take a step. When she almost fell, she'd said, "You may be right. Perhaps I shouldn't walk alone."

Joe had noticed she limped, grimacing with each slow step. Pain reflected on her face. Fearing she'd either broken her foot or ankle, he asked permission to pick her up. When she agreed, Joe carried her to Matt's carriage with the intention of returning it once he saw the young lady home.

"Thank you. My name is Rebecca Taylor."

When they'd arrived at her home, Joe carried her to the front door. Rebecca called out to her father as she began knocking on the oval, etched glass of the door.

Mister Taylor had hurried behind the butler to let them in, but before he could say a word, his daughter told him what had happened and introduced him to Joe. The men retired to the study while their servants and her mother took care of Rebecca.

Joseph and her father had established an instant rapport when they discovered they both loved writing and singing. The time had been past midnight when Joseph left, but he called on the family the next day to inquire about Rebecca's ankle.

She hobbled to meet him and said she felt much better, that the doctor had looked at it, and it was only a bad sprain. At her invitation, Joe entered her home and her life. They'd been courting ever since.

As Rebecca became more comfortable with Joseph, details of Matt's behavior came to light. Joe had been livid when she revealed Matt had tried to rape her. That day, Joe had sworn to kill his own brother. The only way Rebecca stopped him was to point out Joe would go to prison, and they'd never be free to be alone together again.

Later, when Joseph had questioned Matt about his conduct, he threw his head back, and his cold laughter almost shook the room. "Taking my leftovers, huh, little brother? Well, good luck. She's too pious for me. But you go right ahead 'cause I'm through with her, anyway!"

Joseph had squeezed his fists to keep from ripping Matt to shreds, but physically hurting his brother would expunge Joe from the family, and he wouldn't be able to put his plan into action. He vowed that the family wouldn't be defeated by this secret agent of greed who planned to take over the plantation for himself.

* * *

After the boys left, the house had an eerie quietness, and a Cimmerian lethargy settled over everyone, including the servants. Maggie occupied herself with sketching dress designs while Grace read. By late afternoon, the girls wandered outside and sat in the swing.

Maggie broke the silence. "I'm bored. What can we do?"

"Want to go for a walk?"

"No, think of something else."

"How about checkers?"

"No, there's something I want, but you can't help me with it."

"What?"

"To see Charles."

"You're right, my dear, I can't help you with that."

"Then, I'll go in and embroider. You go ahead and take a walk if that's what you want. You like the outdoors better than I do."

The opportunity to have some time alone delighted Grace. She strolled in a lazy kind of way until she got past the prying eyes of the Big House. Then her feet flew. When she reached the circle in the grove, hot and out of breath, she sat down to let her pulse return to normal. Though she was a little disappointed that Jim was nowhere in sight, she knew he wouldn't always be here when she wanted to talk to him.

"Hey," said a familiar voice that could only be Jim.

In an instant, her legs felt numb, her hands dripped with sweat, and her head reeled. She couldn't tell if she felt hot or cold but gave thanks that she didn't have to stand. Grace didn't understand why just a spoken word could evoke such emotions, but in as calm a voice as she could master, she replied, "How nice to see you. Please, come sit." Grace patted the ground beside her.

"I been watchin' out the window for you," Jim said, lowering himself to the soft grass.

"Thank you for coming." Grace's brow wrinkled.

Jim took her hands in his. "What's troublin' you?"

"Our friendship. Why do we have to hide it?"

"Look at my skin. Look at your skin. That's why nobody can never know about our friendship."

"But why should color or social standing dictate how we feel about someone? There's something very special between us. I wanted to teach you to read and write to help you, but more than that, I want people to see we're friends, real friends."

"We can't do that. We can't never do that."

He looked frightened, as if he were going to faint. "What are we going to do? Or, maybe . . . maybe you don't feel the same way about me?"

"I been thinkin' 'bout you ever' minute since the last time we wuz here, even dreamin' 'bout you ever' night. Tryin' to stop thinkin' 'bout you, I been doing two times more work, but…"

He pulled his hands away and began twisting them as he'd always done when nervous or upset.

"But what?"

"But nuthin' can ever come of this. Even friendship could git us in big trouble. We's jes' makin' ourselfs miserable."

"You're right, but there has to be a way we can be friends, very special, spiritual friends."

"How?" In a bold move, he enveloped her small hands once more, holding them in a prayer position under his chin.

"I don't know, but until I have time to think and find a solution, I'm not coming back here."

"Okay, iffen that's what you want to do. Prayin's what I needs to do. The Lord's gonna give me the answer."

They rose together, knowing words weren't necessary as they parted.

CHAPTER NINE

Dinner was a quiet, uneventful affair. Grace had no appetite, pushing her food around on her plate until everyone finished so she could be excused.

"You've hardly touched your food. Are you sick?" Sarah wrinkled up her face as she did when something worried her.

"No, just tired. Think I'll go to bed."

"Want me to come tuck you in and read you a story?" Maggie asked, teasingly.

"No, thank you, little sister."

Grace settled herself in bed long before the sun went down. She intended to use the time to devise a way to acknowledge her friendship with Jim and sever her budding relationship with Paul. Logic and emotions swirled together, muddling her brain. Not being able to wade through the confusion, she gave in to the weariness weighing her down, and blissful sleep took over. She never knew her sister tiptoed in and kissed her goodnight.

Grace begged off going to church with the family the next morning. Sitting alone in the breakfast room, she contemplated her future, a future that had to include Jim in some meaningful way. They could never fall in love or express deep feelings of friendship openly, but outside of her family, he was the most important person in her life, and she wouldn't give him up for anyone. Rising, she walked outside, sauntering along the river before heading to the special circle she shared with Jim.

His voice floated through the air from the tabernacle where he led the singing, and the calming effect on her soul soothed Grace as she sat mesmerized, listening to the clear notes. The moment she relaxed, a plan formed in her mind. With it came the peace Grace had sought for so many days. The problem of what to say to Papa and Paul lay ahead of her. Somehow, she'd deal with them. Noise from the family buggy approaching prompted her to start home.

* * *

Grace excelled in school, but with her new goal, she was determined to move ahead as fast as possible and learn all she could before the summer break. When school dismissed, she didn't resist as Maggie led her to the buggy.

Once they settled themselves inside, Grace noticed that the lively, happy-go-lucky expression on Maggie's face had been replaced with a vision of serious concern and waited for her sister to speak.

"Gracie, I love you. And I'd do anything in the world for you. You seem to be carrying a big burden in your heart. Won't you let me help you? The sadness in your eyes, the frown you wear all the time, not eating, wanting to be alone. Being your sister, I know you're unhappy. Please, tell me what's wrong. Please?"

Tears formed, but Grace didn't dare let them overflow. If she did, they'd never stop. Everything Maggie said was true, but Grace couldn't confide in her. She just couldn't, but lying wasn't an option, either.

"Please don't be concerned about me. Too many decisions have been weighing on my mind, making me so perplexed I don't know what to do."

"What are you confused about?" Maggie took her sister's hand and began rubbing it, hoping to ease her heart in some small way.

"There are so many things I don't want to do."

"What things?"

"Finishing school, forcing myself to marry Paul, and joining all the society groups so Papa and Mama will be proud of me. At this point, I don't even want to have children. But if I give up all the dreams Mama and Papa have for me, what would I do with my life? That's why I need some time alone to try to make some sense out of everything." Grace hadn't lied, but she hadn't told the whole truth, either. Perhaps the words were enough to satisfy her sweet Maggie.

"What a relief. All kinds of terrible things went through my mind. Neither of us wants to disappoint Papa or Mama, but we have to live our lives the way we see fit. If you don't want to marry Paul, then don't!"

They hugged each other, settling back in the carriage for the rest of the ride home.

Grace saw her mother waiting on the verandah and greeted her before bounding upstairs to study until she thought Jim would be finished working for the day. His main job was caring for the horses and keeping the wagons in good running condition as well as serving an apprenticeship in the woodworking shop. A lot of days he was in close proximity to the Big House, making it easy for him to watch Grace's activities, but other times, he had to work near the fields. He never knew how many hours he would work, but most of the time, he was the first one to finish. Making an excuse to go walking, Grace sent a mental message to Jim to meet her. She had something important to tell him.

Deep in the woods, Jim and Grace had stumbled upon a small stand of pecan trees growing in a natural circle. A thick growth of oaks surrounded the little grove separating it from the regular pecan orchard. They consecrated the hidden surround as their sanctuary.

Jim leaned against a large pecan tree.

Grace smiled, wishing she had a picture of him with the branches forming an arc above his head. As she got closer, she noted he was turning a leaf over and over in his hands, his eyes downcast and focused on the nervous habit. Grace stopped and settled herself in order to deal with the deep emotions billowing up inside.

Something was wrong. Could someone have hurt his feelings or found out they were meeting? Anger flared but died down in an instant, replaced by fear—slow, insidious, nauseating kind of fright that crept into her brain, pounding like the great waves in the ocean, reaching all the way down to her toes. On the way back up, the terror erupted into a full-blown earthquake, almost toppling her. She knew. She didn't want to, but she knew. Grace wanted to run, to escape, to be anywhere but here where she'd have to hear his words. Jim looked up. He held out his hand to her. Grace fell to the ground, unmindful of whether she was modest or vulgar, burying her head in shaking hands. Her heart stopped, and she gasped when it started to beat again. Before dying on this spot, she had to tell him what was in her heart. She dropped her hands and looked up. "Jim," she began, but at that moment, he put his finger to his lip.

"Shh." He pulled her to her feet and moved closer. Grace smelled him, but couldn't discern the scent. The aroma was sweet, like flowers, but not as pronounced. The afternoon sunbeams reflected off Jim's snow white teeth, giving his bronzed face and tawny skin an ethereal, golden glow. His personal hygiene had never entered Grace's mind, and she didn't know why it would matter now, but it did. How could he be so clean and pure? He never had the sweaty, dirty smell of the other men after a long day of work.

Jim held her pale, delicate face between his large hands, framing this picture in his mind's eye and in his loving heart, letting the reality of the present etch itself in his brain. The essence of Grace had to be gouged deep enough so he would never forget. Somehow, he knew she understood and wondered if he could even speak. Dropping his hands from her face, he ever so gently pulled her to him. He felt her heart beating out of control as his chocolate-colored eyes met her azure-blue ones. A part of his soul resided there. Jim didn't have to tell her how much he admired her, the way he loved to touch her hand, or his undying gratitude for her teaching him to read and write. Most of all, he didn't have to express what her friendship meant to him. A friendship held deep down in the center of his soul, in a sacred place no one else had ever touched. He knew she already knew. They moved closer together in a forbidden embrace, but with their emotions out of control, reasoning meant nothing.

Silhouetted against the deepening magenta sky, they were one sculpture, black against the vanishing horizon. The embrace lasted all of fifteen minutes, but the memory had to last a lifetime. It had to be enough for now, for tomorrow, and for all of the days of their lives because the color of their skin would never change. When Jim released her, they were both crying in uncontrolled surrender to the moment.

Grace stammered, leaning again into his chest as words and feelings poured forth from the depth of her being. "I don't care if it's wrong. I love you. Instead of going to finishing school, I'm going to normal school to get my teaching certificate. Then I'll leave home and take you with me as my servant. You know I don't put myself above you, but it's the only plan I could think of for us to build a life together."

"Wait," he interrupted.

"No, let me finish. Paul could never make me happy. You and I could jump the broom and what would take place inside our home would be our secret. Normal school takes two years. That's not long compared to a lifetime. And I want to spend my lifetime with you."

Jim took a deep breath, slowly exhaling before speaking. "I love you, too, but God nor man didn't never want two people to fall in love this way. You know I'd wait for you for all the days of my life and all the days in heaven after that. But nothing can make this right. God's answered my prayers powerful strong. His will for me's tore me in two. Please, don't be upset with me, but I jes' had to see you one more time, to hole you close to me, remembering ever'thin' about you, so's the goodbye wouldn't leave me without any mem'ry.

I won't never, ever touch you agin 'cuz it makes it so hard to let go."

Grace knew the end was coming. She could still feel the warmth of his chest radiating through to her cold cheek, and her head was dizzy with feelings she couldn't name, but she knew the relationship was over. She sank to the ground. "Please, don't say that, Jim. How can something be wrong that feels so right?"

"It jes' ain't right, that's all. The Good Book says so."

He sat in front of her.

"Can you read that well?" Grace was miffed at how Jim could put his emotions aside with such ease while he quoted from a Bible he could barely read.

"No'm, can't rightly read all of it yet, though I kin make out some of the words like you taught me to do. But ma... uh, Grace, it don' matter iffen any of us kin read 'cuz we been told what the Good Book says lots and lots of times by folks that kin read. I know what it says." He paused, gaining the courage to speak again. "You boun' to be some kind of angel, teachin' me and all. Then tellin' me you love me. Iffen God took me to heaven right now, my life wouldn't be any happier than it's been the last few months knowing you. I wish I wuz white. No matter much or how hard I scrubbed my skin with a stiff brush and the lavender soap Mama made today, my skin wouldn't turn white. Maybe we both bleed red blood, but we can't make our skin other colors and so..."

Jim put his hands to his face, weeping. Gripping his chest, he writhed in agony. Death had to be on the way, and he wanted it to hurry. The pain was unbearable—the pain of loving her with such reverence, such honesty, with all his heart, and the realization he could never be with her, not even as a friend, much less a husband in public or in private. Nothing mattered now. Jim would've walked three feet behind Grace just to be with her, but still that wouldn't work. He'd thought of everything, and always—always there loomed a barrier, so big, so wide, so unchangeable that he just could not get around it or deny it. She was white.

They held each other and cried for skin colors they couldn't change, for each other's pain, and for love that could never find expression. Each of them wiped the other's eyes, weeping from broken hearts and dying hope. Neither spoke. There were no words, and never would be any, to describe the total isolation they felt, but they knew from the innermost part of their beings that they'd never be this close to each other again. Never.

The sun dipped below the horizon, allowing dusk to settle over them like a pall cloth, completely covering the finality of a doomed love, a severed union of their spirits, a shattered flight of fantasy, of reality. Their dream exploded into a thousand pieces, replaced by a nightmare of desolation and emptiness.

Jim rose, put his hands around his beloved, and lifted her to her feet.

Her reddened eyes were swollen almost shut, making it hard to see anything. Her brain spun out of control. Befuddled she couldn't think or maintain her balance. Grace leaned against a tree, trying to regain her equilibrium.

Jim feared she wouldn't find her way back to the house, so bending down, he picked her up in his muscular arms and cradled her, as a father would hold a child, carrying her to the

Big House. In many ways, that's how he thought of them. She was an innocent child. He was her protector.

Distraught, she laid her face against the skin of his precious neck. She felt so safe, so secure, so sheltered. She never wanted to leave his arms, but as his pace slowed, she knew they were nearing the house. Grace nudged his neck until she found the area below his ear and pressed her warm lips to his cool skin. His body went tense and rigid, but his steps never faltered.

The lights shining from the Big House illuminated Sarah Sullivan sitting in her chair watching Abe pace. The young darkie had never been this close to the house with Grace, nor would he be again. Saying a silent prayer, asking God to forgive both of them and give them strength, he set Grace on her feet at the foot of the stairs going up the side porch. Making sure she was steady, Jim pulled her to him once more, tilting her chin. His strong arms encircled her upper body, and he let his lips brush hers. The kiss was not one of passion, desire, or lust. Not even a full kiss, only a whisper. The loving caress was merely a touch of tenderness that broke free from his heart and came to rest on her lips as lightly as a butterfly.

The kiss was a coming together that brought Grace absolute joy, yet total devastation. Not ever again would she experience this bliss, this utter peace and awe. Total disintegration fractured her heart, the only part of her that mattered.

When they separated, Jim squeezed her hands and disappeared into the night. She made her way up to the porch and slumped on the worn, wooden step where she'd sat a hundred times to sort out life's problems. Her eyelids felt like pillows of wet sand that refused to stay open. They were orbs of dying embers no water could squelch. Grace welcomed pain anywhere else in her body to ease the nauseating, wrenching heartache deep within the chambers of her soul.

Someone sat beside her, and an arm went around her shoulders. Was Jim back? She shuttered. They'd be in big trouble. But the hand felt too small.

"I'm here," Maggie whispered. "I'm here."

"Thank you."

"What's wrong? We've been so worried. Mama and Papa sent me out to look for you, and when I couldn't find you, Papa had decided to send out a search party. Then I saw you sitting here leaning against the stair railing. Where have you been? Please, can't you tell me what's wrong? Whatever it is, is safe with me. I do know how to keep a secret. Honest, Gracie."

The cozy glow from the lanterns inside cast just enough light for Grace to discern the gravity of Maggie's statements as she forced her eyes open to meet those of her little sister. The lies and secret meetings with Jim dug like a heavy anchor into Grace's heart, and she didn't know if she could get up from the porch, much less climb the stairs to their bedroom. "I'm so tired, Maggie. Bone-weary, sick to my soul exhausted. My body must weigh a ton. I don't think I can even stand up."

"Wait right here." Maggie dashed into the house.

Grace put her head in her hands, and let the dark, sinister depression seep into every pore of her body. Fingers of fear and daggers of guilt squeezed and ripped her heart to shreds. Trembling uncontrollably, she gave in to the utter despair that overcame her. Total blackness, replaced in an instant with lightness and peace. The pain was gone. She lay still at last.

Abraham found his daughter crumpled on the porch. Her breath had a shallow, uneven rhythm as she lapsed into unconsciousness. Picking her up as carefully as he would a porcelain doll, Abe carried Grace upstairs to her bed. Leaning over, he placed a tender kiss on her forehead. Together, Sarah and Maggie managed to get Grace undressed and into a thin cotton chemise. Cool washcloths administered to her forehead and puffy eyes lifted Grace back up from the arms of Morpheus, the place of nothingness. The heartache washed over her again with pain so intense, she wanted to die. Beneath the thick washcloth, Grace listened as her mother and sister discussed her condition in hushed tones.

"She's acted withdrawn and worried for the past few months, and she's been crying tonight." Sarah paced, her shoes tapping out a soft, steady beat as her skirt swished about. "I can't imagine what could be upsetting her. Do you know, dear?"

"No. She hasn't said much to me the past few weeks except that she wants to be alone to decide what to do about her life."

"Perhaps she's worried about Paul and the kind of social responsibilities she'd be expected to fulfill when they marry."

Words failed Maggie. She knew full well Grace wrestled with the decision to marry Paul. But no one was rushing her into it, so that wouldn't cause this kind of sadness. Who or what had caused the breakdown escaped her.

* * *

Grace had a fitful night, tossing and turning, alternating between horrible dreams of running through a forest trying to get away from something she couldn't see, and lying awake with so many thoughts jumbled in her mind, she couldn't think clearly. She suppressed the urge to scream and thought of creeping down the stairs into the dark night to find Jim in their special place waiting for her. However, she didn't have the strength, and he wouldn't be there anyway. Had she been in a steamer all night? Given her body and mind were as limp as Miss Daisy's fresh noodles, even the energy to turn over was gone. Her window brightened with the coming daylight, but nothing lifted her spirits.

"Please eat this breakfast. Miss Daisy made these pancakes especially for you," Maggie implored.

"Not now. Let me lie here a while longer."

Maggie hurried downstairs.

"Where's your sister?" asked Abraham.

"She doesn't feel like getting out of bed. I know something's wrong. Gracie screamed out in her sleep several times during the night, and I'm worried about her."

"Time to get Doc Bradley to have a look at her." Abe strode from the room and out of the door without finishing his breakfast.

Sarah and Maggie sat beside Grace's bed until the doctor arrived. He examined her and came out of her room shaking his head, wrinkling his brow, and rubbing his stubby fingers through his frosted, salt-and-pepper hair. "I can't find anything specific," he said, "but she seems a little run down. Give her a teaspoon of this tonic twice a day." Handing Sarah a large, brown bottle flattened on two sides, the doctor gave her a pat on the back. He followed Abraham to the door.

Grace stayed in bed three full days. The family tried to cheer her up and encouraged her to talk, but all efforts failed.

* * *

Jeremiah and some workers finished remodeling Grace's private bedroom the second week after her sick spell. Maggie had finally accepted the separation which gave Grace some peace, but she dared not go to the circle. She didn't want Jim to reject her again, yet she longed to talk to him. A tug-of-war played out in her heart and head, but in the end, she stayed away from temptation.

Paul began driving the girls home in his buggy, but Grace wouldn't allow him to come in or spend time with her alone. She told him she didn't want a formal courtship until after her debut, and Paul, being bound to tradition, accepted her explanation without discussion. The predicament facing Grace was how to dissuade Paul from wanting to court her at all and still please her father.

CHAPTER TEN

Summer came and went in a flurry of activity. Grace hadn't seen Jim or been back to their secret meeting place since the night he ended everything. When she thought about him, the emotional pain caused such physical symptoms she was afraid her chest would explode, so she found ways to occupy herself, which allowed no time for contemplation.

She and Maggie continued their piano lessons, practiced with the church choir, and Grace read or watched Maggie design gowns she'd make as a seamstress.

School started, a welcome diversion making the days go faster. The routine felt good, and Grace looked forward to the crisp, cool days of autumn that brought back memories of when she used to slip out of the house to go for walks in the dark. Though nothing stood out as extraordinary, something about the sameness lifted her taciturn and lethargic mood a little each day.

Getting dressed on a rather brisk morning, familiar smells from the kitchen drifted up to meet her, stirring thoughts of happier times as well as a few hunger pains. As she descended the stairs, she realized half the month of November had flown by, and Miss Daisy had begun the baking she'd always done ahead of time in preparation for

Thanksgiving. Since it was a cool Saturday, Grace decided to let Maggie sleep late.

"Mmm, smells good, Miss Daisy."

Mince pies sat on the cabinet ready to go into the oven while pecan tarts and gooey, sweet rolls, covered with a dish towel, cooled in the open window of the kitchen. Grace stopped, taking in the cinnamon-laced aroma. Looking at the old Negro woman she adored, Grace's mind reverted back to when she and Maggie had first met Daisy.

She'd told them if they drank coffee, it would turn them as black as she was. Then, turning her pale palms upward, she said they were all that was left of her whiteness. The girls believed her about as much as they believed the stories of the leprechauns but avoided coffee for a long time, just to be on the safe side. The memory brought a warm smile to Grace's lips for the first time in ages. She felt alive again.

"My, my, Chile, you sure's up early. I kin put these pies aside and fix your breakfas' directly."

"No, don't stop what you're doing." Grace reached around Daisy's ample waist for a cold biscuit. "Think I'll put some blackberry preserves on this and go out on the porch." She took a white plate ringed with vibrant green shamrocks from the cupboard, put her biscuit on it, poured a cup of coffee in a matching cup, and headed for the back door. Just as she got there, she winked at Miss Daisy and asked, "Still think this coffee will turn me black?"

The old cook threw her head back, and the laughter came tumbling forth.

Being Jim's mother made Miss Daisy even more precious to Grace, but she dismissed the thought of what it would be like to have her as a mother-in-law. If only the coffee would turn her black, she'd drink as much as she could hold.

Grace pushed through the back door of the kitchen and set her breakfast on the small round table on the porch. Sitting down, she let her eyes take in the changing landscape. Some of the leaves had turned from green to shades of yellow and orange, but most of them were drab-brown. Tiny curls of grayish-white smoke rose from several of the huts down in the valley across the river, a sign many of the women had started cleaning and preparing for Thanksgiving since Abe gave them extra time off around holidays. Somewhere from deep inside her soul, Grace remembered the cozy feeling of being close and part of all the activity going on in a small home in Ireland.

Then it struck her. The huts reminded her of their home in County Cork. Knowing how generous her father was in giving each Negro family extra food at this time of year, as well as allowing them to raise gardens in order to can food for the winter, delighted Grace and gave her a warm, glowing feeling. Her father also furnished roomy, comfortable cabins and allowed the darkies the freedom to use anything on the plantation they needed. Abe took them to town some Saturdays where he sold items they had created or canned, and sometimes fresh vegetables. Arriving home, he gave them the money. They couldn't sell outright to anyone in town.

Maggie slammed through the door to join Grace, her plate holding the same breakfast. "My goodness, the trees sure are changing and losing their leaves, aren't they?"

"Yes, before we know it, Christmas will be here."

"How long will the boys be home for Thanksgiving?" Maggie's eyes were shining.

"Mama said about a week."

"Then Matt will only have six months of college left?"

Grace couldn't believe how fast time had flown since last seeing her brothers. Yet in contrast, each hour dragged slower and slower along the track of the clock when she thought of Jim. How strange, she mused. "I think that's right."

"Would you like to go for a walk?"

Grace didn't want to go anywhere near the tree-enclosed circle she and Jim shared, but she agreed to go with her sister because Maggie would never find it. They ambled beside the river, chatting about all sorts of things from school to Christmas activities. Everything looked different in the fall, and Grace, following her sister's lead, hadn't realized they'd turned away from the river and were coming to the special place. Recognizing the grove, Grace stumbled as her knees buckled, and she would have fallen if Maggie hadn't grabbed her hand. Pulling away, Grace spun around to go back, but Maggie, who had skipped ahead, called to her.

"Grace, look! Wonder who did this?"

Her curiosity aroused, Grace made her way to her sister's side. A small heart of smooth, pink, river-washed stones lay in a predominant place on the eastern edge of the circle. The morning rays of the autumn sun dancing through the sparse-leafed branches of the pecan trees ricocheted off the heart giving it the illusion of pulsating. The heart had not been formed for many days or was well maintained since no weeds or grass grew between the stones or around the perimeter. The placement to one side of the entrance to the circle indicated the location had been well thought out. Grace burst into tears and sank to the ground with her head in her hands.

"What's wrong?" Maggie rushed to hold her.

"I've been keeping a horrible secret." Grace wiped her eyes with the back of her hand.

"What? Did you make this heart?"

"No, but I know who did." Sobs overtook her voice and body. When she regained her composure, she looked pleadingly at Maggie. "Before I tell you about this, I have to know you'll never tell a single soul, no matter what. Promise?"

Maggie crossed her arms over her chest. "Promise."

Grace gathered the courage to speak. She shared with Maggie that she and Jim had developed a deep friendship, but she didn't reveal that he had been learning to read and write. Not that Grace didn't trust her sister, but if Maggie got upset for some reason and turned Jim in, or accidentally let it slip from her tongue, he could be hurt quite seriously. Besides, Grace gave her word to him she wouldn't tell anyone, and she'd honor that promise to her death, if need be. With some prodding, Grace admitted that the feelings and emotional bond she shared with Jim had escalated into something precious, but forbidden, ending with the last night she'd seen him.

"His love awakened me to the joy life can hold. For the first time, I felt whole, complete, and free. When he carried me to the house, put me down, and kissed me for the first and last time, I willed my bed to be my coffin for I knew that was the end of me, the me I discovered through him. Now our closeness is over, and I'll go on, but I'll never be the same, having been loved by the sweetest man who's ever lived." She took a deep breath, waiting for her sister's reaction.

Maggie didn't respond, not even with a gasp. She was too angry and shocked. Grace had engaged in a secret tryst with a Negro and had almost died from its ending. Yet as her sister described her feelings for Jim, Maggie realized the two friends had something almost sacrosanct. No wonder Grace hadn't shared it until now, but paramount in Maggie's mind was the irrefutable truth that Jim was a Negro. Maggie liked him. He was one of the kindest darkies. And thinking about it, she believed she wouldn't have judged them if he and Grace had run off somewhere. She had no right since Charles, her own true love, was also far beneath the social standing of the Sullivans, though he was white. How could Grace have kept this to herself? That's what angered Maggie the most. They were sisters and were supposed to share everything. Of one thing Maggie was certain. Her sister would never allow a physical connection with Jim because she wouldn't go against family expectations or social traditions.

Grace rubbed the heart with her finger. A lone tear slid down her face, landing on one of the stones. "This is for me, Maggie. Without words, this is the most profound statement he could have ever made. He still loves me, but our hearts have to be strong and enduring like these stones." She saw Jim's face come to life in the center of the heart.

Maggie nodded in understanding.

"Since this is such a hidden place, away from the regular path, I thought no one would ever find it. So I didn't hesitate to walk with you, but I never wanted to come here again. The thought's been too painful, but look at what he's done. Thank you for bringing me."

Maggie hugged her and said, "You're right. I had no idea this place existed. My intent was just to wander through the woods with you. But while we're sharing secrets, I have something to tell you, too."

"What?"

"You must understand by now how deeply in love I am with Charles. He feels the same, and we're making wedding plans."

"You're too young! Are you sure he's the one for you?"

"Yes, I've known for a long time. Papa and Mama are going to be disappointed, but I don't care. I've been working on my trousseau, and it's almost finished."

"Has he kissed you?"

Maggie lowered her head. "Yes," she whispered, and the scarlet glow that crept up her face like a rising, crimson tide wasn't from the reflection of the of the morning's sun on her red dress.

"Have you set a date? What about your debut?"

"We're taking our time planning that far ahead, and if at all possible, I won't make a debut."

Grace traced the stones forming the outside of the heart before letting her fingers rest on each stone that filled the interior. Her heart's mate had touched these same smooth stones, and warmth radiating from the rocks seemed to caress her cold, melancholy heart. Grace felt the familiar, loving comfort of Jim spread a small light to dispel the shadows of her soul. This meager consolation would have to last a lifetime because she would never touch his precious skin or look into the endless depths of his beautiful, deep-brown eyes again.

*　*　*

Abraham Sullivan had been out all morning, checking on crops and the field hands. Since it had been an unusually dry, hot summer and fall, Abe knew the men would kick up a lot of dust clearing the fields. Not wanting them to dehydrate, he'd left some drinking water with Jeremiah. Starting toward the barn, Abe slowed the horses, giving himself time to think. The open work wagon made him prey to the heat from the sun high overhead even though he wore a hat, but he didn't care. Sweat running down his face camouflaged the tears flowing from his heart. A large pine tree stood some distance from the road. Turning the horses, Abe sought shelter underneath the branches. Pulling a wrinkled, paper-thin envelope from his pocket, Abe held it between his hands. He didn't need to read it. He'd read it a thousand times.

The pains in his chest had worsened over the last few days, an indication of the more serious emotional bombardment on his psyche. Wrestling with his soul, Abe admitted he had to find a way to share this burden with Sarah even though it would change their lives forever. To make matters worse, Miller had lost everything over a bad business deal in another town, which would force Grace to have to wait a year before going to finishing school. The most immediate concern was to finance the remainder of the boys' education, so Abe's savings would have to go toward that endeavor.

He doubled over with a sharp, searing pain that hit his chest. His left arm went limp as waves of blood rushed to his head pounding like a hammer against his skull. He grabbed the old, rusted handle of the seat with his right hand and held on to keep from falling. "Sarah!" he screamed, but no one seemed to hear him because he'd isolated himself in a spot where he could be alone.

Letting himself slip down sideways on the seat made his chest more comfortable but compromised his breathing.

Thoughts of ending his life surfaced, but his selfish nature refused. How could he let go of his family without a fight? Willing himself to relax, the pain subsided. Pulling himself to a slumped, sitting position, Abe dropped the reins, and let the horses find their way home on their own.

He didn't have the energy to unhitch the wagon and was grateful when he saw Jim come out of the barn. In an instant, he rushed to Abe's side to help him down. "Wan' me to go for help, Massa?"

"No, I'll just lean against this tree until I catch my breath." After a few minutes, Abe made his way to the house with slow, weary steps.

CHAPTER ELEVEN

Sarah was shelling pecans for Miss Daisy's next batch of pies. The old cook always started preparing food days ahead of the holidays, and Sarah loved to smell the desserts baking. She sat at a small table made from a giant pecan tree that had been uprooted during the high winds of a storm. The electrical activity had spawned the dangerous lightning that struck and burned the home of Abe's parents, killing them.

Since her in-laws loved pecan trees, Sarah had asked Jeremiah, a talented artisan with wood, to make the table as a memorial to the elder Sullivans. The woodworker designed the round top with a border of pecan leaves uniquely created by carving through the top around the leaves in a cutwork pattern. The center of the table contained the rich pattern of the inner rings of the tree. Tracing and burning out the word *Sullivan* made the name stand out. Jeremiah made a stain by heating pecan bark and hulls in water for days over an open fire. When the mixture had cured enough, he stained the leaves, leaving some lighter and coloring others a deep, chestnut brown. The variation of color gave depth and character to the table, attesting to his expertise. Sarah had presented the small table as her gift to Abe, the way the lavish dining table had been his present to her.

Sarah was bewildered at what could be worrying Abe. She longed to go back to County Cork to the cottage where they started their life together. Before the famine, they had been a happy and close-knit family. Sarah recalled many mornings hearing Abe singing in his loud, off key, bass voice. Lilting Irish songs. He even joined her in the evening, singing lullabies to the girls, unashamed to show his gentle, tender side. Abe hadn't sung since they'd arrived in America. Could it be because of his preoccupation with making money? He seemed to think accumulating wealth was more important than their happiness or his own health. Sarah made a mental note to talk to her husband about returning home since the famine was over.

Glancing up, Sarah saw Abe through the window, stumbling as if walking were too difficult a task. She rushed out to meet him as Jim ran up from unhitching the horses. Together they got him to the table in the breakfast room. "I'm sending Jim for Doc Bradley."

"No, I don't need him."

"Then talk to me, and tell me what has upset you for the past few months."

"Let's have a cup of tea."

"Sure, but then, you talk." They sat facing each other while Miss Daisy prepared them cups of soothing, herbal tea.

Abe fingered the letters in the center of the table just as he'd fingered the letter that burned against his skin through his pants pocket. Not wanting his wife to read the pain that was certain to be visible in his eyes, he kept his head lowered, watching his finger trace the outline of the indented letters. Abe felt Sarah's gentle touch as she reached across the table and put her pale, delicate hand under his chin. Raising it, she forced him to look at her. Concern registered on her face.

A haunting sadness had defined Abe the last several months, and no matter how hard he tried, Sarah couldn't be deceived. Her eyes recognized his pain. Her heart read the words of his emotions.

"I love you, Abraham. Remember our vows? For better or worse? I know you're hurting, but nothing is worth this pain. Please talk to me. What can I do to help?" She began to cry. Moving her chair beside his, she put her arms around him until Miss Daisy brought their tea.

"Let it be, Sarah. When the time is right, I'll tell you everything, but for now, suffice it to say, we don't have a lot of reserves left. Mister Miller and I made foolish mistakes in separate business ventures. Now, he's out of money. One thing bothering me right now is that Grace, and probably Maggie, may not be able to go to finishing school. The rest of my worries will have to wait. Too tired to deal with them, but I do want you to know that I, too, love you, more than my own life. I'm so sorry I've ruined everything, letting our children down and bringing you to a foreign country, but it hasn't been because I don't care for you. If I could ask you to believe anything, it would be to know I will love you until death takes me from you."

"Don't you worry one minute about a thing, and you stop talking that way this instant! Finishing school's a nice thing to do, but if the girls don't get to go, or have to wait for a while, it won't matter to them, I'm sure. Grace is still rather frail, so perhaps it would be best to have her here where we can watch over her."

"Never thought about it that way."

"This may be God's way of telling us this isn't the right time to send them to Miss Bouvier's."

"Perhaps," he whispered, "if God would even speak to me."

Sarah either chose not to hear him or was too preoccupied to pay attention. When she became quiet and pensive, Abe knew better than to interrupt. She seemed to be formulating a plan, and Abe, if he'd been a betting man, would've laid odds it had something to do with their finances. Any time there was a crisis, Sarah's logic and frugality helped pull them through, but Abe couldn't bring himself to tell her the enormity of their present situation.

"Abe, let's go home. I know the land has been scarred with the blood of our loved ones, but God heals all things, and we can start over. Please?"

Her words gripped his heart, but Abe took a deep, cleansing breath, so the pain wouldn't intensify as it had earlier. "No, we can't do that."

"Why? That's where we were the happiest. All of this opulence isn't important to me. I just want to go home to the land we left behind. Ireland will pull us together again as a happy family."

"We'll talk later." Abe put his large, tanned hands on the table, pushed so hard his knuckles turned white, and forced himself to rise. The gripping pains had eased up, but his body felt heavy. Weariness set in, so he made no protest when Sarah helped steady him, leading him to the bedroom.

She removed his clothes, helped him with his nightshirt, and guided his legs down between the smooth, cotton sheets. After washing his face with a cool cloth, Sarah gave her husband a quick kiss before swishing out of the room. "Daisy, have Jim go summon Doc Bradley," Sarah stated in the matter-of-fact voice she used when taking control of a situation. "Abe needs to be examined. His pain is taking its toll on me as well as him, and I want to know what's causing it."

Sarah turned on her heel, returning to the bedroom where she sat in a Bentwood rocking chair, waiting. Waiting, as she'd done so many times for something she couldn't name. Praying silently, she clasped her hands together. Please, God, let this secret surface. Then show us the way to deal with whatever it is. Looking at her husband Sarah noticed the steady rise and fall of his chest and listened to his soft snoring, indicating he was sleeping soundly.

She let her mind wander. Ever since they'd come to America, Sarah had struggled to keep her fear at bay. Having experienced the devastation of the potato famine in Ireland, her in-laws' fiery death in the storm, her own parents' demise, and the burning of the crop at Oak Hollow, Sarah knew everything they had could be gone, wiped out, in only a few minutes. She couldn't stand another crisis like the Great Hunger.

Remembering how mothers died while holding their babies suckling at their breasts was an ever-present picture barely above the surface of Sarah's subconscious. Now, thoughts brought back memories of the way the workers had covered hundreds of the bodies in blankets or tablecloths, burying them together just the way they died. Watching outstretched hands reaching for a bite of anything to eat, and seeing skin dehydrate and wrinkle over brittle bones as screams pierced the silence forever etched itself in her memory, rocking her with nausea when the thoughts arose.

The opening of the bedroom door brought her out of her reverie, and she crossed the room to greet Doc Bradley. "I think it's his heart," Sarah whispered. "He's been having some chest pains and difficulty breathing."

Doc Bradley had been their friend since they'd arrived in Scottsville. If anyone could help Abe, it would be this kind, gentle angel of mercy. He leaned over the bed, pulled the covers back, and unbuttoned his patient's nightshirt. Abe opened his eyes, looked at the good doctor for a fleeting minute, and drifted back to sleep. Sarah stood at the foot of the bed until Doc finished the examination. When the doctor pulled the covers back over Abe and started for the door, she followed him.

In the parlor he turned to face her. "His heart rhythms are a little irregular, but there's a strong beat." He paused, sipping some of the tea Miss Daisy served him. "I've noticed a change in Abe the last few months. He seems to be deep in thought and quite sad. Is something worrying him?"

Sarah sighed, taking in a deep breath. "I know something mighty heavy is on his mind, but he hasn't talked about anything specific, and I can't imagine what it is."

"I'm going to leave some medicine and also want him to take two tablespoons of whiskey just before bedtime." Doc Bradley smiled at Sarah. "I don't think he'll kick about those orders."

Sarah returned the smile. "No, I don't think he'll fuss at all."

"The whiskey may relax him a little, but he must deal with whatever is worrying him." The doctor rose and patted Sarah on the shoulder before walking out to his buggy.

Sarah saw her daughters coming up the hill from the pecan grove. She walked toward them. Her look conveyed her thoughts. Before she could open her mouth, both girls ran to meet her.

"What's wrong?" asked Grace, panting.

"It's your papa."

The girls instinctively separated and went to each side of their mother to help support her, leading her to the back porch. She hesitated as they neared the steps. The girls looked at her.

Sarah turned, pointing to the garden. "Let's go sit where your papa can't hear us." She chose an imported wrought iron bench and sat down.

"Tell us about Papa," Grace prompted.

"Doc thinks your papa is worried about something, and his heartbeat's a little irregular."

Grace put her hand on her mother's shoulder. "If that's the case, then let's just be sure he can't worry about anything ever again, okay?"

"It's not that simple." Sarah played with a handkerchief taken from beneath the sleeve of her dress.

"But it is," said Maggie. "We can pitch in and do a lot of the chores, taking some of the work off him until Matthew graduates."

"Oh my, I'm quite sure he'd like that!" Sarah's voice dripped sarcasm and frustration. "I do know one thing on his mind is finding the money to send you both to finishing school. Mister Miller is having some bad luck with finances."

Grace's shoulders dropped, and she sighed as tension escaped her body. "Maggie and I have been talking about Miss Bouvier's, and we don't want to go anyway. Can't we go back to Ireland and not have to deal with all the fuss and frills of America? Or if we can't go back, can we just live like normal, Irish folk?"

Sarah smiled, relaxing a little before hugging each girl. "What would I do without you two?"

"Will you talk to Papa, please?" Grace asked.

"That's a very good idea," Sarah rose as gracefully as a ballet dancer. "Let's go."

As they entered the bedroom, Abraham appeared to be in a deep sleep, so Sarah and the girls tiptoed back into the hall. They decided not to wake him for dinner, and went to tell Miss Daisy they wanted to eat a light meal outside on the verandah.

"But sake's alive, Miss Sarah, y'all don' gonna get the chilblains. It's right chilly out there." She bustled around as fast as her oversized frame would move.

Maggie whispered, "You'd think she's a mama chicken, and we're her brood."

That wasn't news to Grace. Miss Daisy had been like a mother to the whole Sullivan lot for as long as they'd been here.

Sarah patted the old cook's arm. "Everything will be okay. We'll put on our shawls and promise not to tarry too long over the food."

"Well I never in my whole life…" Miss Daisy busied herself with preparing a simple meal. "White folks jes' don' know what's good for 'em, but I's gotta do what they say." She grumbled loud enough for Sarah to hear her.

She and Sarah made a game of bantering back and forth. Daisy hoped her gentle teasing would make her little mistress smile. The old Negro woman set the teakettle on the stove while she prepared bowls of steaming onion soup and melted cheese toast. She was determined to get something hot down these headstrong, Irish women.

Sarah lowered her voice. "If Papa doesn't get better, we may all have to work in the fields alongside the Negroes. I've sent word for Matthew and Joseph to come home as soon as possible." Sarah's face gave away her feelings that she didn't expect Abe to survive this bout of illness. "He's been having chest pains for a long time now," she muttered, half to them, half to herself.

Grace reached across the table and patted her mother's arm. "We'll do whatever is necessary. The Irish are a strong bunch."

With the finality of that statement, the Sullivan women devoured their toast and soup with abandon, not altogether suitable for true Southern ladies. They talked a little about Irish traditions, at length about what to do with a large Southern plantation, and the approaching homecoming of Matthew and Joseph. When fatigue embraced them, they said their goodnights and went to bed.

Grace couldn't sleep, though she was tired to the bone. Heavy thoughts kept her awake. The trials they'd gone through in this foreign country seemed minuscule compared to the possibility of losing her father. Raw fear he might not survive washed over her in waves so nauseating, she thought she'd throw up. Papa could be stern and demanding at times, but deep down, his heart was as soft as velvet, and his big, callused hands could hold the most fragile flower without disturbing a single, delicate petal. He just couldn't die. They could manage the land without him, but how could they manage their hearts?

Tossing and turning only exhausted her further, so Grace slid from the bed, throwing on her heavy robe. The evenings had turned colder the last few weeks. She hadn't gone outside at night in a long time, but she just couldn't stand the confines of a House of Death as she'd begun to think of the mansion.

Feeling her way in the dark, Grace crept down the stairs and out of the house. How good it felt to be on the familiar path beside the river. When she came to the fork in the trail, she headed straight to her private sanctuary. She was afraid to hope she would find the heart again, but her own heart beat a little faster from the thought. A sliver of moon afforded limited sight, prompting Grace to brush the ground with a foot before placing her weight on it which slowed her progress.

The trees surrounding the small clearing had grown since her last visit, but now that they were bare, the sketchy moonlight cast eerie shadows through their skeletal branches. "Ah, there," she exclaimed to any creature within hearing distance. "There it is." She knelt, letting her hands lightly outline the edges of the heart, which seemed bigger. As before, no weeds, dead grass, or dried leaves touched it.

She felt it again, putting both hands on the stones in the middle. The heart was, indeed, bigger and felt warm. Grace was puzzled. Why would Jim tend the heart? Did he still think about her? She hadn't spoken to him since the night he carried her home to live the life of a Scottsville Southern belle. She'd always done the right thing, trying to please her father and mother, not disgracing them with what she wanted, but her heart felt heavy as if a weight had been placed on her chest.

Sitting by the heart, her only communication with Jim, felt good. How she loved the dark. Leaning against a tree with her eyelids half-closed, relaxing from the turmoil of the day, she jumped when a rustling sound startled her. Adrenaline took over, and she bolted upright, fully alert, waiting for an unknown assailant to attack. Jumping to her feet, Grace tried to run, but something had her arm, holding her back.

"Don't be afraid. It's me," Jim whispered.

"How glad I am it's you and not a large animal about to have me for dinner." Grace smiled.

"You surprised me by coming back here again."

"I . . . I've only been back one other time. With my sister, a few months ago. We found the heart." She stopped, unable to rely on her voice or feelings at this wonderfully blessed moment. God must have been watching over her because He'd sent Jim to her.

"I watched you the day you came." He made no excuse for spying. "Most ever' day, I come sit by the heart. Today, I felt you real strong. You're hurtin' bad, aren't you? Since I couldn't see you, I added some stones to make the heart a little bigger. Did you feel me here?" He was still standing above her, careful not to come too close.

"Yes, but you always seem to be with me. My father's very sick. He may die, and I don't know how to help or what to do. Please sit next to me."

Jim remained standing. "I's powerful sorry. My mama tole me he wuz sick. She tells me 'bout what goes on in the Big House, and my daddy says sometimes when Massa comes out to the fields to bring water, he looks real pasty, like flour. I seen him a time or two, and he don't look good to me, neither."

"He's a good man and a wonderful father. We can't lose him. What would we do?" Her voice reflected the exhaustion and emotion that had spent her energy throughout the day.

"Do you think the Good Lord would understand iffen I wuz to put my arm around you to comfort you 'cuz that's what friends do? Would that help you any?"

"Yes, please hold me."

Moving with a natural ease, he dropped down beside her. His arm scooped her close to him as he placed her head on his chest.

He leaned back against the tree, closed his eyes, and in his soothing, deep voice, prayed the most earnest prayer Grace had ever heard, asking God to watch over her father and to lead all of them in the right direction to be of help to him. Tears erupted unchecked, and she let them flow. Jim dabbed her eyes with his bandana, but didn't try to stop her crying. He only stroked her hair and sang soft, spiritual songs until she fell fast asleep.

The wind picked up, whipping through his lightweight, flannel shirt, as Jim turned his back to shield Grace from the biting gusts. He didn't feel the cold. The body heat he and Grace shared sheltered him from the harsh elements and bleak emotions of his heart.

CHAPTER TWELVE

Jim thought about his life. He, Essie Mae, Lavitica June, and their mother, Daisy, came as chattel of Oak Hollow and Abe bought Jeremiah later. Instilling within her children their African heritage, the old cook taught them many of their customs including the ceremony of jumping the broom. She further demanded that they not have babies until after they'd completed the marriage ritual.

Daisy and Jeremiah had grown up together on another plantation. Jim's early life seemed to pass in a vague blur, but he did remember in vivid detail how their mean overseer, on occasion, whipped his father so hard Jeremiah lost consciousness. Then someone else bought his daddy, and his mama who was left behind had to suffer things no human being should ever have to think about, much less endure. Hatred of slavery and the South burned in his heart, but he loved the Sullivans and would never forget their kindness in uniting all the families, then giving them their freedom.

He looked down at Grace. He couldn't even describe his feelings for her. Now, with her head on his shoulder, his thoughts drifted to rumors of change floating on the winds of time. Some of his people had run away, but he didn't want to leave. The plantation and getting to know this family had brought him more happiness than he could ever have imagined.

Grace awoke with a start. "I'm so sorry for keeping you up."

"Shh. My mind's been filled with thoughts, so's I couldn't sleep, no how."

"Guess I should go in case there's a change in Papa. The family might need me." She stood with Jim's help, gave him a hug, and started for the house.

"Wait. Let me see you to home, so's you'll be safe."

"But you can't be seen walking with me."

"I'll jes go far enough to make sure you're safe. No one's up anyway. I watch all the time from that tree across the river or from the barn."

"You do?"

"Yas, ma'am. I jes' checks to make sure you and Miss Margaret is okay."

Grace smiled. Any other time, she wouldn't have wanted to leave his side, but worry and fatigue had taken over. All she wanted now was to go home. "Thank you," she managed.

Early evening the next day, Jim took some books to the cabin since it had become too dark to read outside. Daisy found him on the porch with a lantern, mouthing the words out loud.

"What you up to, Boy?" Daisy fell into an oversized sturdy rocking chair Jeremiah had made for her.

"Learnin' to read." Jim ducked his head and stared at his feet.

"Don' you be doin' that. You could get us all in a heap o' trouble. Who learned you how to do that readin' stuff?"

Jim never lied to his mama, so he told her the story of how Grace had been teaching him the basics of reading and writing.

"Oh, mercy me." Concern showed on her old, wrinkled face.

"Listen to me. Someday, we kin tell the world we been freed. And maybe, someday our peoples might be 'lowed to go to school and learn just like the white folks do, but for right now, we hafta teach ourselfs."

Daisy had that thinking look about her. Jim sat beside her explaining how the basics of reading and writing could keep them in touch with all their friends and family, even if they never saw them again. "Tha's prob'ly why the white folks don' wan' slaves to learn. Keeping us out o' touch will keep us out o' trouble, and none of us'll know what we's makin' a X for. Why, you know, Mama, they's people runnin' up North all the time, and they ain't slaves up there. Iffen they kin read and write, they kin get good jobs."

"Yeah, but mos' of 'em gits caught and brought back. Then they gits hurt real bad or kilt."

"But someday, that'll all change."

"I don' be gone to Heav'n when that happens." She began to rock.

Daisy remembered the horrible beatings her husband had endured, and her heart felt as heavy as the cast iron skillet she used for cooking. She long ago stopped thinking about the cruel master who had withheld food from her family every time he got drunk, raping her over and over until she thought her insides were going to explode and pour from her. Daisy was his property, though, so she had to endure it.

That ugly master used to laugh at her and tell her she wasn't hurt because her bruises didn't show. Jeremiah didn't find out about the abuse for a long time because the only way they could communicate was by walking many miles to meet or passing the word to a neighbor who'd give the message to their family member.

When Jeremiah finally got the news, he'd wanted to kill Daisy's master and would have if she hadn't stopped him by reminding him how the Good Book said killing was wrong. If families could keep in touch, even passing letters that were more drawings than actual writing, but those notes were looked at over and over to get them through the constant torment of long days and longer nights.

"Jim Boy, I's real worried 'bout this, but what you says makes sense. You bes' be hidin' them books back in the woods and do your readin' away from the cabin."

"Yas'em."

Daisy's thoughts took hold again. She wouldn't have trusted anyone asking her boy to do something illegal, but the Lord above sent the Sullilvans to rescue them, so if Miss Grace wanted to teach Jim, Daisy would keep still. Master Sullivan was raising a couple of brave young women as well as two fine sons. There was nothing she wouldn't do for this family, even to the point of giving her life for any one or all of them.

Not much slipped by the old cook. She watched and listened all the time. Young Joseph had stolen her heart. She loved him as her very own son. She was skeptical and uneasy about the recent change in Matthew, but never spoke her mind, hoping he'd turn back to his sweet ways. Grace had always been the stately and proper one, but underneath that peaceful surface lay a sense of fairness and a determination to make things right when she set her mind to it. And Maggie. There was something very endearing about her, but she could be a stubborn little thing who'd do what she wanted with no regard for the consequences. Jim's voice brought her back to the present.

"I'se gonna talk to Daddy 'bout it, but we's got to educate ourselfs now that we's got the chance. I been thinkin' 'bout having a meetin' down at the tabernacle. See if anybody wants to study on Sunday afternoons."

Daisy entered the house and started making cornbread. "Tha's a good idey, talkin' to yore daddy 'cuz the good Lord only knows what's gonna happen. I's sore afraid Massa Abe's not gonna make it, Boy, and iffen he don' we might haft to go somewheres else unless Massa Matthew keeps us on." Tears welled to just short of overflowing. "Massa Abe's a good, decent man, and he don' deserve to hurt the way he does. I sees a lot of things the family don' see, but I don' say nuthin' to 'em. That man's heart's ahurtin' over somethin' or somebody, and tha's why he's sick."

"Tha's another reason to learn stuff. In case we're forced to leave."

"I also been watchin' Miss Grace. You and her's got some kind of powerful secret. You better know your place, Boy, and not be entertainin' no notions or thinkin' 'bout birthin' no babies. You needs be jumpin' the broom with your own kind."

* * *

The morning dawned clear and cold with a north wind howling around the corners of the house, dressing it in an air of gloom. Daisy heard it blow in and got up extra early so she could have the fire blazing in the wood stove and the fireplaces before the Sullivans awoke. She didn't know what to expect with Master Abe's sickness, but she wanted to be prepared for anything.

The kitchen warmed up as she made biscuits and fried up pork strips. She was startled when Maggie wandered into the kitchen, drew a chair up to the wood stove and put her hands out in front of her to warm them. Miss Daisy glanced at her and smiled. "Tha's a sight for these tired old eyes, Missy, seeing you warmin' yoresef. Brings back mem'ries."

"Feels good, too. I didn't sleep very well last night. Kept having nightmares."

"Well, Chile, I don' want you worryin' none 'bout your papa." She paused with her hands full of dough. "'Cuz we all gonna take care of him and the rest of the fam'ly."

Maggie loved Miss Daisy. She was like a second mama who had a way of telling you something, and whether it was fact or fable, she made you believe it was true and that she had it on good authority.

"May I help you with breakfast?"

"No'm. You don' need to do that, Miss Maggie."

"But I want to learn how to make biscuits like you do."

Miss Daisy's grin lit up her whole face, and she began humming one of her favorite hymns. Maggie joined right in with the words.

"I love to sing your songs." Maggie swayed, her spiral curls keeping time with the music as she kneaded the biscuit dough.

"I guess you wuz boun' to pick 'em up one way or another since I been singin' 'em for so long."

They worked side by side, and Maggie observed each detail. She wanted to be able to cook for Charles when they married, so she had been noticing everything around her with a renewed interest. Maggie was somewhat puzzled, though, when her old mammy took down the bottle of bourbon and added some to the sorghum syrup that would go over the biscuits. Miss Daisy then broke some eggs into a bowl and started whipping them with such fervor that she alarmed her young apprentice. "Why the bourbon?"

"Honey Chile, your poor papa's real bad, and this bourbon'll do him a world of good. I's so angry at that old sickness that's got aholt of his heart." She started the frenzied beating again.

Abraham Sullivan opened his eyes just as the sun peeked through the windows, realizing he'd slept later than he had in a very long time. His memory of going to bed was vague, but in a dreamlike state, he seemed to have seen Doc Bradley. At that moment, his wife entered the room.

"Hey, there, lazybones." She began washing his face with a warm cloth.

Sarah seemed to be in a good humor but always did when in control of a situation.

"Morning." The murmur of his words was a welcomed sound, even to himself. Sarah leaned over, lifted him up a little, and fluffed up the pillows, forcing him into a semi-sitting position. She smoothed the covers over his lap and placed a towel across him.

At the same moment, Miss Daisy appeared at the door with a tray. "Now, Massa Sullivan, you bes' eat all you kin of this here breakfas' 'cuz I done spent a good deal of time a fixin' it."

Abe smiled at her mild scolding but was happy to have her working for them. "Miss Daisy, do I smell whiskey? Whatever have you put in my eggs?" His eyes displayed a twinkle.

"Ain't none in the eggs, Massa. In the syrup. Good for you. Eat." She turned and trudged from the room without smiling at his teasing.

He ate alone while Sarah saw the girls off to school on their last day before Thanksgiving break. As Abe pushed the covers aside to stand up, Sarah came back through the door with her hands on her hips.

"A norther blew in last night. It's cold. The wind's raw, blowing so hard it would whip the skin right off your face. You're going to stay in bed today. I've already spoken to Jeremiah and the other servants, and have told everyone, except the household help, to stay home and start celebrating Thanksgiving early. So there's not a thing for you to do. Now, would you like a book to read, or do you want to go back to sleep?"

"Guess I'll sleep for a while."

"Fine," she said, flurrying out of the room. Abe closed his eyes and was in a deep slumber before another thought formed.

* * *

Sarah had spent most of the day knitting to take her mind off her troubles. Listening to the chiming of the grandfather clock, she stood, stretched, got her shawl from the hall, and stepped out on the verandah, waiting for the girls to return from school. The sun had begun setting much earlier lately, announcing the coming winter. This day had been a bleak, drawn-up-in-fear kind of one for Sarah, and the strong bite of wind, striking her face and going right through the wrap, chilled her, but she didn't care. Her heart had felt cold for a long time.

Sarah's hands shook as terror filled her soul. Abe lay on his deathbed. She knew nothing about business. Oak Hollow would be up to Matthew once he graduated and came home. He'd be the glue to hold the family together. Grace would be fine. She'd marry Paul and live in town, but would be close enough to help out if needed, and who could know what would happen to Maggie or Joseph.

Seldom did Sarah take spirits, but she wanted some Irish coffee. Giving up her watching post, she went to the kitchen where Miss Daisy rustled about cooking the evening meal.

"Set yoresef down here," the old Negro woman blurted out, "and tell me what you been thinkin' 'bout."

Sarah began to sob. "I'm so afraid. My heart feels like it's been twisted right in two. What shall we do?"

"Everthin's gonna be fine, Missy. You wait and see. We'll make do, that's all."

"I want some Irish coffee."

"Well, I'll certainly fix you a toddy, but you bes' not have too much before dinner." Daisy opened the cabinet and pulled down one of the small, pottery mugs brought from Ireland.

When it was ready and steaming, Sarah picked up the heated cup, marching back to the verandah. She sipped the hot drink, savoring the fiery liquid sliding down her throat. The alcohol warmed her, dulled the ache in her chest, and settled her nerves. She seemed to be forever waiting for one thing or another. Waiting for the children to come or go. Waiting for Abe to check on the fields or come in for the evening. Waiting to see what new trial another day would bring. Why did women always wait?

Before she could further ponder this great mystery, Paul's carriage pulled up, and he jumped out almost before the driver had stopped the horses. He gave his hand to Maggie, who alighted first, and then to Grace.

As he followed the girls up to the large portico, he extended his hand to Sarah. "Grace tells me Mister Sullivan's not feeling well, ma'am. Is he better today?"

"Thank you for asking. Yes, he's somewhat better. Keeping him in bed is a true challenge, but this weather's too brutal for him."

Paul nodded. "Well, I'll be running along. If you need anything, anything at all, you send one of the servants. I'll come as fast as lightning." He bowed, took Sarah's hand, gave it a quick kiss and a squeeze before walking back to his carriage.

Sarah turned to her older daughter. "He's such a nice young man, Grace. I'm glad you like him." A large sigh escaped from the deep recesses of Sarah's lungs.

Grace didn't say anything as she breezed into the house followed by Maggie with her mother bringing up the rear. Her first stop was the kitchen where Miss Daisy had steaming hot chocolate waiting. Picking up a cup, Grace led the way to a breakfast room that had been built adjacent to the kitchen with a large arched doorway. Abe had told the children he wanted something to remind him of the cozy one room cottage they'd shared in County Cork, and it had become a favorite gathering place.

Grace started talking before anyone could sit down. "Mama, we need to talk to Papa when you think he's strong enough." She encircled her cup with her hands to warm them. "I don't want to put off telling him Maggie and I have decided not to attend finishing school or have a debut. The sooner he accepts it, the better matters will be."

Sarah looked at her older daughter. That's Grace, she thought. Direct, to the point, and move on to the next challenge. Felt good to have her take charge. Sarah had no energy left to make decisions.

"I agree," piped up Maggie. "He's just outnumbered, that's all."

Sarah nodded. "He's been sleeping most of the day, and I think it's best to let him rest until the boys come home, so perhaps, you can talk to him tomorrow."

"Fine," Grace said. "But you need rest, too. You look tired, Mama. Let's have dinner as soon as possible, so you can go to bed early."

The girls put their arms around Sarah's frail shoulders, trying to shield her from what they all knew would be the eventual death of their beloved father and husband. Miss Daisy prepared a simple supper of potato soup with fried cornbread pancakes and hot tea, which she served to the three ladies of the Sullivan plantation at the small breakfast table rather than in the formal dining room.

Gliding noiselessly into the darkness occupying the bedroom she'd shared for so long with her husband, Sarah donned her gown and slipped between the soft, cotton sheets that carried a faint smell of her wonderful Abe. She lay still, listening, making sure his respirations remained regular and peaceful before allowing herself to relax.

Sleep overtook her at last, and she, along with a young Abraham, frolicked among fields of romantic wildflowers and English heather growing on craggy cliffs overlooking a rough, cerulean sea.

* * *

The girls didn't feel sleepy. Depression hung like a shroud in the house, and the loud ticking of the grandfather clock in the hall seemed to mimic Abe's heartbeat. Needing to escape the confines of the mansion, they took a large quilt, wrapped up in their heavy shawls, and sat huddled together on the oak swing.

Grace couldn't bear to bring up the gravity of their father's illness, so she steered the conversation in a different direction. "You never talk about Ireland anymore."

"Living there seems like a dream. I do miss the Isle and sometimes wonder what our life would've been like if we'd stayed, but you seem to miss it far more than I do."

"You've adapted to America more easily, that's all."

"True, but I'm glad we've decided not to go to finishing school or have a coming-out ball. I'm not that American yet!"

Grace laughed before turning serious. "Paul has done a lot for our family, and I'm grateful, but I'd give anything to return to County Cork."

"I can't wait to marry Charles. Are you going to go ahead and marry Paul?"

"That's too big a decision for me to make right now, but one thing is certain. You're too young to be thinking of marriage, young lady, to Charles or anyone else."

"Not me." Maggie's eyes sparkled.

Darkness embraced them, and as stars winked through the clouds, the two sisters wrapped up their visit and headed to bed.

CHAPTER THIRTEEN

Abe Sullivan didn't object to staying in bed. His color and appetite had improved, but he felt too weak to stand without help. He spent the majority of his waking time either reading the Bible or praying he could live long enough to prepare Matthew and Sarah for running the plantation. He never should have shielded his precious wife from the harsh realities of business or his burdensome secret.

* * *

The familiar sound of horses' hooves beating on the ground signaled Jim's arrival from picking up the boys at the depot. Miss Daisy enlisted the help of her daughters, and the three of them flew into a cooking frenzy to prepare the evening meal. Sarah had changed her dress, redone her hair, and now pinched her cheeks to color them, hoping her efforts would camouflage the lassitude penetrating her frail body. Calming herself, she sat on the sofa in the parlor, while the girls ran out to greet their brothers.

Joe jumped down almost before the carriage stopped, wearing a mask of worry and confusion.

"Papa's some better," Grace said, explaining before he had a chance to ask.

"What a relief!" Joseph's breath gushed out as if it had been dammed up behind his throat.

Matthew stepped out of the carriage, his gaze sweeping the landscape. Staring, his icy-blue eyes turned to a chilled slate-gray. "Where's Mother?"

"In the parlor waiting for both of you." Grace pulled back a little from her older brother's glare.

"Fine. I'll see her there." Maggie, Joseph, and Grace followed Matthew as his deliberate footfalls pounded up the stairs, his long strides propelling him across the wide verandah, down the hall, and into the parlor. Tension elongated his lips into a thin line below eyes void of emotion. His demeanor was brusque, formal, and almost mechanical as he crossed the room and bent to kiss his mother. Straightening up, Matt's grim expression told his siblings the conversation with Sarah would be a private matter.

As if reprimanded, they backed out of the room and closed the door. When they got to the porch, Maggie and Joseph stared at each other, Irish fire blazing mischievously in their eyes, and motioned for Grace to follow them back into the house. The closed parlor door didn't stop three ears pressed against it from listening to every word spoken on the other side.

Matthew began pacing as a look of concern crossed his features. "How's Father?"

"Resting at the moment." Her son's uncharacteristic behavior confused Sarah, but she attributed it to his worrying about Abe's health.

"Mother, I want to see him, but you look tired. You need to rest."

Sarah didn't understand why he acted so formal toward her. But he was taking over so she wouldn't worry. "He's asleep. I don't think you should wake him."

"Perhaps after dinner, but matters need to be settled soon. I spoke to the dean before coming home. Due to the circumstances, he's agreed to let me graduate early, so I won't have to return to school after the Christmas break."

"What about Joseph?"

"Well, who knows, Mother, what Joseph's going to do? I hope there'll be enough money to get him through school. After that, as far as I'm concerned, he's on his own." Matthew inhaled and held it before letting it out slowly. Not wanting his mother to see the animosity he felt toward his brother, Matt fought hard to conceal it. "I don't mean to sound unkind. He's certainly welcome to come back home and help me with the farming, but I don't think it's in his blood. I'd like for him to find a career that suits him, so he can be happy." Matt smiled at his mother, hoping to allay any malice his face might have revealed.

"The girls don't want to go to finishing school." Sarah's lackluster monotone reflected the debilitating exhaustion coursing through her small frame.

"We'll see about that! No matter what, we have our name to uphold. We'll find the money to do what is right in order to maintain our place in the society of this town."

"I'm so glad you're here to take care of us." Sarah patted the sofa beside her.

Matt sat down, and as his mother's delicate hands embraced his face, he marveled at how cold they were, like packs of ice on his heated skin. Though he was tired, a weighty matter lay on his heart, making him uneasy. Managing the land would occupy a lot of time, but his biggest concern was how to manipulate the family.

"Let's join the others." Sarah stood, hoping he would follow. "I haven't even seen Joseph since your arrival."

The three eavesdroppers made a hasty retreat to the porch. They barely got seated before Matt and Sarah came down the hall.

Joseph rose to hug Sarah. "We're here. Just relax, Mama."

The boys went upstairs to freshen up while Sarah headed to the bedroom. She wanted to check on Abe. He sat propped up reading the Bible, looking better than he had in the three days spent in bed.

He smiled at her as she came across the room to kiss his forehead, something he adored and had come to expect. "Are the boys here?"

The bright beam from his eyes lifted Sarah's spirit. "Yes, they arrived a little while ago."

"Good. I shall go to the table for dinner tonight."

"Please wait a few more days."

"No, my boys are home. I'll sit at the table to discuss some important matters with them."

When Abe made up his mind, Sarah knew nothing would change it. Against her better judgment, she helped him to the washbasin where he washed his face and combed his hair.

Abe's eyes met hers in the antique, oval mirror. "Thank you for helping me. I'm a little unsteady on my feet from staying in bed so long."

"I wish you'd wait one more day to get up, but since you won't, let's make a grand entrance."

Arm in arm, they walked down the hall, entering the dining room where their children sat waiting. Miss Daisy almost dropped Matt's favorite potato casserole as Abe came through the door.

"Land's sakes, Massa Sullivan, you lookin' right good there, suh." The old darkie's eyes lit up at seeing Abe take his place at the head of the table.

About halfway through the meal, Abraham spoke. "I know dinner isn't the time to discuss business, but I feel we can make an exception this evening." He noticed everyone had stopped eating and turned their full attention to him. "As you know, I haven't been feeling well and have spent the last few days in bed. Doc examined me, and I'm on the mend now, but I may need some help running this place. I'm also not sure whether Mister Miller is going to be able to help much financially, so I may have to change some plans." He paused and ate a bite of bread, watching his family to see if they'd read between the lines.

Matthew cleared his throat. "I've arranged to graduate early and will be home shortly before Christmas. You've worked hard, Papa. Now it's time to rest. Let me take over the worries and burdens of Oak Hollow and see what I can do." As a hasty afterthought, he turned to his brother. "Certainly, Joe, if you'd like to help, I'd be happy to have you do so."

Joseph didn't say a word. What sprang to the forefront of his thoughts was the conversation he and Matt had on the train going back to school after the end of their last break. Without warning, his gut swirled and his head felt light and dizzy. The sick feeling wasn't from Miss Daisy's cooking. Though Matthew didn't know Joe was aware of his expulsion, telling the family would devastate them, so Joe decided to keep quiet, at least for the time being. Perhaps, he thought, Matt would come forward with the news. But reality told Joe that wouldn't happen.

His thoughts wandered back to the day he'd been walking by the dean's office a few weeks after returning to school. Dean Porter, apparently thinking the boys lived together, had invited him into his office to inquire whether Matthew was ill or why he'd stopped attending class. Not wanting to divulge information that might jeopardize his brother's collegiate standing, Joe told the dean he'd been so busy he'd hardly had time to speak to Matt, but he would make an effort to find out about the problem. Matt was never home even though Joe went by several times. He finally caught up with him in a bar.

Asked about his absences, Matt told Joe he'd fallen and injured his arm, and since he couldn't write to take notes, he thought it best to stay home, but that he'd check with the dean the next day. Joe noticed he could lift the drink with his writing hand, but said nothing.

Running into the dean a couple of weeks later, he asked if Joe had heard the news. Thinking he meant about the so-called injury, he assured Dean Porter he knew everything. The dean shook his head, looking at the floor before he told Joe he would never have figured Matt for a cheater and slacker, and he was sorry he'd had to expel him. Joe almost choked on the revelation, but realized now Matt was covering his secret by lying about early graduation.

Now his parents would never know the truth. Shaking the upsetting thoughts from his head, Joe concentrated on his father's reply to Matthew wanting to run Oak Hollow.

"I don't think I'm ready to simply give up, Matt. Help, though, would be wonderful. You'd need to be shown a thing or two first before I'd bow out altogether."

"Of course, Papa." Matthew played with the food on his plate.

Abe's mood lightened following Matthew's agreement to assist him. Turning to Joseph, Abe asked, "Son, Matt's extended you an offer to work with him. What do you say?"

Joseph swallowed hard, taking a sip of tea before speaking. "Papa, Mama, everyone, Oak Hollow is beautiful and has provided a refuge for our family. I love to walk over this earth. It's almost sacred, but my heart's not in tilling the soil. I'm sorry." Pausing, he glanced down at his hands resting in his lap. Raising his head, his face seemed to have taken on a golden glow, and he looked straight into the eyes of his beloved father.

Abraham sat transfixed by his younger son's countenance and waited with his fork in midair.

"I'm going into medicine. I believe my calling is in caring for people, not crops. Watching mankind prosper, grow, and live is what's important to me." His voice had lowered to almost a whisper, and his eyes glazed with misty film, waiting for Abe's disapproval.

A hush fell over the room, not the kind of shocked silence he'd expected, but a reverence, as if some kind of miracle had taken place. Softness blanketed everyone's face, except Matthew, who appeared stunned and speechless. The girls smiled. Maggie winked at Joe.

Abraham regained his composure, put his fork on his plate, letting Joseph's words sink into his tired brain. "Medicine?"

"Yes. I know times are bad here. The crops aren't doing well from what I can see with the drought and other problems, and you can use Matthew. There isn't anything for me to do that would help. A scholarship should get me through the rest of undergraduate school, and if I can keep my grades up, my hope is to go to medical school back home."

"Home?" Abe asked. "This is your home."

"No, Ireland is home, and I've already applied to the Medical School of the Royal College of Surgeons in Dublin. They also have some scholarships available, so I shouldn't have to trouble you for any education money."

Sarah's hands flew to her face, a gesture she used when words failed her, but tears of happiness spilled forth from her lavender-blue eyes. She'd tried not to show partiality to one son over the other, but Abe had groomed Matthew to be at his side while Joseph had been left to sort of tag along wherever life took him. Folding her hands, Sarah gave silent thanks that her favorite of the boys had made his announcement.

Determined to help him through medical school, nothing would stop her. Finding her voice, she turned to Joseph. "Don't you worry about the money. We'll find a way."

"No, Mama. I can make it on my own."

Abe's eyes never left Joseph's face. His voice grew husky as he spoke to his younger son, the son he thought would never amount to anything substantial. The son, who now would make more difference in the lives of people than any of the other children. "I could never have imagined this is what you'd been thinking. I assumed you were playing at school instead of studying. But here you are, a serious, dedicated scholar with such high ambitions. I'm proud of you. Very proud. With Matthew's help, I'm sure we'll get the plantation going again. Tuition won't be a problem." He turned to his older son for confirmation.

Matthew hadn't moved. He knew from Joe's expression and the careful words he'd chosen that his younger brother remembered their conversation on the train. Now, he was trying to outdo Matt by becoming a doctor. Make their parents proud. Curly-headed, little do-gooder. Well, he'd show them all a thing or two. If his little brother wanted to be a doctor, then he could take care of the family. As of right now, this plantation belonged to Matthew Sullivan by reason of his birthright of being the first-born. And as soon as he could transfer the deed to his own name, he'd send the whole group to live with Doctor Joe.

Patience was the answer. Not letting his true feelings show, Matt pasted a false smile on his lips. "Well, dear brother, you're full of surprises. Of course, we'll make every effort to get you through medical school. And Dublin? That's wonderful. Mama might like to go over with you and visit some old friends and relatives in County Cork."

For now, the volcano brewing just beneath the surface of Matthew's calm exterior hadn't gained enough fury to explode, but how long he could control it, he didn't know.

* * *

Later in Grace's room, Maggie discussed the events of the evening with her older sister. "When do you think it'll be our turn to tell Papa we don't want to go to Miss Bouvier's or have a debutante ball?" Maggie asked.

"I don't know. Tonight, somehow, didn't seem to be the right time. Did you notice Matt? He looked angry. Wonder why?"

"Maybe it's because he always wants to be the center of attention."

Grace agreed, but thought something else prompted the look. He'd seemed cold and power-hungry, almost as if he wanted Oak Hollow for himself. She didn't say anything else about the subject, deciding to wait until she could concentrate on it in more detail. As soon as the conversation lagged, Grace shooed Maggie out of her room. She wanted to go to the grove to think, so she left her dress on but removed her petticoats, allowing her to move easier and quieter.

The weather had warmed up following the norther that had bombarded them earlier, and her feet craved the roughness of the weeds and grasses growing along the path as much as her mind longed for the peace she felt when surrounded by nature. Grace had become adept at finding her way downstairs through the dark and out of the house.

Walking in the blackness, she contemplated the meeting with Jim that had taken place a few nights ago. Having him hold her while she slept awoke emotions she'd tried to suppress. While she knew there'd never be anything physical between them, Jim's gentle, caring always supported her with no demands.

Paul, on the other hand, paid his due respects but didn't seem to have any sentiment invested in anything other than winning her hand in marriage and someday being president of the bank. The cold, misty grass tickled her feet, and she felt more at peace than she had since her papa took ill.

The river gurgled to her, the moon held high a bright, round lantern to guide her, and a moisture-laden breeze caressed her cheek. She found the clearing, sat down, and began to rub the smooth rocks of the heart as she did each time she sat in the circle.

Grace needed to decide what to do about Paul and why she didn't feel the way about him that she did about Jim. Was it because she couldn't have Jim? Forbidden fruit? Or could it be because she didn't want to be an American society lady? If only she could go to Dublin with Joseph. Perhaps she could marry a young man in Ireland and never set foot back in America. Could she forget about Jim and he about her? The cold sent shivers down her spine, causing her to tremble. Was it the weather that caused her chill, or was it the injustice she saw in America that triggered a physical response?

A faint noise interrupted her thoughts. Focusing her attention, she listened intently, trying to decide where it came from. Over there. No, behind her. No, in front of her. Where? She strained her eyes to see who or what was coming.

"Hey." Jim knelt beside her. Over his arm, he carried a thick quilt while balancing a tray containing a big cup of steaming tea. Setting the tray down, he picked up the cup, put his hand under it to shield it from spilling on her, and offered it to her along with a clean rag.

If it had been a pot of gold at the end of the rainbow or a wildflower growing beside the road, it wouldn't have mattered. He'd just handed her the world. As Jim spread the quilt around her shoulders, she pulled her feet up under her, and he tucked them in too. The hot tea tasted perfect, laced with cream and sugar. Grace sipped it, savoring each tiny drop of warmth as it slid down her throat. "How did you know I was here?"

"I always knows where you are. Maybe I can't rightly see you, but I kin feel you. Seems like the good Lord done made me His servant to watch out for you. Sometimes my heart gits real heavy, and other times, well, it ain't quite so sad." Putting his hand on his chest, he continued, "I felt you here, felt you being cold, so I come over to he'p you out."

"You're so sweet. Such a dear friend."

"I ain't gonna stay. Sure would love to, but you got a heap of thinkin' to do, and I don' wanna mess you up with it."

"Please stay."

"No'm, I bes' be runnin' along. You think 'bout things, but if you need me, I'm over yonder, and all you got to do is call my name. You leave ever'thin' right where it is, and I'll clean it up later."

Grace knew begging him was futile once he'd made up his mind, so she sipped the tea thinking about the past few weeks as well as wondering where Christmas would find them. She felt as if a heavy, steel bag had been thrown onto her back, dragging her down more and more each day, and Maggie had indicated she shared the same feelings. They had to talk to Papa soon. Grace finished the tea and realized she was sleepy. Rising to her feet, she folded the quilt, put her empty cup beside it, blew the stone heart a kiss, and walked back to the house.

CHAPTER FOURTEEN

As soon as her head touched the pillow, she fell asleep, dreaming of being in a warm meadow with a huge river running below her in a deep valley. She and Jim ran free, clasping hands and twirling around, then holding each other to keep from falling while dancing to music heard only by them, seeing dreams only their hearts knew. He was white. She was black. How she loved the feel of her own skin!

The dream vanished into the dawning of reality when Maggie shook her awake. "Grace, it's ten o'clock in the morning. We thought you'd died or something. Mama says you need to come downstairs this minute."

"I don't want to get up."

"But you must. Papa wants us to see us. He's back in bed."

Grace threw back the covers, running to the washbasin. "Quick, get me that pink dress hanging over there, will you?" Splashing cold water on her face, she ran a comb through her tousled hair, twisted it into a bun at the nape of her neck, secured it with combs, and pulled her dress over her head. She was ready in fifteen minutes.

"My goodness, you dress fast," Maggie said as they hurried down the stairs and into their parents' bedroom.

Abraham motioned to them. "Come sit by me. Let's talk."

The girls positioned themselves at the foot of his bed.

"Your mother tells me you don't want to go to finishing school, Grace. Is that true?"

"Yes, sir. I'd rather go to normal school. Perhaps it's not fashionable to have a career, but teaching is a suitable profession for a woman if I should ever need to earn my own keep."

Abraham paused. "And I've been told you don't want to have a coming-out party. Is that true as well?"

"Yes, sir. I don't see much point. It's only a formality. Besides, Paul is already courting me, so why bother?"

Abe rubbed his chin with his right hand as the crease between his eyes appeared to deepen. After a few minutes, he turned to Maggie. "And you, young lady; you don't want to go to finishing school or make your debut, either. Is that correct?"

"Yes, sir."

"I guess it's no secret. You're both observant young ladies, and you know our crops have suffered from the dry weather. I'm hoping Matt and I can come up with something to turn our financial situation around, but if not, then I'll abide by your decisions. If we have the resources, though, I'd like for you to follow tradition, go to Miss Bouvier's, and have your coming-out parties before you decide what to do with your lives. After all, that's what is expected by society here in America."

"Yes, sir," they said in unison, walking over to kiss their father's forehead.

*   *   *

Matthew Sullivan's mood turned more sullen. He didn't like the turn of events at the dinner table the night they got home. Realizing he and Joseph would be leaving soon to go back to school, Matt waited until everyone was asleep and then skulked into his father's study. Wanting to go through Abe's desk to find out the plantation's actual state of affairs and the amount of money in the bank, he sat in his father's high-backed chair. Though he went through every side drawer, he found nothing other than some papers and receipts. Since no checkbook or ledger entries were there, Matt wondered if Abe kept them somewhere else.

Pushing the chair back, he reached for the middle drawer to open it. Locked. Trying to pry it open with his knife, the thing wouldn't budge. What was his father hiding? And from whom? He wouldn't keep a large sum of money in a drawer, would he? His mother, he was certain, never bothered with their financial affairs, so why was the checkbook hidden? And the girls. They were too preoccupied with school and looking pretty to bother with business. The servants couldn't read or write, so what was in the drawer? Matt became obsessed. Finding out what secret lurked beyond his reach became his mission.

* * *

Insomnia had plagued Grace for a long time, so most nights she left the house. Since the weather would be too cold after the first frost, she took advantage of the crisp evenings while she could. Starting for the circle, Grace noticed a soft light shining from inside the study. Creeping to the window, she expected to see her father sitting at his desk. Instead, she saw her brother trying to force open a desk drawer. How could he invade Papa's privacy? What could he be looking for? Grace didn't like what she saw, but she couldn't walk through the door to confront him. After all, she was supposed to be in bed asleep.

Leaving the verandah, she fumbled in the dark, finding a small stone. Backing up, she tossed it against the window. Hiding behind a bush, she watched Matt. He almost jumped out of his seat when the stone hit its mark. Quickly, he extinguished the flame in the lantern. Grace could hear him bumping into the wall, trying to find the door. When she saw a light in an upstairs window, she knew he'd gone straight to his room, probably too afraid of being caught to venture back downstairs tonight, but what had he been up to?

She ran to her spot in the grove and found Jim waiting for her. She told him what she'd just seen.

"Good gracious. That's not right at all. He's up to no good, and you bes' watch him real close. I wonder, does Massa Joseph know 'bout this?"

"I'm sure he doesn't." She was glad Jim listened to her concerns. He could always see a situation more clearly than she could, and they talked for over an hour trying to sort out what was happening in the Big House. At the end of their conversation, Jim advised her to bide her time, watch Matt, and if it happened again to tell her father even though she would have to explain her own actions of being out of her room.

Back in her bed, Grace lay awake, contemplating the feeling that an unknown event was about to shape the destiny of Oak Hollow.

* * *

The boys went back to school after the Thanksgiving holidays, Abe's health improved, and Grace and Paul began to sit with each other at social events.

He treated her as if she were a queen, causing Grace to reassess her judgment of him. Had she been too harsh? But sleep still eluded her, and she escaped to the circle three or more times a week to try to sort out her life.

Some nights Jim stayed with her, but they took care to keep their friendship casual. A single unguarded moment could sweep them back to the threshold of dangerous abandon, a point from which they knew they'd never return. They lost track of the times they talked. Other times, they were silent. Much to Grace's surprise, she, too, could feel Jim's presence and knew when he would be at their special place, when he had a problem, or when he felt happy. They didn't talk about their intuition but accepted it as part of their special bond. She knew how Jim felt about jumping the broom. He'd do what his parents had done and solemnize his vows before having children. Rather than let herself think about him having a wife, Grace vehemently pushed the thought aside when it came up.

Jim also thought a lot about Grace and the decision she'd make about marrying Paul. Though he understood why she might agree to the union, it saddened him. As the nights grew colder, he stayed with her more often and longer to keep her warm for the several hours she'd spend in the dark. Sleeplessness was a sign to Jim of Grace's troubled mind. Even though, she'd shared her concerns with him, he had no right to say anything to her or to influence her decisions.

As a surprise for Grace, Jim made a lean-to that would shield them from the wind. He had tacked a piece of canvas he'd found between two thin branches cut from a tree. The temporary shelter could be leaned against a couple of trees when they needed it, or rolled up and hidden when not in use. Jim had also begun covering the heart of stones with leaves. They needed to be careful. Distressed that Maggie would say something after they had discovered the heart caused Jim some anxiety, but Grace reassured him, recalling a conversation with Maggie.

While sitting beside the heart, Grace had mentioned what she considered to be the truth at the time. That the friendship with Jim was over. Maggie had apparently accepted the explanation and asked about Grace's upcoming betrothal to Paul but didn't appear to listen. Her own plans for the future apparently occupied her mind, and Grace was sure her sister had no suspicions of her meetings with Jim.

The news eased Jim's mind, but he was still wary of their friendship being discovered.

*   *   *

The weather turned unseasonably cold as Christmas loomed around the corner. The house took on a festive mood as if waiting for the boys to arrive from school. Abe gave thanks he'd been able to put his troubles to the back of his mind. He went with Jeremiah and Jim to cut a beautiful pine tree he'd spotted last week. Putting it on the bed of the wagon, they hauled it to the house and into the parlor. Abe held it steady in a large bucket while the two darkies tamped in dirt and sand.

Maggie began making decorations from bits of paper along with stringing popcorn while Grace went to the head of the stairs and circled garlands of greenery around the banister. Big red bows placed every few feet along the handrail and mistletoe tacked above the parlor door completed the festive look of the room. As a surprise, the girls made a very large wreath for the front of the house and had it hidden in Maggie's room.

Preparations came alive in the kitchen as Miss Daisy worked her magic, delegating chores to her daughters as well as tending to the pre-holiday baking. Lavitica June polished the silver pieces for the table while Essie Mae shelled pecans for the pies as a way of helping their mother.

Though Sarah didn't voice it, she dreaded the day when one of her children would leave to make their own life. As a way of making this the best Christmas ever, she vowed to have the favorite dish of each of her children placed on the table.

* * *

Abe rode into town to purchase the supplies Miss Daisy had requested for the rest of her holiday cooking and to catch up on the gossip, but after gathering the mail, he didn't want to return home. A letter had arrived from Joe telling them Matthew wanted to spend Christmas with a young lady he was courting and had asked Joe to write for him. As for Joseph, he had been helping a professor for extra credit and couldn't get away until the day after Christmas, but they'd be home as soon as they could.

Abe sensed Joseph's loneliness, knowing he'd have to return to school alone while Matt moved home to begin his new career. But what about Matthew? Who was this girl he fancied? Why hadn't he mentioned her before, and why would he start a courtship with someone when he was leaving? And wouldn't he be eager to come home and show his diploma?

Another thing that struck him as odd was Matt asking Joseph to write for him. Abe sank deep in thought all the way home, trying to read between the lines and figure out what was wrong. Maybe the news wasn't negative, and Matt wanted to stay with his brother knowing this would be their last time to come home together.

The wagon pulled up, and as if a trumpet sounded, servants appeared from everywhere to unload the groceries and other things Abe had bought. The weather was cold and crisp, exactly the way he liked it. Puckering his lips, he blew little smoke puffs from his hot breath and savored the invigorating sting of the wind on his face. Scooping up the mail, he started for the house. Abe loved winter, and Christmas had always been a very big event in their home. He entered through the kitchen so as not to track mud through the main house. Womenfolk got out of sorts with that kind of thing. Besides, Miss Daisy had made a fruit cake and was pouring the rum on it as he walked in, ready to let it ripen, as she called it. The smell was almost more than he could take. Worst yet, he'd have to wait a week, or more, to cut into it.

Ambling over to the cupboard where she worked, Abe pinched a small piece off the bottom, even though Miss Daisy glared at him, swatting his hand with her spoon.

"Now you knows better'n to do that in my kitchen, Massa. You jes' git on with your stuff 'cuz I'm too busy to fool with you right now." She'd become comfortable enough over the years to tease him as if he were a child. Wide grins danced on their faces.

"Yes, ma'am." Abe turned to leave the kitchen, but glanced back over his shoulder. "Oh by the way, Merry Christmas." He winked at her, and gave a little wave as he went to find Sarah. She was sitting in the parlor, staring at the tree.

"Isn't it beautiful?" Her eyes were beaming.

"Yes, the prettiest one we've ever had."

She looked radiant. Sarah. His Sarah. Petite, yet strong, always amazing him. Through all the trials and hard times, she'd maintained her beauty and grace. Now, she sat in a chair by the tree, her skin glowing as the winter sun shining through the window rested on her face. How he dreaded to break her heart with his news. "Let's go for a walk." Abe reached for her hand to help her to her feet.

"Are you out of your mind? It's freezing outside, and you want to go for a walk?"

"Just a short one, please?"

Sarah never could refuse her husband, so she smiled, went to find her heavy, hooded coat, and put on her warm, fur-lined boots. Seemed to take as much time to get ready to go out in the cold for a short walk as it did to get dressed in the morning. But it was Christmas, her husband felt fine, the boys would be home soon, and she was happy. They walked in silence beside the river on the well-worn path the girls had made going down to the pecan grove.

The drought had continued into the winter, and the only moisture on the ground was the dew from the night before. Abe had prayed for some kind of precipitation to provide moisture to the fields but pushed that worry to the far recesses of his mind for now. A more pressing issue had to be resolved. Since the temperature hovered on the brink of freezing, they kept up a brisk pace to warm themselves.

Sarah broke the silence. "What's on your mind?"

He couldn't bring himself to tell her, so he handed her the letter instead. They'd stopped by a big boulder jutting out into the river, and she leaned against it to brace herself. When she'd finished reading, Sarah folded it in the original creases, tucking it back inside the envelope. She wore a blank stare. So deep in thought her eyes seemed to be looking right through space and time. Coming back to reality, she handed her husband the letter, and they held each other in a tender embrace.

"Are you okay?" he asked.

"Yes, I'm fine. We knew the time would come when the family wouldn't be able to be together, and I've tried to prepare for it, but I have an idea." All of a sudden, she became animated, her eyes regained their sparkle, and she started talking nonstop as she hastened their pace back to the house. "The boys can't come home for Christmas, so we'll go to them."

She paused to let her voice warm up. "We haven't taken a trip in a while. Wouldn't it be nice to pack up all the presents and visit the boys at school? The girls could see where they live and what college is all about." Since Abe seemed to be thinking, she didn't wait for his reply. "Besides, if Matthew has a lady friend, I think we should meet her, don't you? And poor little Joseph having to work right up until the holiday seems unfair. Maybe Matt and his friend will spend

Christmas Day with Joe, but it's not the same as family. Let's go, please?"

The cold wind had turned her cheeks rosier than ever and made her bright eyes stand out like beacons of love looking straight into his heart. How could he refuse? "Let me think about it."

"No, don't think. Just say yes!" She threw her arms around his neck.

He twirled her around and set her down as if she were a priceless piece of art. They both knew she'd get her way.

Sarah was all aflutter when she came into the kitchen, and Miss Daisy knew something had happened on their walk but couldn't make any sense of it. Sarah and Abe pulled off their boots and coats while Daisy poured them cups of steaming coffee. Sitting at the little pecan table in the breakfast room, Sarah relayed the news and their plans. "Daisy, that means you'll have the holiday all to yourself, and you can use whatever you need from this kitchen. Fix yourself the best Christmas dinner you've ever had. Why, you're even welcome to invite everyone and use our dining room and all the crystal and china. Whatever you want!"

Daisy didn't understand this unpredictable behavior but was grateful the upcoming trip had excited Miss Sarah. She knew how much her sweet mistress wanted to go home to County Cork for a visit. While this excursion wouldn't be the same, maybe the break would be a good substitute to take Sarah's mind off her troubles for a while. Daisy looked up to see Grace and Maggie enter the breakfast room with eyes all aglow, standing very close together holding something behind them.

"Merry Christmas," they shouted and turned around, revealing the gigantic wreath they'd made.

"It's beautiful!" exclaimed Sarah. "Abe, take it and put it on the door this instant while I tell the girls the news."

Abraham smiled as he took hold of the large evergreen decoration and made his way down the hall. Sarah explained about Joseph's letter and their plan to visit the boys. "We can stay at an inn and take some little presents with us. We'll have a grand adventure. Joe can join us in the evenings after work, and we can meet Matt's lady friend."

The girls sat for a time pondering the idea, sipping on the hot tea Miss Daisy put in front of them. In an abrupt move, Maggie jumped up and twirled about. Grabbing Miss Daisy around her rather generous waist before she could escape, Maggie led the surprised cook in a shuffling dance. Everyone clapped and laughed. "I think it's a splendid idea," Maggie shouted.

Grace smiled, too, but her first thought was how much she'd miss seeing Jim. Not having to spend time with the Scotts, however, would be wonderful. Thinking of visiting her brothers for Christmas prompted her to ask her mother, "Are we going to surprise them?"

"Of course, we shall. What great fun that will be! And I didn't even think of it until this minute, but we'll get to see Matthew's diploma and maybe make a little party of it since he won't graduate at the same time as his classmates."

Sarah became animated as she scurried around, deciding what to take and changing her mind at every turn. She reminded Daisy of a bee buzzing from flower to flower, ascertaining which had the sweetest nectar. Poor Lavitica June had a hard time keeping up with her.

Abraham appeared in the kitchen with a stern look about him. "Miss Daisy, I shall expect, no I demand, some of that fruit cake be saved for me." He broke into a smile.

"Yas, suh. I be guardin' it wit' my own life."

CHAPTER FIFTEEN

Grace wanted Christmas to be special for Jim. She picked out a songbook, a small New Testament, and a wool scarf for him that she embroidered with a small heart on one corner to remind him of their heart of stones. On the first page of the Bible, she wrote a simple note.

Knowing he wouldn't be able to take his gifts home, Grace put them all in a tin container that would be easy to hide yet would protect everything from the weather. She wrapped the box in midnight blue velvet, symbolizing their nighttime meetings. Later, she stole out of the house with his gift. Jim was already in the grove when she arrived, and she was somewhat surprised to find him there.

"I knowed you wuz comin' 'cause Mama tole me y'all was goin' away the day after tomorrow."

"Yes, we are. And I have to spend a little time with Paul and his family tomorrow, but I wanted to share Christmas with you tonight." She handed him the box. The moon wasn't bright enough for Jim to read the inscription, so Grace recited it to him.

"To Jim, the best friend God above could ever give me. You have my heart always. Grace."

Jim listened to her, turning his head to hide strong emotions. After a few minutes, he rose and walked behind a tree, returning with a small, round jewelry box made of pecan wood. Carved leaves adorned the outside edge of the circle of wood with the word *Grace* etched in the center. The pattern looked identical to the breakfast table Jeremiah had made.

Grace appeared overwhelmed yet somewhat upset. "This is so beautiful, but you shouldn't have asked your father to make this. Your parents might get the wrong idea of our friendship."

A grin covered Jim's face. "No, I didn't ask him to do nuthin' for me. I made this for you, myself. My daddy showed me a long time ago how to carve, and I been workin' on this all year."

His gift touched her heart so tenderly that Grace cried in spite of herself. Jim brushed her tears away with the edge of his finger. What would she ever do without him? He epitomized every trait she thought a man should have. Not fake like Paul who was interested only in money and possessions. She and Jim knew the other's heart and shared every aspect of their lives. Well, almost every aspect. Some things could never be shared, but if she had to choose, she'd rather have the spiritual bond than the physical one anyway.

Grace got up early, bound herself in her uncomfortable corset and best petticoats before donning a vibrant green dress and little black boots. After sweeping her hair up into a chignon, she pinched her cheeks even though she knew the cold would make them rosy. Sarah was having coffee in the parlor when Grace entered to retrieve Paul's present from under the tree. Donning her heavy, hooded coat, she bent and kissed her mother. "I'll be back soon."

* * *

Paul looked out the window, startled by the early arrival of Grace's carriage. Had she told him she was coming to see him? Looking into the mirror, his eyes refused to hide the red lines indicative of his drinking the night before. Pressing a washcloth to them, he tried to make the red marks disappear, but his efforts proved futile.

Paul couldn't imagine why Grace had come uninvited unless her father was ill again. By the time he got downstairs, Grace was sitting in the parlor waiting for him. Her smile told him Abe wasn't the reason for her visit.

She looked into Paul's bloodshot eyes as he sat beside her, but made no comment about his appearance.

"Hello Paul. I'm sorry to come so early without an invitation, but we got word my brothers can't come home for Christmas. Since this may be the last holiday we'll all be together for a while, we're going to surprise them with a visit." She stuck a small package in his face. "Merry Christmas."

The box contained a beautiful, oak inkstand with a black pen engraved with Paul's name on the side in gold leaf letters.

"Thank you. This is beautiful." He kept running his fingers over his name. Crossing the room to a magnificently decorated tree in the corner, Paul poked among the gifts. He picked up a gaily wrapped present and handed it to her.

A large, crystal candy box with roses etched on the top and sides peeked out from the inner tissue paper, and

Grace knew he'd paid a handsome price for it. "Thank you so much. It's lovely." She wrapped it up for the trip home. Her thoughts went to the hand-carved box Jim had made which held more meaning than the expensive one Paul had just given her.

Paul sat beside her. "I'm sorry I haven't spent much time with you the last few weeks. Trying to decide whether to go to college or just start at the bank and work my way to the top has taken priority over everything else. You know my ambition is to become president when my father retires, and it seems it would be easier to learn from the bottom up. I've already started working there after school and on Saturday mornings. Papa's trying to find a way I can work every day and still graduate from high school. What do you think?"

Grace mulled over his question. "You need to make this decision regardless of what I think because this is your future, not mine, but I'll abide by whatever choice you make. I've had some decisions to make, myself, weighing whether to go to normal school instead of Miss Bouvier's."

Paul didn't respond. He was puzzled as to why she would want to be a teacher. If she married him, she'd have the best of everything. He contemplated proposing as soon as possible if Grace had decided not to go to finishing school.

Mister and Missus Scott entered the parlor. Grace and Paul stood to greet them. They discussed the weather, the upcoming trip, and the Sullivan family. Grace could tell they liked her, and they were nice enough, but the atmosphere felt stiff and formal. She envisioned how the men would act if she grabbed Louise Scott and shuffled her into a dance as Maggie had done with Miss Daisy. Grace smiled. After a proper length of time, she rose, wished everyone a pleasant Christmas, and gave Paul a hurried hug before leaving.

* * *

Maggie also rose early. She devised an excuse to go to town since she and Charles had agreed quite some time ago to meet on this particular day to exchange gifts. With the unplanned trip, the perfect timing made it seem like a Christmas miracle, and Maggie said a prayer of gratitude. She told Sarah she wanted some embroidery thread to take with her on the trip, and since the servants were busy helping with last minute preparations, Maggie begged to drive herself to town. She'd lifted some floss from her sewing basket, tucking it into her pocket, so on her return, she could produce her purchase. Sarah contemplated her young daughter's request and finally gave permission. "Don't tarry too long. We have a lot left to do."

"I won't."

* * *

Maggie raced to the appointed place and maneuvered the buggy into an open spot on the edge of a wooded area. Jumping down, she smoothed her skirt and petticoats. Trying to stuff her ringlets back under her bonnet proved more difficult than straightening out her clothes. The bouncy curls refused to stay, but Maggie was so excited, she didn't care. Watching Charles approaching on his horse, she marveled at how handsome he looked, his red-gold hair shining like the copper pots Daisy polished. His smile lit up her morning.

Maggie stood still until the horse came to a halt, and Charles dismounted to embrace her warmly. The wind had kicked up, taking a cold bite out of their warm skin, so he moved his horse along with her horse and buggy to a more sheltered grove of trees. The couple climbed onto the buggy, where they found a heavy blanket to put over themselves. "You know any other time we wouldn't be under a blanket together, but the Good Lord knows I love you and want you to be my wife. Just don't want you to freeze to death before that happens."

Maggie laughed. She loved this man with all her heart, and it didn't matter one bit to her that Charles' family wasn't in the elite social circles in town. She watched a slow smile grace his features as his hand went into his pocket. He fumbled around for something, but she couldn't figure out what he was doing. When he withdrew his hand, he held a tiny package. The paper was loose and the ribbon almost untied. Obviously, he'd wrapped it himself. He kissed her cheek as he handed it to her. "Merry Christmas to the sweetest girl in the whole world!"

Maggie's eyes misted over, and she was glad it didn't take much effort to open the gift. She pulled the wrapping paper off a small box and caught her breath. A heart-shaped, golden locket engraved with a rose on the front and inlaid with a tiny ruby in the middle of the flower rested upon a black velvet cushion inside the box.

"This is the most beautiful thing I've ever seen, but it must've cost you all your money."

"No, there's still some left over, and I'll save more by the time I can properly ask you to be my wife. Will you wear this locket close to your heart to remind you of me?"

"I'll wear it always, but my parents can't see it, or they'll make me give it back and won't ever let us get married. Maybe I can hide it under my dress." She turned for him to fasten the clasp. After tucking it next to her skin, she produced his gift. "My present to you isn't so grand, but I made it just for you."

Charles unwrapped the gift, ripping into the paper with abandonment. When he opened the box, his face reflected surprise and awe as he held up an ivory-colored, brocade vest. He fingered the front of it. "Sure would like to put this on right now, Honey, but it's a little cold to take off my coat." Holding it up, he said, "This is the prettiest thing I've ever had, and it'll be perfect to wear for our wedding. Don't want people to think I bought it, though. I want to shout from the rooftops that my Maggie made it!"

"Then, do that. When someone asks you at the wedding where you got this vest, you tell them your new wife is in the business of designing and making clothes, and she made her first piece for you!" As the wind grew stronger, they huddled closer. Maggie knew there was a reason winter was her favorite season, and it wasn't only because of Christmas that she was elated. She loved the way Charles smelled and how strong his arm felt around her shoulders. "I have something to tell you. Matt and Joe can't come home for Christmas, so we're going to Clinton. Since you and I weren't going to be able to see each other anyway, I know it won't make any difference to you, but I don't know when we'll be back. So if you don't see me for a while, don't worry."

"Honey, you know I'll worry until you're back home where I can put my arms around you. The weather bothers me, too, with this wind kicking up. A man from up north said this morning that our sky looks like snow's coming. This trip makes me uneasy."

"We're going by train, so it'll be safe, and Papa will watch after us. Wonder what the boys will say when we surprise them? Maybe we'll get to see the college. Do you want me to come by the general store when we get back?"

"No, I have a new job."

Her eyebrows arched in surprise.

"A cabinet maker has accepted me as his apprentice. He also builds houses, and that's what interests me the most. Why don't you come by the shop, instead of the general store, when you get back? It's that one on Main Street."

"Okay. Watch for me the first minute I can get away. Learn all you can from him. You house people, and I'll clothe them. We'll both provide a sort of shelter." She chuckled, thinking about it. "Wish I could stay longer, but we don't want Papa to come looking for me."

Charles reached for her, pushing her head under his chin and stroking the curls that had escaped from the bonnet. "I'll miss you more than you can imagine."

Miss Margaret Sullivan then raised her head, turned toward the love of her life, and planted a long kiss on his lips. "Don't forget me," she said, winking at him as she prepared to leave.

He winked back, tucked the blanket snugly around her, handed her the reins to her horse, and hopped down. "Be careful going home and remember I love you, Maggie Sullivan."

"You be careful on your new job. Merry Christmas. I love you, too, Charles Burton." Maggie waved and headed her horse into the wind.

CHAPTER SIXTEEN

Matthew sat slumped over a small table in a brothel, drinking with one hand while the other rested on the neck of a young, sad-faced prostitute. "You sure ain't no virgin, Mary," he roared, almost collapsing with laughter. Leaning toward her, he planted a wet kiss on her red, painted lips. She tasted like berries.

He tasted like leftover whiskey. Mary thought she'd gag, but this was her job. She just wanted to get it over with. Time seemed to stand still, but from experience, she knew hurrying him wouldn't work. The only thing that kept her going was that Matthew had been a regular customer since September, always asking for her. She'd been little more than an adolescent when her parents died, but she vowed to care for her younger brother. When food and money ran out, she searched for work. The only thing could she could find was working in the brothel. She dreaded it every night, but it kept Luke with her and out of an orphanage.

After a few more drinks, Matt stood to go to her bedroom. Since he was drunker than usual, Mary had to support most of his weight to get him up the stairs. By the time they reached her bed, she was spent, wondering if she'd have the energy to please him and watched as he slouched on the edge, holding on to the iron bedstead for support.

"Listen," he said in a slurred voice, "I'm going home soon. Won't be coming back, but if you ever get to Scottsville, you come see me, and we'll have a rollicking good time." He'd just pulled off his shirt when he pitched forward, passing out on the floor.

Nudging him with the toe of her shoe to make sure he was unconscious, Mary slipped the wallet from his pocket and stripped it of the money she felt she deserved. She hated taking money she hadn't earned, especially from Matt who was halfway decent to her, but he'd said he was leaving town after Christmas. This would probably have been his last visit. Sitting on the bed for a while, she took her time in leaving the room, so she wouldn't have another customer right away. When she felt she couldn't tarry any longer, she walked to the landing right outside the door and signaled for two, large, well-muscled men to come up and get Matthew.

In one smooth motion, each man grabbed a leg and arm, hauled him down the stairs, and dumped him outside beneath a beautiful, winter moon. The prince of the Sullivan clan had been treated no better than the garbage the saloon threw out each evening.

* * *

Matthew awoke the next morning, cold, chilled-to-the bone cold, with only his shirt thrown over him while his coat lay piled in a heap beside the building. The hangover pounding behind his eyes in a never-ending, staccato rhythm was only a forerunner to the certainty that his head would explode any minute. Waves of nausea rose like a dragon breathing fire from the innermost part of his being, forcing him to throw up like a wretched animal. How he found his buggy or the small flat he'd rented with his gambling winnings was a complete mystery.

The money his father sent would've provided basic necessities, but he always wagered the lot thinking he could make the allowance grow. Sometimes he won, but more often, he ended up on the losing end of the deal. Pulling off his vomit-covered clothes, he fell into bed before passing into oblivion.

* * *

Rebecca and her younger sister, Susan, waited for Joseph to grade the last paper for his professor. Deciding to take a break, he grabbed both their hands pulling them to each side as he dragged them through the door and down the street to the general store. A few, small trees stood against an outside wall. This was his favorite time of year, and knowing he and Matt wouldn't be going home until the day after Christmas, he couldn't bear the holiday without a tree.

Thinking about Matt, Joe knew the story of courting a young lady was a lie. He had the feeling his brother wanted to attend a big gambling event he had mentioned. Or maybe it was because he wanted to put off telling his parents he didn't graduate, though that would entail being honest, not one of Matt's traits lately.

Amid much laughter and discussion, the trio picked out a little scraggly pine. Joseph swung it over his shoulder as the three of them made their way back to his small cottage. They spent the rest of the afternoon decorating the tiny tree with homemade ornaments and some fresh popcorn garland to drape around the irregularly shaped branches. While Rebecca straightened up the kitchen, Susan stuck cloves into a whole apple. Attaching a ribbon, she hung it on the doorknob. The fragrance of the spice imbued the humble abode, evoking an inviting feeling; a warm, glowing feeling of love Joseph knew reflected the true spirit of the season.

Admiring their handiwork, Rebecca started humming "Silent Night," but when Joe and her sister joined in, the lyrics tumbled forth from their enthusiastic three-member choir. More songs followed until each of them had to pause to catch a breath.

"This is fun," Rebecca said, her eyes twinkling. "I'm so thankful you're not like your brother."

Joseph was fond of Becca, his nickname for her. Since she'd already attended finishing school and made her debut he knew he was free to ask for her hand if he chose. They'd spent many hours talking about their goals and dreams, and Joe felt more than blessed that Becca never tried to change his mind about his career. He'd never met such an unselfish girl. This was going to be a good Christmas in spite of not being able to go home. He'd spend the day with the Taylor family.

A loud knock, followed by high-pitched yelling, which Joseph couldn't distinguish, interrupted the little celebration. Voices sounded female and frantic. With some hesitation, he opened the door, trying to take in what his eyes and ears observed. He was so shocked to see his family laughing and shouting Merry Christmas that he forgot to invite them in.

"For heaven's sake, Joseph, it's freezing out here," said his mother, pushing directly past him. She stopped when she saw a young woman and a girl standing behind her son.

Extending her hand the young lady looked into Sarah's eyes. "Hello. I'm Rebecca Taylor, and this is my sister, Susan." Her voice had a lilting quality.

Sarah smiled as she introduced Grace and Maggie. Joseph regained his composure and introduced his father. With so much activity, he wasn't sure what was happening or why, but he was filled with happiness. Obviously, his family liked his guests, and they felt the same.

"Joe, why don't you drive Susan and me home so you can visit with your family?" Becca put on her coat and bonnet. "It's very nice to have met you, and I hope to see you again." She helped Susan with her hooded cloak.

Joe glanced at his mother and could tell she approved of Rebecca's impeccable etiquette.

Sarah took the young lady's hands. "Why, thank you, Rebecca. We certainly hope to see you again, too. Merry Christmas to both of you."

"The same to all of you." She and Susan curtsied before starting out the door.

"Rebecca's house isn't far, so I'll be back soon," called Joe, ushering his two guests out the door.

Alone in their son's apartment, the family began to relax and look around. In the confusion, no one had mentioned Matt. Even though his belongings weren't visible, the family didn't appear suspicious. Grace and Maggie amused themselves by placing gifts under the tree and looking around while the whistle of the teapot on the stove's back burner called Sarah to the kitchen. The warmth of the cottage and the tea heightened the awareness of their fatigue, and they were grateful for a respite before Joe returned.

Sarah sized up the small house. Even in the limited space, she'd have enough room to cook a good meal and would send Abe for supplies tomorrow. A nagging thought of Matt's whereabouts kept intruding into her mental list making until she finally decided he must be at the parents' home of his lady friend.

* * *

Matthew woke up, cold and shaky from not eating. His head still throbbed but was somewhat better than it had been when he'd collapsed. Grabbing the wool blanket from his bed, he wrapped himself in it, and made his way to the kitchen to put the teapot on the stove. Matthew Sullivan. What a name! What a majestic name! The first-born! The heir to the throne! Royalty! A hollow laugh escaped from his throat as reality smashed into his headache. He wasn't a blessing . . . or even a graduate. He sat at the table, remembering recent events.

The dean's words expelling him still tore at Matt's heart. Only a few weeks and he would've graduated. If only he'd attended class and studied instead of copying from other students. But how many people got caught cheating? Not that he cared about finishing Mississippi College. He just needed a diploma to show his parents. Drinking in the bar one night, he'd met an artist who agreed to help him out for a price but told Matt he'd have to wait until after Christmas. That's why he'd made up the story about a lady friend and not wanting to go home before the holidays. He had to wait until he got the fake certificate.

As it turned out, the young man delivered the copy two days before Christmas, stating he needed the money to buy gifts. The document, forged onto the same lambskin as the original ones, looked identical to the college-issued diplomas. Though it cost Matt a big portion of his money, he'd still had enough for a last celebration with Mary. Too bad, he didn't remember the evening. At least, his perfect little brother knew nothing about the banishment from their alma mater. The decision to go their separate ways had allowed Matt to keep his activities and problems to himself.

Mail was the only tie he had to Joe since the family wrote to them together. His brother would pick up the mail at the post office, read it and deliver it to Matt's house. Seldom did their paths cross, so Joe would just leave letters inside Matt's unlocked apartment.

The kettle demanded attention. Matt pulled himself to a standing position, forcing his stiff, aching legs to carry him to the stove. Placing a tea ball into a mug, he poured the boiling water over it and placed a saucer on top for it to steep. Sitting down again at the table, Matt looked through the window watching a group of children playing outside. Bundled in their heavy, winter clothes, they laughed and chased each other, falling down and getting back up over and over.

Matt's mind wandered to a happier time. A time when he, Joe, the girls, and their friends played at the edge of the bog while their father tended the potato crop. Those were times when it was fun to have little sisters. They were close and secure in a small stone house back in their mother country. He'd have been a good farmer there. But here in America, people valued ambition and power.

Being the oldest, he had to uphold the family name, accumulate wealth, and make sure his sisters were well cared for until they married. How he wished he could have been as carefree as his brother always appeared. Joseph's decision to go to medical school was a big blow to Matt's already plummeting ego, a lost ego that he wondered if he'd ever recover.

Here he sat, sick with a hangover and not a soul to share Christmas with unless Joseph happened to come by, an unlikely prospect. Matt recoiled, thinking how ashamed his parents would be of their eldest son being such a miserable failure. The hot tea parched his mouth as he sipped it, trying to shake off the effects of the alcohol. Even though his throat tightened, rebelling against the searing liquid, it felt good.

He seemed to be in some kind of vacuum with no emotion, no feeling. Nothing seemed real. Christmas used to be his favorite holiday. Now, he didn't care. This was just another day of lies and pretense, spent with no one. Staring once more at the children, he ate a slice of stale bread before heading back to bed. "Merry Christmas," he said, smirking to the ghosts from his past.

What he wanted was a drink, a good, strong whiskey, but the liquor and his money were all gone. Besides, the bone chilling cold saturated him, tea or no tea. Had the Lord changed his bones into shards of ice as a punishment of sorts? His chest hurt, and his throat felt raw, causing Matt to wonder if he'd burned it with the hot liquid.

Just as he settled into bed again, he heard a light tap at the door. His brother could pick some of the most inopportune times to come by. Since he didn't want to see Joe or have him know his condition, he chose not to get out of bed to answer the summons. "Go away," he shouted.

"Matthew?" The voice was female.

He tried to recognize it through his muddled brain, but nothing computed.

"Matthew?" Again, so sweet, so feminine. He dragged himself from the bed, wrapped a quilt around his torso, and cracked the door. Mary stood there, holding a basket in front of her, bundled up like a Christmas present in a red, hooded coat and black gloves.

"What do you want?"

"To be invited in. It's very cold out here." Mary didn't wait for an answer, but brushed past him into the small, shabby abode. She caught her breath to keep from throwing up at the foul smell of vomit, strong whiskey, and rotting food. Setting her basket on the small table by the door, she pulled off her coat and gloves.

"Look, I don't have any more money and don't feel well. So if you need some Christmas business, you'd better look somewhere else." Matt couldn't control his shivering and crawled back into bed.

Mary smiled at him. Even in his crapulent state, he noticed an emotion within her that he'd never seen until now. Her beautiful, brown eyes shone like those of an innocent child. Moving into the kitchen, Mary refilled the kettle and put it on the stove to boil before cleaning up the mess of dirty dishes, molded food, and empty whiskey bottles. Then she filled a basin with hot water and marched over to the corner that served as the bedroom area of the efficiency apartment.

The warm, wet cloth felt good on Matt's face and he didn't complain when Mary pulled the covers back to expose his chest and arms. She washed him with some kind of soap that smelled good, though he couldn't name the scent. The aroma reminded him of some of the herbs Miss Daisy cooked with. Fatigue and cold prompted him to give up thinking about the fragrance. Mary patted his upper body dry before attending to his lower anatomy. By the time she'd finished, Matt realized he felt better. Gazing at her, he wished she'd stay for a while.

"You're burning up with fever." She smoothed the sheet and covers over him before disappearing back into the kitchen.

Matt could smell something cooking, but he couldn't stay awake long enough to find out what she had on the stove.

Mary woke him with a tender kiss on his forehead. "Wake up," she whispered, arranging a clean tea towel over the bedcover. She placed a tray in front of him.

Matt's nose detected the aroma of food. There was a bowl of hot soup and warm, buttered bread as well as a cup of tea sweetened with honey. "What's this? And what are you doing here?" Matt was confused and tired. Had she been here before? Yesterday? His mind refused to function.

"This is food for you, and I'm here because it's Christmas Eve, and you're sick. You've been so good to me the past few months. Had it not been for you, there would've been no money to feed my brother or buy him a Christmas present.

He would have been taken away from me. My conscience has stabbed me all day for taking money I didn't earn last night, and my heart wouldn't let me rest after they told me you were dumped on the street. I had to come see about you and bring your money back along with some hot food."

She guided a spoonful of creamy potato soup into his mouth. "Luke and I have no one to share Christmas with, so I came to check on you. Now I'll spend the money on a doctor and medicine."

The soup tasted good. Matthew began to remember answering the door and how weak he'd felt. The hot meal seemed to be giving him strength. Letting his eyes wander over her face, he saw Mary in a different light. She was a pretty girl, in spite of the hard life she'd chosen for herself. Selling her body couldn't be an easy job, and it was strange to think she had a brother. "Where are your parents?"

"They both died of a terrible disease. Consumption's what the doctor told me. They had a long, painful death. I was fourteen when I started taking care of them and Luke. Then, after their deaths, I had total responsibility for our livelihood. I'm not proud of what I am, and though my services are just a paid pleasure for you, I am a human being."

She fed him as she talked. "We had no relatives or anyone to help us after our parents passed. In order to provide enough money to support us, I took the only job offered me. Made me grow up in a hurry. I brought your money back, so you won't have to ever see me again, but first, I'm going for the doctor."

The food seemed to clear Matt's head, and when he spoke, his voice sounded soft and gentle. "Yes, Mary, please leave. You need to spend time with your brother." He paused. "Thank you, though, for what you've done for me. You keep the money and buy Luke something with it. I don't need a doctor." He knew it was the last of his money, but he was too sick to care, hoping for his own death angel to arrive by morning.

"Am I intruding on the few remaining days you have here before going home?"

"No, but I'm sick and don't want to contaminate you."

"Yes, you are sick. And Christmas is no time to feel this bad." She bent over, kissed his forehead, as she removed the tray. Tucking him in, Mary waited until Matthew drifted off to sleep before going to get her brother, and then on to the doctor's home clinic.

CHAPTER SEVENTEEN

When the three of them entered the small apartment, Matthew was almost comatose. Doctor Middleton threw back the covers, listened to Matt's chest, and took his pulse. Mary's eyes brimmed over as she turned to the window.

In a timid voice, she asked, "Is it . . . uh . . . consumption?"

"No, I'm fairly sure it's pneumonia." Opening his black bag, he took out a bottle of liquid and gave Matt a dose. Leaving instructions about administration of the medicine, he shut his bag and walked toward the door. "I'll be going now, but if he gets worse or you get worried, come get me again."

Mary rushed to him, extending Matt's money. Doctor Middleton put his hand up, refusing it as he pointed to Luke. "It's Christmas. You keep the money and buy the young man something. Merry Christmas to all of you."

"Thank you, sir, and a happy holiday to you, too." Mary would have enough money to buy food for the small Christmas dinner she wanted to make as a surprise for Matthew and her brother. She set about making a list of things she'd need.

Matthew woke dripping with perspiration that had dehydrated him.

"Hello, sleepyhead." Mary sat in a chair beside his bed, and a young boy sat reading a book in the armchair across the room.

"What time is it?" Matt felt like a ton of dirt had been piled on top of him and noticed coverings that didn't belong to him.

"Four o'clock in the afternoon."

Matt looked around. The small, dowdy flat was immaculate and smelled good. A tiny tree stood in the corner. He couldn't believe his eyes. She'd been with him when she could've been making good money.

"You know, Mary, you're okay." Matt grinned at her.

She smiled back at him. "I brought over some extra quilts. Since your fever broke a little while ago, you can put on some dry clothes now, and we can remove some of the covers. Also, the doctor came." She measured out a teaspoon of the liquid for Matt.

While she and her brother went to the kitchen, Matthew slipped out of bed, took off his wet clothes, and put on the dry ones she'd laid at the foot of the bed. "I'm dressed," he announced in his strongest voice, a tad louder than a whisper.

Coming toward him, Mary pointed to the bed. She didn't say a word, but Matthew knew he was supposed to get back into it, and did so without argument. His Highness had fallen, and the star he'd fastened his dreams to seemed to have dropped from the sky, leaving him shattered and hurting.

Matt rubbed his chest. A team of horses must have been tramping on it while he slept, and breathing was a struggle. "There's no amount of money that could pay you for what you've done for me. You're an angel sent here at Christmas time." He pulled up the covers, closing his eyes.

Mary Kelly put her fingers to her lips. "Shh. Go to sleep." She returned to the kitchen.

* * *

Joseph didn't know what to tell his parents about Matt's behavior and their living arrangements. Asking Rebecca's advice when he took her home, she confirmed what he already knew. He had to be honest even if hearing the truth upset the family so much they'd never forgive him.

"Where's your brother?" Abraham had a quizzical look about him.

"Papa, we need to talk." Joe began pacing.

Sarah headed toward the kitchen. Joe's voice relayed something ominous, and she didn't want to hear it.

"Mama, please sit down. The girls can make the tea or coffee or whatever you want, but you should hear this, too." He stopped pacing and sat across from his parents. His eyes clouded, and his speech came out low and shaky.

"Is Matt okay?" Sarah asked in a meek, frightened voice.

"No." It was all Joe could manage at the moment.

"Where is he?" demanded Abraham, jumping to his feet.

"Sit, Papa." Joseph paused. "He and I lived together for a few weeks when I first came to college, but he started hanging out with some pretty unscrupulous characters, people I didn't like, so I got this place for myself. I wanted time alone to think and study. Matt moved to another little place. Well, he's moved a lot. Sometimes he can't pay the rent, so he has to move. Most of his time is spent drinking a lot and seeking pleasure. Pleasure I won't discuss in front of you, Mama. Gambling usually pays for most of his needs, but sometimes, when he's down on his luck, I take food to him."

Joseph stopped speaking to regain some composure before continuing. "He doesn't think I know about his behavior, and I'm certain he wouldn't want you to find out. Breaking this news to you is the hardest thing I've had to do, but I'm concerned about him. We seldom see each other. That's his choice." Joseph waited for a response from his parents.

He'd chosen not to tell them Matt had been expelled. No matter what, he couldn't humiliate his brother that much more. Matt needed to be the one to tell them. Joe's objective wasn't to hurt his brother, but to see if their parents could help.

Abraham hung his head, and Sarah's face contorted into a frown. Joseph wondered if she would suppress her feelings as was her way out when worrying about something.

"There isn't much food in this kitchen, but that doesn't matter. We'll simply get some supplies and make do." Sarah wrote some items down on a piece of paper, and told Abraham and Joe to go get them for her, picking up Matt on the way back. She delegated chores to Grace and Margaret, and soon, Joseph's little house was a scene of pre-Christmas activity.

* * *

Mary was talking to Matthew when she heard a knock. Before she could open the door, two men burst in. Abraham Sullivan stood, looking at his son lying in bed. A strange woman also occupied his tiny apartment. "What are you doing in bed?" he demanded.

"I'm sick. But I'd like to introduce you to Mary, my friend, who's been taking care of me." Matt didn't want to admit he didn't know her last name.

"Very happy to meet you." Mary extended her hand to both Abe and Joe.

Joe moved away from the foot of the bed and turned toward her. She was a pretty girl, but he knew his brother and the services Mary must have been performing for him. Still, she looked so young and innocent. Her auburn hair glistened with golden highlights, and her light brown eyes held messages he didn't want to read or know about. He was, however, grateful for what she'd done for Matt, given his illness.

A young boy, introduced as her brother sat in the corner by the tree. Joseph couldn't figure out why he was there rather than at home with their parents, but he let that thought drop. "Thank you for watching after him, Mary."

Abraham said nothing, just raised his hand, and waved his thanks.

"You're welcome. We'll be going now." Holding out her hand with a small bottle in it, she handed it to Abe. "The doctor left this medicine and wants Matt to take a teaspoon twice a day. He's had today's dose and will not need another one until morning." She motioned to her brother. Putting on her coat, she murmured, "Merry Christmas to all of you."

Mary, not quite a virgin but maybe an angel of mercy of some sort, tucked the money inside her coat pocket, slipped from the house and out of Matthew's life.

"Your mother wanted us to take you to Joseph's, but I don't know if you should get out of bed."

"I'm sorry. I didn't know you were coming." Another chill shook Matt's body.

"You stay right here," said Abe. "We'll be back."

* * *

After discussing Matthew's illness with Sarah, they decided Christmas dinner the next day would be served at Matt's apartment, so he wouldn't have to get out of bed. Abe made sure the girls and Sarah were settled at the inn, and then he and Joseph went to check on Matt. They found him feeling a little better, but weak and groggy. His sallow complexion had been replaced with a pale rosy tint. Since Matt wanted to sleep, Abe went to join Sarah while Joe went home for the evening.

* * *

Sarah bustling around Joe's kitchen seemed happier than Abe had seen her in a long time. "In spite of everything that's happened, you seem very happy, my dear."

"I think it's because this is going to be a simple Christmas. Joe's small place reminds me of our home in Cork. Knowing Matt felt better last night is the most wonderful news." A smile softened her face as she wrapped up the meal to take to her eldest son's apartment.

* * *

Testing his strength, Matt sat on the side of the bed. He looked forward to his mother's cooking and a visit by the entire family, but what he wanted more than anything was to get drunk and bed Mary. If he couldn't do that, he realized he'd just like a chance to visit with her. He pushed the thought of dealing with his troubles to the back of his mind, knowing he'd have to face his failures at some point in his life. Now didn't seem like a good time. He'd wait until he felt better. That way a plan could be formulated and a decision made about whether he'd tell the family of his dismissal from school.

* * *

Daisy didn't know what to do. The small home they'd been furnished was the nicest one she'd ever lived in, and she loved spending time with her family on Sundays and holidays. As was his custom, Master Sullivan had given each family a turkey or a ham, so no one needed anything from the Big House. But she knew Miss Sarah had been serious about them having Christmas there.

After the Sullivans left, Daisy finished her chores and started home. She seldom went outside during the waning hours of the morning and found it relaxing just strolling along the path beside the river under the branches of the cypress trees until she came to the little bridge she crossed each day. Humming a Christmas carol almost under her breath, Daisy looked up to see her son, her pride and joy coming toward her.

"Hey, Mama, we all been talkin' 'bout having a community Christmas this year. What you think 'bout that?"

Daisy mulled the proposition over in her mind before breaking into a smile that lit up her whole face. Giving Jim a hug, she said, "That's a dandy idey. Since the Sullivans done gone, us womenfolk kin combine the cookin' for all of us."

Jeremiah called all the workers together because he was the closest thing they had to a leader. He put the plan to a vote, and it was unanimous in favor of the first ever Community Christmas. The cold, crisp air took on an ambience of festivity. Women huddled together talking about the menu while the men, not used to being idle, stood around waiting to be told what to do.

All of a sudden, Jim broke into song, and soon everyone joined him singing and clapping hands. Plans were put on hold for a while.

"Stop!" shouted Miss Daisy. "I got a idey. Miss Sarah said we could use the big kitchen. We kin git ever'thin' cooked there and have Christmas in the Big House."

There was dead silence like the stillness preceding a tornado. Time seemed to be trapped, whirling in a vacuum. No one moved or said a word. There were just about a hundred eyes, it seemed, focused on her. Not one of them blinked.

"Well, I's only gonna say this one more time. Now, listen up here." She repeated her idea.

A man in the back broke the trance that held them captive. "I don' reckon it'd hurt none to go to the Big House. We been invited. Le's go."

Cheering and laughter broke out among the men as they hurried off to cut and haul wood for the stove. Serious planning began among the women and girls. Several turkeys and hams had been hung in the smokehouse, pecan and mince pies were ready in the pie safe, and the cornbread had been cooked for the dressing. Yams were brought up from the cellar along with some onions and Irish potatoes. A few last minute things to do on Christmas Day, and they'd all be ready. Christmas Eve wound down with everyone gathering in the tabernacle to sing carols. This year would be the finest Christmas ever for the Negroes of Oak Hollow.

Jesus' birthday morning crept in on a melody provided by small snowbirds. A special gaiety pervaded the air as the Negroes stirred, opening sleepy eyes. Dressing was accomplished in record time as they bundled up to shield themselves from the brand new snow, which had fallen during the night, laying a gentle blanket over God's creation. What a miracle for the South. Snow! Some of them had never seen the soft, white stuff before. They all headed to the wagons for the trip to the Big House and were as excited as if they were following that star to Bethlehem. Even the young children seemed to sense this was going to be a most special Christmas. The tree in the corner of the parlor stood regal and beautiful, watching over presents for everyone left by the Sullivans. Some of the men started playing Christmas carols on their crude instruments while Jim led the singing. Women talked as they cooked, and broke into singing and laughing on occasion.

Every once in a while, a husband would come in, grab his wife, twirl her around in the large parlor before kissing her under the mistletoe. Young ones played games, laughing and chasing each other through the house.

Jim smiled, letting go of the heavy thoughts burdening him these last few months. "Mmm, they sure's some good smells comin' outta that kitchen," he shouted over the din of merry making, hoping the women would say dinner was ready.

"Now, you jes' go on 'bout your business, Mister Jim. We be lettin' you know when we ready." Miss Daisy loved teasing her son, but she was in charge of the monumental task of overseeing the preparation of food for all of them. When lunch was ready and laid out on the beautiful buffet, Jeremiah stood up and announced that Brother Robert would lead the prayer.

Forming a circle, they joined hands. Voices of old and young alike silenced in reverence to the occasion in honor of the birth of a Baby they knew would bring their friends freedom and give all of them eternal life.

The man who had charge of transporting the girls to school began to pray. "Our Father, on this beautiful Christmas mornin',' of the day Your Son was born in a stable with only hay for a bed, we come before You in this unbroken circle, thankful we got a good life here with the Sullivans. And we jes' ast you, Lord, to bless them as they all get together for their Christmas with the boys. We ast that You watch over us and keep us safe. We been hearin' 'bout some uneasiness. You know, we scart for our friends, but we know You'll direct ever'thin' for Your glory and for ourselfs. Thank you for this food and for the chance to all come together to honor You and Your Son. In Jesus' name, Amen."

A loud echo sounded as each person voiced a hearty Amen at the prayer's end.

"Now, y'all come on and get you a plate and he'p yourselfs, and we ain't gonna have no talk 'bout work or anythin' unpleasant. This here's the best Christmas we ever gonna have, so le's us make it merry." So spoke the matriarch of the Negroes. Miss Daisy was the queen, and no one disputed that.

This Christmas marked their debut of equality, if only for a single day. After the last dish had been washed and dried, the food put away, and the wrappings from the gifts disposed of, the families gathered their young and helped the older ones into the wagons for the ride home. A dream had come true for all of them. They'd come of age, but they'd soon lose their innocence, and some of them, along with their white brothers and sisters, wouldn't see many more birthdays.

Had they had a crystal ball to see into the future, their perfect Christmas would've been ruined by the blood yet to be shed in a Great War to come.

"Now, we ain't gonna talk 'bout it tonight," piped up Robert, "but tomorra, we got to start makin' some plans. I been hearin' some things that really gits to me 'bout slave peoples runnin' away."

"Well," said his wife, a heavy drawl accenting her words, "we sure ain't gonna talk 'bout it tonight 'cuz we all full and happy, and I think we all gonna sleep real good."

"Amen," came a loud cheer. Soon, the old familiar strains of "Amazing Grace" were lifted up to heaven, sung in slow, reverent tones, wooing the youngest children to sleep and touching the hearts of some of the older ones who knew this might well be their final celebration before walking on those streets of gold. As the small caravan of wagons headed home, most everyone sang, making it the perfect ending to a day that would live in the hearts' memories of the young, innocent children, who had no idea they needed to be saved from anything and had no concept of being someone's property.

The day was most profound for Jim, calling up memories of his own amazing Grace, who saved him by teaching him to read and write. And showing him what love was, what real, abiding, straight-to-the-heart love felt like and how it surrounded a person for a second and for all eternity. He couldn't lead the singing, too choked by the tears in his throat. The others carried on, but his mama leaned over and put her arm around his shoulders.

No need to talk. She knew something was bothering him…had been for a long time. There was a change in him, not a good change or a bad one, but one she couldn't describe. When they reached home, Jeremiah kissed his family and went straight to bed, happy and content because this Christmas had been so special. Special because his friends from the neighboring plantation had joined in their celebration and because they had a good master. And the ones here had been freed. None of them would ever have to carry the long, raised lines that formed a shiny gristle on the backs of slaves beaten for no reason by cruel white men. Happy because no woman or girl on this soil would ever have to endure the degradation, the inhumanity, the pain and agony of rape, only to be thrown out like a bucket of soured milk. Content that no child conceived of such a heinous man would ever again be aborted, and the mother killed. Though his back had healed many times and the scars had faded a bit each year, the ones in his heart of hearts would always live.

Jeremiah vowed after he passed on if God would allow it, he'd look down just once as the men who did this to his people cried out from the depths of hell. Just one look from heaven, and he'd be vindicated. His people would sing praises from their mansions in heaven and reap those treasures waiting for them. He closed his eyes, wearing a smile. His family singing Christmas songs with their neighbors under the tabernacle was what he last heard before peaceful sleep paid him a visit.

As people began to drift toward their cottages, Jim turned toward the woods. The only way he could spend time with Grace was through his thoughts, and he drew her to him by their heart of stones as Christmas night passed into a bright morning.

CHAPTER EIGHTEEN

"Hurry up, Luke." Mary was putting food into a large wicker basket.

Her brother looked puzzled. "Thought you weren't going over there again."

"I wasn't because I didn't want to embarrass him, but what if his family doesn't come see him?" She paused, covering a pumpkin pie with a tea towel. "If they're there, we'll leave. If not, no one should spend Christmas alone, especially being sick."

"You shouldn't say we'd embarrass him. We're as good as he is—maybe better. Just because we don't have parents doesn't mean we're bad. I'd much rather stay home." Luke tried to be good without causing any grief for Mary. He didn't know exactly what she did for a living, but she must not like it. He'd hear her in the early morning hours when she came home, crying as if her heart were being cut out of her chest. But when you had a life without parents, you did what had to be done to survive, so crying was never mentioned by either Luke or Mary, at least not to each other.

* * *

Sarah cooked roast beef with carrots, Irish potatoes and onions along with other fresh, winter vegetables, which Abe found at the general store, but there wasn't time or space to make pies. Being together would make this Christmas a festive occasion even without all the trimmings. No sooner had the Sullivans started eating than they heard a small knock on the door.

Matt prayed it wasn't Mary. She didn't need to be subjected to scrutiny by his parents, sisters, and brother at this moment.

Sarah rose to answer the door. A cold wind whipped around the corner, almost knocking a young lady off her feet. She stood, holding a basket and clinging to the boy beside her. From their holly-bright noses and crimson cheeks, it was evident they'd walked for quite some distance. No snow covered the ground, but sleet was coming down strong and razor sharp.

"Hello, Missus Sullivan."

Was this girl Matt's lady friend? "Come in, both of you. The weather's miserable."

Everyone came from the kitchen to see who was visiting.

"Thank you." Mary came in, her eyes darting from one person to the next. With a deep breath, she put her basket down before taking off her heavy coat. She walked over to shake hands with Abraham and Joseph, then introduced Luke and herself to Sarah and the girls.

She crossed the room to Matt's bed. "How are you feeling?"

Matt had never seen Mary so radiant and sophisticated. She looked like high society with the manners to challenge any debutante. Dressed in a beautiful, forest-green gown with touches of gold trim around the high-collared bodice and a dropped waist, she was a portrait of beauty and elegance. Luke was dressed in a classic gray suit, white shirt, and crimson tie, topped with a heavy, black overcoat. Subtle smells escaped from the large basket Mary had set down by the coat rack.

"Did you bring food?" Sarah asked.

"Yes, ma'am. I didn't know you all were coming over, or we wouldn't have intruded."

"Nonsense. We'd love to have you eat with us if you don't have to get back to your family."

"Thank you, but we just stopped by to check on Matt. We'll be running along, so you can finish your meal."

"Do you have family waiting?"

"No, ma'am. It's just Luke and me."

Sarah's face glowed, and her wide, blue-violet eyes twinkled. "Then, you'll join us. We'll simply add what you brought to our spread and have a dandy Christmas."

After eating, the kitchen chairs were moved into the large room that served as a parlor and bedroom. Joseph and Abraham sat on opposite corners at the foot of Matthew's bed while the rest of the group occupied the chairs. Stories of Oak Hollow and the home they left behind in Ireland filled the blessed day.

When they started singing a few Irish songs, Matt was too weak to participate, but Mary stepped in and took his place. Her sweet, soprano voice sounded as clear as the finest church bell. Everyone hushed, mesmerized by her gilt-edged voice. How surprised they were to find Mary knew the words to the songs, including the Celtic ones.

y regained their composure, Sarah asked a
ions, trying to find out as much as possible
o obvious.

ervousness was relieved. Mary handled
y and finesse, avoiding lying, but skirting
not to embarrass herself or him. She
parents and how someday she hoped
h she revealed that her family was also
to give her a hug.

amount of time, Mary rose, stating
leave while it was still light to avoid

home in the buggy," Sarah offered,
She gave Luke a pat on the back
oming to take care of her son on

h again," Grace said, smiling.

. Thank you for allowing us
ry curtsied and Luke waved

ling ever since the family
istmas meal. Though Joe
l childish, it seemed tha*
nanipulated the
rance, Jo*
, ٩ٮ

for him, and
n this special
a dark, heavy
reminded him
nclusion whe*

st
ner
nts
this
up.
what
, but
were
n well
on. At
Ve were
mpting
e won't
vhat you
like this

nuge blue
oft glow of
the parlor.
's story was
d so hastily

d
e

gracious of you to take care of Matt, I'm sure you were p
well. Your performance today must have provided him so
entertainment."

Joe realized he was being unreasonable, but his dis
with Matt's prostitute coming to his family's Christmas di
still bothered him. "And the story about your dead pa
and this kid being your brother. Quite a story. Who
boy anyway?" He turned to Luke, whose eyes had well

Mary spoke in a soft, deliberate voice. "I don't car
you think of me. Doesn't matter, one way or the oth
this is our first Christmas without our parents. The
wonderful, but all the money went to try to make th
and then to bury them, leaving us very little to liv
least my father paid for the house a long time ago.
trying to make the best of this lonely holiday by at
to bring a bit of cheer to your brother. Though
admit it, I know he's sad as well as sick. Believe
wish, say what you will to me, but never again ta'
in front of my brother."

She directed him around the corner to a
house adorned with white gingerbread trim. The
lanterns shone through the sheer white curtains
Seeing the luxurious house, Joseph realized Ma
'e, and he wanted to eat the cruel words h

'ior tonight was out of characte
 his temper had flared
'red his psyche lik
 'ier, and it
 'ng c

"You're right, ma'am," he said, extending his hand to help her down. "There was no call for me to speak to you in such a manner, and I beg your forgiveness." He turned to Luke. "I'd also like to apologize to you, young man. You have a fine sister. Please allow me to wish you both a Merry Christmas."

"Same to you, sir," replied Luke.

Joseph couldn't wait for the chaos of this holiday to be over. He much preferred the peace and quiet of his own place with Becca coming over from time to time. Now the whole family had met Matthew's friend and found her to be a delightful, well-polished, young lady. He still felt terrible over the way he'd treated her.

When Joe walked into Matt's apartment, he expected everyone to be winding down from the big meal, but instead, the place seemed to be in a state of upheaval.

Sarah hugged Joe. "We're taking Matthew home with us, but we can't move all his possessions right now. May we leave some of his things at your place until we can come for them?"

"Of course, Mama."

Sarah spent the remaining two days packing Matt's belongings. When time came to leave, Joseph took the family to the depot and waited until the train was out of sight before turning for home. He was alone at last.

* * *

The trip to Oak Hollow further weakened Matthew, but with Doc Bradley's new medicine combined with rest and Miss Daisy's cooking, Matt rallied fast and managed to go with Abe for a quick survey of the lands.

Sarah met Matthew as he came down the stairs one morning. "While you father goes to town, I thought it might be nice to have your diploma framed, but I can't find it."

Matt produced the fake.

Abe brought the framed certificate home. It hung in the hall, a constant reminder to Matt of his lying.

*   *   *

The winter turned out to be the coldest anyone could remember and was the topic of conversation for weeks with the townspeople complaining incessantly. Abe's dwindling money worried him, but with some careful planning, he felt sure they'd be able to make it until the next crop was harvested.

Fatigue and sadness continued to plague Abe. He kept his feelings to himself, thinking with the advent of spring, he'd fare much better. More and more time was spent alone in his study reading a few wrinkled letters, one in particular. When finished, he'd lock them up until the next time. The ritual, combined with a generous shot of whiskey each evening, seemed to keep him going.

Abe calculated his bank balance. The situation had become critical, and he needed to have a meeting with Matthew since they were going to manage Oak Hollow as a team. He hadn't broached the subject while his son was healing, and now that Matthew had recovered, Abe could find no good time to tell him the news. Besides, he rationalized, the final solution to the problem would be his own decision, so why bother Matt?

He recalled the events that had transpired since Christmas. Matt had been restless as he started feeling better, but occupied himself by spending a lot of time in town. He and Paul Scott had developed a close friendship, and Matt spent a lot of evenings at his new friend's house. Abe was concerned about where his son was getting his spending money.

Gossip had it Matt was gambling and spreading himself thin among the ladies of Scottsville. When quizzed, he patted his father's shoulder and laughed. Explaining that the money came from savings funded by some part-time work while in college seemed to ease Abe's mind. Though Joe's disclosure about Matt's actions rang loud in Abe's ear, he believed Matt had changed since coming home. And he knew his son wouldn't take a chance of lying, knowing the gossipmongers would hunt Abe down to relay news of one of his children's indiscretions. But on the other hand, gossips could fabricate stories out of jealousy, so Abe chose to bide his time until he had more information.

Spring tiptoed in on a gentle whisper of a breeze, but went unnoticed until the fruit trees budded, and the grass woke up. Flowers burst forth, parading their beauty and fragrance like fine Southern belles, and following such a nasty winter, the welcome rays of sun warmed more than a body. This was a time of renewal, a time of hope, a time of new beginnings for old, worn out, souls. A time to stop and listen to the high trill of the first birds, to lean back and breathe in the pure, life-giving air, a time to give thanks to God for getting Scottsville through the brutal winter.

During the past few months, Abe had prayed harder than he'd ever done in his life. Not a night went by that he didn't petition for himself, his family, the ability to keep food on the table, and for his hired help. Increasing discontent among the Negroes was common knowledge. Abe heard of more runaways each time he went to town. Fear rose in his chest when he thought of the slaves because most got caught and were tortured when they were brought back.

Abe never forgot to pray for those he loved who were left in Ireland, but most of all, he begged for forgiveness for his past and the inability to share his burden with his family. He sat in his study, head resting in his hands. With sudden clarity, the realization that the fields were in excellent shape for planting popped into his mind. The winter moisture had penetrated to the deepest level in a few seasons.

But despair took over as Abe realized he had no money to buy seed. If he used all his money, they'd only be able to plant a small portion of the fields, leaving nothing to live on. Worse, there'd be no resources with which to pay the Negroes' salaries. They'd work for nothing. Abe knew that, but he couldn't let them. They'd have to find work elsewhere. Where, though? Who'd treat them as well as he did? He had to find a way out of his predicament. He'd put off telling Matt as long as he could. He'd have to reveal their situation soon.

Sarah knocked and entered the room, interrupting his concentration. Abe's eyes drank in his wife's presence. She was flawless, warm, loving, and understanding. How could Abe live without her? Yet, leaving her would be better than having her stay with him and starve. They'd already been through that possibility in Ireland. He'd almost lost her. He wouldn't, couldn't, do that to her again. She deserved much more than he'd ever been able to give her, and Abe knew plenty of men who'd jump at the chance to be Sarah's husband. She could find a wonderful man who would provide well for her, one who would find favor with God.

"I have a present for you." Sarah handed him a purple velvet bag tied with a gold drawstring.

At first, he assumed it was her purse, soon realizing it held more significance than that. "What's this?" Estimating the weight of the few coins he felt through the fabric, he knew they wouldn't be of much help in this crisis. "You're such a good manager, my dear, and I do appreciate your effort, but I hardly think there's enough change in this little bag to save us." How long had Sarah known the circumstances of their financial state? She stood still, her hands gently clasped, her mouth tilted into a sweet smile.

Abe opened the bag expecting a few coins. All he saw was paper currency. Dumfounded, he stumbled backward to the sofa. Sarah rushed to his side to help him sit down. With shaking, hesitant hands, he reached into the dark interior of a little bag that would change the course of their existence. He started counting. This just couldn't be! There wasn't enough time for Sarah to have saved this much money. Yet, here it was, waiting to bail them out. "I don't understand."

Sarah's explanation made Abe's heart sing. "Sometimes a wife knows a long time before her husband when things aren't going well. I started this little account for myself a long time ago, and with the exception of Thanksgiving and Christmas, I've managed to save a lot on the management of the house. This is my contribution to our livelihood!"

There was more than enough for seed, living expenses, and Grace's debut. Abe jumped up, hugged his wife, swinging her around the study. "What a lucky man I am to have such a perfect wife!"

CHAPTER NINETEEN

Grace continued to see Paul, even though she hadn't made her debut but she refused to give up the secret meetings with Jim. Their relationship had deepened to the point where it sometimes frightened her, especially since Jim confessed he'd had the same feelings. Must be something sacred was how he'd put it.

The ease with which they could talk about any subject delighted Grace. No pretense, no expectations, only simple, but deep communication.

More and more, Jim wished he could spend a whole day just talking to Grace. The intimate, magnetic bond they nurtured had sustained them throughout the cold, harsh isolation of winter. Meetings took place while their households slept, and though they were careful, Jim had the feeling his mama knew how he felt about Grace. Trying to hide anything from the two most important ladies in his life was impossible. His connection to each of them was unmistakable. Daisy periodically dropped little hints about Jim jumping the broom.

Daisy mentioned more than once he needed to marry his own kind. His mama was right, as usual. Since there was no doubt that Grace would wed Paul, Daisy didn't have to get specific. The most important thing, she told him, was she didn't want him hurt because of something he could never change.

Maggie and Charles grabbed secret moments when they could get away from prying eyes and wrote love notes to each other in between. Charles liked his new job. Woodworking came naturally to him, and he worked as many hours as he could. Together he and Maggie designed the home they wanted, so Charles put his extra money on materials to build it.

Mister Burton had offered his son an oversized lot on the edge of town as a building site, which would be a perfect place for Maggie's seamstress business as well. Charles was an only child, and everything his parents owned would go to him eventually, so it made sense to go ahead and use the land. When Maggie told him she loved his family because they reminded her of the way people were in Cork—down-to-earth, friendly, and genuine, Charles' chest had swelled with pride.

* * *

Grace had consented to a debutante ball, and she sat with her mother and Maggie in one of the extra bedrooms upstairs going through boxes of lace and bolts of fabric. A sketchpad lay on the bed for Grace to design what she wanted the seamstress to make.

"What kind of dress would you like?" Sarah asked.

"Something simple and elegant. Nothing too frilly. The only reason I'm doing this is to please you and Papa because if the decision were left up to me, I'd rather not have a party at all."

"The debut marks the end of your adolescence and announces your blossoming into a proper young lady. My feeling is that as soon as the time is right, you and Paul will marry, so you'll need to fit in with the society ladies."

Grace rolled her eyes upward, but didn't say anything. Abe and Sarah had promised her she wouldn't have to go to Miss Bouvier's if she would go ahead and have a coming-out party. Grace handed the pad to Maggie, asking her to sketch a dress.

Spreading bolts of fabric out on the bed, Maggie asked, "What do you have in mind?"

Grace picked up a roll of ivory linen. "How does this look?"

Maggie furrowed her brow as she drew. "Why don't you have a square neckline with horizontal tucks to the waist, short, bell sleeves and an overskirt, pulled up in places with tiny satin bows, parting in the center front of the gown. Like this."

"Perfect!" Grace spun around with the bolt of fabric.

Sarah didn't like Grace's choice. She thought the ivory linen was too close to her daughter's skin color, but as Grace held it under her chin, the slight nubbiness of the linen brought out the pale pink of her cheeks against flawless skin. If Sarah had been designing it, she would've put ruffles and lace on it, but the choice belonged to Grace, so she kept quiet. "I'll take the fabric and design to town tomorrow." Sarah gathered up the sketch, fabric, lace, and thread.

After thinking all night about the design of her dress, Grace sat with her mother in the breakfast room talking over coffee and biscuits. "I don't see why Maggie and I can't make our debut together. I'd think it would be less expensive on Papa."

"You've inherited the Irish practicality." Sarah paused. "Perhaps you're right. I'll hold off going to the seamstress until we talk to Maggie."

"Thank you, Mama."

Maggie came into the room, still rubbing sleep from her eyes, asking what they were talking about.

"How would you like to combine our coming-out parties?" Grace waited for her sister to answer, but Maggie sat down and stared into space, seemingly in no mood to discuss her upcoming presentation to the community.

"She's still sleepy." Sarah offered an excuse as if Maggie weren't able to speak for herself. "Let's give her some time to think about it."

On the way to school, Grace approached Maggie once more. "Please, think about it. We could make a big production, be done with all the rituals, and I wouldn't have to go through it by myself."

"Think anyone will say anything about my age?"

"What if they do? It's our party."

"Okay, let's do it together! That'll please Mama and Papa. Maybe help with customers when I open my shop."

Grace breathed a sigh of relief. "Thank you."

An impish sparkle registered in Maggie's eyes. "The sooner we're presented to society, the sooner Charles can officially court me. Then, as soon as it's fashionable, we can marry."

"You wanted to do this all along!" Grace was perturbed that her younger sister would be so conniving.

Maggie smiled. "I couldn't act too excited, or Mama would want to know why since I've been so opposed to the whole situation. Acting disinterested meant I didn't have to lie to her, and you would talk me into it."

"You're terrible!"

Robert pulled the carriage into the schoolyard where Paul waited to assist the girls. He turned to Grace.

"We need to have an important talk. May I come to your house this evening and spend some time with you?"

"Let's talk about the details after school." Grace knew what his visit held in store for her. She'd dreaded this day forever, it seemed. That's why she'd avoided him as much as possible, but she'd run out of excuses to avoid making a decision. "Dear Lord, please help me," she whispered.

*   *   *

After school, she told Paul he could call around seven that evening. Arriving home, the girls informed Sarah of Maggie's decision, and the three of them pored over the fabric and lace again.

Maggie selected a coral satin.

"What kind of dress do you want?" Grace asked.

"No ruffles for me, either. What about this?" She drew a dress with a scooped neck and dropped waist. Vertical pleats made up the entire bodice, over a plain tightly gathered skirt. Short, puffed sleeves completed the outfit.

"Hold the fabric up to your neck." Grace handed her the bolt.

As Maggie placed the bolt under her chin, the sun hit her hair, bringing the fabric to life. "It's beautiful, dear." Sarah's eyes beamed.

"Maggie, do you think you could make them? It would save some money, and we'd have such fun. I'll help." Grace was trying to introduce her younger sister's talents to their mother without being too obvious.

"I'd love to try! Would you mind, Mama?"

"Do you think you can handle such a big task? You've never made a gown before."

"Grace will help. We can do it."

"If you're that sure, then it's settled." Sarah rose and bustled out of the room.

The girls were ecstatic and danced around, holding hands, and twirling each other. Paul arrived right on time and handed Grace a small bouquet of seven white roses. He took off his light coat, and while Grace went to get a vase, he entered Abe's study, placing his coat on a chair. As he came out, he met Grace.

"Your father has a very nice study. I'd like to have one just like it someday. I hope you don't mind that I put my coat in there. The hall tree seemed to be full."

"That's fine. And I'm sure your comments would please Papa."

They sat in the parlor where a cozy fire kept them warm on the cool, spring evening. Paul appeared nervous. From time to time, he'd stand and pace.

"Paul, for heaven's sake, please sit still. What is it you wanted to talk about anyway?"

"This is hard to say. Everyone in town knows we're sweet on each other, but I don't know how you feel. Father has given me more responsibility at the bank, and it won't be long until I'm working full time."

He had taken Grace's hands in his, squeezing with such force that it took her by surprise. She'd never noticed how hard and unrelenting they felt. Seemed out of character for a banker's hands, but his eyes held affection and a questioning look, so Grace blamed his grip on nervousness. When she pulled back a little, he eased his grip. She almost felt sorry for him. "You've been so patient with me. Never asking me any personal questions, but at the moment, I'm concentrating on my debut. After that, it would be proper for us to talk about our feelings. Can you wait that long?"

"Of course. I'll wait as long as you need me to. You'll soon be a leader in the social world, with or without me, so I think it's important that you're presented in the traditional fashion. But please make it as soon as possible."

He cleared his throat, cast his eyes to the floor, and rubbed his hands on the front of his pants. "I didn't want to bring this matter up, but I think you should know your father's in serious trouble. We need to get married as soon as possible, so I can give him some help, financial help as a family, I mean."

Grace sat up straight.

Paul tensed. "I shouldn't have said anything. Please forgive me. Don't tell your father I told you."

"How do you know this?" Grace's eyes flashed, demanding an answer.

"Matthew and I have been socializing. He's been concerned because your father never talks about the state of his affairs. He asked me to check on the account at the bank. The result shocked both of us."

"You two shouldn't be doing that." Grace tried to hold back her tears. Paul took her in his arms, pressing her to his chest. Even through his expensive shirt and vest, he felt like unsanded wood. His arms were so strong, they reminded her of Miss Daisy's nutcracker as it crushed pecans. Her neck hurt, but Grace attributed the pain to her emotional state. If only she felt more comfortable around this man. Still, Paul was the answer to preserving the family's social standing and saving her father's business. She had no choice. "We can make our betrothal official right after my debut," Grace mumbled, half hoping he wouldn't hear.

Satisfied with the answer, Paul got up and retrieved his coat from Abe's study. He draped it over one arm and with his other one, exerted a firm grip around Grace's waist, pulling her with him toward the door.

Grace felt the imprint of Paul's hand long after he was gone. Troubling thoughts assailed her. The house began closing in, and she had to get away. As always, when she needed to think, she walked to the circle. As far as she was concerned, she'd made her real debut the night she first put a naked foot on God's carpet of leaves and twigs. That night her ball gown was a simple chemise. The music and entertainment were the gurgling brook and the twinkling stars.

Grace loved meeting Jim in the circle. Sometimes he listened as he sat across from her. Other times, he held her hands when she was nervous and shaking. Most comforting were the times he let her rest her head on his chest. There was something about the way the beating of his heart seemed to calm her and bring her back to focus on the issue at hand. Grace needed him now. Would his sixth sense direct him to their spot? Knowing there'd come a time when Jim might not meet her, she had a feeling this was the night she'd be alone. Just as well because she needed to make her own decisions about Paul. As she stepped around a big tree, she saw him sitting in their sanctuary. Grace marveled at their unspoken communication skills.

"Miss Grace," he said as if presenting her to royalty.

The moonlight highlighted his teeth, so white they pierced the darkness like precious stars plucked from heaven. "I'm so glad you're here,"

"You needed me."

Sitting beside him, she was surprised to find tears flowing down her cheeks. "I don't want to marry Paul, but what am I supposed to do? Papa wants him for a son-in-law because he believes Paul will take good care of me. He came to call this evening and rattled on about some horrible news concerning our money situation. No matter how hard I try, loving him is impossible. All I feel is pity for him."

"I know that."

The drastic improvement in Jim's language skills since he'd been reading the books Grace brought him amazed her. He'd lost the dialect she was so used to hearing. She shook her head, trying to still her thoughts to hear his words. Being here with Jim was where she felt the most comfortable. They could discuss anything. These feelings would never be the same with Paul or any other man.

"Sometimes, we have to do things we don't want to do because it's right. We have to think of other people besides ourselves." Jim didn't know how to tell her but knew he had to be honest. She'd pick up on anything that wasn't the truth. "You are my precious friend and more than I could ever express in words. My Grace." He pulled her close, allowing her tears to dry themselves on his soft, worn, chambray shirt.

"How I've wished a million times that I was white or you were black, but God didn't make us that way. He made us humans, though, able to be as close as we can be as friends, but we can never marry. So when I'm upset and blue, I think about His goodness at letting us meet. I praise Him for bringing you into my life, but most of all I'm grateful for your friendship. Every minute of every day, I thank Him for these feelings of the heart, the way down deep emotions that go so far beyond the...the, you know...." His words trailed off, fighting his own tumultuous emotions with all his strength.

"The physical part," she supplied. "That's something I don't think I can bear at all with Paul. Living with him and sleeping in the same bed will be hard enough, but I can't begin to imagine anything physical." Saying the words sent frosted fingers of dread down her spine.

"That's exactly how I feel. Mama's been talking to me, too, about jumping the broom with my own kind, but I don't have the desire for that."

Their time was spent expressing their feelings for each other and what the future might hold if each of them married someone else. They also talked about whether Paul had been truthful with Grace and what kind of friendship he had with Matthew. As the night waned, it alerted the two friends their meeting was over. They stood as one. Hand in hand Jim walked with Grace as far as he dared. Standing behind a tree, he watched her enter the house through the back door.

He walked at a slow pace back home with his thoughts on what it would be like to be with someone else, his own kind, as Mama said. There didn't seem to be any room in his heart for another girl, and Jim was glad he didn't have to make an immediate decision.

CHAPTER TWENTY

Abe and Matt headed into town. "I think it's time we stopped by the bank and put your name on the account, so you can write checks if you need to."

When they entered the building, Matt watched his father deposit Sarah's savings before walking over to an office marked PRESIDENT on the open door. John Scott, Paul's father, came around his desk to shake hands before offering them a seat. After obtaining Matt's signature, John smiled and turned to Abe. "I don't think it's going to be too long before Paul pays you a visit."

"Probably not, from what I hear, but Sarah says we have to wait until the girls have their coming-out party first. You know how women are." He returned his friend's smile. Following some small talk, he and Matt left.

On the way home, Abe broached a subject he'd been thinking about. "There's a nice girl who goes to our church. Rachael Williams. Would you like to meet her?"

"Sure." Matthew knew where this was going. Marriage. His gambling, drinking, and using women the way he'd been doing for years pricked his conscience, and Matt knew he needed to stop before his father found out. How, though? How was he going to stop?

*   *   *

Matthew asked Rachael to go out on Sunday, and for the next few days, they spent a great deal of time together. Rachael had a pleasing personality, but she and Matt had little in common. No matter how hard he tried, there was no attraction, but they did develop a good friendship. Matt didn't discuss the issue with the family. They'd think what they wanted anyway.

Scottsville's Palace Hotel served as a proud landmark for the town. The two-story, brick building was magnificent with its white-columned front and formal grounds. An elegant ballroom surrounded by a wide balcony was the favorite meeting place for social events and the setting of most debutante balls. Crystal chandeliers holding flickering candles and delicate iron scrollwork decorating the long windows on the three exterior sides of the large room added to the grandeur of any gathering.

Once the girls decided on a date, Sarah busied herself with details. She reserved the room and arranged for small tables to be available on the balcony where people, who were tired of dancing, could retreat for quiet conversation. A woman in town was hired to make the punch and cakes that would be served from a long skirted table at one end of the ballroom. The hotel arranged for an orchestra, wait staff, and servants to clean up.

Maggie finished the dresses a week before the big event. The way they fit each girl gave an unspoken testimony to the young seamstress' expert ability.

* * *

The evening arrived, and everyone moved in a state of heightened expectation. Abraham and Sarah escorted the girls to the hotel early. Cloistered in a room off the mezzanine ready to make a grand entrance in front of their guests, Grace and Maggie reassured each other. The festivities attracted most of the town's elite. Everyone complimented the Sulllivans on the music, refreshments, and beautiful decorations. At the appointed time, the orchestra's conductor raised his hands for silence and announced the girls' names. Hand in hand, sophisticated and poised, Grace and Margaret Sullivan stood at the top of the curved staircase and waved before descending to enter a new phase of life as young women.

Abe danced first with Grace and then Margaret before escorting Sarah onto the floor. "Seems as if life is a series of endings and new beginnings, doesn't it?" Abe said, waltzing with his wife.

"Yes, and that's how it's supposed to be. Just as the seasons follow each other, so our children follow us, and so theirs will follow them. That way, we never die." Sarah ran her hand back and forth on Abe's shoulder as he guided her through the maze of dancers. Tears flowed inside her heart, knowing that after tonight Grace and Maggie would change and move on, but she refused to let the girls see her sentimentality. Pasting on a smile, Sarah seemed the epitome of happiness as both her daughters entered Scottsville's aristocracy.

* * *

The heavenly spring turned into a hell-fire-and-brimstone kind of early summer. By the last week in May, the cotton plants that had emerged lay parched and burned in the dry, dusty fields. Matthew and Abraham sat discussing the failed crop and their shrinking bank account. The somber and depressing atmosphere led them to consider selling part of the plantation when a loud clap of thunder sent them flying to the window.

Rain, blessed rain, began as tiny droplets but soon escalated into torrents of water beating on the roof punctuated by house-shaking thunder which sounded as if it were rolling straight from the floor of heaven. Flashes of lightning illuminated the darkened, gray sky.

Abe had never heard a more beautiful symphony. "This rain is our salvation," he shouted above the roar of the storm. "If we get enough to soak into the ground, we'll have time to replant, but we'll have to get it done before the end of next week. It won't be as much money as the original crop, but maybe it'll see us through."

"How can we plant if we have no money to buy seed?"

"We'll go see Paul for a loan."

"He goes to school during the day, doesn't he? Won't we have to see Mister Scott?"

"No, Paul got special permission from the school to work at the bank during the day. He catches up on his studies at night. Doing business with him will give him a vote of confidence that I'd welcome him as a son-in-law, and I don't think he'd have any reservations about making me a loan."

* * *

The rain continued off and on for two days, but as soon as the roads were passable, Abe and Matt headed to the bank.

"Paul, or I guess I should say Mister Scott, since we're here on business..."

Paul interrupted. "Mister Sullivan, please call me Paul. We're certainly more than business acquaintances, but I can guess why you're here. Crops burned up? Don't worry about a thing. We'll be happy to give you a loan, so you can replant."

Abe relaxed. Matthew wanted a drink.

"The only problem is, so many people have made loans, we've had to raise the interest rate. Now the normal rate is one thing, but I'm going to give you this loan at a five-percent discount. After all, I'm hoping to pay you a call real soon." A smile brightened Paul's face.

Abraham knew there were no alternatives and was grateful for a loan at any rate. His family was safe, at least for the time being. As soon as they arrived home, Matthew greeted everyone before dressing and leaving without eating dinner.

The girls smiled at each other over their plates. Grace lowered her voice. "Probably going to Rachael's house for dinner."

"Maybe they'll get engaged." Maggie's eyes danced.

"Wouldn't that be nice?" Sarah smiled.

"Now don't be jumping to conclusions." Abe tried to look earnest, but securing the loan earlier had put him in a relaxed mood, and he smiled along with the rest of the family.

Changing the subject, Maggie asked, "Isn't Joe coming home for the summer?"

Sarah smiled. "No, he's still working for that same professor and has to stay there."

* * *

Matthew arrived at the tavern for the poker party a little early and ordered a drink to calm his nerves. He'd tucked a check into his pocket in case he needed it, but felt with his luck, he'd win big and be able to bed one of the girls upstairs. This night Matt would memorialize becoming a man just as his sisters had celebrated their entrance into womanhood. He could sign checks. He was a man, a Sullivan, a man to carry on the name.

By the time the game began, Matthew was well on his way to intoxication. Losing a couple of big hands, he became desperate, placing foolish bets until he had nothing left except the check. But Matt knew he could bluff the other three men. Taking the check out of his pocket, he laid it in the center of the table. As the game progressed, two men folded, leaving Will Tollivar and Matt to determine the winner. Will called Matt's hand.

When they laid down their cards, even through blurry vision, Matt knew he'd lost. He begged Will to let him pay it out, but he refused. The young man was also inebriated, became belligerent, pounding on Matt's face until he agreed to write the check. In spite of his drunken state, as he filled in the amount, Matthew knew he'd just jeopardized his family's livelihood.

He picked up a full bottle and staggered from the tavern, vowing to finish this one and never drink again. Holding the saddle horn and raising his leg, it took several attempts before Matt found the stirrups, pulled himself up, grabbed the reins with one hand and held onto the bottle with the other. His head was spinning, his speech slurred and incoherent. Since he couldn't keep his balance, Matt placed his head on the horse's neck, hoping the animal could find her way home. Somewhere between throwing up and passing out, Matt had the sensation of separating from his horse. Dark sleep overtook him.

* * *

Abe awoke to a pristine morning, raising his spirits and filling him with energy. He looked forward to having the darkies prepare the land so they could replant. Abe knocked on Matt's door. No answer. Puzzled, he opened it and discovered Matt's bed hadn't been slept in. Looking out the raised window, he saw Jim loading a wagon with hoes and other tools needed to start work on the land. "Jim," he yelled. "See if Matthew's horse is in the stall. Hurry."

Heeding the urgency in Abe's voice, Jim ran as fast as he could, returned so breathless he couldn't speak, but shook his head.

Cold fear gripped Abe Sullivan, and his hand went immediately to his chest. He flew down the stairs and out the door. "Ready me a horse! Quick!" he shouted.

Sensing something was wrong, Jim had saddled one as soon as he'd reported Matt's horse missing. Abe mounted and raced the horse out of the plantation without a word to anyone. Panic set in. What could've happened between the Williams' plantation and theirs to keep Matt out all night? Fear rode as a heavy companion with Abe, but movement ahead of him interrupted his thoughts. He pulled back on the reins to slow his horse. A worried-looking Paul came into view. Matt had been tied onto his saddle and lay still, slumped against his horse's neck as Paul led the mare with the reins.

"What happened? Is Matt okay?" Abe asked.

"Yes, sir, I think so. I went to the bank this morning. The minute I discovered what transpired last night, I knew I'd better check in with you and Matt. On the way, I found him. He must've fallen off his horse and rolled into a rocky depression. Mare stayed with him. Don't think I would have seen him if she hadn't. I couldn't rouse him, and his face looks like he got the worst end of a fight, but at least, he's still breathing."

"Thank goodness, you were coming to see us." Abe turned his horse, and they rode side by side. "What were you coming to tell us?"

"Sir, I don't know if this is the time or even how to tell you, other than just to say it outright. Matthew wrote a check last night to cover a poker debt, and it wiped out about half your loan money. I'm so sorry."

The news stunned Abe so much that he couldn't even comprehend what Paul had said at first. "Matt went to call on Miss Rachael Williams. This isn't possible. There's some mistake. How could he be gambling when he was with Rachael?"

"Rachael? He's only had a few dates with her that I know of. I've seen him gambling and drinking almost every night, but I always left early. Since I'm an official banker now, I have to study at night and be fresh each morning for work. I had no idea things had progressed this far with his habits." Paul paused, letting his words sink into Abe's head. "Sir, I had to honor the check, but I wanted to come to Oak

Hollow as soon as possible to offer my support. Perhaps we can work something out so you can secure another loan, but you might have to put up part of the plantation as collateral. I feel terrible. Matt's my friend, and I should've been watching out for him." He hung his head.

A pain in his chest gripped Abraham, but he managed to hide it from Paul by holding back a little and turning his face. "No," he reassured Paul when he could speak. "I should've noticed."

Sarah heard the horses and went to the door. When she saw Paul with Matt over his shoulder, she screamed, asking questions nonstop. Abe asked Paul to carry Matt upstairs while he gave Sarah a sketchy description of Matt's drinking and the accident. He didn't mention the lost wager. When Lavitica June came in to see what all the fuss was about, Abe sent her to find Jim.

Abe willed his voice to a soothing pitch. "I think you should stay down here until Jim gets him washed and changed. He's a pretty big mess right now."

She nodded and sat down in the parlor with her hands covering her face.

Abe was deep in thought as he mounted the stairs to the room of a son he'd placed all his trust in. A son who'd help him run the family business and push them to wealth beyond what Abe had been able to do, who'd be a leader in the community and take care of his parents in their old age. A son who'd fill the house with laughing grandchildren and happy parties at Thanksgiving and Christmas. Matt lay motionless. Abe waited for Jim.

The stench of whiskey mixed with dried blood and vomit nauseated him, and his belly rolled and tied in knots.

To think the money was gone—so foolishly this time. Try as he might, he could make no sense of the events. Were all the rumors true? Abe assumed the news had traveled to the general store, and the whole town knew now. Matt's indiscretions would make the Sullivans the joke of Scottsville. The reputation he and Sarah had worked so hard to build was gone. Matt had shamed himself and the Sullivan name. Did he hate his family that much? Matthew stirred and opened his eyes. Hurt, disappointment, betrayal, and anger boiled above the surface, manifesting in Abe's voice. "Why, Matthew? Why did you lie to me? Why did you destroy us? Why?"

Mumbling something incoherent, Matt tried to focus his eyes. Words tumbled from Abe's heart. "I don't know what we're going to do. Guess the only thing left is to sell the plantation or get another loan and put it up as collateral. Either way, we've lost our land, our reputation, our daily bread. All I ask you is why? Can't you just answer that one simple question?"

Matt lapsed back into unconsciousness. Abe couldn't stand to look at him at the moment. His emotions were too charged, and he couldn't even discern his own feelings. He turned and walked to the door as Jim entered.

Once he was cleaned up, Sarah went to his room. Matt seemed comfortable and his sleep peaceful. She asked Jim to sit with him while she finished the mending projects she'd started downstairs, but before she left, she bent over and kissed Matt on the forehead.

Matthew opened his eyes mid-afternoon. "Where am I?"

Maintaining his former colloquialism, Jim replied, "You're to home, Massa Matthew. Does you hurt anywheres?"

"No. What happened?"

"You had a accident, suh, and you wuz thrown offen your horse. Massa Paul foun' you and brought you home."

Matthew tried to turn his body to see Jim, but only part of him would cooperate. He could turn his head and upper trunk, but his legs refused to move.

Seeing him struggle, Jim moved closer to the side of the bed.

"Jim," he pleaded, grabbing his arm. "Please, help me. I can't seem to turn on my side. Can't imagine what's wrong. The sheet must be wrapped too tight around my legs."

"Naw, suh, they ain't no sheet wrapped 'round you." Jim held on to Matthew's waist with one hand digging his fingernails into the back of his knee with the other while turning him. Matt showed no signs of discomfort, so Jim extended his hand down to his feet and raked his bent knuckle along a bruise. Still, Matt made no face. Obviously, he didn't feel a thing. "Suh, I bes' go down and tell the womenfolk you's awake, so they can bring some victuals to you. I be right back." He rearranged the sheet over Matt before he walked at a normal pace to the door. Once outside the room, Jim flew down the stairs and out to the barn as fast as he could run.

"Massa! Massa Abe!" Jim was shaking. "Massa Matthew can't feel his legs. Can't feel nuthin' from his middle down to his feet."

"Are you sure?"

"Yas, suh. Sure as kin be."

"Go get Doc Bradley, will you? Hurry!" The young darkie mounted a horse and rode out at a hard run.

Abe walked toward the house, worry gripping him like an eagle's talons around its prey.

Sarah saw Abe, and as she'd done so many times, she went into the kitchen and told Miss Daisy to make tea. She met her husband at the door. She noticed the scowl and the deepening wrinkle between his eyes. "What's wrong?"

Abe didn't answer. He strode down the hall to the staircase, motioning for her to stay in the parlor. She assumed Matt had asked for his father when Jim went running out of the house, but Abe's behavior confused her. Maybe it had to do with Matt's drinking. This was a thing between father and son, and she thought it best to let them work it out.

"I can't feel my legs," Matthew whimpered.

"Doc's on his way to see you." Abe slumped into a chair.

"What's wrong, Papa?"

"What do you remember about last night?"

"Having a drink. That's all. What happened?"

"You lost a bet, a big one, and you wrote a check for about half of our replanting money. You wiped us out with one little signature. One stroke of your hand, and we're done for. That's what happened."

The enormity of the situation almost covered the hurt, but enough was left to squeeze Matthew's heart as fuzzy memories of the night before began creeping into his recollection. "Don't even bother with the doctor. Just let me die. I don't deserve to live." He turned his head to the side; tears streamed out of a blackened eye making geometric salt rings on his pure, white pillowcase. Matt never lifted a hand to feel his swollen face.

"I need to talk to your mother."

When Sarah met him at the foot of the stairs, she mistook the look on his face as one of disgust for their son's drinking too much. "It's going to be okay," she said, patting his shoulder. "You'll see. All of this will blow over, and no one will remember." She led him to the breakfast room.

Falling into a chair with his head in his hands, he let out the most heart-rending moan Sarah had ever heard. She called to Daisy. The old maid brought in two cups of freshly brewed mint tea.

"You don't understand," Abe said in a colorless voice. "It's never going to be okay. Matt's never going to be okay. We're never going to be okay. Not now. Not ever." He pushed the cup of tea away. "He's paralyzed and he's almost wiped out our bank account to pay a gambling debt. We're ruined." Even as he spoke, guilt and sorrow replaced his resentment, and he longed to hold Matt as he had done when he was a youngster.

Sarah's hand went to her mouth to cover the silent scream she felt start in her heart and move upward. She rushed upstairs to Matthew's bedroom. The door stood ajar, and she could see her first-born crying in his hands as if his heart had broken. She flew to him, and in spite of his size, cradled his shoulders in her small, delicate arms. They didn't speak. Sarah hummed a soft, Irish lullaby until she felt Matt relax. After he drifted off to sleep, she slipped from the room.

She was worried about her men. Matthew and Abraham. In all the years they'd been married, she'd never seen Abe so troubled. Sarah moved to the back porch. Staring at the landscape, she walked toward the river, and dropping to her knees, she prayed for strength to endure the crisis, asking the Lord to heal Matthew's wounds and Abraham's heart. Entering the house, she searched for Abe. He sat in his study, and through the partially opened door, she could see him poring over some kind of letter. She wouldn't disturb his privacy.

CHAPTER TWENTY-ONE

Doc Bradley arrived and examined Matt. In the parlor, he turned to the Sullivans. "You know Matt is paralyzed from the waist down, but it's too soon to know whether this is permanent. Only time will tell if the injury he sustained merely traumatized the spine causing inflammation or whether this is a more serious injury and will be the way he lives for the rest of his life. I'm sorry I can't be more specific. What concerns me more right now, though, is his state of mind. Someone should keep a close eye on him because he told me he wants to die." The doctor sipped fresh coffee Daisy made for him before rising to leave.

Abe closed the door, hung his head, and let a beautiful dream float out an open window. Fear, guilt, and profound sadness for his son's condition overwhelmed him. He put his head into his hands and prayed for forgiveness for confronting Matt in anger. He loved his son. He was heartsick.

* * *

The Sullivans wouldn't have picked Charles for a suitor for Maggie, but once he began to call, they changed their minds. Charles and Maggie's love for each other radiated outward warming everyone near them. Many evenings they entertained themselves sitting in the parlor pouring over some kind of drawing or visiting with Abe and Sarah. When Matthew needed to be moved, Charles carried him in a dignified way. He also made a chair from fine, seasoned oak, which he sanded as smooth as the tumbled river rocks. Varnished to a lustrous shine, he attached two large wagon wheels, making it into a rolling chair, so Matt could move around on his own. Maggie had designed and made two comfortable cushions. Though Matt could feel nothing, she wanted to guard against pressure sores.

Matthew seldom spoke or asked for anything. Jim came every morning and cleaned and shaved Matt before carrying him downstairs. In the evening if Paul or Charles were visiting, they carried Matt upstairs, but if not, Jim would come. Jim and Grace didn't speak for fear of being caught, so they continued to meet in their grove when they could get away.

*   *   *

Joseph fanned the papers he had to grade for the professor. A knock startled him. Becca stood, holding a large, brown basket with a hinged lid. A bright red and white gingham napkin peeked from one corner.

"Mmm. Something smells wonderful." Joseph took the basket.

Becca reached for his free hand, pulling him from the cottage. "Come on. Let's have a picnic." They walked to a small clearing near the creek that ran through town. The sunny day came complete with a soft, scented breeze that caressed every flower and tree before settling on their faces. A happy kind of day for them just to be together.

Spreading out a large red and white checked tablecloth that matched the napkin Joseph had seen before, Becca took out fried chicken, potato salad, fresh yeast rolls, and homemade pickles. She prepared the plates and poured lemonade into sparkling glasses.

"What's the special occasion?" Joe pretended not to know the date.

Becca lowered her eyes, her cheeks turning the color of cardinals winging overhead. She didn't want Joe to know how important this day was to her if he'd forgotten.

In an exaggerated gesture, Joe put his hand on his forehead. "Oh, Becca, I'm so sorry. I was so caught up with school and everything. We've been courting sixteen months today! How could I forget?"

Becca struggled hard not to let her disappointment show. She looked at the small creek, not trusting herself to speak.

"My, what's this?" Joe produced a small box from his pocket. "Hmm. Wonder what could be in here and where it came from?"

Becca turned to face her beloved, her curiosity getting the better of her. She reached for the box, but Joe put his hand in the air so she couldn't touch it. He jumped up and started running, but not so fast she couldn't catch him. She managed to grab his arm and as Joe turned, he helped her sit on the stump of a fallen tree, dropped to one knee, and took her hands.

"Becca, you're my best friend and the light of my life. Your support and encouragement have sustained me while

I'm trying so hard to get ready for medical school. I don't know what my life would be without you, and don't want to find out. I love you more than words can say. Will you be my wife? Will you share my life and lend me your smile to light my way home each night?"

Becca was so surprised all she could do was nod as tears of happiness glistened on the soft, smooth curvature of her face.

Joe opened the box and took out a sparkling emerald ring, which fit her finger perfectly. He helped her up from the stump, wiped her eyes with his handkerchief, and held her for a long time. "Remember last week when your father helped me with a new project?"

"Yes. You two locked yourselves in his study. Why are you bringing that up now?"

"The project was to ask for your hand. He gave his consent!"

"You're terrible. Making me think you forgot, meeting with my father, and now giving me this exquisite ring. Whatever am I going to do with you?" Her whole body seemed to be laughing.

"Love me? Marry me?" His eyes twinkled like new candles.

"Well, that might be possible, if you're very good from now on!" They strolled arm in arm back to the picnic site and sat next to each other.

"Why was the ring in your pocket?"

"I had planned to propose to you on a walk this evening, so I'd slipped it into my pocket where it's been all day. But going on the picnic this afternoon made it easy for me to pretend I'd forgotten and make it more of a surprise."

His mood shifted, and the smile faded. "Seriously, Becca, we need to make some decisions. If they accept me to medical school in Dublin, we'll be apart for a long time. Being separated from you will be harder than any subject they could throw at me." He took her hand, fingering the ring. "I chose an emerald because of Ireland—the Emerald Isle. Will you think of me each time you look at it? Or if you don't like emeralds, I can exchange it."

"You're not getting this ring off my finger! Emeralds are my favorite gem. I thought that's why you chose it and wondered how you knew. As far as medical school in Dublin, let's get married beforehand, and I'll go with you."

"They won't allow me to be married in medical school, but if you join me, at least, we could be together until I graduate."

Returning to Joe's small home, they spent the rest of the late afternoon and early evening making plans. Letters were written to Irish relatives to ask about housing.

* * *

Grace had begun to feel pressure from Paul about marriage. His restlessness intensified with each passing day, almost frightening her, but she kept the goal of helping her family foremost in her mind and would do whatever was necessary to attain it. Paul could provide funds to save the plantation, and based on that alone, Grace decided to marry him.

Sitting in the swing one evening, Paul took her hand. "I'm a patient man, haven't asked you to do anything dishonorable or rushed you. But I'm ready to get married and would like your answer. You've seemed hesitant, so if you don't want to be my wife, please tell me now, so I can have the opportunity to find someone else."

Grace let his words sink in. Knowing Paul's hard-nosed approach to most planters, she felt if she refused his proposal, her father would have a difficult time obtaining a loan in the future. Could she live with Paul even though she didn't love him? Placing her hands on either side of his face, she looked into his eyes. Instead of seeing love and devotion, a harshness narrowed them, and a frown covered most of his face. "You look so intense. Are you afraid of my answer?"

"No, I'm simply ready to start our life together."

She hung her head, and tears welled from a deep chasm of despair. Fighting for composure, she whispered, "Then ask me."

"Will you be my wife?"

His voice sounded mechanical, devoid of emotion, the same way Grace felt. Oak Hollow's land painted a visual image in her mind, and the key to saving it sat next to her. She took a deep breath before giving her answer. "Yes, Paul, I'll be your wife." She'd passed the point of no return. They entered the house.

Abe and Sarah sat, lingering over a cup of tea with Matt in the dining room when Paul and Grace walked in.

"Sir," Paul began, "I'd like to ask your permission for Grace's hand." He wore a genuine smile. Grace forced hers.

"You not only have my permission but also my blessing." Abe shook Paul's hand before embracing him in a short hug. "When is the big event?"

The couple moved to the table. Grace sat next to Sarah, and Paul sat across from them next to Matt.

Abe spoke, "We haven't discussed it, but I see no reason for a long engagement. You've been seeing each other a long time." Paul was his salvation to restore the plantation he'd lost.

Talk turned to the events of the day. Paul spoke. "I hear more and more darkies are rebelling against their masters, breaking tools, starting fires, faking sickness, even running away. They always get caught, though. Not a pretty sight when their masters get through with them, but if they don't live through it, no one can blame the owners. Slaves not working cost planters money." His grin indicated Paul viewed the situation as a funny joke.

Grace and Sarah put their hands over their mouths to keep from retching as Paul described the torture. Abe turned away. Matthew registered no emotion.

Undaunted, Paul continued, "I don't think anything will come of it, so there's nothing to worry about. The Negroes are too dumb to get organized, and those radicals in the North don't have enough jobs or places to house the slaves anyway. It's too bad they're against the notion. Slaves are here to stay, and I'll bet it won't be long before the people up there realize it."

"Why don't we put the kettle on for more tea?" Sarah took Grace's hand pulling her toward the door.

In the kitchen, Grace said, "Please, don't tell him our Negroes are free. Promise me?" Her hands shook as she reached for the cups.

"Paul will never hear a word from me, my dear. But don't worry, I think he's just trying to impress your papa." Sarah smiled, but the little wrinkle between her eyes betrayed her thoughts.

"He wants to get married immediately, but I'm barely finished with my debut."

"We'll take our time planning the wedding. That way, he'll have to be patient. Maybe you're just worried about the details, but you look unhappy. If Paul isn't the one for you, don't marry him."

"Paul can help us financially, and I don't think I could do much better." Grace threw her arms around Sarah to hug her, wishing she could curl up in her lap like she'd done as a child. "I love you, Mama."

Charles and Maggie sat in the parlor whispering, unaware of what had been announced in the dining room.

"I know Papa's forgiven Matt, and spends a lot of time with him, but I don't think Matt has forgiven himself."

"He probably needs some female company."

"Who'd want to be around him? He's morose all the time—and crippled...." Her voice trailed off. All of a sudden, she gripped Charles' arm as a pixilated twinkle lit up her eyes. "I know what to do! When we visited the boys at Christmastime, there was the sweetest girl and her little brother. What was her name? Mary, yes, that's it. Mary and Luke lost their parents. She and Matt were going to spend Christmas together. Of course, he didn't know we were coming, and he got real sick, so Mary came over to bring him some food, and she saw we were there, so she and her brother were going to leave right away, but we insisted they stay, and we all ate together."

"Whoa. Slow down a minute. Take a breath," Charles smiled at her antics.

She inhaled, letting her breath out slowly. "Christmas turned out to be wonderful. She's so sweet and sings like a songbird from heaven. Joe took her home, so he knows where she lives. We could write her and send it to Joe to deliver. Wonder if she'd come see us?" Maggie's animations pulled Charles into her festive mood.

"My goodness, Miss Maggie, you do go on about things you feel real strong about," he said, grinning and shaking his head, but it was clear he adored his future wife. "When do you think we should write to this young lady?"

"Tonight!" Maggie looked as smug as if she'd just solved some undiscovered puzzle of antiquity.

"There's something I want to make official." Charles' tone turned serious, and his eyes betrayed his question as he slipped to one knee.

"Before you ask, I think we should give Grace time to marry first, but if she and Paul aren't engaged in a month, then we'll announce ours. Have you been able to do any work on our home?" Maggie pulled on his hands.

Charles sat back on the sofa. "It's almost finished, but I'm sure you want to buy some things for it."

"Yes, but I've started making a lot of the things too. You did leave that room up front for my sewing studio, didn't you?"

"Sure did, but I changed the plans and enlarged it to make sure you'd have plenty of space. You're going to get real busy once people find out how beautiful your work is."

The opening of the parlor door interrupted them. Grace and Paul stood for a moment before entering the room. Both of them were smiling, but if Maggie had been asked to classify their looks, she wouldn't have used the term happy. Grace looked as if someone had pasted the smile on her face, and Paul had a sinister look to his grin.

"Paul's asked me to be his wife. I've accepted."

"It isn't completely official because I have to get her a ring, but Mister Sullivan did give his consent." Paul had his arm around Grace's waist holding her so tight against him, it looked as if she were in a vise. Maggie jumped up and hugged her sister, forcing Paul to drop his arm while Charles extended his hand for a congratulatory handshake.

"I have to get up early tomorrow, so I'd best be leaving now. Goodnight to both of you." Paul dragged Grace after him as he headed for the door leading to the hall and the front entrance. "Decide what kind of ring you want." He gave her a quick kiss on the cheek and waved goodbye.

Paul became a dark silhouette against the magnificent, golden sunset, and Grace watched him fade from sight. How she wished she could erase him from her life as easily. "Don't bring him back," she whispered to his horse that could neither hear her nor obey her commands.

* * *

Much to everyone's surprise, Paul presented Grace with a ruby ring on a wide gold band which had taken residence on her fourth finger, left hand as she and Maggie pored over a sketchbook on the breakfast table.

"Are you sure you want me to design and make your wedding dress?"

"Of course. I want my dress to be the first paid one you do." Grace's face brightened a little as she raised her left hand to push a wisp of hair from her face.

Maggie's eyes were riveted to the ring. Against Grace's white skin, the band appeared to choke her finger, and the blood-red stone glared at her. "Why did you pick such a wide band and why a ruby?"

"Don't ask." Grace glanced down at the monster resting on her finger.

"Seems such a strange choice. So unlike you. Your jewelry is feminine and dainty, and you seldom wear red. Or did Paul pick it out?"

"No, the choice was mine. Let's take a break." The two girls headed for the path beside the river. Grace burst into tears the minute they left the house.

"Whatever is the matter?"

"I don't love him, Maggie. But this is the only way to uphold the family name and be able to get some money for Papa, so we won't lose the plantation."

"But Papa would never want you to marry someone you don't love. You know that."

"Yes, but since being with the man I love isn't a possibility, I'll do something to help everyone else."

"You and Jim are still seeing each other, aren't you?"

Maggie's accusation carried a note of pity.

"Only occasionally. Other than you, he's the best friend I've ever had." Her face softened, lit by a glow straight from her soul.

"He's more than a friend, isn't he?"

"No, that's all he'll ever be. Jim would be beaten and probably killed, and our family's name ruined if we were to marry. I'd never put him in jeopardy, nor would he allow me to be held up to ridicule. Our friendship will never be more than a deep, spiritual bond."

Maggie's voice broke, "Oh, Grace." She didn't understand her sister and never would. Choosing between the richest man in town who treated her like a queen and a Negro who had nothing made no sense to Maggie until she thought of Charles. He wasn't rich or a Negro. Working as a common laborer, his family's social standing was so far beneath the Sullivans, no one would think of them marrying. Yet, Maggie loved him with all of her being. What if she and Charles couldn't openly see each other? Maggie's very soul tore apart over fate's cruelty toward her sister. Grace's conversation continued. Maggie focused on her words.

"Choosing the wide, gold band represents the treasures I'll lay up for myself in heaven where all God's children will be the same, no color, no barriers. And waiting to meet Jim there where love abounds, with no bodies or social status, but spirit alone, is what gives me hope. The ruby stands for giving up my life's blood to marry Paul."

"Please, please don't do this." Maggie grabbed Grace's arm, frantically pleading with her.

"I have to. This will help the family. But don't confide anything to Paul and never tell him Papa freed the darkies. Give me your word, okay? And promise, not a single word to Mama or Papa about this."

"Promise, yet I do worry about you. Paul treats you like royalty, but sometimes, his eyes look mean, frightening. I'm sorry. I shouldn't say things like that."

"I've noticed the same thing. The thought of being a wife to him repulses me more every time I see him, but I'm afraid to say no to him, not for myself, but for what he could do to Papa."

Maggie changed the subject, telling Grace about the plan to invite Mary to visit Matthew.

"That's a grand idea. Maybe she could stay for the wedding and coax Matt out of the house to attend."

"That would be something!"

CHAPTER TWENTY-TWO

Sitting down at the breakfast table, the girls took up the sketchbook to finish the design they'd started. Sarah strolled in.

"What do you think of this design?" Grace asked.

Sarah looked over Maggie's shoulder. "Hmm. Isn't it a little simple? Since you're marrying the most eligible bachelor in town, this wedding should be the talk of the town."

"We don't have the money for a big wedding."

"Still, you mustn't embarrass Papa with a cheap showing. If Maggie makes it, you'll be saving a lot of money." Sarah would never hurt Maggie or Grace, but she had reservations about Maggie undertaking such an important dress. At least, Grace had agreed to marry Paul, so she soothed her nerves and tried to relax.

When Paul came to call, he wanted to discuss their plans. "My dear, how long will it take you to put our wedding together? Now, mind you, I want the very best wedding Scottsville's ever seen. We owe that to our families."

Grace buried her head in her hands, crying.

"What's the matter? Did I say something wrong? Please, talk to me." Paul didn't know what to do with such emotion.

Wiping her eyes, Grace itemized each obstacle, though she knew Paul was already aware of them.

"Matt's gambling, losing half the replanting money, and now he can't even help Papa because of the paralysis. We have no savings and counting on something as uncertain as a small, second crop doesn't leave money for a big wedding without borrowing from the bank. I won't stand for that, so we'll have a nice wedding, but not the elaborate kind you want."

"Oh, my pretty Grace! Don't you know families stick together? There's not a thing going on in this house that I don't know about, so I withdrew money from my account today." He extracted a thick wad of bills and handed it to her. "This should cover everything, but if you need more, just let me know. Let's do this right. And since we're almost family, if your father needs some money to live on, you tell him to come see me tomorrow morning."

Grace looked at her betrothed. His actions were kinder tonight. Maybe she could learn to love him, and everything would work out in the end. "Thank you, Paul."

"You're most welcome. Tell Mister Sullivan to come by whenever he's ready."

"Okay."

"I love you, Grace, and I'm going to take care of you. Wait and see. Everything will be wonderful. However…"

"Yes, Paul?"

"Would Saturday, the seventh of June be agreeable with you for our wedding?"

"I'll try for that date, but it'll depend on how quickly my dress can be made. June is only a little over a month away, but if that date's important to you, I'll try."

"Thank you. The date is quite important to me. My mother would also like to assist in wedding preparations, so please ask her if you need anything."

"Of course."

Grace felt a sense of peace about her decision. Though she knew he'd understand, telling Jim hung heavy in her thoughts. She was surprised he didn't receive the news as well as she'd hoped.

"I'm still very much against it. There's just something about him I don't trust." Jim paused a few seconds. "He's taking the only person I care for more than anything in the world, so maybe I'm just jealous. Please watch him. He could ruin your father with a single mark of his pen, and I don't even like to think he might hurt you."

"I'll be careful." Grace's body rebelled with fatigue. Jim walked with her to their stopping place. Back in her room, Grace sat in the middle of the bed, counting the money. There was enough for Scottsville's most elaborate wedding. Crossing the room to the connecting door, she gave a soft rap.

When Maggie answered, Grace stood there holding out the money, wearing a big grin. She watched Maggie's eyes open as wide as the full moon outside. They jumped in the middle of Grace's bed while she explained why Paul had given her the cash. Since the next day was Saturday, they stayed up most of the night making detailed plans until falling asleep surrounded by Paul's money.

Sarah seemed surprised to see her daughters up before dawn.

Grace bent and kissed her, telling her what Paul had said about the loan. "Will you tell Papa?"

"Why don't you tell him?"

"Because Maggie and I are going shopping. Paul gave me some money for the wedding, so Papa won't have to worry about paying for it." Grace buttered a biscuit.

"You're going into Scottsville?" Sarah pushed her food around on her plate.

"No' we're going to Flower Grove since they have better prices and a wider selection of fabric. Would you like to come along, Mama?"

"I'd love to, but there's a luncheon meeting at the church."

Grace and Maggie devoured breakfast, barely taking time to swallow and rushed out the door.

*   *   *

The girls found the perfect fabric, lace, buttons and thread in one store. Shoes, stockings, a new corset, and petticoats in another small shop two blocks away completed the shopping.

Grace fingered the money, noting she'd have a substantial sum left. She'd put it in a little velvet bag, just as her mother had always done in case she needed it for emergencies.

Celebrating their success, they stopped at a nearby home, which had been turned into a small café and enjoyed a delightful lunch, courtesy of Paul.

"Why, thank you, Mister Future President of Scottsville State Bank," Maggie said, teasingly as she raised her fork to her mouth to take a bite of chicken salad. "How nice of you to pay for our lunch!"

"Yes, my Dear Future Husband. My favorite society lady is now Miss Maggie Soon to Be Burton, and we're having a social today." Grace raised her glass in a toast.

The young ladies giggled and gossiped, bonding closer than they'd been for the past several months. Dumping so many bundles into the buggy, they almost didn't have room to squeeze themselves in for the jaunt home.

"I had such fun today, Maggie. For a while, I almost forgot I'm marrying Paul."

*   *   *

As soon as they arrived home, the girls began studying the sketch once more. Finding such good bargains, they'd picked up some extra fabric, deciding to make the dress more elaborate than the original design. When they'd finished, they summoned their mother for her approval.

Sarah looked at the drawing, running her hands over it. "I can't believe my eyes. This looks like something from the Old Country. The design is beautiful and most appropriate. Did you have enough money for the fabric?"

"Oh, yes. Look!" Grace led her mother to the bed where they had spread out the fabric, along with lace, buttons and thread.

Sarah ran her hands over the material, holding the lace up to the window, viewing the exquisite detail of small roses embedded within it. "Reminds me of Irish lace. It's perfect," she said with a faraway look in her eyes.

*   *   *

The mild, spring temperatures, cooled off by the recent rain, provided the ideal conditions for replanting, and Abe sat at his desk calculating their finances. With such favorable soil conditions, he knew he could turn enough profit to pay off the original loan at the bank, and with Sarah's careful management of the household money, they'd manage through another season. Paul's offer of an additional loan cemented Abe's opinion of his future son-in-law's generosity and kindness, two traits Abe admired, but he didn't want to start off Grace's marriage beholden to the young man. Abe had thought about Matthew many times since the accident. Seeing his son unable to move his legs broke Abe's heart. Matthew's behavior indicated he was his own worst enemy, but his mood seemed to be getting better every day. Sometimes, he even expressed some enthusiasm when Abe included him in decision making and ideas he'd been contemplating regarding the plantation. The two men had healed their emotional scars as far as Abe was concerned since they shared time together with light banter as well as serious plans for the future. Sarah knocked on the door of the study, and when Abe opened it, she stood with two glasses of iced tea.

"Would you like to sit on the swing for a few minutes?"

"That'd be nice. I'd also like to talk to you about something." Abe took a glass from his wife as they moved to the verandah.

"What's on your mind?"

"Jeremiah's rheumatism is causing him a lot of pain when he climbs into and out of the wagon, so I've decided to train Jim to take over as foreman. He's a younger copy of

Jeremiah…dependable, honest, well liked, and respected by the workers."

"That's good. I know Daisy's been worried about Jeremiah, but she'd never ask for a favor."

"He can work full time in the woodworking shop, sitting on a stool while he carves to his heart's content, or if he feels good enough, he can create beautiful furniture, resting when he gets tired. Who knows, we might even sell furniture if times get too bad."

"Wonder if he could teach Matthew to do something like that?"

"What a good idea. I'll see if Matt is interested."

* * *

The next day, a letter arrived from Joseph saying he'd be home in a few days for Grace's wedding. He sounded happy and wrote he was bringing Rebecca Taylor with him. Mary and Luke had also agreed to come, and Joe asked his parents to keep the visit a secret from Matt since the girls wanted to surprise him.

"I like Mary and Luke. Playing Cupid is just like our girls, but perhaps seeing Mary will brighten Matt's days." Sarah folded the letter.

"Even though his mood is better, I agree Mary's visit will be good for him."

"Has he told you he's had a few tingling sensations in his feet?"

"No. Don't get your hopes up, though. Remember, Doc warned us not to count on anything."

* * *

Matt grew tired of reading, so upon hearing his parents come inside, he rolled himself out to the verandah. Staring into space eased him into an almost trance-like state, and he ruminated over the past few months. The image of a conversation he and Abe had when Matt asked him for a pistol played out in his mind. It took a lot of laughing and joking to convince his father that he wasn't depressed and that he only wanted the pistol for protection. He mentioned he might need to shoot a snake or signal for help. Asking for one of the men to go with him until got used to rolling his chair over the terrain clinched it. Also venturing out to the woodworking shop, Matt expressed an interest in learning the trade, knowing the information would get back to his father. Jeremiah built a ramp on the side porch so Matt could roll onto the lawn independently, and after a few outings of marksmanship training, fishing, or just talking to the man who accompanied him, Abe agreed to let his son go outside on his own. Matt could tell his parents were pleased with his elevated mood and was relieved that they hadn't guessed the truth. He was tired of being a burden and thought if he weren't around, perhaps the family could recover from the pain he'd caused. Though he still had fleeting thoughts about gambling and drinking, each day his cravings lessened, and now being free from the restrictions of the chair was the only thing occupying his mind. Freedom. He could hardly wait. The chariot the darkies sung about was going to carry him home very soon. He didn't want to spoil Grace's wedding, and he liked Paul, so he'd decided to wait until they were married and settled before he took action.

The light breeze felt good, but he noticed a puff of dust rising down the road. Squinting to see who was approaching, he remembered Jim had gone to the depot to get Joe and his lady friend, who were coming for Grace's wedding. Even before the carriage stopped, he could hear singing and Joseph calling out a greeting. His brother still acted the clown.

The horses came to a stop, and Joseph jumped down to help a beautiful girl from the carriage. Matthew stared at her, and a vague memory surfaced. Was she the one who ran away from him so long ago? Rebecca? No. Couldn't be. Matt knew Joe had dated her a few times, but he didn't realize they were still seeing each other. His stomach rose, threatening to choke the breath from him. Trying to relax, he inhaled deeply before blowing his breath out in a sigh, hoping he was wrong.

Before Matt regained his composure, he realized Joseph was helping another young lady down, but a boy jumped to the ground, creating just enough haze to obscure Matt's vision. As the group made their way up the steps, Matthew recognized two women he didn't want to see. He didn't want Mary to see him crippled, and what could he say to Rebecca after his past behavior with her?

"Hi, brother. Look who followed me home!" Joe seemed to be in a very good mood. "You remember Rebecca Taylor, don't you? And as a special gift, I persuaded Mary and Luke to come also. Grace should have a fine wedding with all of us here, don't you think?"

Mary came over to Matthew, bent down and kissed his cheek. She still smelled like fresh berries, and the sight and scent of her roused feelings within him that had lain dormant for so long, he'd thought they were gone forever. Her soft, melodious whisper reminded Matt of how often she'd tried to calm him from one of his drunken rages. "If you don't want us here, Luke and I can go into town and stay until Joseph gets ready to go back to school."

Matt shook his head, trying to keep his voice steady. "Please, stay," was all he could manage. Turning, Matt rolled himself to the door.

The others followed. They were all talking at the same time as they entered the house where Abe, Sarah, Grace, and Maggie came from the other end of the hall to greet them.

"Okay, so where's the groom?" Joseph asked, jokingly.

"At the bank making money to support me, so I can buy everything I want!" Grace wore a fake smile, hoping no one would notice.

"I'm happy for you." Joseph wrapped her in a hug.

The whole party moved into the parlor where the family exchanged greetings with their guests. Everyone seemed at ease and happy with the homecoming. After refreshments, Grace invited Mary and Rebecca to her room for a look at the completed wedding dress.

Maggie had done a superb job. The gown was made from fine white satin. Covering the high-necked bodice and long sleeves was an overlay of heavy lace, encrusted with seed pearls. A red velvet sash tied in a large bow in the back marked the waist and trailed to the end of the skirt. The bell-shaped, skirt had medallions of white lace scattered over it and was the essence of femininity designed to cover Grace like a soft mantle of womanhood.

Sarah had discussed the use of red, mentioning some people might consider Grace non-virginal for having such a bright color on a white dress and asked why her oldest daughter hadn't chosen a pale blue to match her eyes.

Grace explained red would match her ring.

"And the younger people might consider red the color of love," Maggie added. She was the only one who knew the symbolism behind the colors Grace had chosen. They'd talked about it when they were picking out the fabric. Besides the red indicating Grace giving up her life's blood, she had decided on white to represent bandages to heal her broken heart and to tie up the plantation's wounds. She swore Maggie to secrecy. No amount of persuasion would alter Grace's resolve to go through with the marriage.

Completing the ensemble was a floor-length veil, which would fall from a circle of red roses in Grace's hair.

Maggie would be her only attendant, wearing a simple, crimson taffeta dress she'd made some months before Grace became engaged. When Mary and Becca saw the wedding gown, they both gasped at its beauty and showered Maggie with compliments. The four of them had a grand time, talking and laughing until they heard dinner being announced.

Just as everyone gathered to enter the dining room, Sarah took Matt's diploma from the wall and passed it around for everyone to see.

Matt, though confident no one had guessed his secret, still felt uneasy. He wanted his mother to put the certificate back on the wall and forget about it.

Joe asked to hold it. "Nice to see what they look like. Not too much longer until I have mine." Wheels spun in his mind. Where did Matt get the diploma? Had to be a forgery.

CHAPTER TWENTY-THREE

The evening meal was lively with animated conversation sprinkled with lots of laughter.

Charles brought his cousin, Seth, who was about the same age as Luke while Paul rounded out the guest list. After dinner, Matthew asked Mary to join him on the porch, and everyone smiled as she pushed his chair through the door.

"Tell me why you decided to come? To see an invalid? To gloat over the idea that my wild days are over?"

Mary looked into his eyes, the eyes she'd never forgotten, and even in the bright moonlight, she could still see the pain…not the pain of being paralyzed, nor the pain of having his dreams shattered, but the pain that had always been there. In some strange way, she'd often thought of them as two souls lost in some kind of void. Looking into his eyes the first time he'd paid for her services, the first thing she noticed was the anguish. No matter how sophisticated or arrogant he acted, Mary always knew the real Matt lay buried under the behavior he exhibited. In spite of talking about becoming rich, in a rare, drunken moment, he'd admitted he didn't want to till the soil or work as his father's apprentice. But since he didn't know what else to do, he'd uphold the

Sullivan name as was expected. Mary had learned to read Matt through his eyes rather than believing his boasting.

Speaking in a soft voice she said, "I didn't come here to cause you additional pain. The girls invited me, and the thought of seeing your parents and being able to thank them again for the wonderful Christmas that we shared made me decide to come. You have no idea how much that meal meant to Luke and me after losing our parents."

"Sorry. Guess I just don't like for anyone to see me like this."

"Like what, Matt? Like a man sitting in a chair? Like a man who's had some terrible luck but is very handsome with a wonderful brain? Like a man who can still move his arms and feel with his heart? Should everyone feel sorry for you? Well, I don't. You have a lot of potential, and you could certainly put it to good use rather than sit here and beg people to sympathize with you. Look, I had to do something I'm not proud of, not at all, but what choice did I have? Feeling sorry for myself would've weakened me, and Luke needed me to be strong. So, I locked away my feelings, did my job, and we survived. Finally things got better. Don't sit here and expect me to weep at your feet. You're still a man. You just don't act like one."

Matthew hadn't expected her to be angry, but she was right. He looked at her. She was absolutely beautiful, and he wanted to hold her. Any other time, he would've thought of bedding her, but she looked different tonight. Maybe he could just touch her. Matt extended his hand. Mary walked over and took it, pulling him to the side of the wicker sofa as she sat.

He readjusted the chair to an angle where he could see her face in the glow of the rising moon, but he remained in the shadows. "How are you, Mary? What's happened since I left?" The softness of her hand, like a fine deerskin glove, soothed him, and he relaxed in spite of himself.

"My life is fine now, but it's taken some time. I worked hard at the tavern, but I felt death waiting to steal me each night. Every time a man came in, it made me violently ill, but I managed to smile, to think of it as a job, to make myself numb to any feelings, and once it was over, I'd throw up, and go to the next customer. You know my story and why I worked there. That filthy job kept a roof over our heads and food in the pantry. Luke's been able to stay with me, and I've put away every penny I could spare. Now there's enough for Luke's first two years of college, and I've quit that job."

"What are you doing for a living now?"

"Teaching piano and voice lessons, and while it doesn't pay a lot, it's enough for us to get by. The horrible memories of the past have been replaced by hopes and dreams for the future. I've thought of you many times. You were the only one who ever tipped me. In spite of your anger and drinking, I didn't feel quite so used with you. How very different you were."

"I wasn't a very nice person when you met me. Believe me, I've had more than enough time to think about those days and why I had such crazy notions."

"Perhaps you were trying to decide who the real you was. Maybe you were trying to impress your friends. Most likely, you were trying to run away from yourself."

Matt didn't acknowledge Mary's observations. How could she know all that? "But you came to see my parents?"

"Well, yes, but also to see you. To thank you for what you did for me by letting us share a little of your life last Christmas and to see if maybe we could remain friends."

Matthew was glad it was dark because his face could convey feelings he'd have to deny if she saw them. Since his accident, Matt had attempted to push all thoughts of his former life to the back of his memory and felt tonight as if a wooden stick would have more personality than he had. Putting on a happy act seemed to drain his energy, but Matt took comfort in the idea that shortly he'd have real peace. A sort of elation usually swept over him each time he fingered the icy steel of the pistol he kept under the cushion in his chair. But now, touching the deathly cold weapon, outlining it with his index finger, he was surprised it repulsed him. He jerked his hand away, out from under the blanket covering his legs.

"Are you in pain?" Mary asked at his sudden movement.

"No, no pain. No feeling at all."

"That's strange. Joseph said Maggie had written that you have had some tiny feelings or sensations in your feet."

"Well, yes, and sensation is the right word. Feeling would be too strong."

Mary wanted to change the subject to a lighter note. "Did you know Grace asked me to sing at her wedding?"

"She did?"

"Yes, I'm so happy to be a part of her big day." They spent the rest of the evening engaging in happy, lighthearted conversation that infiltrated Matthew's heart, giving him some pleasure instead of the terrible sadness that had swallowed him for so long, even before his accident.

Joe and Becca sat side by side on the sofa visiting with the rest of the family. Sarah marveled at how right they seemed for each other. Joe would start a sentence. Becca would finish it. They delighted in showing off her ring and recounting the story of the engagement picnic and about their plans for going to Ireland.

"But you can't get married over there. None of us could come to the wedding." Maggie's eyes misted.

"Don't worry. We can't get married until after medical school anyway, so we may be back here for our wedding." Joe had been told Maggie's wedding was in the planning stages also. "So tell me, when is your big day, Miss Magpie?"

"We want Grace and Paul have theirs first."

"Don't you two wait too long because I'm leaving for Dublin right after the Christmas break. I won't get to come back very often once classes start." Though he acted as if he were teasing her, he truly wanted to be at her wedding. In his opinion, Charles was a lot more likeable than Paul, though he'd never voice that to Grace.

The hall clock sounded midnight, prompting everyone to end the evening. Charles and Seth, along with Paul, bade the family goodnight.

Abe had retired somewhat earlier with the excuse he had to get up before daybreak to get the workers organized. But before leaving, he made sure everyone knew how his future son-in-law had offered financial support to save them from sure disaster and was a welcome addition to the family. Paul volunteered to carry Matt up to bed, so Jim had the night off. Paul hoisted Matthew, roughly threw him across his shoulder, and rushed up the stairs so that Matt's chest bounced against

Paul's back. Matt remained silent, but his grimace conveyed his pain. The incident did not escape his future wife's notice.

* * *

Heavy clouds hung low on Grace's wedding day creating a dismal backdrop for the social event rolling off the tongues of most all the women in Scottsville. Several ladies from Sarah's church group arrived early in the morning to make pew bows and flower arrangements to display at the church. The women spread their supplies out on the dining room table. The talk turned to the possibility of rain, and one of the ladies became hysterical.

"Means God's crying over the union, and the wedding will have to be postponed."

Before breakfast, Sarah had picked deep crimson red and delicate white roses from the formal garden at the side of the mansion. Now she worked at putting them together for Grace's bouquet and headpiece. All the talk of bad luck had her in a panic because she didn't want Grace upset. Taking a deep breath, Sarah turned to face the ladies.

"Personally, I hope it does rain. In our country, it's said a wet knot is harder to untie, so rain's a good sign."

Grace entered the room in time to hear the conversation and stated emphatically, "Doesn't matter whether it rains or not. We're going through with this wedding today." She picked up the headpiece and motioned for Maggie to follow. Becca and Mary had been helping with last minute preparations, and they joined the two sisters in Grace's bedroom. Maggie put Grace's hair up into a soft chignon with curls framing her face. Then Becca and Mary helped both girls dress. Essie

Mae and Lavitica June went with Miss Daisy to the hotel ballroom to oversee preparations for the reception since Grace had asked that they serve the food.

A hush fell over the house as the ladies left for church with the decorations. When the family was ready to leave, Abe sent for the white carriage he and Sarah would share with Grace. To keep her dress from getting dusty, Abe picked his daughter up and carried her to the carriage. Once she and Sarah smoothed her dress, Abe gave the word for the procession to start.

Sarah laid the veil and bouquet on the seat beside her daughter. A large sigh escaped from Grace's lips, but then she settled down, a true picture of composure.

Becca, Mary, and Maggie rode in the small buggy behind Grace, singing all the way to the church, but Maggie knew no amount of merriment could dispel the gray clouds in the sky or in her sister's heart.

Joseph lifted Matthew into the large wagon, putting his chair in the back, and they followed the smaller buggy. The wedding party wound its way to the church.

Sarah studied her daughter in great detail. The way Grace had her lips pressed into a tight line, the tiny frown opaquely covering her ivory skin, and dull eyes that held a depth of utter oppression broke Sarah's heart. She longed to stop this day and go back to a happier one. Her daughter should be getting married at home. At home in Cork to a nice Irish farmer.

Grace reminded Sarah of the ghostly still before a thunderstorm, mirroring the weather. What storms lay ahead for her beautiful daughter? "Are you going to be okay, Grace?

You look a little pale but don't seem to have the jitters most brides get on their wedding day." Sarah patted Grace's cheek.

Grace smiled, looking off in the distance as if in a trance. "I'm fine. Don't worry about me."

Abraham even acted concerned. He reached over and took her hands in his. "You're marrying well, and that's what we've always wanted for you, but I want to be sure this wedding is what you want. There's still plenty of time to change your mind. Your happiness is the most important thing. Heaven knows, your mother and I had to work for what we have, but we've always had love. Lots of love. Love above all else is our wish for you."

Abe handed Sarah a small coin, a sixpence for good luck, brought from the Old Country, and she slipped Grace's shoe from her foot to place it inside. "Just tradition," she said smiling, but it was clear to Sarah this wasn't a glorious occasion. This event felt more like a funeral procession, and she was sure the clouds were going to smother all of them.

As soon as they were on the road, Matt cleared his throat to speak. He didn't want to depart this life without making amends to everyone, and now was a good time to get things straight with his brother. "I didn't know you were serious about Rebecca. Can you both forgive me for the way I treated her? I'm so sorry."

"You did us a favor. We probably wouldn't have met, otherwise." Joe smiled, remembering that night. "Of course, the minute she found out my name was Sullivan, she almost had a fainting spell. She couldn't run, though, because of her swollen foot and sprained ankle. She had to let me carry her, whether she liked it or not!"

They rode in silence for a few minutes until Matt pursued the issue. "But you forgive me, don't you? And Becca? Think she does?"

Joe had never seen his brother so solemn, but he knew that asking forgiveness had to be hard for him. The urgency in Matt's voice bothered him. "Sure, we both do. You're our lucky charm."

"That's good."

Joseph was puzzled. The family said Matt seemed resigned to his fate, acting happy and productive, but Joe had the uneasy feeling something was bothering his brother that no one had noticed. "What about Mary?"

"What about her?" Matthew shrugged his shoulders as a slight shiver shot up his spine.

"I think you like her a lot more than you're willing to admit."

"Wouldn't make any difference. She doesn't live near us, and I . . . I can't really be a man so...."

Joe changed the subject. He'd picked up on a few innuendoes about Grace's wedding that caused him concern. Knowing he might just be sensitive to his sister's moods, and not knowing Paul very well, he wanted Matt's opinion. "Do you think Grace and Paul will be happy?"

"Who knows? We aren't promised anything when we're born. But she's marrying well, so Papa's pleased. From a financial standpoint, she'll be taken care of, but whether Paul will be true to her is anybody's guess. I used to see him at the tavern a lot, drinking and talking pretty intimately with the girls, but I never saw him go upstairs. Doesn't mean he didn't, though."

"I'm concerned about her. She doesn't seem happy to me."

"I used to worry, too. But Joe boy, life's a fleeting thing, and it'll all be over before we know it anyway. So what difference does it make?"

Matt's dark mood put a damper on the conversation, and Joe decided to remain silent for the rest of the ride. After the festivities, he'd talk to Matt and see if he could get to the bottom of what was troubling him.

The small, white, clapboard church sat on a slight hill, shared by a small stand of willows, transplanted from the pond at the base of a rise. Backlit by thin rays of light peering through the pewter-colored clouds, the lone building stood stark and barren, giving an eerie impression to the guests arriving for the momentous event.

Grace made no mention of the weather but alighted from the carriage with Sarah and Abe on either side of her. The three girls carried her veil and bouquet, as the wedding party entered the vestibule, darkened by the weather. The doors leading to the sanctuary were closed, allowing for last minute adjustments to hair and clothes. Maggie placed Grace's veil underneath the circle of roses in her hair and straightened her dress. Charles met Matt at the side door and wheeled him to a reserved spot at the end of the first pew before lighting the tall, red tapers held by two, white candelabras. Entering through the same side door, Mary took her place beside the piano while Becca sat near where Sarah would be seated. Joseph waited in the vestibule with the wedding party to escort the mothers to their respective places at the appointed time.

Before Paul's mother arrived, Sarah pulled Grace aside. "Don't marry him. I have a bad feeling." A tear trickled down her face.

"I have to, Mama. It's okay."

Each pew was marked with white satin bows while baskets of red rosebuds graced the pulpit. The only light in the sanctuary came from the glow of the crimson candles, giving the room an atmosphere of warmth and love, but the heavy fragrance from the roses, pungent and sickening, lent a funereal quality to the room. Strains of music filled the church, the doors were opened, and Joseph Sullivan seated Louise Scott. Returning, he escorted Sarah to her place, kissing her on the cheek before she sat down. Next came Maggie who stood across from Paul's father, the best man. The sweetness of Mary's beautiful soprano voice filled the room, an overlay to the sepulchral environment descending on the event and a stark contrast to the dark day.

As the processional music rose above booming thunder, Abe leaned over and kissed his daughter on the cheek. "I love you, Grace. My wish is for all your dreams to come true, each day happier than the last."

Grace looked at him with a vacant stare, mechanically returning his kiss. Starting down the aisle, Abe couldn't help but notice she was as stiff as Miss Daisy's starched apron, moving with measured steps as if marching off to the gallows. He wanted to pick her up and run back to the safety of the carriage. "Relax, honey."

"I'm trying, Papa." In order to control her heartbreak, she remained rigid, eyes fixed straight ahead.

As Abe gave Grace's hand to Paul, the flower stems of her bouquet shifted. Though her mother had cut the thorns from the stems, she must've missed one, and Grace jumped as a barb ripped her flesh. Instinctively, she put her finger into her mouth. Abe, seeing what had happened, wrapped his white handkerchief around her finger to stop the bleeding.

Blood and bandages crossed Grace's mind. She glanced at Maggie who must have been thinking the same thing. The ceremony continued, but a bride's bleeding finger caused a little stir in the audience, especially since the red blood glared out on the white ribbon of her bouquet as she and Paul exited after reciting their vows.

CHAPTER TWENTY-FOUR

In contrast to the dark wedding, the reception at the hotel ballroom was spectacular with plenty of light and merriment in spite of the weather. Miss Daisy, Lavitica June, and Essie Mae stood behind the large buffet, serving the guests. The old cook beamed at Grace, telling her how pretty she looked.

After the couple cut the cake, John Scott proposed a toast, and the dancing began. When Paul noticed Grace getting tired, he stopped the band, thanked everyone for coming and whisked his bride away to begin their new life together while their friends continued with the festivities.

Matt had been carried up and now sat alone on the balcony watching people pass below. Joe took the opportunity to confront him. He drew a chair close to his brother.

"On the way to the church, you were so intent on Becca and me forgiving you. Made me think. Are you rectifying your sins for a reason? Does that include admitting to everyone your diploma is a forgery?"

Matthew was speechless. How did Joe know? Maybe it was a trick to get him to confess. "What are you talking about?" Matthew hedged answering until he could think.

"Dean Porter thought I knew due to a misunderstood conversation on both our parts. I know why you were expelled, and it's obvious what you're planning. Don't even think about it, but if you don't tell the family soon, I will."

Joe's words screamed in Matt's brain. How could he know what he was planning?

* * *

Paul purchased a lavish house in town as soon as he went to work for the bank. Without consulting Grace, he furnished it with the finest appointments available and selected imported china and crystal. All the linens bore his monogram, embroidered with white silk thread. He and his mother chose the furniture, and she organized the kitchen. A windowless hut at the back of the property housed an older slave woman and her two sons, a gift from Paul to his new wife.

Arriving at their new home, he picked up his bride, carried her over the threshold, and set her down at the base of a curved staircase leading to the upstairs bedrooms. "Would you like some tea?" he inquired in a polite and formal manner.

"Yes, thank you," Grace replied in the same formal tone. They made their way to the kitchen where Paul introduced Grace to a large Negro woman, waiting to serve them a small meal before they dismissed her for the evening. She had a kettle of water boiling on the stove, ready to make the tea.

"My name is Grace."

"I be Lizzie, ma'am, and I be servin' the dinner when you's ready." She backed away as fast as she could without taking her eyes off her new mistress.

"We'll have tea in the parlor first," Paul stated in a curt voice.

The old slave bowed, keeping her eyes glued to the floor. "Yas, suh."

Grace followed Paul into the parlor where he went to a beautiful, hand-carved cellaret. Removing a large, crystal decanter of Irish whiskey, he poured himself a glassful while Grace sipped the tea Lizzie brought her. As soon as Paul finished his drink, he led Grace to the dining room, filled with dark oak furniture. A seven-branched candelabrum graced the middle of the table furnishing the light for the room. The menu consisted of smoked pork, fresh tomatoes and squash along with some crusty bread…Paul's favorites and their first meal together. Grace marveled at how good everything tasted, even though she was too nervous to eat more than a few bites. Paul didn't eat much, either, but consumed plenty of the Irish whiskey to make up for his lack of appetite.

After dinner, Paul dismissed the cook, and they ascended the stairs. Walking into the bedroom, Grace had a vision of how hell, without the fire, might look. The wallpaper was red velvet brocade, which served as a backdrop for the mahogany bed with its bright, red spread, edged in heavy, black fringe. Black velvet drapes, embossed with a red fleur-de-lis pattern, hung at the windows, and red and black brocade pillows tossed on the bed added the final touch to the most repulsive room Grace had ever seen. The only pretty decoration was a large white rug in front of the dresser, which seemed as out of place as Grace felt.

"You get ready first," Paul ordered.

Grace reminded herself she was saving her family, and it was her duty to do what her husband wanted. With sheer determination, she entered the dressing room, removed her clothes, and put on a long, pink gown and peignoir, trimmed with matching lace. As she stepped out, trying to still her shaking body, she noticed Paul was gone. A few minutes passed before she heard him coming up the stairs. Framed in the doorway, he paused for a moment as if trying to retain his balance.

Grace ran across the room, helped him to the bed, and between them, they managed to get his clothes off and his nightshirt on. She tucked him in between the sheets. He passed out almost before his head hit the pillow, and Grace knelt beside the bed, saying a silent prayer of thanks for not having to consummate the marriage.

She wasn't so fortunate the second night, but focused her thoughts on the beauty of Ireland to help her endure the ordeal. It was the worst ten minutes she'd ever spent.

*   *   *

The next week, Grace realized what Paul expected of her and performed her duties mechanically without emotion. When she heard his steps on the porch at the end of his workday, she met him at the door, handed him a glass of whiskey, and escorted him into their parlor while listening to him discuss his day. Each night she attempted to engage him in a lengthy conversation, refilling his whisky glass enough times to get him inebriated so that he'd eat very little supper, and nothing physical would be possible or expected. Praying she wouldn't conceive a child, Grace became adept at devising ways to distract her husband, and liquor was her best ploy. Whether he was drinking or sober, Paul didn't show much interest in the physical side of their marriage, and Grace gave thanks that he never took much time. She assumed being drunk affected his performance, and preoccupation with business and making money interfered with his libido when he was sober. Anything that spared her having to perform in his bed gave Grace reason to rejoice. She fulfilled the role of wife by entertaining Paul's elite customers, becoming known as the most gracious and charming hostess in Scottsville. All of the prestigious societies vied to gain her membership, envying Grace's impeccable taste. Paul was very generous with money, demanding Grace wear the finest gowns money could buy, and though many of the women commented on her clothing, they were too polite to ask where she purchased her finery.

Gossip circulated around town that she had her clothes imported from France. Little did anyone know her sister designed and made all of Grace's dresses. Although she wanted to advertise Maggie's business, her primary goal was to stockpile large sums of money to go into her little velvet bag for emergency use after paying her sister a handsome fee.

If Paul found out Maggie was making his wife's clothes, he'd cut the money he gave Grace in half. Maggie assured her sister she had more than enough work to keep her busy, even without Grace's business. "I'll always put your clothes first, but word of mouth is spreading.

* * *

All in all, Paul was content. Since his marriage to Grace, his father had never suggested college again. Knowing Grace had become the center of attention in town, Paul was pleased. He knew he should pay more attention to her, but he had to concentrate on getting the rest of what he wanted while Grace seemed able to amuse herself, which was a big relief to him.

*   *   *

On their first month anniversary, Grace and Lizzie spent all day preparing a gourmet meal. The old cook boiled a shoulder roast with potatoes and onions, carving little roses out of radishes and cherry tomatoes from the garden. Fresh yeast rolls, made the day before, sat in the breadbox while a subtle aroma circled through the house from a fresh molasses pie made from Miss Daisy's recipe. Since it was the seventh day of the seventh month, Grace knew the date would be especially meaningful for Paul, even if she didn't understand the significance of the number.

She heard Paul's carriage pull up outside. Dressed in a pale blue dress with ecru lace edging the collar and sleeves, she rushed to greet her husband. Paul burst through the door before she could open it, and the force knocked her against the wall. He stormed into the parlor, threw his leather case on the sofa, and stomped upstairs without a word to his wife. Dumbfounded, Grace made a mental list of anything she thought might have precipitated such behavior, but nothing came to mind. She ran to the parlor and poured a drink before ascending the stairs to find out what had Paul so upset. He was pacing in the bedroom, muttering under his breath.

Handing him the drink, Grace asked in a soft voice, "What's wrong?"

Paul grabbed the drink, threw the contents in her face, and hurled the glass across the room.

Shocked and confused, Grace stood with whiskey dripping from her face, down her elegant gown, and onto the soft, white rug.

Paul glared at her, becoming even more furious. "You look like a clown, and you're always meddling in my business, you nosy little witch. You're always trying to catch me in some shady deal while pretending to be so interested in what happens with my day."

Before Grace could comprehend what he'd said, she felt the back of his hand on her side and across the front of her breasts. The pain was so severe, she almost lost her breath as she fell to the floor. Paul picked her up and slammed her head against the wall. She went limp and slid down the wall, landing in a crumpled heap on the floor. Trying to avoid further torture, she pretended to be unconscious.

Paul cursed under his breath, left the room, and slammed out the front door. Her head was pounding, she was dizzy, and her side was burning. She knew some of her ribs had been broken, but her main concern was for Miss Lizzie's safety.

Leaning onto the railing with one arm and holding her side with the other, she managed to make her way down the stairs to see about her slave. Opening the pantry door, she found the old Negro, her eyes as wide as carriage wheels, trembling like an oak leaf in a cyclone.

"It's okay. He's gone. You go on home. He'll probably spend a lot of time at the tavern tonight." Grace leaned against the wall to catch her breath.

Lizzie rushed to support her mistress and half-carried her upstairs. Tucking her in, she wet a washcloth to put on Grace's head. "Ma'am, I don' want to leave you. He's done hurt you real bad."

"Please do as I tell you, or he could come back and hurt me worse."

"Let me fix you a tray before I go."

"I'm not hungry. Please just go."

Lizzie crept down the stairs, a prayer for her mistress on her lips.

Left alone, Grace Sullivan Scott tried to make sense out of what had transpired. She couldn't get comfortable. It hurt to breathe. To take her mind off her pain, she read the Bible until her eyes felt heavy, and deep slumber eased her suffering.

The noise of Paul coming home woke her, but she lay still with her eyes closed. He fumbled in the dark to get his clothes off, threw them on the floor, and crawled into bed beside her.

"Grace, are you awake?"

Not trusting him, she didn't answer.

"Please, wake up. I'm so sorry." He wrestled his arm underneath her and began rocking her, kissing her hair while he stroked it.

Any movement compromised her breathing, and when Paul started hugging her, she couldn't stay still. She moved away from him before willing her voice to sound normal. "What made you so angry?"

"I don't know, but there's no excuse for taking my frustrations out on you. Can you forgive me? This was a bad day, a business deal went wrong, and my father was upset with me, but that's no reason to hurt you. I'm so very sorry."

He leaned on his elbow above her, and Grace felt his tears fall on her face. "No one has ever beaten me. I don't think I could stand it again. Maybe I should go back to Oak Hollow."

"No! Your place is here with me, not with your father. I'll never lay a hand on you, again. I promise, but please, forgive me."

"The pain is so intense. Maybe Doc Bradley could see me tomorrow. There may be some broken ribs."

"No! You want the whole town knowing I accidentally hurt my wife?"

Paul's behavior turned erratic, and Grace felt fear rise in her throat. Assuring him she wouldn't see the doctor, she rubbed his forehead until he passed out.

Thoughts tumbled over each other in her brain and she lay awake all night. Finally, a plan formulated and Grace swore to herself she'd go home, or what she still considered her home, tomorrow.

At breakfast, she made the excuse of wanting to drive to Flower Grove with another lady to look at lamps for the parlor. Pain stabbed her with every breath, but she tried to appear cheerful as if nothing had happened the night before. She counted breaths until Paul rose to leave for the bank.

Smiling, he patted her shoulder, and threw a large sum of money on the table. "Buy whatever you want, my dear. I'll have lunch at the Gentlemen's Club." He crossed the room and vanished.

Pain slowed Grace's movements, but with Lizzie's help, she managed to get into her buggy and head for Oak Hollow. Taking the back way into the plantation, skirting her parents' house, she drew the horses to a halt as she peered into the fields. Shielding her eyes, she saw Jim standing at the head of a cotton row, watching the men hoeing weeds. Hiding her buggy as much as she could behind a clump of fragrant crape myrtle bushes, she eased herself down and picked up a small stick, throwing it with all her might. Landing just short of its mark, the movement blinded her with pain, and she bent over to catch her breath.

Jim turned and nodded as Grace pushed herself to a standing position. Rushing to her, he looked into her eyes. "What are you doing here?"

"It's Paul." She was shaking.

Jim pulled her to him, even though sweat poured from him like a waterfall. Under normal circumstances, he wouldn't have allowed her to touch him until he'd bathed, but something was wrong. He felt her flinch in his embrace. Lightening his touch, he listened as she told him about the temper tantrum. She refrained from telling him about the beating.

"He hurt you, didn't he?"

Grace turned her head.

"Didn't he?" He was demanding, projecting his voice louder than he'd meant to, but since no one stopped working, apparently they hadn't heard anything.

Grace nodded, wiping away uncontrollable tears with the back of her hand.

With a gentle touch, Jim felt her side. "I don't mean to be familiar with you, but I think you have some broken ribs. You need it bandaged."

"That's not what worries me. I've seen the way Paul treats our slaves and heard him when he's drunk. He wouldn't think twice about hurting Lizzie or her sons or even killing them. He doesn't consider them human. Will you help me free them?"

Jim wiped his forehead with a handkerchief, deep in thought.

Grace took a shallow breath. "I'm afraid Paul is going to cause trouble. If he finds out Papa has freed all of you, everyone will be in danger. He could even start rumors in town, whether they're true or not. I hate for you to leave, my dear friend, but maybe all of you should run away to the North. And please take Lizzie and her sons with you."

"Let me think about it. I'll bring it up to the men at our next Sunday meeting. We'll pray over it and see what's best for everyone."

"Please don't mention I was here because I'm not going to the Big House. Paul would be furious if he thought I ran home, and I don't want Papa to know I'm hurt."

"Before you go, may I do something?" Jim took off his shirt and ripped a couple of strips from the bottom of it.

If Grace hadn't been in so much pain, she would've loved to touch his bare chest. "What are you doing?"

He tied two strips together, binding her midriff with the makeshift bandage. "Have Miss Lizzie do this better when you get home."

"Thank you. I'd better go."

"Go then with my prayers."

"And your love, Jim? Go with your love?" Tears dripped from her heart and clung to her soul where they would forever remain. She didn't have to be told that Jim shared in her sorrow.

"With my love, Grace. Always, with my love." He turned and walked back to the edge of the field.

CHAPTER TWENTY-FIVE

A blistering hot June turned to a cooler July, the rains came at the right time, and the crops prospered. Sitting on the front verandah surveying his land, Abraham smiled. Best crop he'd produced in a long time, even though it was half the acreage of the original. Most of all, he was grateful for Mary's presence in Matt's life. She refused to feel sorry for him, or if she did, she didn't show it. Quite a remarkable young lady.

Sarah had persuaded their guests to spend the summer and was delighted to see a friendship developing between Mary and Maggie. Life felt good.

Mary's presence made putting Matt's plan into action harder by the day. Why did she evoke such feelings in his heart? He could never marry or be productive. He was a burden, so ending his life seemed the best avenue for everyone. Only thing left to do was confess and ask forgiveness from his parents and prepare Mary. Tomorrow evening he'd roll out to the orchard, so they wouldn't hear the gunshot.

After dinner Mary made it her practice to spend time with Luke. Announcing they were going walking gave Matt an opportunity to talk to his parents. He invited them to the verandah. "Something I've done has brought more shame to me than I can tell you, and I know it's going to hurt you. I'm so sorry."

Abe assumed his son was apologizing for the evening he wrote the check. "I've come to accept what happened, and you should too. I hold no animosity, and you shouldn't either."

"Thank you, Papa. But this is about something else. Joe found out, and it's time you know, too." He took a deep breath. "I didn't graduate. The diploma hanging on the wall is a forgery. The friends I chose in college had loose morals, and I got caught up in that lifestyle, so I missed classes and even resorted to cheating. The dean dismissed me." Matt hung his head.

Abe felt his world crash. How could Matt have almost ruined the family with his gambling and drinking, and now admit he'd lied to them as well? "I don't know what to say."

Sarah sat with her hands over her face.

"My life has been nothing but a failure and a burden. I don't deserve to be part of this family, and if you disown me, I'll understand."

Abe glared at his son. "Is there anything else you haven't told us?"

"No."

Sarah read her son's eyes and knew the demons he'd been fighting. "Give us time. Everything will be fine once we get over the shock."

Abe willed himself to check his anger. After all, Matt was paralyzed as a result of his own actions and adding to his pain wouldn't help either of them. Besides, he could always go back and finish one semester. "Son, I'm glad you were man enough to admit what you've done. We'll work through this and come out better for it."

Matt didn't speak, just rolled into the house. He wanted a whiskey but knew the liquor cabinet was locked because of his drinking. Realizing he'd part this life without a drink seemed fittingly ironic.

Sarah removed the diploma from the wall before following Abe into the bedroom.

Mary resolved to make Matthew productive. She'd found the gun when plumping up the pillow in his chair, waiting for Jim to bring him downstairs. Hiding it in the folds of her skirt, she took it to Grace's former room, which she now occupied.

Taking some deep breaths to calm her nerves, she walked down the stairs and came face to face with Matt. "I found your little toy, Matthew. It's no longer available to you, so don't ask for it. You plan has suddenly become obvious. How could you even think of doing such a thing?"

"Leave me alone, Mary. You're not part of this family, you don't know what's going on, and you don't own me." He tried to roll the chair out of her sight, only to have her block him.

"Then suppose you tell me what is going on, Matthew, or would you rather take this up with your father? I've seen the way you look at each other. There's a lot of hurt between you. Of course, no one owns you, but I'm not going to let you kill yourself, either. So you decide. Talk to me, or I talk to your father."

Matthew's frustration level had almost reached its peak. She'd taken away his solution. The only way to get it back was for her to leave, but she had a right to know what a rotten man he was first. Would the truth push her away? He hoped so. Matt recited his confession to her almost without emotion.

When she didn't comment, he continued. "I'm the biggest failure in the world. Failed in school, failed my family, myself, and even failed at love. I'm not sure I even have a soul." Matthew's heart felt like the anvil in the blacksmith shop, but at least he'd confessed. He met her eyes. "Well? When are you leaving?"

"Leaving? I've been invited to spend the summer. Think that's a good idea, given what we're up against."

"What do you mean?"

"You can feel something. I've watched when Jim carries you up and down the stairs, and no matter how gentle he is, you sometimes wince. People who can't feel don't make faces. We're going to work on these feelings or sensations as you call them."

"No, we're not going to work on anything. I feel nothing. You're reading something into my face that isn't there. I've been honest with you up to this point, so now, please just leave me alone."

"Never, Matthew Sullivan, or at least not for the rest of the summer."

Swishing her skirt, Mary left him. He watched her exit, and her body language said it all. The woman was strong and refused to be deterred by his gruff behavior. When Miss Daisy brought his meal, he couldn't take a bite, uncertain of what this determined young lady was going to do.

Mary found Jim between two fields, manning the water bucket for the men and women who would drink a dipper full at the end of a long row to keep from dehydrating in the sweltering heat. "Anythin' wrong, Miss Mary?"

"No, I just wondered when you get Matthew dressed if he acts as if he feels anything?"

"Yas'em. I been noticin' and wuz gonna say somethin' to Massa Abe when I wuz sure."

"You think he might walk again?"

"Yas'em, if you have anythin' to do with it." Jim grinned.

"Will you talk to Jeremiah about making Matt some crutches?"

Back at the house, she enlisted the help of Maggie, Essie Mae, and Lavitica June. She didn't ask Sarah because she'd have too much sympathy for Matt and would make them stop treatment if he yelled. And Daisy had her hands full with the cooking. She was given the duty of providing plenty of iced tea.

Day after day, the makeshift nurses began the ritual of raising Matthew to his feet, making him lean on the crutches with Essie Mae and Lavitica June behind him, Jim in front, and Maggie and Mary on each side. Matt had no choice but to stand. At first his feet dangled, and he held his weight up with his armpits, but as the days passed, he began to bear some weight on his feet. He admitted some feeling was returning, but it wasn't enough to have him up and walking. The women took turns rubbing his legs and feet with camphor oil until their hands numbed. Then Jeremiah and Jim would take over. At night in his bedroom, Mary massaged the oil into his back.

Matthew humored all of them, but had to admit he felt better.

Several weeks had passed, and he and Mary were sitting on the back porch talking while she embroidered. He was teasing her just to see her eyes sparkle when she reached over and pricked him with her needle. His leg hurt and he yelled in pain. Mary threw down her needlework, jumped up screaming and dancing all over the porch. The commotion brought Maggie and Miss Daisy on the run.

"Good gracious, Miss Mary, what's the matter? A bee done got you?" Daisy bent to catch her breath. Maggie ran to see if Matt was okay.

"He felt it!" Mary erupted into loud laughter.

"She's trying to kill me!" Laughing with her, Matthew put his arms around Mary as she knelt in front of his chair.

Maggie and Daisy shook their heads, not knowing if Mary and Matt had been in the sun too long, if they'd been drinking, or precisely what might be causing such a clamor.

"I pricked him on the leg with my needle, only playing, and he felt it."

Exercise of his legs increased the next few weeks.

Summer was kinder to the farmers than spring had been. Crops flourished, and as the hot days gave way to cooler temperatures in the fall, the Negroes put in longer hours picking cotton. Abe figured he'd have more than enough to repay the loan. How different everything would have been if Matt hadn't had the accident! Forgiving was one thing, and Abe was sure he'd done that, but he wasn't sure about trusting Matt again. But he was grateful for Mary. He'd watched her coax his son to take a few steps with the crutches. A long battle lay ahead of him, but most of the household had dedicated themselves to Matt's recovery.

Sarah cried the first time she saw Matt struggle to stand and walk a few steps, realizing it was all because of Mary's pushing and never letting Matt give up. She'd make a fine daughter-in-law if she could get Matt to ask her.

Joining her husband on the verandah, Sarah asked, "What are you so deep in thought about?"

"Maggie and Charles. He asked for her hand, and I gave my consent. Not many things escape my notice, and he's no exception. Charles is a fine young man. Built Matt his chair and Maggie a house. I think he'll make an excellent son-in-law!"

"What a relief you feel that way. He loves Maggie. You can see it in his eyes every time he looks at her."

"Grace is my big worry. She's losing weight and looks tired. Is that what happens when a woman first gets married?"

"Sometimes, but she's probably working too hard with all the social activities and the entertaining she's doing."

*   *   *

Maggie's wedding plans were progressing. She joined her mother for tea on the front verandah, waiting for Grace's visit. Most of the details were finalized, and Maggie had designed and made her dress but wouldn't let anyone see it until Grace gave her approval. All she'd told Sarah was that she wanted to use fall colors. Maggie looked forward to seeing Grace since her sister seldom had time to return to Oak Hollow.

When she arrived, Maggie gave Grace time to greet Sarah before pulling her through the house, upstairs to her bedroom. Draped over a large chair in one corner was Maggie's wedding dress of ivory voile, a masterpiece reflecting her simple taste. A slightly rounded neckline marked the elongated bodice above a tightly gathered skirt that fell softly to the floor. Long, full sleeves ended in wide cuffs at her wrists. Both the sleeves and the bottom of the skirt were edged in wide, heavy lace of the same color. Maggie would wear an everyday petticoat, and following Irish tradition of carrying a horseshoe, she embroidered one on the edge of her sleeve as a symbol. Her veil, made of the same heavy lace, would cascade from a band of fall flowers and leaves in yellow, orange, brown and ivory. Topping off the trousseau was the traditional Irish hooded cloak made from brown lightweight wool, which Maggie would wear when she and Charles left the reception. Grace would wear a simple V-necked dress of deep bronze taffeta, and they would both carry chrysanthemums in various shades of yellow, bronze and ivory in a nosegay backed with red oak leaves.

Grace stood still, staring at her sister's creations.

Maggie couldn't wait. "What do you think?"

"Everything is so beautiful. It reminds me of home, especially the cloak. I hope you'll be the happiest bride in the world."

"Me, too! Now let's go back and join Mama."

Miss Daisy appeared with Grace's favorite tea as she settled herself in a wicker armchair on the verandah. "When will Joe and Becca be here?"

"Tomorrow."

Mary walked through the door, and turned to Grace before sitting beside Sarah. "Have you heard that Matt's been taking a few steps?"

"Yes! Papa stopped by the other day and told me. I couldn't be more excited. I know you agreed to only stay for the summer, but you can't leave. You're the reason Matt's improving, but more than that, we love you and Luke."

"And I love all of you, too. Matt helped me at a very low time in my life, and anything I can do to help him is a small payback." She sipped her tea.

Sarah patted Mary's arm. "We don't want to be selfish, but all of us want you to stay. Luke could go to school here, and I'm sure you could teach music if you wanted."

Grace wore a soft, cotton blouse and a full, gingham skirt. As she shifted in her chair, Maggie noticed bruising around her neck and asked about it.

Anxiety flushed Grace's face, and the heightened color accentuated the dark marks. She stammered, trying to think of a plausible answer. "Oh . . . it's nothing. I was out in the yard the other day, and the clothesline broke. The wire sprung back at me and wrapped around my neck. Lizzie had to untangle me." Her nervous laugh failed to conceal the lie.

"That must have been a funny sight." Maggie didn't believe her for a moment.

Grace rose trying not to let the pain and stiffness show. "I'd like to take a walk if you girls don't mind. It's been a long time since I've been here, or at least it seems that way." Grace's heart soared when no one objected. She loved the solitude of Oak Hollow and headed down the path beside the river. Though Jim wouldn't be in their circle, she wanted to see the heart one more time. The unspoken communication it represented made her feel closer to her former life and her bond with Jim.

When she entered the clearing, she found it had, as usual, been tended with love and care. She smiled through her tears, knowing she could endure anything to keep her feelings for Jim sacred and to keep all the Negroes safe from horrible masters.

After Grace became mistress of his house, she learned Paul had beaten the young slave boys repeatedly for no good reason, and that's why Lizzie was so terrified of him. Grace had witnessed it only once, but that was enough. She persuaded Paul to stop after three lashes, and though he promised he'd never touch them again, he took his wrath out on her, leaving red, blue and black bruises, but at least, he spared her face.

Grace despised him and wanted to leave, but he'd made it clear he'd kill anyone who tried to interfere in their marriage. She knew Oak Hollow would be his first stop, so she'd stay to protect her family. The last time he got angry, Paul had almost killed her when his hands went around her neck. Grace could never tell what would trigger the attacks, but they were becoming more frequent. In the end, after every attack, Paul begged her forgiveness. Something had to cause him to lose his temper. Maybe she could talk to him when he was in a calmer mood. She meandered back to the Big House, reluctant to go to her own home.

* * *

The day of the wedding found Maggie up early making last minute preparations. As they had done with Grace, Abraham and Sarah now shared the carriage with Maggie. A feeling of excitement and anticipation hung in the air, energizing everyone.

Maggie's face radiated her happiness. She laughed and made small talk in the carriage on the way to the church. Sarah smiled and slipped her younger daughter's shoe off to put in the lucky sixpence.

* * *

Talking and giggling filled the vestibule. Sam and Alice Burton entered the small area and headed straight for Maggie. Alice kissed her on the cheek, looking as if she would cry at any moment, and Sam hugged her, patting her on the back.

Abe and Sarah had entertained the Burtons a few times and had been to their home in town on several occasions. Even though they didn't socialize in the same circles, the two couples developed a deep friendship, which delighted Maggie and Charles. Joseph, again, was appointed usher to seat the mothers while Becca lit the candles.

The ceremony began. Mary's voice filled the tiny chapel as Grace started down the aisle.

Alone for a few minutes, Maggie squeezed Abe's arm in a silent expression of her love for him. He bent and kissed her. "I wish for you the same thing I wished for Grace. May all your dreams come true, and you find each day happier than the last. I love you very much."

"I love you, too, Papa. If only you loved Charles more."

"Maggie, I was worried about his providing for you. He's proved me wrong, and I do welcome him with open arms now, as a part of this family. Even if I didn't feel that way, the way you look today would change my mind. I'll be proud to call him my son."

The tears Maggie shed were for what she'd longed to hear from the first man she'd ever loved, the one who'd kept her safe until this day when he'd turn her over to another man, the other half of her soul. She happily walked with her father down the aisle toward the arms of her beloved.

In a surprise move, when Abe reached the altar, he shook hands with Charles, followed by a warm embrace before giving him Maggie's hand.

The deepening rays of the sun caught one of the facets of the stained glass window, showering a soft rosy glow over Charles and Maggie as they stood at the altar waiting to recite their vows. No one else was illuminated, and throughout the audience, audible gasps were heard coming from some of the women, who called it a miracle. This simple ceremony would long be remembered as the loveliest wedding in Scottsville's history.

The reception was a plain, no-frills affair without dancing or drinking, held in a large room of the church, more like a reunion of friends and family. The buffet, served by Daisy and her daughters, held trays of hearty food, and people lingered to catch up on the latest news including births and deaths.

Daisy had tears in her eyes. "You wears love real good. That's why yo face glows."

The newlywed couple seemed eager to leave, but they managed to pull Abe and Sarah aside for a personal goodbye.

"Papa, thank you for giving me away and for blessing our marriage," whispered Maggie.

"Sir, I'm going to take real good care of my wife, and thank you very much for your show of acceptance at the altar. That means a great deal to me." Charles fought to keep his voice steady.

Abe also struggled not to show emotion and in a hushed voice said, "You two are going to be fine. I couldn't be happier or more comfortable that you've made the right choice."

Sarah looked at the happiness radiating from her daughter's face just as it had on her own face when she and Abe had married. "I love you both. Be well and most of all, be happy."

"We love you, too, Mama." Maggie kissed her mother as Charles placed the cloak around his new wife's shoulders before escorting her from the church hall.

CHAPTER TWENTY-SIX

Joseph and Rebecca were preparing to leave the next day to return for Joe's last semester of college. Sarah hugged her son, knowing he'd be off to Dublin in a few months.

Tears spilled down her face. Mary came up and put her arms around Sarah's shoulder as Joe and Becca waved from the buggy. "Too many changes, but I'm glad one of them is that you and Luke are staying here." Sarah sighed and entered the house.

* * *

A month after Maggie's wedding, Paul came home drunk and late for dinner. Grace steeled herself for his beating. She'd learned certain words and actions would set him off like a volcano, so avoiding them was a must. Sometimes, though, outside events caused his rage. Pasting on a smile, she went to the door to let him in but didn't say a word as she helped remove his coat.

"Where's that nigger?" he yelled at her.

"Miss Lizzie's her name. She left you a nice supper if you want it."

"No, what I want is for all those niggers out there to do what I say when I say it. You're treating them like they're as good as we are. They're chattel, Miss Grace Almighty. Chattel. Not worth a drink of water in the middle of July if you ask me." Paul's voice rose to crescendo pitch, his face the color of a rotting tomato.

Grace kept still, seething inside. She hated this man with an all-consuming passion, and she prayed he would have to pay for his actions one day. Glancing at her ring, Grace noticed the band seemed to be cutting off her circulation, and the ruby had turned almost black, both signs of an unhappy union. She didn't need an old wives' tale to point out the truth.

Turning to Paul, she put on her best act. "You're right. I'm much too kind to them. I'll try to be harder starting tomorrow."

For once he seemed satisfied as he staggered upstairs and fell into bed with his clothes on. When she was sure he was asleep, Grace crept out to the shack. She hesitated before knocking for fear Paul would wake and hear her.

Lizzie's son peeked out of the door, his eyes so big they seemed to cover his face. Grace knew he expected to be jerked from the shadows and beaten. "Let me in," she whispered.

He opened the door. Grace remembered the day after Paul had brought her here. She'd asked to see Lizzie's living quarters and couldn't believe what her eyes told her. Paul wouldn't allow them to have water to wash clothes or bathe, except once a week, and they lived with moldy linens and clothes with a stench unfit for human habitation. Grace used part of her money to replace the rags in their shack and allowed them all the water they wanted. Keeping it secret became a bond of trust between the two women.

Grace took Lizzie's hands in hers while instructing the older boy to saddle a horse as fast as he could without making too much noise. Whispering to her friend she said, "I don't have much time, so listen carefully. Master Paul is drunk and sleeping, but he's getting more out of control every day, and I'm afraid for your safety. I have a friend who can help you, but you must travel light, so pack only what you need. Do you understand?"

"Where we gonna go, Miss Grace?" Lizzie's eyes displayed her terror.

"I don't know yet. After I check on Paul, I'm going to see my friend. Watch the house, and if you see a light in the window, run. Run anywhere, but get away from this place. I'll be back as soon as I can."

Grace ran to the stable, mounted the horse and walked him out of hearing distance before letting him run. Twilight faded into a surreal landscape of shadows and distortions. Though there was a bright moon, she rode with fear in her heart, a prayer on her lips, and a very fast horse.

Reaching the plantation, she took the back road and went across the small bridge to Daisy and Jeremiah's house. Jim was sitting on the front porch, and she could hear his plaintive singing before she ever got there. Breathless, she dismounted as Jim ran to greet her.

"What's the matter?"

"I had to come."

Jeremiah struggled to stand on his arthritic feet, and he and Daisy limped out to see what was causing all the activity.

Grace had almost finished her story. One look at her, and the old couple knew something terrible had happened. She briefed them about her concern for Lizzie and her family. "I'm so afraid he'll kill them. Please tell me what to do."

"I'm gonna go back with you and take care of 'em. Get 'em to a safe place. We been hearin' rumors. They's an uneasiness raisin' up its head. We got friends buildin' hidin' places and helpin' people go up North." Jim fell back into his colloquialism and hadn't wanted to worry her with all the details, but now it was time to be honest and to act.

Without thinking of how it would look, he jumped on her horse and drew her up behind him. They rode to the barn. Jim bridled four horses but didn't take time to saddle them. He mounted one horse, leading two others while Grace took the reins of the remaining one. They walked the horses at a brisk pace.

"I don't want to run them so they'll be fresh when we get to town. Are you sure Paul is sleeping?"

"He was when I left."

"Please be careful. You're a brave woman, but you also must think of yourself. I know he's been hurting you."

"Yes, but he'll come to his senses soon. There's something I'm doing he doesn't like, and surely I'll figure it out before long."

"No, it's him, not you."

They arrived back in town, and Jim waited near the depot with the horses while Grace went home by herself. A quick check on Paul while Lizzie's son unsaddled her horse proved she had nothing to worry about. Paul had passed out. Creeping across the yard to the shack, she gave Lizzie directions to where Jim waited. They hugged, tears flowing down both their faces.

"Hurry, Lizzie, but remember, when this is all over, I want you to come back and sit in my parlor and have tea with me." Grace watched them melt into the shadows without making a sound, and a weight lifted from her heart.

* * *

Paul was not in a good mood when he awoke. His head hurt, and his clothing felt stiff. He heard Grace humming and smelled fresh coffee. After washing up and changing clothes, he entered the kitchen, expecting to see Lizzie waiting to serve breakfast. Instead, his wife put plates of food on a tray to take to the breakfast room.

"Where's that woman?" he demanded.

"She wasn't feeling well yesterday. I'm afraid she has something contagious, so I told her not to come into the house today. She might even die. That would be terrible because I'd have to break in a new cook." Grace hoped her lies would appease her husband.

"Well, keep those boys busy. Don't want them idle. Have them chop wood and stack it by the carriage house."

"Don't worry about things here. Just have a good day at the bank." As soon as he left, Grace rushed to her buggy, and drove to see her father. He was ready to mount a horse. Jim stood beside him holding the reins.

"I was on my way to see you, but since you're here, let's go to the house. We need to talk."

Abe helped her down from the buggy. As she looked back, Jim mouthed that Lizzie's family was safe. Grace smiled and winked a thank you.

As they passed through the kitchen, she hugged Miss Daisy and smiled, hoping she couldn't tell her pale lavender dress covered black and blue marks. As her father's stern gaze caught her eyes, Grace sat down at the table where Miss Daisy had placed a cup of steaming tea.

Clearing his throat, Abe patted her shoulder. "I'm not good with words so I'm just going to get to the point. Jim came to me last night and told me you'd been here."

Grace knew she'd hurt her father by not coming to the house and letting him know what was happening. She interrupted before he could get another word out. "I'm sorry. I didn't want to involve you, and time was short. Please forgive me." Her body ached, but she stiffened to conceal the pain.

"Asking Jim to get your slave woman and her family out of that situation was the right thing, but that's not what worries me. I haven't said anything to your mother, but I know Paul's been hitting you. Jim didn't want to go behind your back, but he fears for your safety, as I do."

Grace started to cry as her father got up and pushed his chair closer to hers, guiding her head to his chest. When she caught her breath she whispered, "You work too hard making the plantation productive. Paul can lend you any amount of money you need. That takes a worry off of me, and I'll figure out what I'm doing wrong in my marriage."

"Your mama told me you married Paul out of my stupid expectations and out of duty to the family. That was unbelievable to me. Even though I told you not to worry about Oak Hollow, your determination to marry Paul made me think you loved him. You go pack your clothes and come home."

Abe's eyes misted, touching her more than any of the words he'd spoken. "Lots of people stay in marriages without loving each other. Thank you for offering to let me come back, but I have to stay with Paul since we're married."

"No, you don't. This matter will be settled tomorrow. The time has come for me to pay Paul a visit, and we'll see how *he* looks in black and blue."

"No, please don't do that. Let me talk to him."

"Okay, but if he hits you again, John Scott's going to know, once I drag his son through the streets in front of the whole town. One more payment, and we're out of debt to that bank. So don't worry about my problems." Abe smoothed her hair away from her face.

She smiled. It felt good to be back home with the comforting smells drifting out of the kitchen, and the happy and peaceful atmosphere even in the midst of turmoil. She longed to walk along the river but knew she should go home before Paul returned from work.

* * *

Grace pulled the buggy into the carriage house and entered her home through the back door. Paul wasn't there. What a relief. She was glad Jim had told her father about Paul's behavior, but she hated for Abe to worry. Just as she started making dinner, she heard Paul's carriage approaching the house.

Running to the parlor, she poured him a drink and was standing by the front door when he entered. "Hello, Paul," she said, flashing him a fake smile. "You're home a little early today, but it won't be long until dinner."

"Why are you cooking? Where's that nigger?"

"I told you," she said, trying to sound calm, though her heart was pounding. "She has a bad illness, and I don't want us to get sick from it. She may die." She handed him the drink.

He took it, gulped it down, and turned to her. "You know what, Grace? I don't want your cooking. You're a lot of things, but you're not a cook, and I won't eat it. We have slaves. They should work, but you're too soft on them and let them lie around in bed."

Grace flinched and braced herself for the blow. It didn't come.

Instead, Paul sneered at her, shaking his head. "I'm going to the Gentlemen's Club. Don't wait up for me."

Grace knew he'd be drunk and stagger in later that night which was fine with her. She ate by herself. Lighting a couple of candles, she pretended Jim and Lizzie were sitting beside her. She carried on a conversation with them as if there were no more slaves, and whites and Negroes were equal. The fantasy made her laugh out loud. Her play-acting relieved the almost intolerable stress bestowed upon her by a marriage which never should have happened. Grace felt free from her own slavery as she rose from the table, waved her hands and moved her feet to a beat playing in her head. Holding a tall glass of lemonade in the air, she twirled and bowed as she danced with it. The glass became Jim. What a life she'd created for herself where memories became a momentary reality.

Grace settled in bed early, basking in the freedom of aloneness. Unfortunately her enjoyment was short-lived as Paul entered the house. Most of the time after going to the club, he came home drunk, stumbling and bumping into furniture before making his way upstairs. Tonight was an exception. He was quiet when he came home and ascended the stairs with surefooted finesse. When he opened the door to the bedroom, Grace tensed. "Hello, Paul. Did you have a pleasant evening?"

"So, you're awake." His concern sounded genuine.

"Yes, I've been waiting for you."

"Well, I'm here now, and we need to talk." He undressed, throwing on a blue silk nightshirt. "You've mentioned you'd like to go to Cork, and since Joseph is going so soon, why don't you go with him? You could see your homeland and have a nice visit before coming back. By that time, everything will be in place for me to take over the bank. With a little persuasion, I'm sure Father will retire."

Grace sensed an underlying hostility and nervousness in Paul's voice, but chose not to acknowledge the change, waiting to see what else was on his mind. "Going to Cork would be wonderful but not fair to you since we've been married such a short time. And Joe won't be ready to go until a day or two after Christmas."

"Then go with your mother. And don't worry about me. I have so much work to do, learning new things and organizing accounts that I wouldn't be here much, anyway. If Lizzie doesn't get well, we need to sell her. As far as meals, the Gentlemen's Club prepares excellent food."

"Let me think about it." Paul drew her to him, gave her a tender kiss, and released her. Why didn't he demand a physical encounter? Why did he want her to go to Ireland? If only she could talk to Jim, he could make sense of the whole thing. Sleep eluded her, but going outside at night here wasn't the same as it was at Oak Hollow. She stayed inside.

CHAPTER TWENTY-SEVEN

Abe saw John Scott drive up in his buggy. "Morning." Abe was puzzled at such an early morning visit.

"Good morning, Abraham. You're aware of why I'm here, aren't you?"

"No, not exactly, but after speaking to Sarah the other day, we decided to make it a point to have you and Louise visit us more often now that our children are married. Maybe you had the same thoughts?" Abe couldn't stand the Scotts, especially knowing how violent Paul had become toward Gracie, but he wouldn't breathe a word about that until the time was right.

"I'm here to repossess the plantation. Neither Paul nor I want to do this because of Grace, but business is business." He got out of the buggy.

"What on earth are you talking about?" Bewilderment clouded Abe's face.

"Since you haven't made one payment, not one, on the loan we made you when you put up this place as collateral, I'm here to repossess it. Simple as that."

"Wait a minute. I never put Oak Hollow up as collateral. Paul said my signature was good enough for him. Besides, the loan is paid in full. Ask Paul. He took my checks. When he wanted to lend me more money, I refused. Instead, because of Matt's foolishness, I just bought half the amount of cotton seed from the original loan."

"Before Paul left the bank yesterday, at my insistence, he finally told me when he asked you to put down a little good faith money, you said he owed you something for Grace's hand, so he had to insist on your putting up Oak Hollow."

"What? That makes no sense, whatsoever."

"We've been friends a long time. I wish there was some other way."

"Will you give me a little more time to see what's going on? There's a terrible mistake. Maybe tomorrow Paul and I can make some sense out of this."

John hesitated, but agreed. They shook hands on it before he left.

Abe walked into the house and sat in his study. Why would Paul say those things? As a father, he hated Paul for what he'd done to Grace, but that had nothing to do with business. Paul surely wasn't being vindictive because he had no idea Abe knew about the beatings. He'd go tomorrow and demand to see the payment checks in the bank statements Paul had been holding. That would prove payment, and everything would be resolved.

He started pacing. Meanwhile, he had more pressing things to worry about than the plantation. Thinking about the letter he'd received in yesterday's mail, a stabbing pain hit him, causing him to career against the door.

The noise alerted Lavitica June and Miss Daisy, who had just come into the main house from making preserves in the kitchen. Daisy sent Lavitica June back to the kitchen for the whiskey bottle reserved for cooking. Mary and Sarah had reached Abe first and managed to get him to the sofa as Miss Daisy shuffled in and took over. She opened the bottle, placing it to his lips.

"Drink, Massa," she ordered.

Abe complied without hesitating.

"Lavitica June, go find Jim. Have him go for Doc." Sarah's voice was stern.

"No, that won't be necessary. The pain's gone now, and I need to have a serious talk with Miss Sarah. All you women are more than enough doctoring for one man, anyhow." Smiling, he scooted them out of the room, motioning Sarah to a chair. "No matter what happens to me, I want you to always think of me as a good man, a man who loved his wife and family very much."

Sarah rushed to him, putting her small, pale hand over his mouth. She was frightened by his words. Was his health issue worse than he'd let on? Had he been hiding pain since his sick spell? "Don't be talking like that." All of this had to do with the secret, and she needed to find out what was troubling her sweet husband. "Something's bothering you, has been for a long time. We had a good crop this year, you paid off the loan, and our daughters are married and settled. Matthew's getting better, and Joseph is thinking about his future. What else could we want, darling?"

"That's just it. You don't know what happened today and what's been going on under our noses. I'm going to go see Paul tomorrow morning and get this straightened out. When I come back, we'll have a private lunch. There are things I've kept from you for longer than you know." Abe got up and walked out to the barn to clear his head from the stuffiness of the house.

Sarah's curiosity gave her an uneasy feeling that something monumental was about be revealed, but there was a certain peace in knowing she'd find out the secret that had wedged itself between her and Abe almost from the time they'd arrived at Oak Hollow.

*   *   *

Abraham Sullivan walked into the bank and saw John Scott sitting behind his desk wearing a scowl as he talked with Paul, who sat across from him.

"Good morning, Abe," John said, changing his expression as fast as a chameleon could change its colors.

"Morning."

Paul squirmed in his seat. "Good morning, Mister Sullivan."

"Now Paul, is that any way to greet your father-in-law? No need to be so formal. Isn't that what you said the other day? That we're family? So let's sit down and talk."

"My office is next door, Mister Sulli . . . I mean, Abe." Paul rose and extended his hand.

Abe refused the phony gesture. "No, that's not necessary. We can settle this right here in a short time. When you came to me and said you'd manage my affairs and watch out after my interests following my sick spell, a sense of relief washed over me like a cleansing breath of spring. I thought you'd been sent from the good Lord above. How reassuring to know my new son along with my first-born would take care of the plantation and my Sarah in case something happened to me.

When you mentioned keeping my statements at the bank in case we had a fire at the house, given the one we'd had in the field earlier, that seemed reasonable as well. You gained my trust, Paul, and making payments to you gave me a sense of closeness, of family. The check numbers are all recorded, but I can't produce them since you hold the records. John says there are no payments reflected on the note, and that you said none had been made. Give me my statements back, now, and tell me what happened to the checks I wrote you for the note. Obviously you weren't sent by God. He doesn't send cheaters and liars!"

At Abe's scathing look, Paul diverted his gaze, lowering his eyes, but not before Abe saw the cold, calculating, tempest of anger boiling just below the surface of the young man's face.

John rose. "That's uncalled for, Abraham. You will not speak to Paul that way."

"Until he finds my payments, he's cheating me." Abe fought to keep control. He needed to be careful so as not to put Grace in more jeopardy.

Regaining his composure, Paul raised his head and looked directly into Abraham's eyes, man to man. "So that's what this is about. I'm sure there's been some kind of error. If you'll give me some time, we'll get to the bottom of it. Don't worry. I'll check the statements again, and in the meantime, I'm sure we can extend the note for a few days. By that time, it should be straightened out."

"No, I want my bank statements along with my balance right now."

"Please calm down. Let me go through the records for the last several months. Then, I'll turn everything over to you. I'm sure there's been an oversight, which will be easily corrected."

Abe thought it over. The logical thing to do would be to give Paul the benefit of the doubt and allow him to rectify his mistake. That would also give him time to face Sarah. He had to get out of the bank, out of the vision of deceit Paul exuded. Money and the plantation were not his priority at the moment. Talking to Sarah was.

Paul followed Abe out of John's office. "One more thing before you go. My wonderful wife would love to go to Cork for a visit. I've suggested she go with Joseph, but she said he would have to wait until after Christmas. Perhaps Missus Sullivan would go with her. Grace has taken on a lot of causes, and she needs some rest. After all, we may be starting a family soon, and she should go while she can. This trip could be my special present to two of my favorite ladies." A phony smile took up most of his face.

Abe felt uncomfortable. When something wasn't quite right, little prickly feelings popped up on the back of his neck, and they were starting now along with uneasiness in his gut. Rather than dealing with the issue, he said, "Let me talk to them, but you know women." Abe couldn't wait to get outside. The atmosphere had gone stale in the bank, and he felt as if he were choking.

* * *

After Abe left, John called Paul into his office. "Why did you tell Abraham there might have been a mistake?"

"Merely trying to avoid a scene, Father. What would my life be like with my wife if that had happened? If Grace and Sarah go to Ireland for a while, perhaps Abe will listen to me and understand the gravity of the situation. Even though his attitude upsets me, my making a few payments to tide him over might help, but for my wife's sake, I don't want his dignity destroyed. If only this could have been worked out before you visited him."

"That's very honorable and just the thing I'd expect from you, my fine son. Though it's only a formality, let me ask. Are you telling me the truth about the whole situation?"

Paul's posture and the beads of sweat that broke out on his forehead indicated nervousness. "What do you mean? Of course, I'm truthful. Abraham Sullivan thinks he can do no wrong. Oak Hollow means nothing to me, but it might be nice for Grace to live there one of these days, and it'd knock Mister Sullivan off his towering pedestal, I'd say."

John didn't like his son's tone, nor could he imagine why Paul would want to hurt Abraham. Had Louise been influencing Paul again? The two of them had exhibited some mild jealousy toward the Sullivans over the past few months, but John hadn't confronted them since they were so hard to live with when they were upset. He turned toward his son. "Fine, see what you can find in Abe's records, and let me know."

Paul stood, still visibly shaken as he left his father's office. "I will."

* * *

Abraham entered the parlor where his wife was sewing buttons on a flannel work shirt. He walked over to her, took her chin in his hand, and raised it so her eyes met his. "Time to talk, Sarah."

His voice sounded tired. "I told Daisy we'd eat on the porch. That seems to be your favorite place for discussions, and the servants can't hear us."

"Good idea. You go ahead. I'll be there in a minute." Abe disappeared into his study. Taking a smooth key from his pocket, he opened the drawer to his desk, the one that held his secret and his future. With shaking hands, he removed a packet of letters bound with string, holding them to his chest for a moment. Stuffing them into the pocket of his black leather coat, he walked to the back porch to join his wife.

Sarah wore a heavy, hunter-green shawl over her shoulders. Draped in front, it accentuated her beautiful face, emphasizing her pale skin and blonde hair highlighted by only a few strands of silvery-white. The illumination from the rays of the winter sun gave her an ethereal appearance, but her presence still sent Abraham's body reeling as it had done all of their married life.

He sat down to a meal of fried chicken, potato salad, and green beans, toying with the food before speaking. "We're truly American. Never thought I'd look forward to fried chicken!"

Sarah reached across the table and patted his arm. "That's true, but part of me will always consider Cork home." They finished their meal in silence.

The time had come. He placed his hand over his heart and gazed at Sarah.

"What's the matter? Are you in pain? Is it your chest?" She jumped to her feet.

"No, sit down please. There are so many things, it's hard to know where to begin."

"Start with what's bothering you right this minute, and go from there."

"You're so practical, my sweet Sarah." He drew in a deep breath of fresh air, hoping his lungs could take in enough of the rich oxygen to clear his cluttered mind. "First of all, you know the relief that paying off a debt brings me. John Scott came by yesterday and told me they have no record of having received any payment on the loan. He wanted to repossess the house and land right then. You know I'd never pledge our home for money to finance a crop. Naturally, I was furious and questioned Paul this morning. Since he's married Grace, he's been taking care of our affairs, but he never asked me to put up the house or the lands of Oak Hollow as collateral, yet John insists that's what is shown on the note. None of this makes sense because the last few times we've sold cotton, I've made double or triple payments. According to my records, the note is paid in full."

Daisy came out, removed their plates, placing hot coffee in front of them.

Abe paused and drank some of the fresh brew. "After John's visit, to prove this place wasn't put up as collateral, I went to my desk to find the deed. It's gone. Can't find it anywhere."

"Maybe you moved it and don't remember."

"No, it's always been in a tin box inside the top right hand drawer. But there's something else. When that sick spell landed me in bed, I was afraid I'd die and wanted to make sure someone would be able to manage this place for you. Paul offered to keep our statements and watch over our financial affairs until Matt gained enough strength to take over the plantation. He promised he'd discuss any decisions that needed to be made with Matt and you. He took a big burden off of me, so I agreed. Besides that, he had earned my trust as if he were my own son. Since that fire we had, losing records has concerned me, so I've continued to let him manage our finances. I'd periodically ask for the balance, and the amount he told me always matched my records, so I didn't worry."

"This is probably a simple mistake."

"What if Paul can't produce the canceled checks? I keep a ledger here to show our bank balance and the deduction for the payments. So what happened to the money? Did he take it? Why would he do something like that? He doesn't need the money, and what would he do with this plantation? You'd think he'd be happy we paid off the loan seven months early. They've extended the note a few days in order for Paul to look into it, but something tells me, he won't find anything. He wants this plantation for some reason which escapes me."

"They'll find the mistake, and everything will be back to normal in a day or two." Sarah knew Paul adored Grace and would never do anything to hurt any of them.

"That may be. We'll deal with it later. Right now, I want you to listen without interrupting. This is a nightmare."

Sarah put her hands in her lap. By the look on his face, she had a sinking feeling a hole was going to open up and suck her inside. A dark, ugly foreboding engulfed her. Her wedding ring caught her eye, and she concentrated on it, turning it over and over while she waited for the secret that sounded so ominous.

"Paul's been hurting Grace. She asked Jim to help her slaves run away because of Paul's cruelty to them. She was afraid he'd kill them. Jim only confided this information to me when he noticed some bruises on Grace's skin. I cornered her when she came by the other morning and made her talk to me. She confirmed it. Sarah, she married that contemptible, overbearing, pious, lying man to save our souls and this plantation. I listened to her words instead of my heart telling me how she felt about him. Now for some reason, Paul wants to send you and Grace to Ireland for a visit. He's devious and up to no good."

Sarah let Abe's words sink in. She wanted to kill Paul. Thoughts of his attention to Grace and his persistent begging her to marry him made all of this revelation seem unreal. Her head was spinning, but she regained her equilibrium before speaking. "There's a solution. We'll pack up Grace, Matthew, Mary, and Luke, and go home to Cork. We still have our land there, the famine is over, and we'll make a living just fine. If Maggie and Charles want to join us, that'll be wonderful. Since Joseph's going to medical school there, Becca could live with us. We'll make sure all the servants are safe here, and then Paul can have this whole plantation. I'll start preparations in the morning."

"Wait, you don't understand."

Sarah sat back down. There couldn't be more. Abe's face told a different story.

CHAPTER TWENTY-EIGHT

From the inside pocket of his coat, Abe produced the letters. Holding them between his broad hands, his thumbs rubbed over the front of them. His voice was low. "There's no land to go back to, Sarah."

"What do you mean?"

"The land no longer belongs to me. It belongs to Sean O'Malley."

"Who's he, and when did you sell it?" she demanded, confusion swirling through her head.

"This is the hardest thing I'll ever have to say, and the worst thing you'll ever have to hear." Abe's eyes misted, and he wiped his nose with his sleeve as he had done when he was a youngster. "You remember when we were courting in Cork? How I used to drink so much?"

"Yes. Thank goodness, you don't drink very much any longer."

"A couple of months before we got married, my friends threw me a big party in that small pub around the corner from the church."

Sarah nodded.

"Besides my male friends, there were some nice girls there, too. Some of them were friends, some strangers. Of all the new girls, there was one who looked so sad. She'd just moved to town and didn't know anyone except the girl who brought her. Bridget was her name, and everyone tried to cheer her up. We walked outside together, talking and sharing some drinks. She told me about being beaten by her father, and that's why the family left him and came to Cork. Of course, she knew about our upcoming wedding since that was the reason for the party. We kept drinking, and the next thing I knew, Sarah . . . I just can't tell you." He put his hands to his head and shook with such overwhelming sorrow, Sarah was afraid he was going to die.

"What, Abe? What happened?" Sarah felt a slow bonfire of anger forming in the depths of her being and struggled to keep it from erupting. She took a deep breath and stared at the river.

"The next morning, we woke up together in a little out of the way lodge. Neither of us had ever been there before, but we were heartsick. She'd never been with a man, and I was engaged to you. Though we couldn't remember anything, we hoped against all hope that nothing had happened. That we'd just passed out. But we were naked. There were still a couple of months before the wedding, which would be plenty of time to find out if she were carrying my child. I saw her twice before you and I got married, and both times, she assured me everything was fine. I married you, Sarah, full of guilt and remorse for what I'd done. But praying for forgiveness, I swore never to get that drunk again. That promise has never been broken." Abe rose and started pacing.

Sarah sat as still as a marble column, trying to comprehend what her husband had said. At last, she found the strength to move. She straightened her dress with mechanical hands. She did the same with her hair. Straightening everything she could because there were some things that could never be fixed or straightened out again. Abe had dropped his burden in her lap, and she didn't know if she could hold the weight. He was speaking again and she forced her mind to concentrate.

"I didn't see her again until we'd been married for a year. You were carrying Matthew. Then one day Bridget appeared on the edge of the bog. She looked as if she were an apparition. She cradled a baby wrapped in a blanket. My son." Abe stopped, waiting for some response from his wife.

Sarah sat unmoving and unemotional. "And?"

"And she told me she'd named him Sean and given him her name of O'Malley. Her family disinherited her, but she worked to support herself and rear him. I helped her with finances and saw the boy every week when I'd go to town. I wanted him to know his father, though I couldn't give him my name. The last time I saw him was two days before we sailed."

Sarah rose and turned. Looking straight ahead, she was about to enter the house.

"Wait, Sarah, there's more."

Her eyes glazed with ice. "More? You have more confessions, Abraham? What else have you done behind my back? Is it not enough to break my heart in two? Now you want to shatter it into pieces? Maybe your confessions are good for your soul, but what about my heart, Abraham? Shall we trade places? Your heart for mine?"

"I deserve that, Sarah." His body blocked her from going into the house and with a gentle hand pushed her back into the chair. "When we left Cork, I gave Sean and his mother enough money to go to England until the famine passed, and I also put the Irish land in trust for him until he was of age with his mother as administrator. That was the least I could do."

Sarah shifted in her chair. Nausea rose in her throat, but she forced herself to concentrate on Abe's words.

"We've been writing, and he wants to come for a visit. Sean believes it's time to reveal the secret, and I agree with him because I'm weary of keeping everything inside. He's on his way and will rent a carriage in Vicksburg, once he gets there. I don't know the exact day of his arrival, but you will be civil to him, won't you? My sins are not his fault."

Abe dropped to one knee, taking Sarah's hands into his own. "Can you ever forgive me? I'm so sorry for what I've done, but regret even more that I had to tell you. Yet it isn't fair for you not to know. I love you, Sweetheart, more than anything. I've thought many times of ending my life rather than having to tell you what a horrible thing I'd done."

Sarah pulled her hands away, rising and turning before he could see the seething hatred flowing from her eyes. She spoke without facing him. "You've made a mockery of our marriage, and now our children have no heritage. We have one in a wheeled chair and one who's being beaten, and all you can do is tell me some tale from a drunken party that produced your first-born son. So the boy...the man is coming here. Is that why you decided to confess, Abraham? What about me and my firstborn son? What shall we tell our children? My identity is gone. I don't know you or myself, anymore. I do know, I don't like you very much right now."

Opening the door, Sarah entered the kitchen that smelled like the cherry cobbler Miss Daisy had cooling. The room felt cozy and warm from the embers of the wood-burning stove, but Sarah was chilled to the bone, shivers playing a scale up and down her spine. She accepted the cup of tea Daisy poured her without a word. Perhaps, the whole scene had been a bad dream, but it seemed too real. She had to think. Taking her tea upstairs to Maggie's bedroom, she sat in the middle of the bed and held the cup, both hands wrapped around the warm porcelain. Her gaze took in all the details of the room…her room, now. Never again would she share a bedroom with Abraham Sullivan. Her marriage, as she had known it, was over.

Jim walked onto the porch, surprised that Abe was so deep in thought he didn't appear to hear him. "Massa?"

"Yes, Jim?"

"I don' want to overstep my boun's, but I don' trust that Paul fella. Would you let me borry one of your horses to foller him ever' night and see where he goes? I's 'fraid he's up to no good and feel someone needs to watch Miss Grace's house in case he tries to hurt her again. I kin do my job in the daytime and still keep an eye out for her at night. That is, iffen you want me to."

Abe motioned for Jim to sit down, and even though he was young and an employee, Abe felt grateful for someone to listen. He relayed the strange feelings he got around Paul and spilled the details about the Scotts trying to repossess Oak Hollow but couldn't bring himself to mention Sean. "So if you want to take a horse and check on my Gracie, I'd appreciate that."

Jim rode fast and hard. Now that twilight was fading, he wanted to know where Paul Scott spent his time. What was he was doing when he wasn't at home or work? Suspecting he might be at the Gentleman's Club, Jim rode down the street to the back of the building. Paul's carriage stood in plain sight. Creeping behind a hedge flanking one of the windows, Jim watched Paul's activities. He appeared to be drunk and yelled for more liquor and something to eat.

A young darkie brought him a light supper, which seemed to calm him. Although Jim couldn't hear what was being said, he noticed the boy was shaking his head so hard he almost lost his balance. Paul grabbed him by the arm and dragged him outside. The boy was wailing, struggling to get free, but Paul slapped him across the face with the back of his hand. The little body went limp for a few moments. Jim changed positions to get a clearer view.

He heard the boy's ululated crying while Paul cursed. "Shut up, you dumb darkie." Paul stumbled, taking the boy down with him, stripping off his clothes. Jim knew the truth at last. Lunging at Paul, he shouted to the boy, "Run! Run!"

Jim fought with a vengeance he didn't recognize as his own until Paul fell and stopped moving. The tormented screaming of the young boy reverberated in Jim's head as he raced to get Grace out of her house.

Answering the door, she looked more beautiful than Jim had ever seen her. The flowing, white dress and flickering light from the lanterns in the parlor gave her an angelic appearance, and she appeared to float as she moved to let him inside. "What a surprise. Come in."

Jim shook his head, bringing himself back to the present. "Go around to the back. Hurry. We've got to talk." He moved his horse to her back yard.

"What is it?"

He gave her a quick rundown of what had transpired at the bank and what Paul had attempted to do to the young darkie. "I'm worried about you." He tried to calm his shaking hands.

"Don't be," she said, touching his arm. "This explains a lot of things. Paul never pressures me to do…the wife thing." She blushed. "No wonder, he's been aloof. You should leave, though, before he finds you here. Is Miss Lizzie safe?"

"Yes, everyone's fine. I'm staying in your barn tonight to keep an eye on him. If you need me, all you have to do is yell. Better yet, let me take you home, the home where you belong."

"No, I've handled Paul many times, so I know what to do. You're so sweet and kind, but don't worry about me." She gave him a quick hug, pushing him toward his horse. "Hurry before Paul comes home."

Jim mounted his horse. "You can't stay married to this man. He's going to kill you!"

"I need some time to collect my thoughts and make plans. He's talking about sending me to Ireland. Maybe I'll go for a while, but you must get out of here."

* * *

Paul woke up, staggered back into the club, grabbed his bottle, and somehow climbed onto his carriage, not even aware of where his home was. The voices in his head were becoming more pronounced. They wanted him to die and to kill everyone with him. As his mare made her way home, he saw the lights in the parlor shining through the thin, shimmering, white curtains flowing in the breeze from open windows. Paul managed to get up the steps and across the porch to the front door. He hated the curtains. They were going to blow around him, choking him and then become wrappings for his dead body. That's what the sneering voices said.

"Grace!" he screeched at the top of his voice. "Come here!" To Paul's psychotic mind, instead of Grace wearing a white dress, she appeared to be wearing the curtains, the same flowing, white death clothes. No, they weren't curtains. They were twisted white ropes, and he hated her for what she could do to him with them.

Paul put his hands on either side of his head, attempting to stop the voices confusing and frightening him.

As Grace approached her husband, she noticed his cut and swollen face. His clothes were torn, dirty, and covered in blood. This was the result from the fight he and Jim had, but she acted unaware of the situation. "What happened to you?"

She'd never seen him like this. His eyes held a mad, crazed look, and he was acting strange, even for him. Fear crept up her spine taking goose bumps with it as it traveled to the area of her throat where it lodged. She grabbed her neck, realizing she would choke at any minute. Why hadn't she let Jim stay?

"Someone attacked me! I fought back, but you've stolen my thoughts!" He was screaming and appeared to be talking to a nonexistent person.

Paul lurched into the parlor, and with one swoop, grabbed the curtains and tore them from their rods. The rank odor coming from him repulsed her. Fumbling with buttons, he tried to get out of his clothes, cursing at the top of his lungs. Grace pulled him away from the windows out of sight of people passing by, but he pushed her aside and managed to remove the rest of his garments. Paul Scott stood naked in front of the biggest window in his house, facing the street with his arms spread wide, a bottle in one hand and a dark, evil smile on his face.

"See me!" he yelled. "See Paul Scott, the soon to be president of the bank. Take a look, all you small town fools."

Grace ran to the foyer's hall tree, grabbed her shawl, and attempted to drape it around his waist to cover him.

"Leave me alone, you whore," he sneered. He grabbed her dress at the neck and ripped it down to the hemline. The elegant white gown puddled at his wife's feet, as soft snow would do.

Grace dared not move. Paul seemed to have acquired superhuman strength. She felt his puffy, blue-white, long-nailed hand groping for her thin, everyday chemise. Latching onto a strap, he forced the undergarment down around her hips, leaving a long, bleeding gash on her skin. After he stripped her of the last garment and all her dignity, he physically forced her to stand with him. Grace prayed like she'd never done before, for her safety and for no one to see them. "Paul, please, everyone can see us naked." She tried to position herself, so she wasn't quite so visible through the window.

He shoved her, pinned her against the wall with his body and squeezed her face with his free hand. Grace could barely breathe. His face was inches from hers. She was the reason for the voices, and he'd tell them a thing or two. "You're a whore 'cause you never loved me and never gave me a child. And you're all crazy. Shut up!" Paul took a long drink from his bottle, "I've found plenty of people to satisfy me. I don't care who it is. A young boy or an old woman. They're all the same. Understand me, whore? Miss Pure and Better'n I am? Well, you're not, and as of today, I own you and your plantation. Want to go home, Little Princess? Home to your poor, broken down, old papa?"

He was weaving, and Grace waited, praying he would pass out. "You've been drinking. Let me help you." She moved him toward the stairs. The secrets he continued to blurt out appalled Grace, but she was too terrified to try to sort truth from fantasy. She'd never seen her husband this way. Paul crumpled in a heap at the foot of the stairs.

The voices and strange surroundings had abated to a dull roar, but they were still there. Crawling up the stairs, he shouted above the hallucinations. "Everything would've been fine, but your father had to come into the bank and make a fool of Paul Scott. Nobody gets away with that." Halfway up the staircase, he turned his bottle up to drink, but it was empty. "Go! Get my friend," he commanded.

Grace rushed to the parlor. Running back, she handed him a full bottle. Please pass out, she silently begged. Helping him to his feet at the head of the stairs and supporting him as he made his way to the bed, Grace yanked back the covers, hoping he'd collapse into oblivion. Instead of lying down, he sat there, holding onto his bottle, swaying back and forth.

The voices were replaced by an uncontrollable fury. He hated everyone except his mother and vowed to return to her fold, just the two of them. "I wanted you to go away, but no, you wouldn't go, so you can certainly stay here and see the show, Little Lady."

"What show are you talking about?"

"What show? My papa's going to have an accident. I'll take his place. Your papa lost his plantation today, thanks to me, so he'll have to go, too because he made my father suspect me. Want to bury 'em side by side?"

He laughed with a deep, guttural sound that seemed to come from the very bowels of a soul trapped in hell. If he'd breathed fire from his nose and sprouted horns, it wouldn't have surprised Grace.

"You want to be the High Queen of the Sullivan Plantation? You shall have your wish, my little harlot. We're going to live there. I can't wait to beat some sense into your slaves. Did you ever see skin come off in long threads? It looks so funny."

He threw his head back and made a noise that filled Grace with a fear she didn't even know existed. Unspeakable terror tensed every muscle of her body, and she tasted it on her tongue. Backing away, she looked around for something, anything, to hit him with. Paul sprang from the bed, snatched her hair, forcing her to stand on the white rug at the foot of the bed. He stumbled over to the dressing table and picked up a brush with his free hand.

"Don't you ever back away from me. Brush your hair," he demanded. "I hate how it looks."

Grace brushed and cried at the same time. Between sobs, she begged, "Please, let me put you to bed."

"No! You're not going to do anything with me, except what I say. Get on your knees. Now." he bellowed, hitting the bottle on a chest. The force of the blow caused it to break into two jagged pieces.

Grace knelt as he ordered but raised her eyes, pleading with him, trying to talk sense into him. He took a handful of her hair, pulling with all his might, laughing as she screamed in pain. A million thoughts went through her mind. What could she do? Where was Jim? She saw Paul raise his hand, holding the bottle, and watched it coming down to meet her. That was the last thing Grace Sullivan Scott saw. The clock in the downstairs hall registered well past midnight when Paul, his anger sated, left his house, naked and carrying a full bottle of the finest Irish whiskey.

CHAPTER TWENTY-NINE

Jim rode slowly back to Oak Hollow, thoughts heavy on his mind. Grace needed protecting, but he didn't have a right to go against her wishes. She'd always told him she could handle Paul, but seeing the incident with the young boy, Jim knew she was in danger and no match for a madman. Maybe not tonight, but sometime soon, Paul would snap, and Grace could die. Stopping at the circle, he went to the heart to think. As he bent to clear the weeds and dead grass from the stones, Grace's frightened face appeared through what appeared to be white clouds. He had no choice but to return to her home, whether she liked it or not. He couldn't let her die.

*   *   *

The front door stood wide open, no lights burned, and Paul's carriage was gone. Jim entered with dread and caution, calling Grace's name. No answer. Lighting a lantern, he noticed curtains and clothes all over the floor in the parlor. Puzzled, an unknown dread rising in his chest, he looked left and right before rushing upstairs. He paused on the landing, listening for sounds of life. Nothing. Pushing the door, he entered the first bedroom and reeled backward, almost fainting from shock. He struggled to hold the lantern until he could put it down.

Grace lay in a heap on the floor, naked. She was covered in blood, her face so swollen he didn't recognize her at first, and a huge, jagged gash in her head lay open, oozing blood into her hair and onto the white rug now dyed dark crimson. If Jim hadn't known her, he would've thought she was a Negro from the dark bruises covering her body. He was too late. His beloved had died a horrible death, and Jim couldn't stand it.

He grabbed a robe to cover her bare body, and then put his head in his hands. Wailing, his heart broken, Jim prayed to join her. When release didn't come, he picked up his precious Grace to hold her one last time before taking her home. As he lifted her, she stirred and a moan escaped her lips. She was alive! He gently placed her on her bed and covered her. Running as fast as he could, he mounted his horse and sped straight to Doc Bradley's house. He sprung to the door, yelling and beating on it.

"What's going on?" Doc opened the door, rubbing sleep from his eyes.

"It's Miss Grace, Doc. She's done been beat up real bad. Please, come quick before she dies!" Jim was covered in blood, trembling like a building about to topple in an earthquake.

The physician threw on his pants, grabbed his bag, and rode double with Jim to the house.

Very few things upset Doc, but Jim could tell he was having a hard time examining Grace.

"When did you find her, Boy?"

"Jes' a few minutes ago. Massa Sullivan ast me to check on her 'cuz Massa Paul's been acting strange. Is she alive?"

"Yes, but go hitch up her buggy and hurry! We've got to get her to my clinic."

Jim bolted down the stairs and out to the barn. Bringing the buggy to the front, he rushed upstairs to carry her down as gently as he could.

Blowing out the lantern before he slammed the door, Doc drove while Jim held Grace. When they arrived at the clinic, Jim placed her on a white bed in a small room illuminated by a lantern placed on a bedside table.

"You'd better go for her folks. She's in bad shape. Tell them to hurry if they want to see her alive." He began working on her, assisted by his wife who had readied the room.

Jim drove the buggy back to Grace's house, jumped on his horse, and raced as fast as it would carry him. How was he going to tell her parents? What was he going to tell his heart? He chanted and prayed all the way. "Hold on, Grace. Hold on, Grace."

* * *

Jim ran to the Sullivan's, pounding on the front door, calling to Abe. "Massa Sullivan. Please wake up! Massa! Massa!"

Abe lit a lamp and peered through the etched glass of the front door. Jim knew the light blinded him, so he called out again, "It's me, Jim. Come quick!"

Abe, sensing the urgency in Jim's voice, threw on his robe and ran outside. The young man stood on the verandah, breathless and smelling of blood. "What in the world's the matter? You could wake the whole plantation with that hollering."

Jim thought Abe smelled like whiskey, but he didn't take time to ponder the situation. "Massa, we gots to go."

"Go where? Calm down. Tell me what's happened. Is it Grace?"

"Yas, suh, Miss Grace's been hurt bad. Doc says hurry fast. I be tellin' you what happened on the way. You get Miss Sarah while I bring the buggy. Hurry!"

Abraham ran upstairs and pounded on Maggie's door. "Sarah?"

"Go away. This is my room now, and you're not welcome."

She still sounded mechanical. Abe pounded harder and yelled louder. "Grace's been hurt. There's no time to waste!"

The door flew open. Sarah had never undressed. She brushed past him, ran down the stairs, grabbed her shawl, and was on the verandah before Abraham could even get his pants on.

Jim drove the buggy to the front and helped Sarah into the back seat. Abe scrambled onto the seat beside Jim and they sped away at a full run. Shouting above the pounding hooves, Jim gave Abe a shortened version of what had happened.

"Massa Paul tried to do some bad things to a young boy, but he run away when I hit Massa Paul. I went to see Miss Grace, and she tole me she could handle Massa Paul. But when I got back home, I had a bad feelin' and went back, and now she's hurt real bad." Jim didn't mention she might die. He couldn't bring himself to say the words.

* * *

When they reached Doc's home clinic, he ushered Abe and Sarah into a small room. Grace lay still on a white bed, her face, arms and hands covered with bruises and cuts, her face swollen and unrecognizable and her head wrapped in a turban of white guaze. Sarah collapsed. Abe caught her and laid her on a sofa while Doc crossed the room to get a cold compress for her. Jim stood just inside the door, wringing his hands.

"Grace's lost a lot of blood in this brutal beating. If Jim hadn't found her when he did, she would've died in a short time. She's still critical."

Jim felt his life force being pushed out of him as the pain Grace must've suffered before lapsing into darkness, twisted him in agony. He had to get outside.

"What can we do for her, Doc?" Abe brushed his hands through his hair on both sides of his temples.

"I'll keep her here. I couldn't even do a proper examination because of her condition, but I got her cleaned up and the bleeding stopped. I don't know if she has any broken bones or what her internal condition is, but she's safe here. If she regains consciousness, and when some of the swelling goes down, I'll be able to tell more. But you need to be prepared. She could slip away from us at any time. Any idea who did this?"

Abe relayed Paul's violence toward Grace over the last few weeks ending with Jim's account of the attack on the young darkie. "When she's able, I'm taking her home with us. Paul Sullivan will never see her again."

Abe's tired voice masked a controlled anger, but Doc didn't blame him. No one should see another person in this condition, much less one's own child. "I suspected as much when I saw her. Rumors have been flying around about Paul's behavior. Now, it's easy to believe them. There's pretty strong evidence he either has no conscience, may be insane, or both. I haven't treated the darkies, but I've heard some horrible tales." He shook his head.

Grace stirred and moaned, sending all three to her bedside. Abe bent over his daughter, whispering soothing words to her. She seemed to relax and became quiet once more.

Sarah stood on the other side of the bed, tears streaming down her face, with a heart so heavy, she feared it would break from the sheer weight of all the burdens heaped upon her. She took her first-born daughter's hand and silently beseeched God to heal her.

Checking her pulse and breathing, Doc eased from the room leaving Abe and Sarah alone with Grace.

Abe tried to convince Sarah to go home and come back later, but she wouldn't hear of it.

She sat down to maintain a vigil for as long as it took for her daughter to recover. "I'm staying here, Abraham. I don't really have a home now. My daughter needs me, and I'll be by her side until she's well. If you want to do something, ask Lavitica June to pack some clothes for me, and have Jim take them to the hotel."

Abe nodded and walked outside. He wouldn't blame Sarah if she never forgave him, but he'd wait for her the rest of his life.

Jim sat in the buggy. Looking up at the sky, Abe watched dawn just beginning to break. "Let's go to Miss Maggie's."

Abe's voice steeled with determination. "I'm going to find Paul and kill him for what he's done to my Grace."

"Iffen you can't find him, Massa, I kin track him down at night and take care of that for you. Miss Grace an' this fam'ly mean an awful lot to me. After I seen what he did to her and to that boy, I don' think he needs to live."

"What exactly did he do to the boy, Jim?"

"He was trying to have his way with him, but I stopped it quick as I could git over there. I believe I knows the boy, but the bartender in that club place knows him for sure. Last I saw, that little chile was runnin' fast as he could. People says they heard Massa Paul does the same thin' to women of the evenin' and to young darkie girls. Guess he don' much care who he hurts."

"Rape is what it's called, but it doesn't matter if it has a name. It's still a horrible thing to go through, so I've been told. Doc Bradley's also heard or seen some of the same things you're talking about."

"Yas, suh."

They reached Maggie's house. She served them hot biscuits and tea, then sat quietly as Abe told her the news.

"What would we have done, Jim, if you hadn't gone to check on her?" Maggie shivered.

"Well, ma'am, after I seen Massa Paul, I become worried 'bout Miss Grace."

"You saved her life. There's no way to ever express enough gratitude for what you've done." Maggie didn't voice her opinion, but she knew it was Jim's love, prompting him to check on her that saved her sister.

"Iffen she's well and safe, tha's enough for me."

Abe finished his tea, handing the cup to Maggie. "The bank's open. We'll pay a visit to the Scotts while you go see about your mother and Grace. I'll telegraph Joe to come home. When he gets here, I want to talk to all of you. Can you and Charles come over late this afternoon?" Abe's voice reflected his mental fatigue and physical exhaustion.

"Of course. And I'll go see Mama and Grace right away, but I'm concerned about you, too."

"Don't worry about me." He bent and kissed her cheek before he and Jim headed to the buggy.

* * *

Abraham Sullivan strode into the bank with such an aggressive and authoritarian demeanor that everyone froze. He went straight to the office of the president and opened the door. "John, I'd suggest you come with me and have a look at your daughter-in-law."

"What's the matter with you?"

Abe tried to control his voice, but it got louder as he spoke. "What's the matter? Your son's a rapist and almost killed my daughter! He's swindled me out of my money, and he'll stop at nothing to get what he wants! He's crazy, John, crazy and dangerous. Do I need to go on?"

"No, of course not. But please, lower your voice. Why are you blaming all this on Paul?"

"Just come look at Grace, that's all I ask." Abe had regained some control, but he was still smoldering as he stamped from the bank, pushing John in front of him. Jim drove. Abraham stared straight ahead. John looked down at his shoes. They walked into the clinic.

John saw a badly swollen, bruised and cut face on some girl with puffy hands. "Poor girl," he said, "but where's Grace?"

"This is Grace. This is what your son did to her."

"Now wait a minute. You're a little premature on this," Haughtiness tinged John's voice.

"No, I'm not. Did you ever uncover Paul's embezzlement of my money?"

"You're upset, and I don't blame you, but Paul didn't do this to Grace. Something else must've happened, and I am quite concerned also." He paused, and the wrinkles on his face seemed to burrow their way further into his skin. "Paul didn't come to work today. I thought maybe he was sick and was going to check on him at lunchtime. Now I am wondering if they were robbed, and maybe the thieves kidnapped him. If you'll excuse me, I'm going to the sheriff and start looking for my son. I just pray Grace gets well real soon, and that I don't find my son beaten unconscious or worse." He rushed from the clinic on foot.

Abe followed him through the door and turned to Jim. "Take me to the Gentlemen's Club." When they arrived, Abraham got down and went in.

Jim saw Abe and the bartender shake their heads, looking at the floor. After a short while, Abe came out, eager to tell Jim everything. "The bartender confirmed what you've heard. Paul's been buying women for a long time. Not long ago, one of them was going to have his baby, but she was so afraid of what he'd do, she ran away to relatives in another town. She had a miscarriage, and when she came back, Paul was very mean to her. Right after that, he started doing strange things. Raping women and young Negro children, but no one said anything because Paul let it be known no one would believe them since his name was so important in town. The slaves were afraid of being beaten or killed."

"I knowed he wuz a bad man."

"He was very superstitious, too and made Phillip, he's the bartender, serve him seven drinks at once. They had to be lined up in a row of six, side by side, except for the seventh one, and it had to be behind all the others. Paul made him put a napkin over each glass and he would lift the napkin, breaking the seal as he called it. After he finished the six, he'd have the glasses taken away and make a big production of breaking the seventh seal. Phillip said he did a lot of things like that."

"Massa Abe, I don' know nuthin' much, but he and Miss Grace wuz married on the seventh of June, and yesterday wuz also the seventh day of the month."

"You're right! The number seven has something to do with Paul's thinking. He's mentioned it a lot. First time I heard about it was at Grace's sixteenth birthday party. I've just realized that's how many payments I made at the bank."

They rode in silence for a few minutes. Abraham looked old and drawn, his hands clasped as if to keep from hitting something as they stopped by the telegraph office. "Joseph should be here late this afternoon. I'm going to have a family meeting and tell everyone about the repossession notice."

"Yas, suh."

"I don't know what's going to happen to us, but I don't want any of your people around if Paul comes out here to run this place. Call a meeting, and you and Jeremiah make plans to take everyone North. You'll be safe there, won't you? I'll help any way I can."

"You don' have to worry none 'bout that, Massa Abraham."

"I don't want you getting into the middle of anything concerning Paul. They'd lynch you for sure. Just let me handle it."

Neither man said a word, but each knew the other's intentions.

CHAPTER THIRTY

John Scott went by his son's house. The front door was closed, but not locked. He called to Paul as he entered the foyer, stumbling over Grace's discarded clothes, a whiskey bottle thrown on top of them. Where were the slaves? They must've run away or been killed. Apprehension shook him to the core. As he moved into the parlor, the drapes and Paul's clothes lay strewn about the room. In a panic, he rushed through the dining room, down to the kitchen and out the back door.

A cursory search of the back yard, the stable, and the slaves' quarters revealed nothing amiss except the servants, but a cold feeling competed with John's breakfast. He managed to stumble to the side of the stable before vomiting. Surprisingly, he felt better.

Back inside the house, he climbed the stairs to the bedroom. With the exception of a hairbrush on the floor, a broken whiskey bottle, and the dark-stained rug dried to a sticky mat, everything seemed normal. The couple's jewelry rested intact inside a crystal box on top of the dresser. John looked at the rug, spellbound. The blood-soaked runner seemed to glare at him, a tangible reminder of the macabre events that took place in this brothel-looking chamber. Who could sleep in such a hellish room? He knew the answer. Grace didn't decorate it.

Downstairs again, he bent over and picked up Paul's clothes. The pockets still had money in them, but he noticed the dried blood on the shirt. Had there had been a fight with an intruder? John bolted as Charles entered the foyer.

"Maggie told me something terrible happened here last night. She asked me to come over to lock the house."

"Thank you. There's a possibility Paul's been kidnapped and beaten or worse. I'm going to help the sheriff look for him." John Scott exited his son's house, never looking back. His heart told him something he hadn't wanted to face, but the memories were too distinct.

Ever since Paul was a young boy, he'd acted strange with an unrealistic affinity about the number seven. There was a mean streak to him, and more than once, John found him torturing animals. Paul would always be stopped and punished, but when John realized the spankings excited his son, he resorted to other methods to reprimand him. As his son reached puberty, he seemed to have settled down, and John was relieved Paul had outgrown his childish behavior. Of course, Louise had always been different, too, and there were many times John was sorry he'd married her. In the beginning, he thought she'd influenced their son. Now, he didn't know. His head told him there was no kidnapping, and Grace could very well die from her husband's own hand. Where was he? The knowledge was too much to bear, and John let the currents of salty tears flow, stinging him as much as any thorn ever could. He looked everywhere he could think of. No Paul. John reported back to the sheriff before going home to tell his wife their son was missing.

* * *

Sarah looked up as Doc Bradley's wife entered and placed a tray of food on a small table near her chair. "Thank you, but I can't eat a thing."

Miriam Bradley patted Sarah's shoulder. "You need to keep your strength up if you're going to care for this precious, young lady. So, eat as much possible, one bite at a time."

Sarah lifted half a small sandwich and took a bite. Fresh cream cheese with crushed pecans melted in her mouth. Did Miriam know how much Sarah loved nuts? The small bowl of steaming vegetable soup and the strong, hot tea added soothing warmth to Sarah's cold heart. She ate everything on the tray, not realizing how hungry she was. The food also seemed to clear her head, giving her clarity to think about what she was going to do.

Whispering to her daughter, Sarah formulated a plan. "We'll sell your house and go home to Ireland where no one will hurt either of us again. And if Paul says one word about it, we'll tell the sheriff what he's done to you."

* * *

Maggie dashed into the clinic. Looking at her sister, she wept so hard Sarah was afraid Doc would have two patients. She held her younger daughter, smoothing her hair as she'd always done. They spent the day talking, taking comfort in the memories from life in Cork to the present. Sarah noticed that look on Maggie's face the moment she came into the clinic but waited all day for her to mention it.

When she said nothing, Sarah asked. Maggie confirmed she was going to give the Sullivans their first grandchild.

"I didn't say anything about it because Grace's condition is more important than anything at the moment."

"But good news takes the edge off bad, and I'm so happy for you and Charles."

"We are, too. Charles will be a wonderful father. He's already started making wooden toys, and I'm beginning to decorate the nursery. I should go soon to prepare dinner for him."

"Before you go, there's one other thing. Your father is planning some kind of meeting."

Maggie nodded and kissed her mother before making her exit. "He told me."

Sarah dreaded the meeting for Abe's sake. Talking about losing the plantation would be hard enough, but how could he tell the children about Sean? Her heart ached for her husband's upcoming ordeal and for her children having to hear the secret.

Why was she so tired? Sarah drifted off into a light sleep, sitting straight up in the high-backed chair that would be her post until Grace was well.

Swirling in her memory was the sensation of floating on the whispers of a green isle far, far away. For the first time in a very long while, Sarah relaxed, and a small smile softened her delicate face.

* * *

Jim couldn't concentrate on work and was thankful Master Abe had told him to take the afternoon off. He couldn't get the screams of the child Paul had hurt out of his mind and he couldn't close his eyes without seeing his beloved Grace lying on that rug.

When he walked outside, he saw Daisy sitting in a rocking chair on their tiny front porch. "Why you not at the Big House?"

"Massa Abe tole me the fam'ly was gettin' together, and he wanted us all gone early. Some's up, but I don' know what. Prob'ly gonna talk about poor Miss Grace. I sure got a heap o' thinkin' to do, Boy."

"Me, too. Think I'm gonna ride, clear my head."

"Now, Boy, don' you even be thinkin' 'bout goin' after that white man." Miss Daisy's voice revealed her apprehension. "Iffen some of his own kind kilt him, that'd be bad 'nuff, but not you. You don' need to get messed up in that stuff."

"Whatever happens don' matter. I be careful, but I don' care what they do to me, anyhow."

Daisy lumbered out of her chair and shook her son hard, as if that would shake some sense into him. "You set down here right this minute. What you mean by that? You and Miss Grace's frien's, I know, but it better not be nuthin' more'n that. You hear me?" She sank back into the chair.

Jim put his head in his hands.

"You done fell under her spell, tha's what. You bes' be fallin' out of it, 'cuz no good's gonna come of it." Daisy paced, wringing a tea towel between her hands, a habit Jim had picked up from her. Twisting hands meant nervous insides.

"Mama, I love Miss Grace with all my bein'. Not jes' how a man loves a woman. Not jes' how a frien' loves another frien' and not how a slave loves his mistress. It's ever'thin' all rolled up together. I can't never begin to describe it. It's more'n all what I said, and it's not any of them thin's outright, either. It's jes' that she's somewhere way down deep in my soul, a part of me."

"Well, you sure can't never jump the broom with her, and you bes' know that. Better not hear nuthin' 'bout you touchin' her neither, broom or no broom."

"You don't understand. I don' have to jump the broom with her, or touch her, or even see her. I know when she's happy, when she's sad, when she's in trouble." He pointed to his heart. "I know it here." A tear slid down his cheek.

Miss Daisy sat, looking at Jim, thinking about her children. She was grateful to have the three that survived with her at Oak Hollow. The day Jim was born came to the forefront of her memory. He'd let out a loud cry and then giggled, letting her know he was a special child. But he couldn't, he mustn't get messed up with Miss Grace. Wasn't right. Yet, she knew that look. Same look Jeremiah had when he'd asked her to jump the broom with him.

Theirs was a love so profound and deep, no words could do it justice. She'd say no more. She knew Jim would do the right thing in spite of how he felt. She'd raised him right. Something else had been nagging her.

Nobody had told her, but she knew Jim and her beloved husband had helped some runaways to escape in the dark of night, and she prayed every day for the safety of all the slaves. Daisy put her hands on the arms of the chair and pushed, forcing herself to stand.

"You're hurtin' in your knees. Let me he'p you." Jim took her arm.

"No, son, it's jes' my rheumatiz." She patted his hand before withdrawing her arm, moving clumsily into the tiny cottage she shared with her husband.

Jim walked at a brisk pace to the barn for a horse. As he drew close to the house, he noticed Abraham Sullivan pacing in the parlor with his children's eyes focused on him. The family meeting must have started.

Anger consumed Jim, and the only thing that would quench the fire, the anger, the uncontrollable rage was the blood of Paul Scott. Saddling up, he rode slowly into town, keeping the horse from tiring. Jim had a lot of thinking to do and many miles to travel tonight. He wasn't in a hurry. If it took the rest of his life, he'd see Paul Scott dead.

Riding by Grace's dark house, he turned down the street leading to the Gentlemen's Club. Neither Paul's carriage nor his horse was there.

Trying to collect his thoughts, Jim walked his horse to a shack at the back of one of the finest houses in town. He dismounted and quietly walked to the door. With a muffled knock, he whispered his name into the vacuum of night. The door opened just a crack until he was recognized, and then he was swept inside.

"Joshua, how's the boy?"

The middle-aged man shifted his weight as he stood facing Jim. "Set down. I'll tell you what a evil man did to him."

"You don't have to."

"Wuz you the one what fought with that Massa Scott?"

"Yeah, but how's your boy?"

"His body's gonna be okay. His head, I don' know 'bout. He still has horrible bad dreams. I put some salve on his cuts where he got throwed down, and he's not so sore now. But that Scott man's done a lot worser to some girls and other boys. He's like the very devil hisself."

"Yas, I'd like to find him and kill him, but my Massa wants to find him first."

"Me and several of the other men has already made plans to go after him."

"What you don' know is my Massa is his daddy-in-law. He's gonna see 'bout bringin' him to the law. Kin you jes' back off a couple days? Then, I won't try stopping you."

Joshua thought for a while. "I guess we kin do that."

After a hasty goodbye, Jim left, turning toward the river that ran through town. There was no sign of Paul.

* * *

John Scott sat in his study, worried about his son. Where was he? What had happened in his home? Where were the slaves? Abraham's note lay in front of him. Collateral was listed as Oak Hollow, including the land and all buildings, which seemed excessive and unusual, based on the amount of the loan. John had always loaned his friend money on his signature. But not a single payment had been made, not at all characteristic of Abe.

Looking at the master ledger in the bank, not one entry of the amount of the payments had ever been deducted. Why would Abe lie when his plantation was at stake, or why would he agree to put the whole thing up anyway? Something didn't add up. Becoming more alarmed, John began to think Paul's story was the problem. An exceptionally large withdrawal had been made yesterday from Abe's account. Enough to pay off the note. Had Abe done it, he would've mentioned what he was going to do with the money or that he didn't trust the bank…something, given the status of the note. Abe must not have known, or he would have demanded it back. Regardless of the mystery, he'd have to repossess. There was little enough money left in Abe's checking account to pay the loan now. His only hope was that Paul would be found safe and Grace would recover. Beyond that, he dared not think.

* * *

Maggie and Charles arrived at Oak Hollow just as the rented livery carriage pulled into the carriageway. Joseph alighted and helped Becca, lifting her down as if she were a soft cloud. She looked radiant as she and Joe climbed the steps to the verandah.

As Charles and Maggie drove up, she put her hand lovingly into her husband's and squeezed. "Guess Papa wants to discuss Grace and what's happened."

Mary and Matthew waited on the verandah, waving as everyone arrived.

"Papa sent for me. What's the matter?" A frown formed between Joe's eyes.

Matthew shrugged. "I think he's going to talk about Grace." He rolled through the door as his siblings followed.

Abraham Sullivan stood in the center of the parlor. His face looked old, his posture, defeated. The late afternoon rays of the sun created shadows on his creased face, seemingly tacking more years onto his age. "Come in and sit down, please. As soon as this meeting is over, we'll eat."

He paced, telling Joseph about Grace's beating and that Paul was missing. "She may not live. If she doesn't, I don't know what this family will do."

Joseph looked at his siblings. Their faces reflected the horror of the event. Nausea rose, stronger than anything he'd ever known. Slamming his clamped fist into his flat palm, he stood. "I've heard enough. I'm going after him! I'll kill him slow. Let him suffer!"

"Wait, Joseph. We'll talk about that later. There's other news."

"What kind of news? What on earth could be more important than Grace?" Joseph voiced the concern of all of the children.

Abraham ignored the questions. He stared straight ahead, showing no emotion. He had to finish what he'd started. "God's been good to us, but He's also given us some difficulties to help us grow. Paul manipulated my trust, making me believe he loved Grace more than anything. She acted reserved, but sometimes she's like that. When I asked her over and over if she wanted to marry Paul, she always assured me she did. Later, she admitted she only married him so he'd give me financing whenever we needed it."

"Aren't you and John Scott friends? Wouldn't he have given you a loan?" Joseph sat on the edge of the sofa.

"Not likely. If Paul and Grace hadn't married, he might've held that against me." Abe summarized how they'd found out about the beatings through Jim. "I tried to persuade her to come home, but she wouldn't listen." Abe walked over to a table where a full fifth of Irish whiskey rested.

He poured an old fashioned glass half full and downed it in one motion, hoping the liquor would bolster him enough to tell them the rest.

"Are you still having chest pains?" Maggie's look showed her alarm.

"Not the kind you're talking about." Putting the glass on the table, he recounted the events of the repossession notice, the missing bank statements, and the note showing no payments had been made.

"Since we've accused Paul of trying to kill Grace, John Scott's not going to do us any favors. I should've paid more attention, but with my sick spell, Matt's accident, the two weddings, and the good crop, questioning Paul never entered my mind. I trusted him as my own son."

"Don't worry." Matthew sat up very straight in his wheelchair. "My legs may not function perfectly, but my mind works fine." He winked at Mary since he was using her words. "We'll get through this. Everyone can pitch in. How much time to do we have?"

"Until tomorrow."

"We may not be able to save it by then, but if we lose it, we'll work hard and buy it back." Maggie's resolve showed in her eyes, and everyone knew she meant it.

"That's not my main concern right now. What I'm about to tell you is the hardest thing I've ever done in my life, outside of telling your mama. Please let me finish, and then judge me any way you see fit. There's been a big secret in my heart from the time your mama and I married. She knows now, and you should, too." He swallowed another stiff drink. Starting at the beginning, he told the entire story of Sean, including turning over the land in Cork to him.

"Your mama barely speaks to me and hasn't forgiven me. There's no way to ever work through the hurt I've caused her. Many times, taking my own life seemed like the best way out, but leaving all of you and your mama to take care of yourselves made it seem like a selfish thing to do. That's why I kept thinking the good Lord put all these trials on me. To punish me for my transgressions." He was so choked up he couldn't speak. After bolting down another fiery shot, he sat with his head in his hands.

Regaining his composure, he looked up and saw the torn hearts of his family reflected in their faces. "Sean will be here tomorrow or the next day. I hope you all know this is not his fault. No child is ever responsible for what parents do, so please don't hold any hatred against him. Judge me. Hold me accountable because I don't deserve to ever have your trust or love again. The only thing I have a right to ask is that you take care of my Sarah." Abe unashamedly let the tears flow and made no effort to wipe them away. He was spent.

"But Papa, what are you going to do?" asked Maggie.

"I don't know, my child. No one knows what will happen to Oak Hollow, and there's no land for me in Cork, so I have no home."

"You're drinking more than usual. Don't you think you should slow down?" Joe walked over and put his arm around Abe.

"Tonight and the afternoon I told your mama are the times I've felt the need to be excessive, but since the secrets are out, there's no need to drink now more than socially."

Maggie appeared relieved and walked to Abe's other side. She and Joe led him to the dining room where Daisy had left supper on the buffet.

They ate, keeping the sparse conversation as light as the meal.

Abe ate very little, excused himself, and retired to his room behind a closed door. The finality with which the door slammed startled the group.

CHAPTER THIRTY-ONE

Charles and Maggie had come prepared to spend the night, and now Maggie paced, worried about Abe. She addressed her siblings. "I don't think Papa should be left alone. I'm afraid he'll kill himself." She was crying as the words left her mouth.

Quietly, Mary said, "I've already taken care of that, Maggie. I felt a need to secure the guns a long time ago." No one asked why, and she offered no explanation. Matt's gaze hit the floor.

* * *

Gray clouds of winter ushered in a cold, dreary morning. Miss Daisy busied herself with the big breakfast crowd. A knock at the door interrupted the meal, and Abe rose to see whom Obadiah was admitting. Before the old butler could announce him, a handsome, red-haired young man rushed into the room.

"Father!"

"Sean, how nice to see you! You've grown up over the years since we left Cork." Abe embraced him. "Come meet everyone." He introduced him and called for Miss Daisy to bring another plate.

All eyes focused on Sean. Neither Matthew nor Joseph acknowledged his extended hand and averted Sean's attempt at making eye contact. Maggie dug the nails of one hand into the palm of the other to keep from screaming at him to go away. If Abe or Sean noticed the icy tension that spread over the room, they appeared oblivious to the change.

Asking about Grace and Sarah, the young man expressed an interest in seeing both of them. Abe had the loathsome chore of telling him about Grace's beating. He also told him that Sarah was not receptive to seeing him, and Grace hadn't been told about him because of her condition.

"But I want to see my sister, and perhaps Sarah wouldn't find me so horrible if she would only talk to me."

"Don't count on that!" Maggie piped up.

"Honey!" Charles almost never raised his voice to his wife, but he didn't want her to say something she might regret later. He squeezed her hand under the table, letting her know it was time to be silent. Without anyone noticing, Charles ran his hand over Maggie's slightly rounded belly in a caress he hoped his unborn child could feel.

Joe exchanged a look with his older brother and through a bit of body language, they decided to exit the meal.

Before they could take their leave, another knock sent Obadiah to the front. Within a few moments, John Scott entered the dining room.

"Would you care for coffee?" asked Abe.

"No. Nothing, thank you. Let's get this matter over. As of today, I'm taking possession of your property." He handed him the note and the notice of the previous extension naming today as the date for execution of the papers.

Abe sat down and tried to read, but the words blurred. All he had worked for in Ireland and in America was flitting away. The only person who could clear him had almost killed his beloved Grace, and was now conveniently missing. This was too much to handle all at once. "John, as long as we have been friends, I can't believe that you'd do this so close to Christmas and with my daughter lying near death at Doc Bradley's clinic. Didn't you find my checks in the statements Paul kept for me?"

"No. I went through every drawer in Paul's desk, as you asked me to do, and none of the bank statements are there. I went over the note again. No payments are listed. I'm sorry, but it looks as if Paul was right. When someone finds him, I'll ask him, but for now, this plantation belongs to the bank."

"If no payments have been made, I should have more than enough money to write you a check."

"I'd already thought of that, but since you made a substantial withdrawal day before yesterday, your account is very low."

"I haven't taken any money out. Where's my money going, John? And what's happening at the bank?" Abe turned. "Time to go to the sheriff."

"There are no answers, Abe. I don't know where your money is or where my son has been taken. Maybe the money was for the kidnappers. I honestly don't know."

"Excuse me, sir. May I see those papers?" Sean rose, and Abe handed them to him. In a few moments, Sean faced John. "Sir, I believe you are in error. The extension reads you cannot assume ownership until midnight of this date. Therefore, Mister Sullivan still owns this property. Counting the few day's interest for the extension, what is the total amount owed on this note?"

"Who is this man?" asked John.

"Never mind. Just answer his questions." John produced a figure and Sean said, "This matter can be resolved immediately, if you'd like."

"What do you mean?" asked John, somewhat confused.

"I'll pay off the loan right now. Is that agreeable with you, sir?" Sean had turned to Abraham.

Too bewildered to say anything, Abe nodded his head. Sean produced a checkbook and made out a check for the amount. He started to hand it to John but withdrew it. "On second thought, I would much rather come to the bank this afternoon and get a receipt plus the deed."

"Suit yourself." John turned to go. "Don't you know Paul would've let you live here, Abe?"

"No, after what's happened, I don't think Paul would want anything to do with me. Or you, for that matter."

John left without another word. Conversation buzzed. Abe walked out on the back porch to take in what had just happened with his oldest son. Through letters, Abe learned Sean had continued his education, become a barrister, and kept the land in Cork. When he mentioned he and his mother had been living in the family home since the famine eased, Abe wasn't surprised. Now here this mature, young man was about to save the plantation in America. Abe was proud to call him son.

Matt rolled onto the porch to face his father. "I speak for everyone here. We don't know Sean, but we don't want him to pay off the loan, especially if he'll be holding the deed. Let the bank have it, and maybe someday we'll buy it back."

"If Sean pays off the note, at least Oak Hollow will still be in the family, and we won't have to move right away."

"I don't trust him." Matthew forced his emotions under control, but his eyes glowered and his nostrils flared.

Abe looked him directly in the eyes. "I don't trust John Scott or his son. But I'll drive to the bank with Sean and then see Grace. My decision as to what will be best for this family will be made on the ride into town."

Matthew turned without a word and rolled back into the house.

* * *

As Abe and Sean strode across the bank lobby, John Scott walked out to meet them, ushering them into his office. He looked sad and weary. "Abe, I've been through Paul's desk and the safe twice and can't find the deed anywhere. He told me you put it up for collateral, but it's missing."

"Exactly like my bank statements are missing, and exactly like your son is missing."

"I don't suppose you can repossess without a deed, can you?" Sean assumed a legal posture.

"We can say it was lost and get a replacement. You don't have the deed, do you, Abe?"

Abe rubbed his chin. "No, I couldn't find it, either. Something's not right, John."

Sean took control. "We're going to settle this for the time being. Here's my check, and I want a receipt that I paid off this loan. Then, when the truth comes to light, I want my money back with interest and the deed. Is that understood?"

"Yes, that's fine, but I doubt you'll find any payments Abe has made."

Sean insisted on witnesses before handing over the check. The loan was noted Paid in Full, signed by John Scott. As the two men left the bank, Abe asked Sean what he intended to do with the plantation now that he technically had it as collateral against the note he just bought.

"Don't worry about that." He laughed. "The plantation will never be put in my name. My only intention is to help out. Besides, what would I do with land in America?"

"But there's a possibility you'll never be repaid if we have a few lean years. And you might decide to come to America."

"I would never leave Ireland. You've already more than paid me by introducing me to the family. Even if they hate me, I don't have to be in the shadows any more. That's worth the price of the plantation three times over."

"Forgive my manners. How's your mother?"

"She's fine. We struggled for the first year in England but your money and the land in Cork helped put me through school. My grades and passing the bar opened up a good job, and now I take care of Mum. She's here with me at the hotel. Since she'd be lonely left at home, I brought her along. Of course, neither of us expects the family to meet her."

"Let's go by and check on Grace. I pray Sarah will be civil to you, but don't get your hopes up. After that, perhaps in a few days, I'd like to visit Bridget."

* * *

When Abe and Sean arrived at the clinic and entered Grace's treatment room, Sarah sat straight up, steeling herself for the encounter. Introductions were made, and with all the activity, Grace opened her eyes and turned her head.

"Mama, Papa?" Her raspy voice was little more than a whisper.

Elation replaced all other emotion as Abe and Sarah rushed to her bed.

"Hello, darling. How are you feeling?" Sarah smoothed Grace's hair. Abraham held her hand.

"Sleepy." She drifted off again.

Sean bowed to Sarah and kissed her hand. "Meeting you is a great honor, Miss Sarah. Thank you for allowing me to visit in your home."

Sarah just stared at him.

"Sean has just paid off our loan at the bank. The Scotts will never be able to cheat us again if I can help it. There might be a way now to keep Oak Hollow. He and his mother are staying at the inn for a few more days."

Fatigue saturated Sarah's voice. "That's good."

"We'll go. If there's any change in Grace, or if you need anything, let me know. I'll be back soon to check on you both." Abe bent over and kissed Sarah's forehead. "And never forget how very much I love you."

Sarah watched Abe and Sean head to the buggy, trying to imagine how Sean had looked as a youngster. How hard it must have been to be reared by an unmarried mother. Worse than that, though, was to know he had a father who saw him three or four times a month and brothers and sisters he could never see or play with. He didn't deserve that.

Sarah was still hurt, but there were many corners of her heart being pounded in different directions, and she'd been left unable to sort out her feelings. Her thoughts turned to her own children. First to Grace and what a good child she'd been…actually her best child. She didn't deserve this.

Then, there'd been Matthew's accident, and his battle to learn to walk all over again with sweet Mary remaining by his side through it all. Neither one of them deserved this.

Joseph and Rebecca. So much in love, yet they couldn't marry until Joseph finished medical school. They didn't deserve this, either.

And Maggie. She and Charles were about to start a family, and they didn't deserve to be worrying about all the turmoil in this family.

Abe was a different matter. By himself, he'd killed a part of her heart. But she thought about his chest pains as well as the agony his eyes had portrayed the afternoon he confessed the secret. What was she to do? She was such a part of him, and there was no doubt he'd rather die than hurt her. He didn't deserve what he'd held inside as a means of protecting her from his sins.

Sarah tried to put herself in Bridget's place. No woman deserved to be betrayed, disinherited, or abandoned. No mother should have to feel the heartache both of them had endured. Perhaps, in time, Sarah would heal. Maybe she could regain some feeling for Abraham. She'd forgiven him already, though he didn't think so, but she couldn't trust her feelings at the moment. She and Grace would heal together.

* * *

The day had been unusually long for Abe. He sat in the parlor with a blank look shadowing his face, resting, while the children visited. The young men, including Sean, played dominoes while the young ladies talked over cups of tea. The good news that Grace was slowly waking up had put them all in a jovial mood, and conversation flowed easily between the young people.

A knock sounded on the front door. Obadiah answered it to find Jim standing there, twisting his hands.

"I needs to talk to Massa Sullivan."

"He's busy right now. Come back tomorrow."

"Naw, I needs to see him, now!"

Abe recognized Jim's voice and went to the door. "What is it?"

When the young darkie didn't say anything, Abe stepped out onto the porch.

"Thinks we foun' him, Massa Abe," Jim whispered.

"Where?"

"You bes' come with me."

"Okay, let me get the boys. They'll want to be in on this, too." Abe rushed back into the room. "Jim thinks they may have found Paul. Let's go!"

The young darkie went to hitch up the big wagon. Tying Matt's chair on the rear of it, they helped him into the back seat. Joe and Charles sat with him while Abe rode up front with Jim and Sean. They traveled at an easy, steady pace.

"Don't we need to hurry?" Abe asked.

"Naw, suh. Don' reckon that'll be necessary." About two miles out of town, Jim turned off the road onto a seldom traveled path and slowed the horses. He came to the bank of the river and pulled back on the reins.

The late afternoon sun cast an eerie light through the tree branches. Everyone, except Matt, jumped down. The men only had to walk a few feet. A carriage robe was thrown over two people. Abe lifted the blanket. From the gasp of astonishment escaping the men, Matt realized Paul was dead.

Abe surveyed the scene. His horse must've gotten spooked and started running at full speed before the carriage sideswiped that tree over there. The shattered tongue could've freed the animal. Abe made a mental note to see if the horse made it back to its stall at home. Paul and a young male darkie under him were naked. Each had been shot in the head. Most of Paul's face was erased, though there was enough left to identify him, but no one recognized the boy. A pistol was thrown across Paul's back. Could it be some eerie sort of calling card? They'd been dead a while.

"You didn't move anything, did you, Jim?"

"Naw, suh. Me and some of the slave men whose kids has been hurt wuz lookin' for Massa Paul. When we come up on this horrible thing, we didn't even raise the blanket. I recanized Massa Paul's carriage. Then I come got you."

As twilight gathered, the men climbed back onto the buggy, heading for the sheriff's office. Because he didn't want to give the sheriff any reason to blame Jim, Abe said he and the boys had found Paul. When Abe described the scene, the sheriff shook his head as if to clear the news from his mind.

"I'm on my way, but don't say anything to John Scott. They've been through a lot. I'll tell them tomorrow. They deserve one more night of sleep."

* * *

Before leaving town, they stopped by Doc Bradley's so Abe could tell Sarah.

"What do you want?" she asked as he walked in.

"To talk to you. We've found Paul."

Sarah brightened somewhat. "Did you talk to him? What did he say about what's happened to our Grace?"

"No, none of us talked to him," he whispered. "He's dead." Abe described as gently as possible what they'd found and told her the sheriff had bound them to silence until he told the Scotts.

Sarah gasped, throwing her hand to her mouth. "But who, how, when...."

"We may never know. At least, though, Grace is getting better." Abe held Sarah for a moment before she pulled away.

CHAPTER THRITY-TWO

Sheriff Robertson and his deputies rode out to the scene. Nothing Abe could've said would have prepared him for the sight, even in the scope of a lantern and the moonlight. The situation was bad. A child was involved. Thank goodness, the cold weather had kept the bodies somewhat preserved, though the malodor of death filled the air. He lifted the pistol and rolled Paul's body off the boy.

The sheriff directed his men to wrap the bodies and put them in the wagon for the somber trip back to town to leave both bodies with Odis Ritaker, the undertaker. As morning dawned, Sheriff Robertson drank coffee, waiting for the bank to open. When the employees said John Scott hadn't been in to work for two days, the sheriff drove to the Scott home. As kindly as he knew how, Robertson told them their son had been murdered. "If there's anything we can do, or if you want me to send the minister over, just let me know. This has to be the hardest thing a parent ever faces."

Missus Scott was inconsolable. She buried her head in John's shoulder, weeping hysterically. John sat unmoving on the sofa as if nothing had registered.

* * *

Paul Scott's funeral the next day drew most of the townspeople. Other than stating he'd been murdered, no details were released to save the family embarrassment. No mention was made of the boy who was returned to his parents for a simple slave ceremony. Louise Scott placed seven bunches of dried lavender atop her son's casket. John Scott stared into space.

Almost as a dirge following the church service, a cold, windy mist started to fall, but the nasty weather didn't deter the people from following the Scotts to the cemetery, forming a circle around them and the coffin of their only child. Just as the minister finished his words to the family, a powerful gust of wind swept through the crowd, picking up a bunch of lavender. It hit Paul's father full in the face before dropping at his feet. Louise bent, picked it up, held it to her breast for a moment, and then replaced it on the coffin. The funeral of Paul Scott was over, his body committed to the earth.

* * *

Grace Scott had a fitful night, tossing and turning. Sarah didn't sleep at all, as was typical of her ten-day vigil beside her daughter's bed, afraid Grace would thrash around and fall off the narrow cot.

As dawn broke, cold and windy, Grace opened her eyes and looked at her mother. "I had a dream Paul was falling into a pit, and I'm frightened. Where is he?"

"Honey, there's been a terrible accident. You've been hurt and need all your strength to get well. We'll talk about Paul when you feel a little better. Do you think you could eat something?"

"Maybe some tea and a biscuit. Would you ask Daisy or Essie Mae to bring it?"

Sarah explained to Grace she was in the clinic before going to find the doctor. Doc Bradley rushed into the room, a big smile replacing the worried frown he'd carried since his young patient had been brought in. "Well, well, what have we here?" He walked over to take a closer look at Grace.

"May I have some tea, please?"

"By all means, my dear. What would you like to eat?"

"A biscuit might be lovely, thank you. When can I go home?"

"Hmm. Let's see how quickly you recover. Then we'll talk about it."

When Abe came to see Grace, Sarah asked him to follow her outside. "Doc will probably release Grace in a day or so. Will you take us to her home here in town? If I should need Doc, we'd be close, and Grace might rest better in her own home among her own things."

Abe took his wife's hands. "That house is a mess. Blood's everywhere . . . our Grace's blood. Since there hasn't been time to get Lavitica June and Essie Mae over to clean it, I don't think either one of you should see that. The sight might bring back horrible memories and cause Grace to have a relapse."

After mulling over her husband's words, Sarah agreed.

* * *

Doc Bradley released his patient three days later, and Abraham and Joseph made a bed in the back of the large wagon before going to the clinic to get her. Charles and Maggie stopped by Grace's house and collected some clothes and personal items to take to her. Waiting for the homecoming, Miss Daisy plodded around the kitchen, making two of Grace's favorites. A buttermilk pie and potato soup. Essie Mae and Lavitica June moved Mary across the hall and busied themselves with cleaning the rooms.

When Grace asked why she was going to Oak Hollow instead of her own home, Sarah explained there were more people to care for her at the plantation. Grace sighed with relief when the wagon stopped. Joseph had walked the horses, trying to keep the ride as smooth as possible, but every small bump caused Grace pain. She was grateful when they stopped, and her brother carried her up to her old room.

Essie Mae stood grinning, ready to put her mistress to bed after helping her into one of her favorite gowns. Lavitica June brought up the food, and Mary, Becca, and Maggie sat in her room, making light conversation while Grace ate.

She'd never tasted anything as good as the meal Daisy prepared, but all she could manage was a few bites. The girls tucked her in and left the room so Grace could nap. In her dream, she and Paul were in a valley. He walked toward her holding a sheaf of papers in his hand. When Grace reached for them, he ran to a cliff, scaling the craggy face of it until he reached the top. He looked down at her, threw the papers in the air and jumped, falling through space. With a loud thump, Paul hit the ground. Grace awoke with a start.

Trying to come back to reality, she noticed her mother sitting in a wicker rocker close to her while her father sat on the foot of her bed. She told them about the dream and how real it had seemed.

Abe looked at Sarah. She nodded her head. Taking his daughter's hands in his, Abe explained about the accident and told her Paul was dead.

"He was drinking. I remember that. He was very, very upset. Did his drinking cause the accident?" Grace asked.

"No one knows for sure. We'll get the details later. Try to rest now."

Grace didn't shed a tear for her husband's passing. She couldn't remember what had happened to her, but Paul had something to do with it. A vague memory of Jim coming by her house flashed through her mind, but she couldn't remember why he had come. How she longed to see him. Most of the night was spent awake, trying to remember details of how she got hurt. The bed stifled her, and she wanted to get up to look out the window, but after pulling herself to a sitting position on the side of the bed, Grace decided she'd need help walking.

Content to be sitting, she ran her foot over the hardwood boards of the floor, watching the pattern her foot made. Her big toe outlined the shape of a heart. She smiled, remembering a simple heart of stones in a secret place in the woods and within her own heart.

Miss Daisy pulled herself up each stair trying to ignore her arthritic feet and knees and greeted Grace the next morning. She hummed an old Negro spiritual as she pulled back the heavy draperies, to allow the scant sunlight to enter the bedroom. "God's healing rays, my baby," Daisy said, cooing while she washed Grace's face with a warm, soft cloth.

"I missed you so much, Miss Daisy." Grace held out her arms for a hug.

The old woman enveloped her in a tender embrace so as not to hurt her. "We missed you, too, Missy. Now you bes' get well 'cuz Christmas be comin' in no time at all, and you gots to be up and around."

"How long?"

"Tomorrow's Thanksgiving, and land's sakes, Christmas'll waggle in right behind it. I's so busy, I don' rightly know whether I's coming or going. Sure wish you wuz up to he'p me taste the pies." She smiled at her. "I 'spec mos' of the family will be up here soon 'nuff, so I'll hurry and send up your breakfas' 'fore they all tromp in."

Grace heard soft footsteps on the stairs, and her eyes darted to the door being opened. There stood Jim not five feet from her. This time, she wasn't startled. Her lips curved into a broad smile as he approached her. His eyes twinkled like a crystal chandelier of a thousand candles.

"I have a surprise for you. Close your eyes and wait 'til I count to three to open them. One, two, three."

Grace opened her eyes and gasped. She was laughing and crying at the same time. There stood her beloved Miss Lizzie, accompanied by her two sons.

"We gots a real good hidin' place, and we's been stayin' there. Most of the menfolk are waggin' their tongues about goin' up North, but we couldn't leave without knowing you wuz all right. All the years I worked for Massa Scott, he was a mean and strange man." Lizzie's eyes filled. "But I never thought he'd hurt you that bad."

At that moment, memories came flooding back to Grace. She remembered everything up to seeing the whiskey bottle coming toward her. No accident caused her injuries.

No grief existed for her husband. She looked at her dear friends. "He's dead now. That means I own you. As soon as I can write, you and the boys will be freed. If you want to work in town or go North, you'll have your certificates."

"We wouldn't mind being slaves to you. You's dear to our hearts. Massa Paul jes' scart us."

"But I'm going to free you and make it legal."

"I been tole I could be your servant 'til you get well. Is that okay? We couldn't never be free, though. Agin the law."

"Not if we don't tell anyone! And yes, you may help me as an employee."

The boys left with Jim, and Miss Lizzie set about getting Grace ready for breakfast before going downstairs for her tray.

Grace was happy, at peace.

Sarah came to sit with her, giving her the rest of the news. She told her in a matter-of-fact, emotionless way the details about Sean and how he saved the plantation. "I was wondering if I could live in your house in town because I can't live here after what your father's done."

Grace was moved to tears. Tears for her mama and what the news must've done to her spirit. Tears for a brother she never knew. Tears for the land in her blessed Green Isle that would never be theirs again. Tears for her papa and his long kept bitter secret, a secret that almost destroyed them, saving them at the same time.

"Mama, we've all been through so much, yet we're still together. Everyone's made mistakes, but we need to forgive people who've hurt us and trust God to show us the path. I understand how you must feel, but your place is here to help Matthew and me heal."

She walked to Sarah's chair and knelt at her feet. She ran her hand over her mother's face and traced every little frown line as if to smooth it away. "And help yourself and Papa heal, too. You'll see. Healing together will strengthen both of you."

"I'll give it some thought."

"Who found me?"

The question startled Sarah. She hadn't realized Grace didn't know. "Jim. He said he had a sense something bad was going to happen and stopped by to see you. Told you something horrible about what he saw by the Gentlemen's Club, but you sent him home."

"I remember. Always before, Paul would pass out, so he was no trouble, but that night was different. What made Jim come back?"

"We're not sure. All he says is that he had a feeling and knew he had to go against your wishes, so he turned around and went back. When he found you, he ran for Doc Bradley. They got you to the clinic."

Grace smiled and drifted off to sleep for an afternoon nap.

*　*　*

As Thanksgiving morning lightened the sky, Sarah went to the river and knelt over a large rock, praying as hard as she ever had. She prayed for herself, her children, Abe, and for the inner peace to know what to do. Tears streamed down her face, her knees were numb from her weight on them, and still she prayed, asking for a sign. A shaft of sunlight peeked through the haze, illuminating her bowed head.

Sarah felt the warmth and opened her eyes to see a large cloud ringed with gold. She had her answer, rose from her stiff knees, and marched into the kitchen. "Where's my husband?"

Miss Daisy, elbow deep in cornbread and sage dressing met Sarah's eyes. "I don' know, ma'am. Maybe out to the smokehouse."

"If you see him, tell him I want to talk him this instant." Sarah Sullivan turned on her heel and went to look for him, herself. Entering the barn, she saw Abe, kneeling in prayer as she had done earlier. She heard enough to know her answer was right and backed away before he discovered her there.

Sarah waited in Grace's room because she could see the barn through the window and would see Abe leave. She'd told Grace of her decision. Now she needed to tell Abraham. When he moved toward the house, Sarah descended the stairs and met him in the hall.

"Daisy said you wanted to see me?"

"Yes, let's go for a walk."

"But it's cold outside. I don't want you to get sick."

"Come." Grabbing her cloak, she tucked her arm in his as they walked out the door.

The wind gusts seemed to be getting stronger, so Abe put his arm around her to shield her.

After a long silence, she spoke. "What you did was wrong. Wrong for Sean and Bridget, for me, for our children, but most of all for you. You've hurt me more than you'll ever know, but Grace pointed out we've also been blessed by Sean's presence. His money and generosity have saved this plantation. I know it isn't ours anymore, but maybe he'll let us pay him for it when we can."

She paused, giving her throat a chance to warm up. "I want you to know I forgave you a long time ago, and since we can't undo the past, I'm ready to welcome Sean into the fold. Will you invite Bridget and him for Thanksgiving?"

Abe looked at his wife whose face had a softness he hadn't seen since she'd held each of her children for the first time. "Are you sure you want me to do this?"

"Yes, if I can forgive you and offer Bridget some understanding, then perhaps the children can make peace with Sean."

"You mean Matthew, Sarah. The others don't have a problem with him any longer."

"Yes. Matthew."

*　*　*

Abe arrived at the hotel, but before he had a chance to go inside, he glimpsed Sheriff Robertson approaching him. He had a letter in his hand. "Can we go over to the café and have a cup of coffee?"

"Sure, but I'm on an errand for Sarah and kind of pressed for time."

"It's important. The street isn't the place to discuss it."

Abe followed the law officer to the small café inside Miss Norton's house. After serving them, they were left alone.

"This letter's for you."

"Me?" Abe's face filled with questions. "Who'd send me a letter through you?"

"John Scott. We found him this morning hanging in Paul's carriage house. He left several letters. There's also one for Grace."

Abe was stunned. He couldn't believe John Scott was dead by his own hand. "Why would he do that?"

"Read the letter. It explains everything. I had to read it before giving it to you. Hope you understand."

CHAPTER THIRTY-THREE

Abe opened the envelope. His bank statements, seven uncashed checks, a huge sum of money, and a piece of paper fell out of it. He knew without opening the paper that it was the deed to the plantation. Abe read the letter twice, trying to figure it all out.

Abe,

This is very hard to write, but you have a right to the truth, just as I did. I found my son the afternoon after you and Mister O'Malley were in the bank to pay off the loan. A young slave boy's screams led me to him. Before I could help the child, Paul shot him in the head. Finding out the rumors were true made me physically ill and sick to my very soul. Paul was violent and insane. When I called his name to get his attention, my boy didn't seem to recognize me. I struggled with him to get the pistol, but it went off, shooting him in the face. I tried to stop the bleeding, but there was too much. A man's own flesh and blood, dying in his arms, killed by his father.

Why didn't I turn myself in? Because no justice could ever mete out punishment enough for me, nor could I live with myself for taking my own child's life, for not seeing his problems when he was younger. His blood is on my hands. What father can live with that?

Abe turned to the sheriff. "How horrible for John."

"Yes, I can only imagine what he must have gone through."

Abe continued reading.

After holding my faceless son until his death, I went back to his house, to sit there for a while, to remember, to hold his clothes. Finally, I went to the barn to check on his horse, which had come back. While I unbridled him and looked for feed, I noticed him pawing the ground. I discovered an underground safe holding Paul's important papers. Reading his journal devastated me beyond words. He's been raping young darkies, both boys and girls for years. Said he couldn't get away from the number seven. Dates were listed. Paul would rape seven times, rest for anywhere from seven days to seven months and resume his crimes. He always wanted to get the better of someone and bragged about going to your home, sneaking into your study while Grace went to get a vase for the flowers he took her. He lifted the deed from your drawer and slipped it into his coat pocket, telling

Grace he was admiring your study. My son prided himself on persuading you to let him manage your affairs, which made his plan easier. Your checks were never cashed, so no money was taken from your account or paid on the note, but he kept up with what your balance would have been had the payments been deducted. So when you asked, he could give you what you thought was the correct amount. You were right about his violence, Abe. After withdrawing almost all your money on his last day at work, he went home, planning to kill Grace. Following that, Paul set out to get you and me as well as Sarah, Maggie, Charles, and Matthew. Seven of us. Voices told him to. The plan was to make it look like murder caused by someone else.

I've returned your money in this letter and have put Mister O'Malley's money in a new account, complete with interest as he asked. All he has to do is sign for it. Please forgive me, and remember me as you knew me before when we were friends.

John

Abe folded the letter, returning everything to the envelope. "That's quite a burden he carried, Sheriff. Don't know if I could have written that letter, but I appreciate his honesty."

"I admire him, too."

"What's in Grace's letter?"

"He mainly apologizes to her."

Abe read it, and rose slowly. He felt old. "I'm glad no one else will ever be hurt by Paul, but my heart goes out to Missus Scott."

"Everything's okay. John made arrangements before he died to send her to a sanatorium. We found out she's almost as mixed up in the head as Paul was, but John had managed to keep it hidden all these years. She'll be provided for until her death."

Abe stopped at the hotel, knocked on the door and invited his son and Bridget for Thanksgiving dinner.

Bridget hesitated, not knowing how she'd be accepted.

"Come along, Mum," said Sean. "You'll have two strong men to hold you up!"

* * *

To everyone's surprise, Bridget and Sarah liked each other immediately, and the rest of the family seemed to accept her as well.

Abe gave silent thanks for a small miracle.

After the meal, Sean rose. "As you know, the land in Cork is mine. Obviously that created some hard feelings when you found out, but I hope to set that straight today. When I passed my barrister examination, I put the place in all our names. The only stipulation is my . . . uh, our father and our respective mothers can live there as long as they desire, or if they desire, and only upon their passing, or their consent, will it be divided among us to do with as we see fit. But it's yours as well as mine." He turned to Abraham. "I trust that's okay with you, Father?"

Abe's face was shining. He nodded his approval.

"Now, about Oak Hollow. It could be mine since I bought the note with it listed as collateral, but we all know Paul manipulated the situation. An entire plantation is hardly worth the amount of a note for planting, and upon John Scott's death, I got my money back from the bank. So, your inheritance here is safe. The deed is in Father's name."

A gasp went up from the room as hands flew to faces.

Sean cleared his throat. "I guess Mum and I will be leaving soon as we don't want to impose on you. Since today is a day of counting blessings, I want to thank you for letting us meet all of you, for sharing this wonderful American holiday with my mother and me, but most of all for giving me a family, if even only for the brief time we've been here." Sean sat down, patting his mother's arm.

"Please stay," said Grace. "until after Christmas? As for me, I think Oak Hollow should be split five ways between all of us upon the passing of the three parents."

The group gave a cheer. Abe and Sarah suggested Bridget and Sean move from the hotel into two vacant bedrooms upstairs in Oak Hollow.

* * *

A few days following Thanksgiving, Grace felt strong enough to read her father-in-law's letter. He apologized for Paul's cruelty and told her to contact James Black, a local attorney, when she felt up to it. Everything Paul owned had been conveyed to her, including the horses, which were housed at the livery stable. He told her about Louise and the nice place he'd sent her to live out her life. Their home was also left to Grace. John had freed his slaves, giving them their certificates and knew that would please her. He asked her to let them live at Oak Hollow. Upon Louise's death, everything that was left in the estate would also go to Grace. The last sentence read

> I may see my son in hell, or maybe God will have mercy on my soul, and I'll see you in heaven, but no matter where I go, please know I loved you like the daughter I never had.

Grace read every word of the letter before placing it in her journal. Night came early now that the days were getting shorter, and she spent more time alone in her room practicing walking and moving about, which seemed to help her stiffness. The rest of her injuries were almost healed, and by the middle of December, she was going up and down the stairs as well as taking short walks on the property. The first place she went was to the grove where she found the heart of stones. Jim joined her as he always had, and they spent an early evening reminiscing over happier times. Grace smiled at his perfect diction.

*   *   *

Bridget and Sarah became inseparable friends. Sarah found it very comforting to have someone from Ireland to talk to and confide in. One morning on one of their usual daily walks, Bridget broke the silence.

"Who would have ever thought we'd be friends? I just can't believe we have become so close in such a short time."

"It took me a while to believe you and Abe had never loved each other and didn't remember anything about the night you spent together, but when I met Sean, none of that mattered. You've done a remarkable job of rearing the boy all by yourself. He's a fine young man, and I'm glad the children are accepting him as their brother. We'll have a very nice Christmas. A real family affair."

They continued their walk until it was time to return for lunch.

*   *   *

Following Maggie's wedding, Mary bought some oil paints and canvas, which she had Jeremiah stretch over frames and encouraged Matthew to start painting as a way to fill his time. Much to their surprise, he not only liked the hobby, but he was a natural artist. He moved from simple landscapes to massive portraits and became so well known for his artistic talent people were placed on a waiting list to get one of his pieces.

What started as a simple hobby had become a lucrative business, and Matt was grateful for the opportunity to earn his own money. More than that, he realized painting was his passion and the career he'd been searching for. He'd been frugal with his earnings, but managed to purchase a diamond ring for Mary, keeping it until the right time came to propose marriage.

The perfect opportunity appeared the week before Christmas. Everyone had gone to town, and Mary came from the kitchen carrying steaming cups of hot chocolate to the dining room for the two of them when he interrupted her.

"Why don't we have our drinks on the back porch?"

"Because it's cold out there."

"So we'll snuggle."

He appeared to be in a very good mood. "Okay, but let's not stay long." She placed the cups along with spoons and napkins on a tray and walked outside to put everything on the table before going back in to help Matt roll out on the porch.

Instead when she turned, Matt was standing very tall and straight, holding on to the doorframe. He took a few hesitant steps toward her without the aid of crutches, and arm in arm, they made their way to the table.

As Mary was helping him sit, he extracted a velvet box from his pocket, hiding it with his hand. As the pristine winter afternoon wound down, a brisk breeze swirled around them on the porch, and the sun played hide-and-seek with slowly drifting clouds while points of light reflected off the river below. The setting was almost magical.

"How beautiful. No wonder you wanted to come out here." Her voice was soft, almost reverent. "And you've surprised me walking without the crutches. What a special Christmas this is going to be!"

"I hope so. For as beautiful as today is and as brightly as the sun is shining, nothing could compare to the light you give to me with your love. Will you be my wife?" He opened the box, took out the ring, and waited for her answer.

Through tear-filled eyes, she nodded her head, unable to speak. Matthew slid the sparkling diamond on her finger. "If you'd like, we could move into town since Grace has offered to let me live in her house, and use the parlor for a studio. She wanted you to have the Scott's house. The places would be perfect for you to teach music and me to paint until we get married. Would you like that?"

"That would be wonderful!"

They talked, making plans for their future and decided to wait until everyone came for Christmas lunch to announce their engagement. The Sullivans had agreed to celebrate Christmas on the twenty-fourth to accommodate Maggie and Charles who'd spend Christmas Day with the Burtons. Both families had been told of the blessed event that would occur in early June. Joseph had written that he was coming home alone, so Becca could spend the holiday with her parents. The letter also stated that he'd decided not to go to Dublin to medical school. A scholarship had been granted to him for the medical school in New Orleans, which would be closer to Rebecca as well as his own family. Grace requested that the Negroes be invited to join them for Christmas dinner due to all the events, which had transpired during the year.

Everyone agreed it would be a wonderful way to show gratitude for loyal service and to bring the whole plantation together on one very special day.

* * *

Christmas Eve dawned fresh and still with just a dusting of snow. Every once in a while, the sun peeked out, casting beams of light on the glistening ground, making it look almost as if the snowflakes were dancing. There was a festive air in the house, and Daisy and her helpers were scurrying around preparing the turkey and all the trimmings. Abe and the men went to the woodshed to gather more wood for the fireplace and to talk among themselves.

"I didn't know so many women could move around so much," Abe said and laughed from deep within his soul. He was pleased when the men agreed with him.

Soon, one of the Negroes pulled a harmonica from his pocket and began to play. Male voices filled the air as the men carried wood to the house or just followed along. Matthew was in front, leaning on Sean and Joseph, walking with his head held high singing louder than anyone.

The festivities started with the opening of presents, and then the meal was served buffet style shortly after noon. Tables had been set up all over the house, and Grace and Jim managed to sit together. Though they dared not touch, just the presence of each other was enough to make it the best Christmas they'd ever had. After the dishes were cleaned and put away, the darkies went home, leaving the family gathered in the parlor. Sean and Joseph were playing checkers when Matthew announced his engagement to Mary. She blushed, but extended her hand for everyone to see the ring. The perfect ending to a memorable day.

* * *

Christmas morning, Abe and Sarah sat in the breakfast room drinking coffee and talking before the rest of the household awakened.

"How happy I am you've accepted me for what I am, and you and Bridget are friends."

"Yes, Abe, it's amazing, but it's proof that something ugly always has a bright side, if we simply turn it over to God."

"I have something to tell you. Sean has offered to buy us tickets to go home for a visit. We could leave with them and still be back in time for the birth of Maggie's baby. Would you like to go?"

Sarah smiled and hugged her husband. "Oh yes, my dear. To see our home once more would be wonderful."

He was a peaceful and blessed man, and for the first time in his life understood the true meaning of Christmas.

Grace met Jim in the circle and together, they added a few stones to the heart. They'd made a commitment to each other, not a commitment to marry or jump the broom, but a commitment of love and devotion, to keep what they had sacred and special, knowing it would transcend anything physical. They talked about the future and wondered if anyone hundreds of years from that Christmas would discover their heart of stones and wonder what it meant. Grace told him of her offer to Matt because she couldn't stand to live in either house. Too many bad memories. But she'd decided to stay at Oak Hollow and help her father run the plantation. She'd do the bookkeeping and overseeing the day to day activities. And since Jim had been made foreman, it sealed her decision.

Jim smiled. "I have a surprise for you."

"What?"

"When we thought you were going to die, I vowed to make your life stand for something. I've taught almost all my people here to read and write, and on Sundays we've been going to see my relatives and some friends on other plantations. We set up a little corner of the tabernacle as our meeting place. We call it the School of Grace . . . for you, our Amazing Grace, and for the grace of God to let us learn. Like the song says we've gone through a lot of toil, and strife, and a lot of fears, but you, with the help of the Lord, have relieved them. We're using the Bible for our textbook."

"How wonderful!"

Jim also mentioned a small movement that had started to help slaves escape to the North, but he didn't know if many of his people would risk running away.

"I love you and want to assist with this movement you're talking about."

"I love you, too, but it's very dangerous. We'll decide together later what we'll do. Right now, I'm just thankful you're safe and back home where you belong."

"Yes, home. But more than that, I'm with you." Grace placed her head on the chest of her beloved as the winter sun cast golden rays on their heart of stones.

Author Biography

With roots from Alabama, Georgia and Mississippi, Lanna Richards is truly a Southerner as well as a Native Texan. She has written for as long as she can remember, writing her first three-act play at age nine. It was when her children began pulling her poetry from the trash that she began to save her work.

Unable to sleep during the last months of her husband's terminal illness, Lanna wrote to pass the long nights, and *Heart of Stones* was born.

She counts as one of her greatest joys her children, grandchildren and great-grandson.

She feels blessed to have been asked to design and make clothes, especially Halloween costumes for all her grandchildren as well as her daughter's wedding gown.

She currently lives and writes in Texas.